CHAIM POTOK...

My Name Is Asher Lev

by

Chaim Potok

FAWCETT CREST • NEW YORK

MY NAME IS ASHER LEV

THIS BOOK CONTAINS THE COMPLETE TEXT OF
THE ORIGINAL HARDCOVER EDITION.

Published by Fawcett Crest Books, a unit of CBS Publications, the
Consumer Publishing Division of CBS Inc., by arrangement with
Alfred A. Knopf, Inc.

ISBN: 0-449-23498-3

Selection of the Literary Guild, April 1972

Printed in the United States of America

20   19   18   17   16   15   14   13

Art is a lie which makes us realize the truth.

—PICASSO

*Book
One*

ONE

My name is Asher Lev, *the* Asher Lev, about whom you have read in newspapers and magazines, about whom you talk so much at your dinner affairs and cocktail parties, the notorious and legendary Lev of the *Brooklyn Crucifixion*.

I am an observant Jew. Yes, of course, observant Jews do not paint crucifixions. As a matter of fact, observant Jews do not paint at all—in the way that I am painting. So strong words are being written and spoken about me, myths are being generated: I am a traitor, an apostate, a self-hater, an inflicter of shame upon my family, my friends, my people; also, I am a mocker of ideas sacred to Christians, a blasphemous manipulator of modes and forms revered by Gentiles for two thousand years.

Well, I am none of those things. And yet, in all honesty, I confess that my accusers are not altogether wrong: I am indeed, in some way, all of those things.

The fact is that gossip, rumors, mythmaking, and news stories are not appropriate vehicles for the communication of nuances of truth, those subtle tonalities that are often the truly crucial elements in a casual chain. So it is time for the defense, for a long session in demythology. But I will not apologize. It is absurd to apologize for a mystery.

And that is what it has been all along—a mystery, of the sort theologians have in mind when they talk about concepts like wonder and awe. Certainly it began as a mystery, for nowhere in my family background was there any indication that I might have come into the world with a unique and disquieting gift. My father was able to trace his family line down through the centuries to the time of the Black Death in 1347, which destroyed about half the population of Europe. My father's great-great-grandfather was in his early years the manager of the vast estates of a carousing Russian nobleman who when drunk sometimes killed serfs; once, in an act of wild drunkenness, he burned down a village and people died. You see how a goy behaves, I would be told by my father and mother. The people of the sitra achra behave this way. They are evil and from the Other Side. Jews do not behave this way. My father's great-great-grandfather had transformed those estates into a source of immense wealth for his employer as well as himself. In his middle years, he began to travel. Why did he travel so much? I would ask. To do good deeds and bring the Master of the Universe into the world, my father would respond. To find people in need and to comfort and help them, my mother would say. I was told about him so often during my very early years that he began to appear quite frequently in my dreams: a man of mythic dimensions, tall, dark-bearded, powerful of mind and body; a brilliant entrepreneur; a beneficent supporter of academies of learning; a legendary traveler, and author of the Hebrew work *Journeys to Distant Lands*. That great man would come to me in my dreams and echo my father's queries about the latest bare wall I had decorated and the sacred margins I had that day filled with drawings. It was no joy waking up after a dream about that man. He left a taste of thunder in my mouth.

My father's father, the man whose name I bear, was a scholar and recluse in his early and middle years, a dweller in the study halls of synagogues and academies. He was never described to me, but I pictured him as slight of body and huge of head, with eyelids swollen from lack of sleep, face pale, lips dry, the veins showing blue along his cheeks and temples. In his youth, he earned the name "ilui," genius, a term not lightly bestowed by the Jews of Eastern Europe. And by the time he was twenty he had come to be known as the Genius of Mozyr, after the Russian town in which he lived. Shortly before his fiftieth birthday, he abruptly and mysteriously left Mozyr and, with his wife and children, journeyed to Ladov and became a member of the Russian Hasidic sect led by the Rebbe of Ladov. He began to travel throughout the Soviet Union as an emissary of the Rebbe. Why did he travel so much? I once asked. To bring the Master of the Universe into the world, my father replied. To find people who needed help, my mother said. While on his way home from the Rebbe's synagogue late one Saturday night, he was killed by a drunken axe-wielding peasant. Somehow my grandfather had forgotten it was the night before Easter.

My mother came from a family of leading Sadegerer Hasidim, pious Jews who had been followers of the great Eastern European Hasidic dynasty established by Israel of Rizhin. On her father's side, my mother could trace her family back to the Rebbe of Berdichev, one of the saintliest of Hasidic leaders. On her mother's side, the family line consisted of great scholars down to the Chmelnitzki massacres in seventeenth-century Poland, where it vanished in blood and death.

So, little Asher Lev—born in 1943 to Rivkeh and Aryeh Lev, in the section of Brooklyn known as Crown Heights—little Asher Lev was the juncture point of two significant family lines, the apex, as it were, of a triangle seminal with Jewish potentiality and freighted with Jewish responsibility. But he was also born with a gift.

I have no recollection of when I began to use that gift. But I can remember, at the age of four, holding my pencil in the firm fist grip of a child and transferring the world around me to pieces of paper, margins of books, bare expanses of wall. I remember drawing the contours of that world: my narrow room, with the bed, the paint-it-yourself bureau and desk and chair, the window overlooking the cemented back yard; our apartment, with its white walls and rug-covered floors and the large framed picture of the Rebbe near the living-room window; the wide street that was Brooklyn Parkway, eight lanes of traffic, the red brick and white stone of the apartment houses, the neat cement squares of the sidewalks, the occasional potholes in the asphalt; the people of the street, bearded men, old women gossiping on the benches beneath the trees, little boys in skullcaps and sidecurls, young wives in long-sleeved dresses and fancy wigs—all the married women of our group concealed their natural hair beneath wigs for reasons of modesty. I grew up encrusted with lead and spectrumed with crayons. My dearest companions were Eberhard and Crayola. Washing for meals was a cosmic enterprise.

I remember drawing my mother. Born and raised in Crown Heights, her family high in the ranks of the Ladover aristocracy, she had gone through the Ladover school system for girls, and had married my father one week after her graduation from high school. She was nineteen when I was born and seemed more a sister to me than a mother.

I remember my first drawings of my mother's face— longish straight nose, clear brown eyes, high-boned cheeks. She was small and slight; her arms were thin and smooth-skinned, her fingers long and thin and delicately boned. Her face was smooth and smelled of soap. I loved her face next to mine when she listened to me recite the Krias Shema before I closed my eyes to go to sleep.

I remember those early years of my life, those first years of my efforts with pens and pencils and crayons. They were very happy years; laughter came easily both to me and to my mother. We played. We took long walks. She was a gentle big sister.

I drew her walking with me along Brooklyn Parkway, her coat collar up around her chin, her cheeks flushed in a high autumn wind—two roundish spots of bright pink against the smooth fair skin of her face. In the winter, I drew her tossing snowballs at the trees that lined the wide parkway, her arm motions like those of a little girl. Often we ran through the drifts together, kicking up the snow with our galoshes, and I drew that, too.

"Oh, how pretty," she said to me once, looking at a drawing of herself jumping over a snowbank. "Oh, I like this one, Asher. You made the snow very pretty. And so high. What a jump! Did I jump like that? I'm almost flying."

In the spring, we sometimes went rowing in Prospect Park, not far from where we lived. She was an awkward rower, and she would laugh nervously whenever she fell backward off her seat from a skimming pull at the oars. But we went anyway, and often I took my crayons and pad with me and drew her as she rowed, and drew, too, the look of the water beneath the sky and the surface movements stirred up by her erratic oars.

"Asher, it isn't nice to draw your mama like this."

"But it was the time you fell in the boat, Mama."

"It isn't nice. It isn't respectful. But the shore is very pretty. How did you do that?"

"I used sand from the beach, Mama. Can you see the sand?"

And in the summer I drew her in her light long-sleeved blouses, with the tiny beads of perspiration on her upper lip and brow. Her dresses and blouses were always long-sleeved, for out of modesty the women of our group never wore short-sleeved garments—and she perspired a great deal in the heat, especially on our walks together.

"What is that on my face?" she asked, looking at one of my summer drawings of us walking through the Brooklyn Botanical Gardens.

"Those are the spots, Mama."

"What spots, Asher?"

"The wet spots, Mama. When it's hot, there are the wet spots."

After a moment she said, "But why didn't you draw the pretty birds, Asher? And the flowers, Asher, why didn't you draw the flowers?"

In the very early years, before my mother became ill, my father traveled a great deal.

I asked him once during breakfast, "Is my papa going away again today?"

"To Ottawa," he said, not looking up from his *New York Times*.

"Where is Ottawa?"

"Ottawa is a very important city in Canada." He spoke with a faint Russian accent.

"Canada is a country next to America," my mother explained.

"Why is my papa going to Ottawa?"

"To meet with people in the government," my mother said proudly.

"Why?"

My father looked up from the newspaper. "The Rebbe asked me to go."

He had been brought to America at the age of fourteen, together with his mother and older brother, and had been twenty-five when I was born. He was a graduate of the Ladover yeshiva in the Crown Heights section of Brooklyn. He had earned a bachelor's degree in political science from Brooklyn College and a master's degree in the same subject from New York University. He had earned those degrees at the request of the Rebbe.

He was tall and thick-shouldered. His eyes were sharp, direct, and dark. His untrimmed beard was red, as was the hair on his head. He kept his sidecurls tucked behind his ears. It was from him that I inherited my red hair and dark eyes. My slight features and thinness of build I inherited from my mother.

I came into the kitchen one morning and found him preparing the orange juice. He had his own way of making our orange juice: each of us received the juice of one orange, half a glass of cold water, and a teaspoonful of sugar. It was a refreshing drink to wake up to every morning. Sometimes I was able to determine from the way he prepared the orange juice whether or not he would be traveling that day.

He was in a hurry that morning, so I knew he would be traveling.

"Good morning," I said. "Is my papa traveling again today for the Rebbe?"

"Good morning, Asher. Did you say Modeh Ani?"

"Yes, Papa."

"Sit down. I'll make you your orange juice."

I sat down. My mother was putting dry cereal on the table.

"Your papa is going to Washington today," my mother said.

"What is Washington?"

"The city where the government of America is."

"My papa is traveling to Washington for the Rebbe?"

"Yes," my mother said. She took great pride in my father's missions for the Rebbe.

"Why does my papa travel for the Rebbe?"

My father poured orange juice into my glass. "My father traveled for the Rebbe's father, may they both rest in peace. I travel for the Rebbe. It is a great honor to be able to travel for the Rebbe."

"What does my papa do when he travels for the Rebbe?"

"So many questions," my father said. "Drink your juice, Asher. The vitamins will go away if you let it stay too long."

Sometimes he left after supper. Most of the time, he left after breakfast. My mother and I would go with him to the door.

"Have a safe journey," my mother would say. And she would add, in Yiddish, "Go in health and return in health."

They would not embrace. They never embraced in my presence.

My father would kiss me, take his black leather bag and his attaché case, and leave. Sometimes I would go to the living-room window and see him come out of our apartment house and hail a cab, or watch him walk toward the building that was the international head-

quarters of the Ladover movement a block and a half
away. I would watch him walking quickly beneath the
trees along Brooklyn Parkway, the black leather bag
and attaché case in his hands, a copy of the *New York
Times* under his arm—a tall, broad-shouldered, red-
headed, neatly dressed man in a dark suit and coat and
narrow-brimmed hat, walking with the faintest of limps
from the polio he had been stricken with as a child in
Soviet Russia.

I drew him often during those very early years. I
drew him as he sat evenings with my mother, reading or
talking. I drew him drinking coffee with my mother at
the kitchen table. Sometimes I would wake in the night
and hear them in the kitchen. Often they sat at that
table late into the night, drinking coffee and talking.
And I would lie in my bed, wondering what they were
saying.

I drew my memory of my father and me walking together to our synagogue. He was so tall and I was so
short, and he would incline his head toward me as we
walked. I drew him as he prayed at home in his prayer
shawl and tefillin on those weekday mornings when for
some reason he could not go to the synagogue. He
would stand at our living-room window, his head covered with the prayer shawl, swaying faintly back and
forth, with only the edge of his red beard protruding
from the white black-striped shawl.

I drew my memory of him praying in our synagogue
on Shabbos, garbed in his prayer shawl, only his red
beard visible. I drew my memory of him weeping on
Yom Kippur as he chanted the prayer describing the
slaughter of the ten great sages by the Romans. I would
stand close to him in the white sanctity beneath the
prayer shawl and I would see him cry as if the killing
were taking place before his eyes. I drew my memory of
him carrying the palm frond and citron on the festival
of Succos, the small lemonlike fruit dwarfed by his large
hand. I drew my memory of him lighting our Hanukkah
candles on the sill of our living-room window. He
would chant the blessings and light the candles and my

mother and I would join him in the songs. Then he
would stand a long time at the window and watch the
tiny flames burning against the huge night.

Often on Shabbos or festivals, I would see him in the
living room, studying Talmud or a book on Hasidus.
Sometimes I would find him looking at the passage in
the tractate *Sanhedrin,* "Any man who has caused a single Jewish soul to perish, the Torah considers it as if he
had caused a whole world to perish; and any man who
has saved a Jewish soul, it is as if he had saved a whole
world."

I asked him once, "Is it only if he kills a Jewish person, Papa?"

"No, Asher. Elsewhere the same passage appears
without the word 'Jewish.' "

"Papa, how can a man who kills one person be like
one who kills a whole world?"

"Because he also kills all the children and children's
children who might have come from that person."

"Why do you study that so often, Papa?"

He smiled faintly and his eyes grew dreamy. "My father liked to study it often, Asher."

And I drew my memory of my father studying that
tractate of the Talmud.

He said to me once, gazing at one of my drawings,
"You have nothing better to do with your time, Asher?
Your grandfather would not have liked you to waste so
much time with foolishness."

"It's a drawing, Papa."

"I see what it is."

"A drawing is not foolishness, Papa."

He looked at me in surprise. But he said nothing. I
was almost five at the time.

He was indifferent to my drawing; he thought it
something children did when they were very young and
then outgrew. But I continued to draw him anyway,
though after a while I stopped showing him the drawings.

I drew my memory of him singing zemiros during our
Shabbos meals. My mother and I would sing with him.

He had a deep voice but he sang softly, his eyes closed, his head thrown slightly back so that I could see the white skin of his neck below the start of the thick growth of red beard.

I drew my memory of the first time he sang his father's melody to Yoh Ribbon Olom during the Shabbos meal four days after the death of his mother—a haunting tune that carried with it pain and suffering and faith and hope. "Yoh ribbon olom, ribbon olom veolmayoh," he sang, his eyes closed, his voice soft and quavering, the upper part of his body swaying faintly back and forth between the back of his chair and the edge of our dining-room table. "Ant hu malka, melech melech malchayoh . . ." He paused, swaying. He let the pause linger tremulously, then continued, "Ovad gevurtaich. . . ." Tears flowed from his closed eyes. My mother looked down at the table. I stared at him. I felt my mother's hand on mine.

That melody echoed inside my head for days. Again and again, I drew my memory of my father singing his father's melody.

He sang it again the week my mother was taken to the hospital.

I have only vague memories of the darkness and fog of that week. It was January. I had just turned six. There was a phone call. My father rushed from the apartment and returned a while later, the blood driven from his face. Then my mother began to scream. The phone rang endlessly. The apartment filled with relatives and friends. My mother continued screaming. People moved about aimlessly, their faces filled with horror and shock. I was in my room, peering out the door, which I had opened to a tiny crack. I watched the faces of the people and listened to my mother's screams. A cold uncontrollable trembling took possession of me. Something had happened to my mother. I could not endure the screams. They cut—like the sliver of glass that had once opened my hand, like the curb of the sidewalk that had once gashed my knee. The screams cut and cut. People were becoming frenzied and hysterical. I heard loud weeping. Then, suddenly, the noise died. My mother stopped screaming. There were whispers. I peered into the hallway. Two tall dark-bearded men came along the hallway. Behind them walked a man of medium height, wearing a dark coat over a dark suit. He had a short dark beard and wore an ordinary dark hat. He walked in the path cleared by the tall dark-bearded men. People murmured softly as he passed. His presence seemed to fill the apartment with white light. It was the Rebbe. Behind the Rebbe walked two more tall dark-bearded men. The Rebbe was in my house. I was certain my mother was dead. I lay down on the floor in my room, and wept.

Later, someone remembered me. I was taken to a neighbor's apartment. The next day, I was brought back. My mother was not dead. She lay in her bed, but I could not see her. Uncle Yaakov had been in an accident, my father explained. A car accident. In Detroit. While traveling for the Rebbe.

My Uncle Yaakov was my mother's only brother. He had been to our apartment only three days before. He would visit us all the time. He lived alone two blocks away. He was short and slight and dark-haired, with brown eyes and thin lips. He looked like my mother. He was studying history and Russian affairs. He was to be an adviser to the Rebbe. His favorite expression was "What's new in the world?" He spoke in a soft voice and was gentle. Now he was dead of a car accident at the age of twenty-seven.

The following day, my mother was taken to the hospital. That Shabbos, my father sang his father's melody to Yoh Ribbon Olom. We were in his older brother's home a few blocks away from us, for his sister-in-law would not hear of us having Shabbos in our apartment without my mother. We sat at the table that Friday night and there were long silences and feeble attempts at zemiros by my father's brother. And then, suddenly, my father began to sing his father's melody.

There was an unearthly quality to the way he sang that melody that night—as if he were winging through unknown worlds in search of sources of strength beyond himself. His eyes were open, fixed, but gazing inward. There was a sweetness and sadness, a sense of pain and yearning in his voice—soft, tremulous, climbing and falling and climbing again. And when he was done there was a long silence—and in that silence I thought I heard distant cries, and I was afraid.

Late, late that night, I came slowly awake from dream-filled sleep and heard the melody again and thought I was still dreaming. But even when I knew I was truly awake the melody still went on. It was my father's voice coming from our living room. I saw him standing in front of the window. The huge Venetian blind had been pulled up. It stood rigidly perpendicular to the two tall rectangles that were the window's frames. A single small light glowed faintly in the baseboard socket near the window—the light we left on in that room all through Shabbos. It cast weak shadows across the floor and a soft reddish glow on my father's face. He stood looking through the window at the street outside, quietly singing his father's melody. He wore his dark-red dressing gown over his pajamas. A tall skullcap covered his head. His sidecurls hung uncombed alongside his cheeks. The room was dark save for the single weak night light. I stood in the doorway behind him and saw his face reflected in the window. I saw his eyes and watched his lips move. He held his hands to both sides of his head. Standing there, with the room in shadows and his faintly illumined features reflected in the window that looked out onto the dark street, he seemed to spread himself slowly across the wide night, to embrace and cover the darkness with his blanket of melody and soft light.

My mother returned from the hospital and my father stopped traveling.

The Rebbe's staff had suffered a number of casualties since its reorganization in America after the Second

World War: one of its members had had a heart attack while on a mission in West Germany; a second had been in a serious car accident in Rome; a third was badly beaten one night in Bucharest. There had been others. But my mother's brother was the first to die.

There had been a special kind of relationship between my mother and her brother, and his death almost destroyed her.

She had always been thin; she returned from the hospital skeletal. At first, I did not know who she was. I thought there had been an error, that somehow they had sent back the wrong person.

For the first few days, she remained in her bed. Then she came out and moved specterlike about the apartment in her nightgown, her eyes dark dead pools, her short dark hair uncombed and uncovered by a wig. She would not speak to anyone. I thought she had lost her voice until I heard her talking in the living room late one afternoon and found she was talking to herself.

"You had to go?" she was saying. "Yes? Why did you have to go? How will I cross the street?"

I felt cold listening to her. I said to my father that night as he was putting me to bed, "Is my mama going to die?"

He drew in breath sharply. "No, Asher. No. Your mama is not going to die."

"Is my mama very sick?"

"Yes."

"Will my mama get better?"

"Yes, with God's help."

"I want my mama to get better. I want to make pretty drawings for her."

My father hugged me to him. I felt his beard on my face. "Now go to bed, Asher. And let me hear your Krias Shema."

She wept easily. She tired easily. She cared nothing for the apartment, for food, for the things a person must do to stay alive.

A woman came into the apartment every day to clean

and cook. Her name was Mrs. Sheindl Rackover. She was a widow with married children, short, plump, stern, energetic, and fiercely pious. She spoke only Yiddish. My mother avoided her. My mother avoided friends and relatives. She avoided me. She avoided my father. She seemed to cringe in the presence of another person.

One day, sitting alone in our living room, she began to sing. It was a Hasidic melody, but I did not recognize it. She was imitating a soft voice.

"Why does my mama sing that way?" I asked my father that night.

"What way?"

"In Uncle Yaakov's voice."

He was helping me put on my pajamas. His hands trembled. "Your mother is remembering her brother, may he rest in peace."

"Papa, you remember Uncle Yaakov."

"Yes."

"You don't sing like that, Papa."

He turned his head away for a moment. Then he said, "It's time for sleep now, Asher. Let me hear your Krias Shema."

I found her alone in the living room one afternoon about a week after she came back from the hospital. I said to her, "Mama, are you feeling better?"

She gazed at me but did not seem to see me. Then I saw a flicker of light in her eyes.

"Asher?"

"Mama?"

"Asher, are you drawing pretty things? Are you drawing sweet, pretty things?"

I was not drawing pretty things. I was drawing twisted shapes, swirling forms, in blacks and reds and grays. I did not respond.

"Asher, are you drawing birds and flowers and pretty things?"

"I can draw you birds and flowers, Mama."

"You should draw pretty things, Asher."

"Shall I draw you a bird, Mama?"

"You should make the world pretty, Asher. Make it sweet and pretty. It's nice to live in a pretty world."

"I'll draw you some pretty flowers and birds, Mama. I'll draw them for you right now."

"Never mind," she said sharply. She looked out the window. "It's not complete. Can it make a difference? Tell me how."

And the dead look returned to her eyes.

She seemed to hate the kitchen and would flee from it as soon as she was done eating. She never came into my room. She either lay in her bed, sleeping or staring at the ceiling, or she sat on the sofa in the living room, gazing out the window at the street below.

She began to smoke. She sat in the living room wreathed in smoke, the ashtrays on the end table beside her spilling over. Mrs. Rackover muttered to herself as she cleaned the ashtrays, but she said nothing to my mother. I began to find stubs of gray ash on the floor of the apartment.

About two weeks after my mother returned from the hospital, I came into my parents' bedroom late in the morning and found her in bed. It was a large double bed. She lay beneath the green quilt, looking shrunken. Her face was sallow. Her bony hands protruded from the sleeves of her nightgown. She had seemed dead when I came in, but now her eyelids fluttered open and she raised her head from the pillow and looked at me. She started to speak, stopped, and lay back on the pillow. She gazed up at the ceiling for a moment, then closed her eyes. Her closed eyes looked like ashen knobs in the blue-gray darkness of their sockets.

I stood there for a long time. She seemed to be barely breathing. There was a strange fetid odor in the air.

I had come to show her a drawing I had made earlier that morning. It was a drawing of two birds. One of the birds was in a nest; the other was settling into the nest, its wings wide and fluttering. The nest was pale yellow, the birds were orange and deep blue, and there were green leaves and red flowers everywhere. There was a pale-blue sky and white clouds and birds off in the distance. The bird in the nest had large round black eyes.

I stood alongside the bed and watched my mother's slow breathing.

"Mama," I said.

Her eyes fluttered faintly but remained closed.

"Mama," I said again.

Her hands moved then, and she turned her head toward me and opened her eyes.

I held up the drawing. She gazed at it blankly.

"Here are the birds and flowers, Mama."

She blinked her eyes.

"I made the world pretty, Mama."

She turned her head away and closed her eyes.

"Mama, aren't you well now?"

She did not move.

"But I made the world pretty, Mama."

Still she did not move.

"I'll make more birds and flowers for you, Mama."

Behind me someone came quickly into the room. I felt a hand on my shoulder.

"What are you doing?" Mrs. Rackover whispered fiercely in Yiddish.

"I made a drawing for my mama. I'm making my mama well."

"Come away from here." Her fleshy face quivered. She seemed frightened my mother would wake.

"My mama asked me to make a drawing."

"Come away, I said." She turned me forcefully around. I felt her pushing me out of the room. "What kind of boy disturbs a sick mother? I am surprised at you. A good boy does not do such a thing." She sent me to my room.

I sat on my bed and stared at the drawing. Then I was frightened in a dark and trembling way I had never known before. I went to my desk. A long time afterward, Mrs. Rackover called me to lunch. I found myself in front of a drawing filled with black and red swirls and gray eyes and dead birds.

Relatives and friends came to visit my mother. Often my mother would refuse to see them. Sometimes she would let my father persuade her to join a group of visitors in the living room. She would sit in one of the easy chairs, looking small and fragile, and say nothing. There would be awkward silences, feeble attempts at conversation, and more silences. In those moments, my mother seemed a ghostly spectator, hollow, without a core to her being.

Her older sister, a short robust woman in her early thirties, came in one day from Boston, where she lived with her husband and four children. She sat with my mother in our living room.

"Rivkeh, you have a husband and a son. How can you neglect them? You have a responsibility."

My father was in the room at the time. There were other relatives there, too, but I do not remember who they were.

"Look at the boy," my mother's sister said. "Look at him. He's dirty. How can you let him be so dirty?"

"Asher is always dirty," my father said. "Even after he's bathed he's dirty."

"He should not be left alone. How can you leave a little boy alone?"

"He is not left alone."

"A boy left with a housekeeper all day is alone. A boy without children to play with is alone."

My father said nothing.

"You should send him to your kindergarten."

"Asher doesn't want to go to the kindergarten."

"Then he should come and live with me," my mother's sister said. "We have a big house. There are four children. A boy Asher's age should not be by himself all the time."

"Asher likes being by himself."

"It isn't healthy. It leaves scars. You don't want to leave scars on the boy. Let him live with me."

There was a brief pause. I felt myself shivering inside.

"Let me think about it," my father said.

My mother had been staring blankly at her sister and saying nothing.

"It's wrong, Rivkeh," her sister said. "The boy will have scars." Then she said, "Rivkeh, it is forbidden to mourn in this way."

My mother was very still.

"Rivkeh, the Torah forbids it."

My mother sighed. Her frail body seemed to shrink even more in the large chair.

"Papa and Mama would have forbidden it," her sister said.

My mother said nothing.

"Rivkeh," her sister said. "He was my brother, too."

A dark light flickered in my mother's sunken eyes. "The Torah forbids it?" she said quietly. "It is forbidden? Yes?"

"Yes," her sister said.

"But there are scars everywhere," my mother said. "And who will hold my pennies?" She stared out the window at the afternoon sunlight on the trees below. "Who will tell me about the fox and the fish? Yaakov, you had to go? You left it unfinished. Who said you had to go?"

Then she lapsed into silence and would say nothing more.

Her sister stared at her, open-mouthed. Then she turned her head away and shuddered.

That night, alone in my room, I drew my Aunt Leah. I drew her in the shape of a fish being eaten by a fox.

"What did the doctor say?" I asked my father the next evening as he was helping me out of my clothes.

"To have patience."

"Will my mama get well?"

"Yes."

"When?"

"It will take a long time."

"Will you send me to live with Tante Leah?"

"No. We'll think of something else. Now let me hear your Krias Shema, Asher."

The weeks passed. The visitors ceased coming.

In the first week of March, my father began to take me with him to his office. He worked at a desk in the Ladover headquarters building a block and a half from where we lived. The building was a three-story house of tawny stone, with Gothic windows and a flagstone front porch with a whitestone railing. It contained offices, meeting rooms, a room with about a dozen mimeograph machines, two suites of rooms for the editorial offices of the various Ladover publications, and a small press in the basement. Men came and went all day long. They sat behind desks, met in conference rooms, rushed along corridors, talked frenetically, sometimes quietly, sometimes in loud voices. All the men were bearded and wore dark skullcaps and dark suits with white shirts and dark ties. No women worked inside that building; secretarial work was done by men.

On the second floor of the house, in an apartment facing the parkway, lived the Rebbe and his wife. To the left of the entrance hall beyond the carved wooden doors that led into the house was a carpeted wooden staircase. There was endless two-way traffic up and down that staircase: men with and without beards; young men and old men; men who were obviously poor and men who were clearly affluent; men who were Jews and men, who, it seemed to me, were not; and an occasional woman. Twice during those weeks, I saw a tall gray-haired man in a black beret climb the stairs and turn into the second-floor hallway. I noticed his hands; they were huge, rough, and calloused. I wanted to climb those stairs, too, but my father had told me never to go beyond the first floor of the building. I would wander through the first floor of the building alone, trying not to get in anyone's way. People knew I was Aryeh Lev's son; they patted my head, pinched my cheek, smiled, nodded indulgently at my drawings—I took my pad and crayons with me every day—and fed me cookies and milk.

My father's office was the third along the corridor to the right of the entrance hall. It was a small office, with white walls, a dark-brown linoleum on the floor, and a window that looked out onto the parkway. There were filing cabinets along the wall opposite the desk. The walls were bare, except for a large framed photograph of the Rebbe that hung near the window. My father's desk was old and scarred and seemed a relic of ancient academies of learning. It was cluttered with piles of paper and copies of *Time, Newsweek,* and the *New York Times.* Often he sat tipped dangerously back in his swivel chair, his feet on the desk, his small velvet skullcap pushed forward across his red hair onto his forehead. He would sit reading a newspaper or a magazine and I would worry that he would fall over backward, but he never did.

There were two telephones on the desk. Frequently he would talk into one or the other of them and write as he talked. Sometimes one of the men from another office would come in and sit on the edge of the desk and speak quietly with my father. I heard the word "Russia" often in those conversations.

My father spoke English, Yiddish, or Hebrew into the phones. But the second week I was in his office I heard him use a language I did not recognize. On our way back to the apartment for lunch, I asked him what language it had been.

"That was French, Asher," he said.

"I never heard my papa speak French before."

"I use it when I need it, Asher. I don't need it around the house."

"Does Mama speak French?"

"No, Asher."

"Did you learn French in Europe, Papa?"

"I learned it in America. The Rebbe asked me to study it."

"Didn't the Frenchman on the phone know Yiddish, Papa?"

"The Frenchman on the phone wasn't a Jew."

"What did my papa speak to him about?"

"You are full of questions today, Asher. Now I have a question. Your papa also has questions sometimes.

Here is my question. Do you think Mrs. Rackover made chocolate pudding for dessert? You wanted chocolate pudding."

Mrs. Rackover had not made chocolate pudding.

Even when my father used the languages I understood, it was often not clear to me what he was saying. Calls seemed to come to him from all over the country. He would listen and write. He would talk into the phone about train and boat schedules, about this person flying here and that person sailing there, about one community in New Jersey that did not have enough prayer books, another community in Boston that needed schoolbooks, a third community in Chicago whose building had been vandalized. At the end of a day behind that desk, he would be tired and a dark look would fill his eyes.

"I'm not made for this," he would say. "I need people. I hate sitting with telephones."

He would walk home with me in brooding silence.

One day, he spent almost an entire morning on the telephone arranging to move two Ladover families from somewhere in France to the United States.

"Why are they moving, Papa?" I asked him on the way home to lunch.

"To be near the Rebbe."

"What is the State Department, Papa?"

He told me.

"Why did you talk to that man in the State Department?"

"He's the man who is helping the families to come to America."

"How is he helping?"

"Asher, you've asked enough questions. Now it's my turn. Are you ready? Do you think Mrs. Rackover finally made chocolate pudding for dessert?"

Mrs. Rackover had indeed made chocolate pudding for dessert. My absence from the apartment had begun to mellow her.

Late one afternoon toward the end of March, I sat in my father's office drawing the trees I could see through

his window. One of the telephones rang. My father put
down his pen, picked up the receiver, and listened for a
moment. I looked at his face and stopped drawing.

Lines of anger were forming around his eyes and
along his forehead. Two sharp furrows appeared above
the bridge of his nose between his eyes. His lips became
rigid. He gripped the phone so tightly I could see the
knuckles of his hand go white. He listened for a long
time. When he finally spoke, it was in a voice of cold
rage. He used a language I had never heard before. He
spoke briefly, listened again for a length of time, spoke
again briefly, then hung up. He sat at the desk for a moment, staring at the phone. He wrote something on a
piece of paper, read over what he had written, made
some corrections, then picked up the paper and went
quickly from the office.

I sat there alone. One of the telephones rang. Then
the second phone rang. The first stopped ringing. The
second continued. The ringing sounded suddenly piercing and thunderous inside that little office. I went out
and spent the rest of the day on the flagstone porch,
drawing the street.

On the way home, I asked my father what language
he had spoken.

"When?"

"When you were angry, Papa."

"Russian," he said.

"You were very angry, Papa."

"Yes."

"Did the man hurt you?"

"No, Asher. He was telling me what some people are
doing to hurt others."

"They're hurting Jews, Papa?"

"Yes."

We were walking together along the street. The parkway was clogged with late-afternoon traffic.

"There are lots of goyim in the world, Papa."

"Yes," he said. "I've noticed."

That evening, my mother refused to join us for supper. I heard my father through the closed door of their

bedroom, pleading with her. "Rivkeh, please eat with us. We ask you to eat with us. You can't go on like this, Rivkeh." She would not move from the bed. We ate in heavy silence without her, served by Mrs. Rackover.

Later that night, I was awakened by the sound of my father's voice. I went on bare feet along the hallway and looked into the living room. He was standing in front of the window, chanting softly from the Book of Psalms.

The next day, there were more phone calls in Russian. My father was tense and restless. Between calls, he sat staring morosely at the top of his desk. He went to the window and stood gazing out at the busy parkway. He paced the floor. He seemed caged.

He saw me looking at him. "I'm not made for desks, Asher." He rubbed the side of his face. "I should be there, not here. How can I spend my life talking on the telephone? Who can sit like this all day?"

"I like to sit, Papa."

He gave me a dark brooding look. "Yes," he said. "I know you like to sit."

I held up the drawing I had made that morning of my father behind his desk talking into a telephone. It showed him with an angry face.

"It was before, when you were talking Russian, Papa."

He looked at the drawing. He looked at it a long time. Then he looked at me. Then he sat down behind the desk. One of the phones rang. He picked it up, listened for a moment, then began talking in Yiddish. I went out and spent the rest of the day on the porch, drawing the trees and the cars and the old women on the benches along the street.

My mother joined us for supper that evening. She smoked cigarette after cigarette. She had put on one of her blond wigs, but it was awry and gave her head a grotesque elongated look. My father tried talking to her but she would not respond. Finally, he gave it up. We ate in silence. The cigarette smoke formed an acrid cloud around our heads. Mrs. Rackover moved about quietly. From time to time, I heard her sigh.

Toward the end of the meal, I said abruptly, "I made a drawing today, Mama." My thin voice sounded loud in the smoky silence of the kitchen.

My father had been sitting tiredly over his food. Now he looked at me, startled.

"Yes?" my mother said in a dead voice. "Yes? Was it a pretty drawing?"

"It was a drawing of my papa on the telephone."

"On the telephone," my mother echoed. She looked dully at my father.

"Asher," my father said quietly.

"It was a good drawing, Mama."

"Was it a pretty drawing, Asher?"

"No, Mama. But it was a good drawing."

Her eyes narrowed. They seemed tiny slits in the blue-gray darkness of her sockets.

"I don't want to make pretty drawings, Mama."

She lit another cigarette. Her hands trembled faintly. An odor rose from her, fetid, cloying. I put down my fork and stopped eating. My father took a deep breath. Mrs. Rackover stood very still near the sink.

"Yes?" my mother said. Her voice was sharp. "I want the pennies now, Yaakov."

"Rivkeh," my father said. "Please."

"You should make the world pretty, Asher," my mother whispered, leaning toward me. I could smell her breath.

"I don't like the world, Mama. It's not pretty. I won't draw it pretty."

I felt my father's fingers on my arm. He was hurting me.

"Yes?" my mother said. "Yes?" She stubbed out the cigarette she had just lit and began to light another. Her hands trembled visibly. "No, no, Asher. No, no. You must not dislike God's world. Even if it is unfinished."

"I hate the world," I said.

"Stop it," my father said.

"You must not hate, you must not hate," my mother whispered. "You must try to finish."

"Mama, when will you get well?"

"Asher!" someone said.

"Mama, I want you to get well."

"Asher!"

To this day, I have no idea what happened then. There was a sensation of something tearing wide apart inside me and a steep quivering climb out of myself. I felt myself suddenly another person. I heard that other person screaming, shrieking, beating his fists against the top of the table. "I can't stand it, I can't stand it, I can't stand it!" that other person kept screaming. I remember nothing after that. Sometime later, I woke in my room. My father stood over my bed, looking exhausted.

"Mama," I said.

"Your mama is asleep."

"Mama, please."

"Go back to sleep, Asher. It's the middle of the night."

I was in pajamas. The night light was on near my desk. The slit of window not covered by the shade was black.

"No one likes my drawings," I said through the fog of half sleep. "My drawings don't help."

My father said nothing.

"I don't like to feel this way, Papa."

Gently, my father put his hand on my cheek.

"It's not a pretty world, Papa."

"I've noticed," my father said softly.

My father's brother came over to our apartment some time before Passover. He was about five years older than my father, short, somewhat portly, with a round dark-bearded face, watery brown eyes, and full moist lips that collected spittle at the corners when he spoke. He operated a successful jewelry and watch-repair store on Kingston Avenue, a few blocks from where we lived. He had two sons and two daughters and lived in a two-story brownstone on President Street.

We sat in the living room. The window was partly open. The Venetian blind swayed faintly in the breeze that blew into the room.

My father's brother wanted us to join his family in his home for the Passover sedorim. My father thanked him but would not accept.

"Why?"

"Rivkeh cannot leave the apartment. We'll have the sedorim here."

"Alone?"

"Yes."

My uncle squinted his watery eyes. "Listen," he said. "I don't want to mix into your affairs, but I'm your brother, and if a brother can't mix, who can? Have you talked to the Rebbe?"

"No."

"You should talk to the Rebbe."

My father looked at his hands and said nothing.

"Don't look away from me like that. Listen to me. I know how you feel about such things. But when our father had trouble he went to the Rebbe's father. I remember. You were only a baby. But I remember."

"It's not yet time to go to the Rebbe."

"What does the doctor say?"

"The doctor doesn't say anything any more."

"Then it's time. Believe me, it's time. What are you waiting for? People go to the Rebbe because they have a cold."

"I'm not such people."

"Listen to me. You should talk to the Rebbe."

"The Rebbe has a thousand problems."

"Then one more can't hurt. Listen to an older brother. Talk to the Rebbe."

At that point, my father asked me to leave. I went to my room, sat at my desk, and drew pictures of my uncle. I made him very round and dark-bearded, and I gave him a kind smile and warm eyes. He always wore dark-blue suits, but I made his suit light blue because he did not feel dark blue to me.

I was working on the third picture of my uncle when

he and my father came into my room. They stood behind me. My uncle peered over my shoulder at the drawings.

"This is a six-year-old boy?" he said softly.

My father said nothing.

"A little Chagall," my uncle said.

I felt more than saw my father make a motion with his hands and head.

"I fix watches and sell jewelry," my uncle said. "But I have eyes."

"Who is Chagall?" I asked.

"A great artist," my uncle said.

"Is he the greatest artist in the world?"

"He is the greatest Jewish artist in the world."

"Who is the greatest artist?"

My uncle thought a moment. "Picasso," he said.

"Picasso," I said, tasting the name. "Picasso. Is Picasso American?"

"Picasso is Spanish. But he lives in France."

"What does Picasso look like?" I asked.

My uncle pursed his lips and squinted his eyes. "He is short and bald and has dark burning eyes."

"How do you know about such things?" my father asked.

"I read. A watchmaker does not necessarily have to be an ignoramus."

"It's late," my father said to me. "Get into your pajamas, Asher. I'll come back to put you to sleep."

"A regular Chagall," my uncle said.

I turned in my chair and looked up at him. "No," I said. "My name is Asher Lev."

The two of them stared at me for a moment. My father's mouth dropped open a little. My uncle laughed softly.

"This is six years old?" he said. "Good night, Asher." Then he said, "I want to buy one of these drawings. Will you sell it to me for this?"

He took a coin from his pocket and showed it to me. He picked up one of the drawings and put the coin in its place. "Now I own an early Lev," he said, with a smile.

I did not understand what he was saying. I looked at my father. His face was dark.

"Good night, Asher," my uncle said.

They went out of the room.

The coin gleamed in the light of the lamp on my desk. I could not understand what had happened. I found myself suddenly missing the drawing and afraid to touch the coin. I wanted the drawing back.

My father came into the room. He held the drawing in his hand. Without a word, he put it on the desk and took the coin. He was angry.

"Your Uncle Yitzchok has a strange sense of humor," he said, and went from my room.

I looked at the drawing. I felt happy to have it back. But I felt unhappy my uncle had not kept it. It was a strange feeling. I could not understand it.

My father returned to the room. "I asked you to get into pajamas," he said.

I began to undress. He sat on my bed, watching me. He did not offer to help.

"Is my papa angry?" I asked when I came back from the bathroom.

"Your papa's tired," he said. Then he said, "Asher, would you like to go to Uncle Yitzchok for the sedorim?"

"Will you and Mama be with me?"

"Your mama can't leave the house."

"I want to be with you and Mama."

He sighed softly and was silent a moment. Then he shook his head. "Master of the Universe," he said in Yiddish. "What are You doing?"

The weather turned warm. Green buds appeared on the trees. The sun shone into the living room through the huge window. The rug and white walls and furniture shimmered with light. The light seemed to have a life of its own. On Shabbos and Sunday afternoons, when my father did not go to his office, I stayed in the living room and watched the sunlight. I watched the colors change. I watched new shapes come alive and die in the slow movement of color and light. Sometimes my eyes would hurt after a day of watching.

My mother began to sit in the living room in the sunlight. She sat on the sofa near the window, her eyes closed, sunlight bathing her face. She rarely moved once she sat down on the sofa. Her skin was sallow, translucent. She seemed drained of substance, dry skin and brittle bones surrounding empty space.

One Sunday afternoon, I brought my pencil and pad into the living room and drew my mother sitting on the sofa. I drew the sagging curve of her shoulders and back, the concave depression of her chest, the bony stalks of her arms crossed on her lap, the tilt of her head resting against a shoulder with the sun full on her eyes. She did not appear to be bothered by the sun. It was as if there were nothing behind her eyes for the sun to bother.

I was having trouble with her face. The cheek on the left side of her face dropped sharply into a concave plane from the high ridge of bone. I could not do the shading with the pencil. There were gradations of darkness in the shade which the pencil could not capture. I tried it once and it did not work. I used the eraser. Then I tried it again and used the eraser again, and now the drawing was smudged; some of the line had been weakened. I put it away and on a new piece of paper once again drew the outer contour of my mother's body and the inner contour of her arms. I left the face blank for a while, then filled in the eyes and nose and mouth. I did not want to use the pencil again. The drawing felt incomplete. It bothered me to have it incomplete. I closed my eyes and looked at the drawing inside myself, went over its contours inside myself, and it was incomplete. I opened my eyes. Along the periphery of my vision, I saw an ashtray on the table next to the sofa. It was filled with my mother's smoked-out cigarettes. I looked at the crushed dark ends of the cigarettes. Quietly I went to the ashtray and brought it to my chair. I put it on the floor. Then, holding the pad with the drawing on my lap, I carefully brushed the burnt end of a cigarette onto my mother's face. The ash left an ugly smudge. I rubbed the smudge with my pinkie. It spread smoothly, leaving a gray film. I used the ash from another cigarette. The gray film deepened. I worked a long time. I used cigarette ash on the part of her shoulder not in sunlight and on the folds of her housecoat. The contours of her body began to come alive. I was working on the shadows in the sockets of her eyes when I realized that my father was in the room watching me.

I had no idea how long he had been standing in the doorway. But from the way he was leaning against the wall near the doorway I thought he had been there a long time. He was not looking at me but at the drawing. He could see the drawing clearly from where he stood. There was fascination and perplexity on his face. He seemed awed and angry and confused and dejected, all at the same time.

I thought he would be angry at me for drawing my mother while she rested. Instead he simply turned and went quietly from the room. I heard him walk up the hallway and go into his bedroom.

I put the ashtray back on the table near the sofa, collected my pad and pencil, and went to my room.

That night, as my father helped me out of my clothes, he said quietly, "I wish you wouldn't spend all your time playing with pencils and crayons, Asher."

"It isn't playing, Papa. It's drawing."

"I wish you wouldn't spend all your time drawing," my father said.

"Is my papa angry with me for drawing my mama this afternoon?"

"No," he said wearily. "No."

"I was careful not to wake my mama."

"I saw."

"Mama didn't wake up."

"Who showed you to use cigarettes that way?"

"I thought of it by myself. Once I used sand in a drawing and I thought of it by myself, too. It was when I was rowing with Mama."

My father was silent a long moment. He seemed very tired.

"Did I give you your vitamins today, Asher?"

"Yes, Papa."

He turned off the light. "Let me hear your Krias Shema."

I recited the Krias Shema. He kissed me and started slowly from the room.

"Papa?"

"Yes, Asher."

"I'm sorry for drawing Mama and making you angry at me."

He started to say something, then stopped.

"I wanted to draw the light and the dark," I said.

"Yes," he said softly. "Go to sleep, Asher."

He went from the room.

I'll have to draw it again, I thought. Maybe there is something else besides cigarettes I can use. It's too hard to work with cigarettes. And they smell. There must be something else. I fell asleep. I dreamed of my father's great-great-grandfather. He was dozing in the sunlight in the living room and I was drawing him, when he woke. He went into a rage. He stormed about the room. He was huge. He towered over me. His dark beard cast huge swaying shadows across the rug. "Wasting time, wasting time," he thundered. "Playing, drawing, wasting time." I woke in terror, my heart beating loudly. I lay in bed and could not sleep. I went to the bathroom and urinated. On the way to my room, I saw a dim light in the living room. I looked in. My father stood near the window, swaying back and forth. I went silently back to my bed. I would find something other than cigarettes. I would put all the world into light and shade, bring life to all the wide and tired world. It did not seem an impossible thing to do.

The stores that were run by observant Jews were all closed on Shabbos and open on Sunday. I went with my father early one Sunday morning to the grocery store. It was a cool sunny spring morning. There was little traffic on the parkway. Sunday morning was the only time the parkway rested.

The store was long and narrow and old. Cans and bottles stood on dusty shelves along the walls. Boxes and cartons were stacked in disarray on the floor. Now the store was jammed with kosher-for-Passover foods. Cartons of matzos teetered on both sides of the narrow aisle that led from the door to the counter. The counter was piled with paper bags, bills, boxes of candy. Behind the counter stood a man I had never seen before.

He was short and thin, with large bulging eyes, a beaklike nose, and pinched wrinkled features. A dark stubble covered his face. He wore a dirty white apron, an old brown wool sweater, and a strange-looking cap. His eyes had a nervous look. He kept glancing over his shoulders as we went along the narrow aisle between the cartons of matzos. He nodded his head vigorously at my father and wiped his hands on the apron. He said something in a language I did not understand and held out a hand across the counter.

They shook hands. My father said something to him and he looked down at me and smiled. His teeth were stained and misshapen. He leaned across the counter and extended his arm. We shook hands. His fingers and palms were dry and thickly calloused.

"Asher," my father said. "Say hello to Reb Yudel Krinsky."

"Hello," I said.

"Good morning," the man said in heavily accented English. "A nice morning." He had a hoarse raspy voice.

"Reb Krinsky just arrived from Russia," my father said.

I stopped eyeing the boxes of candy on the counter and looked at the little man.

"I told my son you just arrived from Russia," my father said in Yiddish to the man.

"Thursday," the man said to me in Yiddish, and smiled again.

"How are you feeling?" my father asked him.

"How should a Jew feel?" The man peered down at me. "What is your name? Asher? Did you know, Asher, that your father is an angel of God?" He turned to my father. "How should a Jew feel? There we went through the seven gates of hell for matzos. Here I stand in matzos over my head. So how should a Jew feel? You are an angel of God, and the Rebbe, he should live and be well, the Rebbe made miracles and wonders for me. At night, I tell myself it is a dream and I am afraid to wake up. If it is a dream, better I should not wake up, better I should die in my sleep."

"You should not talk this way," my father said quietly.

"Reb Lev, no man in the whole world should talk this way. But it is the way I feel."

They were silent for a moment. Then my father said, "Here are the things I need," and handed the man a slip of paper.

"Yes," the man said. "Right away." He scurried about for a few minutes. He was putting it all into a paper bag when my father said, still in Yiddish, "You learned the store quickly."

"I have learned more difficult things than this store even more quickly," the man said. "To survive you learn to learn quickly." He handed the bag to my father. "I wish you a kosher and happy Pesach. And I wish your wife a complete recovery."

Outside, I asked my father, "Is that man one of those you helped bring from Russia?"

"Yes, Asher."

"How many came?"

"Three."

"Is he the owner of the store now?"

"No, Asher. He's working there during these weeks before Pesach. We'll find other work for him later."

"Is he one of us?"

"Yes, Asher. He is one of us."

"Why does he wear that hat?"

"He wore that hat in Russia. The Rebbe told him to continue wearing it here. It's called a kaskett."

"Why did the Rebbe tell him to wear it in America?"

"So everyone would see a Russian Jew who remained a Jew."

"Is the leader of Russia bad to the Jews, Papa?"

"Stalin?" He said quickly in Hebrew, "May his name and memory be erased," and went on bitterly in English, "Stalin is from the sitra achra."

I said to Mrs. Rackover when we came into the apartment, "We saw a Jew from Russia."

"Yes," she said. "The man in the store. He is well?"

"He looks very skinny," I said.

"Eleven years in Siberia," she said. "It is miracles and wonders he is alive. Reb Lev, your wife is asking for you."

My father hurried off to the bedroom.

"What is Siberia?" I asked.

"What is Siberia?" Mrs. Rackover echoed. "It is a land like the inside of this refrigerator." She was putting away the milk we had bought. "It is a land of ice and darkness where the Russian government sends people it hates. Go wash your hands and I will give you a glass of milk and some cookies. What is Siberia? No one should know of it. The Rebbe's father sat three years in Siberia. I had two cousins in Siberia. One died; the other returned but could not remember his own name. Go wash your hands, Asher."

I went down the hallway to the bathroom and stood on the wooden stool. I was short and needed the stool to reach the faucets. In the mirror over the sink I was red-haired and had dark eyes. Short and red-haired with dark eyes. Dark burning eyes, I thought. I splashed water on my clothes and on the floor. Dark burning eyes. How do I draw a land of ice and darkness? How would Picasso draw a land of ice and darkness? I dried my hands and came out of the bathroom.

My father was in the kitchen. Mrs. Rackover was putting a cup of coffee and a roll on a tray. My father took the tray and went with it into the bedroom.

"How is my mama?" I asked.

"Your mama asked to eat something," Mrs. Rack-over said. "It is a good sign. Did you wash your hands?"

I held up my hands for her to inspect.

"You washed your shirt and your pants, too. Sit down. I'll give you milk and cookies."

A few minutes later, my father brought the tray back into the kitchen. The cup was empty and the roll was gone.

"My mama is better?" I asked.

"I don't know," my father said wearily. "Maybe a little better."

"Can I see my mama?"

"Later," my father said. "Now your mama is resting." He picked up the newspaper, which he had left on the kitchen counter. "You have something to do with yourself, Asher?"

"Yes, Papa."

"First you will finish your milk and cookies," Mrs. Rackover said.

My father went from the kitchen.

I sat at the table looking down into the milk in my glass. Ice is white, I thought. White like milk. No, not white like milk. There is blue in ice. And gray.

"Asher, drink your milk," I heard Mrs. Rackover say.

"What color is the feeling cold?" I asked.

Mrs. Rackover stopped drying the cup in her hands and peered at me closely. "Ah?" she said.

"The feeling cold," I heard myself say. "And the feeling dark."

"Asher, finish and go to your room. You will make me crazy with your nonsense. Finish and go."

Ice is the color blue and gray and white, I thought. Then I thought, No, it isn't blue and gray and white. I don't know what color it is. It bothers me not to know that. I felt upset and there was a sense of irritation inside me. Ice is what color? I fidgeted on the chair.

"Finish," Mrs. Rackover said.

I drank the milk and ate the last of the cookies.

"Thank God," Mrs. Rackover said, removing the glass and the dish.

"My mama is really feeling a little better?"

"I am not a doctor and I am not the Master of the Universe," Mrs. Rackover said. "I do not know. Go play in your room. Wash your hands and face first. You have as much milk and cookies outside you as you have inside you. Ah, how a six-year-old boy eats! Go, go, go."

Inside my room, I lay on my bed with my eyes closed and thought about the man from Russia. I saw his face clearly: the nervous eyes, the beaked nose, the pinched features. That face had lived eleven years in a land of ice and darkness. I could not imagine what it was like to live in ice and darkness. I put my hands over my eyes. There was his face, very clearly; not truly his face, but the way I felt about his face. I drew his face inside my head. I went to my desk and on a piece of blank white paper drew how I felt about his face. I drew the kaskett. I did not use any colors. The face stared up at me from the paper. I went back to the bed and lay on it with my eyes closed. Now there was ice and darkness inside me. I could feel the cold darkness moving slowly inside me. I could feel our darkness. It seemed to me then that we were brothers, he and I, that we both knew lands of ice and darkness. His had been in the past; mine was in the present. His had been outside himself; mine was within me. Yes, we were brothers, he and I, and I felt closer to him at that moment than to any other human being in all the world.

My mother came into the kitchen as we were having supper and sat down at the table. She did not greet us. Mrs. Rackover put a bowl of soup in front of her. My mother said the blessing over bread and began to eat.

"Asher," my father said. "Eat your soup."

Mrs. Rackover moved about quietly. From time to time, she glanced at my mother.

My mother wore a pink housecoat with lace around

the cuffs of the sleeves and along the collar. She had on a pretty blond wig. She was gaunt and there were dark circles around her eyes. But the sallowness had begun to leave her face; there were small patches of color in her cheeks.

I ate without knowing what I was eating. During the meat course, my father reached for a slice of bread and knocked over his glass of water. Mrs. Rackover wiped up the water without a word and refilled my father's glass.

At the end of the meat course, my mother said to me softly, "How are you feeling, Asher?"

"I'm fine, Mama."

"Are you making new drawings?"

"Yes, Mama."

I saw a faint smile play on her small lips. "Good drawings, yes, Asher?"

"Yes, Mama."

"I must see them. But not now. Tonight I'm a little tired." She turned to my father, the smile still on her lips. "Aryeh, what's new in the world?"

I saw my father's eyes narrow. He looked away from my mother a moment, then looked back. "A lot," he said softly.

"Yes," my mother said. "I'm sure." Then she said, "Aryeh, it is wrong to leave things unfinished."

Slowly, my father rubbed the side of his face.

"You taught me that, Aryeh. It is a victory for the sitra achra to leave a task for the Ribbono Shel Olom unfinished."

"Yes," my father murmured.

"I want you to remember that, Aryeh. Please remember that."

My father was quiet. There was a long strange silence, broken finally by Mrs. Rackover.

"Will you have tea, Mrs. Lev?"

"Yes, please," my mother said, and smiled faintly.

She joined us in the Birchas Hamozon after the meal. She chanted the words very clearly, by heart. When we were done, she got to her feet.

"I'm a little tired," she said. "Good night, Asher."

"Good night, Mama."

"Tomorrow I will look at your good drawings."

My father went with her to their bedroom.

"Master of the Universe," Mrs. Rackover was murmuring to herself as I walked out of the kitchen. "Master of the Universe."

I came into my room. I was trembling. Mama, I thought. What's happening to you? I sat at my desk and looked at the drawing of the Russian Jew. The Jew from the land of ice and darkness. I found myself with a crayon in my hand. I could not remember the color of his hair. I began to color the area between the bottom of his cap and the top of his ear. It was a small area. I used a red hue. Now his hair was red. He had dark nervous eyes and red hair. My fingers were sticky with the wax of the crayons. I did not like the drawing. I went back to my bed. I lay on my bed, not moving, feeling the fear like a presence in the dark places of the room.

When I came back to myself from the darkness where I had been, I looked at my window and saw it was night. I went through the hallway into our living room. The room was dark. The window was covered with the Venetian blind. I adjusted the slats and peered between them to the street outside. A stream of headlights moved slowly along the parkway, warm slashes of light in the darkness. After a while, I found it uncomfortable looking between the slats. I started to raise the Venetian blind, pulling hard on the string alongside the window. It was a very tall window and I got the blind up a few feet over my head, when it jammed. I released the string. The left side of the blind dropped about ten inches; the right side remained in place. I could not move it. I left it that way, a sharp diagonal cutting across the vertical lines of the window. I stood there a long time, looking out at the cars and the people and the houses of the street.

I did not hear my father come into the room.

"Asher," he said quietly.

"Papa."

"It's late, Asher."

"What was my mama saying?"

"I don't know, Asher."

"Why is God doing this to my mama?"

My father was quiet.

"Why should God do such a thing?"

My father turned away from the window and looked at me. I could feel him looking at me. Then he tugged at the cord near the window, and the blind dropped swiftly with a clattering noise. He flattened the slats and shut out the street. Then he bent over me. I turned and saw him bending over me and felt his hands under my arms and I was being lifted by him. He held me to him tightly. I put my arms around his neck. I felt his beard on my face. I buried my face in his neck and beard. He carried me to my room.

Later, lying in my bed, I said, "Mrs. Rackover told me Reb Yudel Krinsky was in Siberia eleven years."

"Yes."

"Will you be able to save more Jews from Russia, Papa?"

"I don't know," he said wearily.

"Would you like to travel again, Papa?"

He looked at me and his eyes glittered briefly. "Yes," he said.

"Does Reb Krinsky have a wife and children?"

"He had. They died in the war."

"How did he know about Mama?"

"Everyone knows about your mama, Asher. Now we'll stop talking and you'll go to sleep. Let me hear your Krias Shema."

The next morning, I went with my father to his office. It rained all morning, a cold dismal rain that turned the trees black. My father sat at his desk, reading the *New York Times*. There were few phone calls. Occasionally, he raised his eyes and stared out the window at the rain on the street. His eyes were dark and somber. He seemed very tired. We came home to lunch in the rain. My mother remained in her room. She refused to see me and would not speak to my father when he came in to ask her to join us.

The rain continued all afternoon. I wandered about the building, spent a while drawing the trees in the rain from the window in my father's office, then stood in the doorway watching the rain fall into the puddles on the flagstone floor of the porch. It was a steady rain and it fell with soft sounds against the stone and the street. After a while, I watched from inside the rain and no longer knew I was watching.

My father found me like that in the doorway. We walked home together. My mother was asleep. We ate supper alone. It continued to rain.

Later, I stood alone at the window of our living room and looked between the slats at the street. The asphalt glittered darkly in the rain. The rain cut through the circles of light around the tops of the lampposts, cold silvery diagonals against the warm yellow-white arcs of brightness. The street seemed to be crying.

My father came into the room.

"It's late, Asher."

"A few more minutes, Papa. Please."

He stood beside me. I watched the rain falling against the gleaming blackness of the street.

"I made a drawing of Reb Krinsky, Papa. But I don't like it."

He put his hand on my shoulder. "Come to bed now, Asher."

The lights came on in the living room. My mother stood in the doorway. The suddenness of the lights in the dark room stung my eyes. My mother had on a pale-blue bathrobe and slippers. Her short dark hair was uncovered and in disarray.

"Why do you stand in the dark?" she asked softly.

My father looked at her for a moment. "We were talking," he said.

She came slowly into the room, hugging the robe to herself.

"You slept all day, Rivkeh," my father said. "Are you hungry?"

"I'm not hungry. How are you, Asher?"

"I'm all right, Mama."

"You look pale. Are they taking care of you?"

"Yes, Mama."

"You should not let yourself get sick, Asher. Why are we standing? Please, let's sit down."

I sat with my father on the sofa. My mother sat facing us on one of the easy chairs. She put her hands on her lap. Wisps of dark hair lay across her forehead. But her eyes seemed clear.

"I must talk to you, Aryeh," she said quietly.

"Asher should go to bed."

"It concerns Asher, too."

My father was quiet. From somewhere along the parkway came the sound of an automobile horn.

"Aryeh," my mother said. "My brother's work is unfinished."

My father looked at her wearily and said nothing.

"I want to finish my brother's work."

My father's mouth slowly fell open.

"Aryeh, don't deprive me of this." There was urgency in her voice. "Please."

My father stared at her and said nothing.

"Aryeh, it's wrong for my brother's work to remain unfinished. I want to complete his work. In September, Asher will enter the yeshiva. Mrs. Rackover will be here when I can't be home." She was silent a moment. Then she said, with a quality in her voice that two people have when they speak an intimate language only they understand, "Aryeh, you'll be able to travel again."

My father slowly rubbed the side of his face.

"Please, Aryeh. Do you know what it's like for something to be incomplete?"

My father looked at her and said nothing.

"Yes," she murmured. "You know what it's like."

"Rivkeh, we should talk about this another time."

"Another time? Why another time? Will another time make a difference, Aryeh?"

My father was quiet.

"It's wrong for this also to be incomplete," my mother said. "It would be a victory for the sitra achra."

"Rivkeh, you're a mother. There's a child to raise."

"I'm also a sister and a wife," she said. They looked at each other then in silence. After a moment, my mother said, "Aryeh, please let me call the college tomorrow."

"Wait until Tuesday."

"Why?"

"I ask you to wait."

"All right," she said. "I'll wait." Then she said, "You're going to talk to the Rebbe?"

"Yes."

I saw the darkness return suddenly to her eyes. "The Rebbe will never permit me to do it." She pulled the bathrobe tightly to her as if she were cold. Then her voice became harsh and malevolent. "The Rebbe killed my brother."

I stared at her in horror. The blood drained from my father's face.

"The Rebbe sent him on a journey and he was killed."

"Rivkeh, please, please," my father murmured. His voice trembled. He said in Yiddish, "Master of the Universe."

"My brother would not have been killed if the Rebbe had not told him to travel."

"Enough," my father said, getting to his feet. "Asher, come with me. We'll talk more later, Rivkeh."

"But his work shouldn't be incomplete. The sitra achra would love his work to remain incomplete. Explain that to the Rebbe, Aryeh."

"Asher, come with me, do you hear?"

"Yes, by all means, put the boy to bed. Look how pale he is. Is he getting his vitamins? Do you get your vitamins, Asher? I think I'll go to bed now, too. I'm very tired." She rose abruptly to her feet, hugging the robe tightly to her small body. "Good night. Please, Aryeh. Please. Explain it to the Rebbe."

She went quickly from the room.

My father stood near his chair and stared down at the floor. He kept rubbing the side of his face.

"Papa?"

He went on rubbing his face and staring at the floor.

"Papa? Will Mama go to school and not be home?"

He did not respond.

"Papa, I'm very scared. Papa?"

He held me to him then, tightly. My face was against his beard. I had my eyes wide open and I saw the skin of his face and the red strands of individual hairs and the pink corners of his eyes. He smelled of warmth; an odor of strength and warmth came from him. He carried me to my room and helped me get into my pajamas. He sat on the edge of my bed.

I said to him, "How could Mama say those things about the Rebbe?"

My father said nothing. He looked tormented. Then, abruptly, he got to his feet, said good night, and went from the room. He had forgotten to ask me to say the Krias Shema.

I remember that night very clearly, the texture of its darkness, the echoing resonance of its sounds. I lay in my bed in the enveloping night and felt myself one with all the vast and endless arc of the universe, felt myself as raw flesh connected to near and distant pain. "The Rebbe killed my brother," I heard my mother say—and it was as if the words came hurtling through the black face of the universe, searing words, demonic words, from the sitra achra, the Other Side, from the region of blackness that spawned horror and evil and the stone hell that enclosed the light.

Sometime in the night, I came out of my bedroom and went through the hallway to the window of the living room. The rain had stopped. A huge three-quarter moon hung in a clear sky and cast a bluish light across the buildings and the parkway below. The night was still. The sky was a tranquil counterpoint to private fears.

I returned to my room. There was the drawing of the Russian Jew, barely visible on my desk. I looked at it and for a long moment felt it as a wedge into the darkness, a light encasing the shell. Uncle Yitzchok had liked one of my drawings. I would work again on the drawing of the Russian Jew. I would learn to draw my feelings of ice and darkness and a street crying. There was nothing I could not do.

Then I was back in my bed and the darkness returned and with it the memories and horror of the night. To draw, to make lines and shapes on pieces of paper, was a futile indulgence in the face of such immutable darkness, a foolishness I would certainly leave behind when I entered the world beyond the window of our living room. Yes, my uncle had a strange sense of humor. The Russian Jew would remain unfinished; the land of ice and darkness, the street crying in the rain—all of it would remain the fantasy of a child. I would grow up.

I lay in my bed in the darkness of the night, praying to grow up.

The Rebbe gave his permission.

That September, I entered the Ladover yeshiva, my mother entered Brooklyn College, and my father resumed his journeys for the Rebbe.

I had stopped drawing.

TWO

My teachers were gentle; my classmates were as friendly and as cruel as are classmates everywhere. I was treated with special care, for I was the son of Aryeh Lev, one of the Rebbe's emissaries who was often not home and whose absence had to be counteracted by teachers; I was also the son of Rivkeh Lev, one of the very few Ladover women the Rebbe had permitted to attend college and one who had recovered from a serious illness and whose life on occasion gave every appearance of remaining in tenuous balance between darkness and light.

I remember little of my first years in school. I cannot remember the color of the classroom walls or the shapes of the windows. I do remember that each room had a framed picture of the Rebbe on the wall near the blackboard. It was a photograph of the Rebbe's face. The Rebbe wore an ordinary dark hat. He seemed to be looking at us all the time. After a while, that picture began to appear in my dreams—though I do not remember ever seeing him inside the school during those years.

We saw a great deal of the mashpia, Rav Yosef Cutler, the one responsible for the development of our souls, and whose task it was to teach us the doctrines of Ladover Hasidism. He was a tall dark-bearded man, with white hands, dreamy eyes, and a soft voice. He came into our classroom once a week and talked to us about the importance of holiness and righteousness. He told us stories about the Rebbe and the Rebbe's father and grandfather. He told us about the hardships and sacrifices of Ladover Jews who maintained their Yiddishkeit despite Communist persecution. His height and dark beard reminded me vaguely of my thunderous mythic ancestor; his dreamy eyes and soft voice made me think sometimes of my grandfather, the scholar-recluse who had mysteriously turned into a journeying Hasid.

The school was in an old four-story red brick building adjacent to the headquarters building of the Ladover movement. I attended that school from eight-thirty in the morning to four-thirty in the afternoon. We were taught religious subjects in Yiddish and secular subjects in English. All our religious teachers were Ladover Jews; the secular teachers were either Ladover Jews or Gentiles. There were no non-observant Jews in our school.

I did no drawing at all during those early years of school, save for indifferent smears of finger paint for art projects the class undertook to help celebrate festivals. The gift lay buried.

I remember that sometime during my first year in school my mother asked me why I had stopped drawing.

I shrugged a shoulder.

"Is that an answer, Asher?"

"I don't feel like it any more, Mama."

"Why don't you feel like it, Asher?"

"I don't know."

"You are really very good at drawing."

"I hate it," I said. "It's a waste. It's from the sitra achra. Like Stalin."

She paled a little and said nothing more.

My father never mentioned it at all. To him, it had been another of the slowly disappearing ills of my childhood, like measles, mumps, and chronic tonsillitis.

In the summers, we lived in a private bungalow colony in the Berkshire Mountains of Massachusetts. It was a small Hasidic colony on the shore of a small lake. The bungalows were a few yards from a sandy beach. My father worked during the week and came up with the other husbands for weekends. Often on Shabbos afternoons, I would see my parents walking along the beach or beneath the tall trees in the nearby pine grove: my father wearing a white shirt and dark trousers, a small dark velvet skullcap on his head, his face surrounded by the red of his hair and beard; my mother wearing a long-sleeved summer dress or a light long-sleeved blouse and white or pale-blue skirt. They never swam. Sometimes they went rowing alone. I would see them on the lake early Sunday mornings when the air was still cool from the night, my father sitting in the center of the boat and facing my mother, leaning toward her as they spoke. Alongside my mother he seemed very tall, and he always inclined his head toward her when they talked.

I played with a few of the Hasidic boys who were my age. Often I wandered about alone. On occasion, my mother and I would walk together and talk about summer things: the sun on the lake, the way grass grew, the insects at night, the heat of the day, the mountain cold of the night. She asked me often why I had stopped drawing. I gave her shrug-of-the-shoulder answers.

She seemed happy during those summers, and I was glad to be near her. But there were odd moments when the dead look returned to her eyes—in the middle of a conversation about butterflies, during a walk beneath the tall pine trees, crossing a graveled country road, watching a bird in flight—and I would want to be far from her then.

We would return to the city at the end of August, and in September I would go to my yeshiva and my mother would resume college. She was no longer a light-hearted elder sister. She had become instead an efficient organizer of the temporal traffic that governed our lives. I was never permitted to stray from the time spectrum laid out for me: rise at a certain time, leave for school at a certain time, return at a certain time. My father's travel schedules were carefully worked out. His trips during those years were brief local journeys. He went no farther than Boston or Washington. If a change in schedule occurred while he was traveling, he telephoned my mother the very first chance he had.

We needed to make maximum use of our time, my mother kept saying. We could each of us accomplish a great deal if we arranged our schedules carefully and made maximum use of our time.

But on occasion I had the feeling there was more to it than that. Once I returned late from school after a wandering detour along Kingston Avenue. My mother met me at the door to our apartment and screamed at me. I did not recognize her then. Her small body trembled with rage. It seemed to me that my minor detour had upset nothing, especially as I had no homework that day. But I did not detour again for a long time.

After supper, she would help Mrs. Rackover do the dishes. Then she would wash the top of the kitchen table. Afterward she would bring in her textbooks and notebooks and arrange them neatly in front of her on the table. Often she hummed a Yiddish tune. She sat down at the table and went to work. She would sit at that table for hours. It seemed to me often then that the kitchen was not a kitchen at all, that the cabinets were library shelves, the dishes were books, the counters were stands for journals, the sink was a librarian's desk, the room was a laboratory of the mind.

I could not disturb her while she studied. I did my own schoolwork in my room. When I was done, I would move very quietly about the apartment. The silence of libraries and archives filled the rooms. She would come in to hear my Krias Shema. Then she would return to the kitchen and her books. There was no more walking in autumn winds; there was no more running through snowdrifts; there was no more rowing in Prospect Park. And there was no more drawing. The gift seemed dead.

My father had resumed his journeys for the Rebbe
the same month that my mother had entered college. He
retained his office, but his main task now lay not with
telephones but with travel. He seemed a different person. He glowed with new life. His first trip was to a
small Ladover community near Tom's River, in New
Jersey. He brought them supplies for the High Holidays
and the Rebbe's blessing. His next trip was to Balti-
more, where he participated as the Rebbe's personal
representative in the cornerstone ceremony for a new
Ladover synagogue and community center. Then he
traveled to Philadelphia, Newark, Providence, Boston,
and Washington. I lost interest in his journeys. Each
journey became for me another day when he was gone
from the apartment.

When he did not travel, he worked in his office. At
night, he often sat in the living room, reading *Time,
Newsweek,* the *New York Times,* Yiddish journals and
newspapers. He would sit slouched on the sofa, the
magazines and newspapers scattered around him, his
slippered feet on the coffee table, a small dark skullcap
on his head, his fingers slowly combing his long red
beard.

He searched constantly through his newspapers and
magazines for news about the Jews of Russia. He
seemed more connected to the Jews of Russia than to
the Jews of our own street.

On Shabbos, he never read anything except the writ-
ings of the Rebbe or of past leaders of Ladover Hasidism. Often he studied the Talmud tractate *Sanhedrin.*

He came home one evening during my second year in
school and told my mother that he had been moved to
an office on the second floor. His face was luminous inside its frame of red hair. I saw a flicker of alarm invade
my mother's eyes. But it vanished swiftly.

I measured time during those years by my tests, by
the holidays and festivals, by the events in the lives of
people around me. Rosh Hashonoh, Yom Kippur, Suc-

cos, Simchas Torah, Hanukkah, Purim, Pesach, the many Ladover celebrations—that was the cycle of my year. On occasion, I heard of the death of a near or distant member of our group. One winter, someone in our apartment building became ill and was taken to a hospital and I never saw him again. My Aunt Leah gave birth to her fifth child, a daughter. My Uncle Yitzchok bought the empty store next to his jewelry store, had the adjoining wall knocked down, and doubled his already successful business. Yudel Krinsky took a job in the stationery store on Kingston Avenue three doors away from my uncle. The store was one of two owned by a Ladover who ran the other, larger store himself in Flatbush. Yudel Krinsky lost his thin pinched look, put on weight, and grew a thick dark beard streaked with gray. He still wore the kaskett. He still glanced nervously around him from time to time. I liked Yudel Krinsky. It was to his stationery store that I detoured the day I came home late and was screamed at by my mother.

Our Crown Heights Ladover community grew quickly during those years. Almost every Shabbos, I saw new faces in the synagogue. They were coming from Western Europe and from those parts of Eastern Europe that still permitted people to leave. Very few came from Russia.

On a Friday in the summer of 1952, my father came up to the bungalow colony from a trip to Washington. I was on the beach, tossing pebbles into the water, when I saw the cab drive up the main road and turn in to our driveway. I saw my father in the cab and ran up the grassy slope to the front of the bungalow. There I stopped and watched my father. He was getting out of the cab, slowly and with care, as if he were in pain. My mother came out of the bungalow and went toward him. He paid the driver. The cab left. My father stood in the driveway, his suitcase next to him, his dark hat tilted back on his head, his dark suit rumpled. He looked moodily around. He seemed dazed.

"Aryeh," my mother said, coming toward him.

"Rivkeh," my father murmured. "They shot the writers."

My mother stopped. Her small body stiffened. Her mouth fell open.

"We just found out. Those who didn't die in prison were taken out and shot." He rubbed the side of his beard and looked around, still seeming dazed. "I can't remember traveling here."

"Aryeh, come inside," my mother said.

"It's the work of the sitra achra," my father murmured. "Why am I here?"

"Aryeh, please."

"I shouldn't be here, Rivkeh. I should be there."

"Aryeh."

He looked at her. "They were shot, Rivkeh. Shot. Just like that. A life is nothing to them. Nothing. Ribbono Shel Olom, who's going to be left?"

"Aryeh, I'm in the middle of making Shabbos."

He closed his eyes for a moment. Then he looked at her again. "Yes," he murmured. "Shabbos." He picked up the suitcase. They went into the bungalow.

I stood near the corner of the bungalow, staring at the closed screen door. They had not even noticed me. I went back down to the lake and tossed stones into the water.

My parents were together a great deal that weekend. My father looked tormented. I was afraid to talk to him. He seemed to need my mother's presence.

I heard him say to my mother that Shabbos afternoon, "They kill people the way people kill mosquitoes. What kind of human being kills another human being that way? To kill a human being is to kill also the children and children's children that might have come from him down through all the generations."

My mother murmured something I could not hear. They were standing near the lake and I was a little away from them along the shore.

"I cannot reconcile myself to it, Rivkeh," I heard him say. "I can't do it."

Again my mother murmured something I could not hear.

"Rivkeh, please," I heard my father say. "I'm not made for sitting still. And my father's work is also incomplete." He rubbed the side of his beard. "They're dying, Rivkeh. Why am I here? Do you know how much work has to be done in Europe?"

I saw my mother looking up at him. She brushed her fingers across his eyes. Then she moved toward him and he held her, his arms around her thin shoulders. She looked so small and frail in his huge embrace. Her eyes were concealed behind his beard, but I saw her holding him tightly. Then he noticed me. He released her. She glanced at him, then at me. They walked slowly away, talking softly. I stood at the edge of the lake and tossed stones into the water.

He left the following afternoon. I said to my mother that night, "What writers were shot, Mama?"

"Jewish writers in Russia," she said.

"Were they our own people?"

"They were Jews, Asher."

"Why were they shot?"

"Stalin ordered it."

The dreaded name again; the demonic agent of the sitra achra. I felt cold hearing that name.

"Is Papa going to Europe?" I asked.

I saw sudden alarm in her eyes. "No," she said, too quickly and loudly.

"I wish Papa wouldn't travel so much."

"Your father travels for the Rebbe."

"I wish he didn't travel so often. I don't like Papa to be away so much."

"You'll get used to it, Asher."

"No, I won't. I don't want to get used to it."

"You will have to get used to it," she said quietly. She was talking to herself, too. "It is your father's work for the Rebbe."

"Why?"

"Because his father traveled for the Rebbe's father."

"Yes, Mama. But why?"

She looked at me and was quiet a while. Then she said softly, "It is a tradition in the family, Asher. We have to help your father. Where are you going?"

"To the lake."

"Asher, we're in the middle of talking."

"I finished talking, Mama."

"It's dark by the lake."

"I know the way."

I left and went down to the lake and threw stones into the water.

There were nights during those years when I could not sleep. Often I would go to our living room and stand by the window and look out at the parkway. Late one night, I woke from a dream about my mythic ancestor and went to the window and pulled up the Venetian blind. It was a clear night with a full moon that cast shadows upon the street. The street seemed deserted. Then I saw a man walking slowly along the street near the house. He walked with his hands clasped behind his back. Some distance in front of him walked two tall bearded men. About fifteen feet behind him were two more tall bearded men. The man had a dark beard and wore a dark coat and an ordinary dark hat. I could not see his face. He continued slowly along the street, a man with a beard and an ordinary dark hat walking alone in the shadows of the trees.

On the last day of the year in which the writers were shot, a storm buried the city beneath four inches of snow. The following day, the first day of 1953, there was a bus strike and a dock strike. The city seemed dead.

I stood at the window of our living room one evening in the first week of January and thought the snow would never end. I walked through it to school the next morning, feeling it against my face and eyes. In the evening, it was still falling as a powdery mist, and the earlier

snow was turning wet on the streets. Then in the night a
windstorm came up. I watched the trees swaying crazily
and heard the sound of the wind as it whipped around
the corners of our building and blew against the windows. The wet snow froze. I walked to school on ice the
next morning and discovered that one of my classmates
had broken an elbow the night before when he slipped
while going with his father to the synagogue for the evening service.

The next day was Shabbos. In the morning, we went
to the synagogue. After lunch, my father went back to
the synagogue to hear the Rebbe's Shabbos afternoon
talk. My mother and I spent part of the afternoon in the
living room. We often spent time together on Shabbos
afternoons. She would tell me about her week in school,
and I would tell her about mine.

That Shabbos afternoon, she told me about a lecture
she had attended on the rise of Islam. One of the leaders of that religion had given orders to destroy the great
ancient library of Alexandria, because he believed that
his holy book, the Koran, was the only important book
in the world and therefore no other book was worth
preserving. The library was burned to the ground. Many
of the greatest books ever written were lost forever because of that fire.

I was looking out the window at the snow on the
trees. Was it the same kind of snow that fell on Siberia?

"Are you listening, Asher?"

"Yes, Mama."

She went on with the story. Does Yudel Krinsky remember Siberia each time he sees such snow? I stared
out the window and felt vaguely entombed.

"Are you all right, Asher?" I heard my mother ask.

"Yes, Mama."

"You look pale."

"I'm just tired."

"You're tired all the time, Asher."

I said nothing.

"Do you want to tell me about your week in school?"

"Do I have to, Mama?"

"No," she said quietly. "You don't have to."

I gazed out the window. "I've never seen so much snow. Is there this much snow in Siberia, Mama?"

She looked at me. After a moment, she said, "More, Asher. Much more."

"More snow than this? How can anyone live eleven years in more snow than this?"

My mother was quiet.

"I'm glad Papa brought Reb Yudel Krinsky out of Russia."

My mother said nothing. I thought I heard her sigh. We sat there together, gazing out the window at the snow.

The next morning, my father flew to Boston on a journey for the Rebbe.

It snowed all that day. A freezing wind blew through the parkway. Standing at the window, I saw the wind blow the snow in white waves across the parkway, saw the snow beating against the buildings and piling in huge drifts along the tall iron fences fronting some of the apartment-house lawns along the street.

I spent the morning doing homework and moving quietly about the apartment, careful not to disturb my mother, who was at the kitchen table surrounded by her books and papers. Mrs. Rackover did not come on Sundays. My mother prepared lunch. We ate on a corner of the kitchen table which she cleared by moving her books aside. After lunch, I read a story about the Rebbe's father in the Ladover magazine for youth which was distributed to all the students in the yeshiva. It told of the Rebbe's father teaching Yiddishkeit in defiance of Communist authorities and being threatened with a bullet from a Russian policeman's pistol and responding that he had no fear of death because he believed in God and knew what awaited him in the next world. Instead of shooting the Rebbe's father, they had sent him to prison.

For a long time after I finished the story, I lay in bed seeing the Rebbe's father with a pistol at his head. I wondered what I would do if a Russian policeman

pointed a pistol at my head and told me to stop teaching
Yiddishkeit. I thought of Yudel Krinsky in Siberia. For
the very briefest of moments, I thought of the drawing I
had made years before of Yudel Krinsky. I did not even
know where that drawing was. Then I forgot about the
drawing and looked at my window. It was dark.

I went to the window. It was still snowing. I saw the
snow falling through the lights of the lampposts. The
night was wild with wind and snow. I wondered how my
father would get home.

I went to the kitchen. The table was cluttered with
books. My mother was not there. Nor was she in her
bedroom. I found her in the living room in front of the
window, looking out at the snow-filled night. The Venetian blind had been raised almost three-quarters of the
way and had jammed again. It lay diagonally across the
verticals of the window. My mother stood with her face
against the window. The room was dark.

Then the phone rang. My mother turned. She was
past me even before the first ring had ended. She gave
no indication of having seen me. I heard the second ring
begin. It was cut short as the phone was lifted. I heard
my mother's voice, thin, tremulous. She listened a long
time. Then she spoke again, in a strange trembling whisper. "I warned you," she said. "I asked you not to go
today." She was silent a moment. Then she hung up.

I heard her go into her bedroom and shut the door.

I waited. I looked out the window at the snow. Slowly, the room began to fill with the noises of night darkness. I turned on the lights. I tried to lower the blind but
I could not release its jammed left side. Finally, I gave it
up and went through the hallway to my parents' bedroom. I listened at the door and heard nothing.

"Mama," I said.

There was no response.

"Mama," I said again.

"One minute." Her voice was soft and quavering. I
could barely recognize it. I waited at the door. I waited
a long time.

"Mama."

"Asher, please go and wash your hands. We'll have supper now." She was still talking through the door in that same faint voice.

"Where is Papa?"

"In Boston."

"Papa isn't coming home?"

"The airplanes can't land in the storm. Your father will come home tomorrow."

I stood at the door and did not know what to say. In a child's panic, I saw my father in snow up to his knees looking for a place to eat and sleep.

"Papa has a place to stay in Boston?"

"Your father will stay with your Aunt Leah."

I had forgotten about my Aunt Leah.

"Please go and wash your hands," my mother said through the door.

We ate cold chicken and vegetables, the leftovers from our Shabbos meals. My mother had put on her pink housecoat; her short dark hair was uncovered. Her face was pale and her eyes were dark. There was about her a little of the dead look she had had during the months of her illness.

Later that night, she came into my room and sat on the edge of my bed.

"Were you frightened, Mama?"

"Yes."

"Were you thinking of Uncle Yaakov?"

She hesitated. "Yes." Her voice trembled. She stroked my face. I felt the delicately boned fingers of her thin hand against my skin. "I'll get used to it," she said. "I'll have to get used to it." She was silent. Her eyes were dark and frightened. "My Asher," she murmured. "I'm sorry to be such a mother."

"Mama—"

"It's not good to be so easily frightened." Her eyes fixed on me intently. "Do you understand, my precious Asher? It's bad to be easily frightened."

I did not respond.

"But I'll get used to it," she murmured. She was silent a long time, staring darkly at the thin hands folded on her lap. Then she stirred and put a hand back upon my face, gently stroking my cheek. "You're not happy, my Asher. I want you to be happy." She sighed and shook her head slowly. Then she smiled through dark moist eyes. "Please, Asher, don't be like your mother. Don't be easily frightened. Now let me hear your Krias Shema, my son. Say it for both of us. Speak to the good angels for both of us. Maybe they'll help us not to be frightened."

I said the Krias Shema. She leaned over me and kissed my forehead. "In the name of the Lord, the God of Israel," she murmured, repeating one of the prayers in the Krias Shema. "May Michael be at my right hand; Gabriel at my left; before me, Uriel; behind me, Raphael; and above my head the divine presence of God. Amen, Asher. For us both. Amen." She went slowly from my room and crossed the hallway into the living room. She was in the living room a long time. Then I heard her go along the hallway to her bedroom. The bedroom door closed softly. I lay in the darkness and listened to the snow on my window.

The storm ended sometime in the night. My father flew back from Boston early the next day and was home when I returned from school.

The following morning, we heard over the radio that nine doctors, six of them Jews, had been arrested by Soviet police on a charge of plotting to murder leaders of the Russian army and navy.

The blood drained from my father's face. "Ribbono Shel Olom," I heard him say. "What do You want from us?"

My mother had been standing near the stove. She sat down slowly. Her face was pale.

The news broadcast continued. The doctors had been accused by Moscow of being connected with the international Jewish bourgeois-nationalist organization called the Joint Distribution Committee, which had been set up, according to Moscow, by the American intelligence service. A Soviet news broadcast had announced that the doctors had confessed to trying to kill top Soviet leaders by harmful medical treatment and bad diagnosis. They were accused of having killed Comrade A. Zhdanov, a leading member of the Politburo, by deliberately misdiagnosing his myocardial infarction.

There was a brief pause. The announcer began a commercial. My father turned off the radio.

"He's going to use this," my father said in a frightened voice to my mother. "He will start a blood bath."

The phone rang. He went quickly from the kitchen.

My mother and I sat at the table in silence.

My father came back into the kitchen. "I have a meeting with the Rebbe and Rav Mendel Dorochoff."

My mother sighed and nodded slowly.

"Eat something first," she said.

"Later."

"Aryeh, have some orange juice."

He said the appropriate blessing and drank a small glass of orange juice. Then he put on his jacket and coat and hat and left the apartment.

"Will Papa go away again today?" I asked my mother.

"There will probably be meetings all day today." She looked at me. "Let's try not to be frightened, Asher. Remember we said we would try?" After a moment, she said, "I think your father will be going away more often now." She said it resignedly and with darkness in her eyes.

Later that morning, I came into my school building and walked along the corridor to my classroom. Most of the students were already there. Some were settled at their desks. Others were running noisily around the room. I took off my coat and scarf and galoshes and went to my desk.

The boy in the desk next to mine looked up from the book he was reading. He was short and chubby and wore thick glasses. I did not like him.

"How much is nine times twenty-two?" he asked.

"I don't know."

"How much is nine times twelve?"

"I don't know."

"You'll fail the arithmetic test."

I had forgotten about that test. "I don't care."

"I wish my father was on the Rebbe's staff. I could fail and get away with it also."

"I wish it, too," I said.

We did not have the arithmetic test that day. A special assembly was called. There were over three hundred boys in our school. We all filed into the auditorium. The mashpia, Rav Yosef Cutler, climbed onto the stage and spoke softly in Yiddish into the microphone.

"Dear children. Today the enemies of the Jewish people have again shown us how much they hate us and our Torah. The Russian bear has cast six of our people into the pit. Our tears and our prayers go out to our brothers the children of Israel in this moment of darkness. For hundreds of years, Jews have suffered from the murderous hatred of the Russians, first under the czars and now under the Bolsheviks. The Russian government is different, but the Russian hatred of the Jew is the same. This morning, the Rebbe asked me to ask all our dear students to plead with the Master of the Universe to spare the lives of the Jewish doctors and return them safely to their families, and to pray for the redemption of all our oppressed people everywhere."

We all stood as the mashpia chanted a Hebrew prayer. Then we answered amen, and filed silently back to our classrooms.

I came out of the school building in the early darkness of the winter day, and instead of turning toward home I went in the opposite direction to Kingston Avenue. I walked quickly along Kingston Avenue, went past my Uncle Yitzchok's jewelry and watch-repair store, and came into the stationery store where Yudel Krinsky worked. I saw him standing on a ladder behind the counter, reaching for pads of paper. There were two women ahead of me. I waited. Looking around, I noticed that a new glass display case had been placed to the right of the door. The case was small and had three shelves filled with art supplies—pencils, crayons, watercolors, brushes. There were boxes with names I did not understand, like Conté Crayons, Rembrandt Pastels, Grumbacher Zinc White. Next to this display case was a tall metal cabinet with an open slanting top divided into sections by metal strips. The sections were stocked with tubes of oil colors.

"The son of Reb Aryeh Lev," I heard Yudel Krinsky say in Yiddish in his hoarse voice. "How can I help you?"

He wore a white frock over his shirt and trousers. He had on his kaskett. He looked relaxed and cheerful.

"I need a notebook," I said in Yiddish.

"A Hebrew notebook or a goyische notebook?"

"A Hebrew notebook."

"Here is a Hebrew notebook for the son of Reb Aryeh Lev."

"I need also a pencil."

"A dark pencil or a light pencil?"

"A dark pencil."

"Here is a dark pencil for the son of Reb Aryeh Lev. How is your father?"

"He is well, thank you. He is at meetings all day long. About the doctors."

"The doctors?"

"The Jewish doctors in Russia."

"Ah," he said. His thin face darkened. "Yes. The Cossacks came out again."

"Will they send the doctors to Siberia?"

"I do not doubt it. If they will not shoot them, they will send them to Siberia."

"Is Siberia really very cold?"

He looked at me closely, his eyes clouding. "Siberia is the home of the Angel of Death. It is the place where the Angel of Death feeds and grows fat. No one should know of it, Asher. No one. Not even my worst enemies, all of whom, thank God, I left behind in Russia. Only Stalin should know of it. But even he should know of it only for a little while. I have a Jewish heart even where Stalin, may his name and memory be erased, is concerned. Now, what else do you need? Paper, pens, erasers? It is a big store and we have, thank God, everything."

I did not need anything else. I thanked him and hurried home in the dark.

My mother was not due back from college until later. Mrs. Rackover met me at the door.

"Where were you?"

"I had to buy a notebook."

"Your mother knew you had to buy a notebook?"

"I forgot to tell her."

"Your mother does not like you to come home late. What shall I say when she asks when you came home?"

"I don't care."

She looked at me sadly. "You are not the boy I thought you would be," she said.

"What do you mean?"

"Take off your coat and galoshes. I will give you a glass of milk. You still care about milk, yes?"

She did not tell my mother.

I slept late the next morning. My father woke me. I sat up in my bed. My father looked upset.

"I saw the mashpia at yesterday's meeting with the Rebbe. He gave me a bad report, Asher."

I looked down at the hills my knees made beneath the blanket.

"Look at me, Asher."

"Yes, Papa."

"Are you feeling all right?"

"I'm tired, Papa."

"The mashpia told me you aren't studying. What would your grandfather say if he knew you weren't studying?"

I was quiet.

My father regarded me silently. His clothes were rumpled. He looked as if he had been up all night. "I'll talk to you more about this another time," he said. "I'm disturbed by what the mashpia told me."

I lay back on my pillow and covered my eyes with my hand.

"Asher, today is a school day," I heard my father say.

"I'm tired, Papa."

"Are you sick?"

"I don't know."

I felt his hand on my forehead. His fingers were dry and cool.

"You have no fever."

"I'm very tired, Papa."

"I want you to get up and get dressed and go to school."

The phone rang.

"I want you to get up now, Asher."

"Aryeh," my mother called.

My father went from the room.

Now, I thought. Now now now. But I'm tired. And I don't care. And what difference does it make? Oh, I'm tired. Why am I so tired? Maybe I'm sick. Maybe I should ask Mama to take me to the doctor. Mama wouldn't take me to the doctor. Mama has no time. She'll ask Mrs. Rackover to take me to the doctor. Then I thought of the Jewish doctors in Russia. Then I thought of Siberia. Then I thought of Yudel Krinsky. I sat up on the edge of my bed and began to get dressed. I heard my father go through the hallway and out of the apartment. I dressed quickly.

Later that day, I came out onto the street after school and walked along Brooklyn Parkway and Kingston Avenue to the stationery store. Yudel Krinsky was behind the counter, stacking reams of paper on a shelf.

"Sholom aleichem to the son of Reb Aryeh Lev," he said.

"I need another notebook," I said.

"Yes? What kind of notebook?"

"A Hebrew notebook."

"And a pencil? You need a pencil?"

"No, thank you."

The store smelled of paper and pencils and crayons. It was a warm smell. I liked being inside that store. Yudel Krinsky looked across the counter and smiled at me.

"What else can I do for the son of Reb Aryeh Lev?"

"Did Stalin send many people to Siberia?"

He blinked. Then he said, nodding, "Ah, I understand."

"Did he?"

"Many millions."

"Did he kill many people?"

"Tens of millions."

"Did the world do anything?"

"Exactly what it did when Hitler killed Jews."

"What?"

"Absolutely nothing."

"I do not understand."

"What do you not understand?"

"Why the world kept silent."

"I also do not understand."

We looked at each other across the counter.

"I have to go home," I said.

"Do not forget your notebook."

I picked the notebook up off the counter.

"Asher, you do not have to buy something each time you want to come in to talk to me."

"Thank you," I said.

I went out of the store and ran home.

"Another notebook?" Mrs. Rackover said.

I showed her the notebook.

"I see. And what shall I tell your mother?"

I shrugged.

"I should tell your mother you made like this with your shoulder?"

I said nothing.

"Asher, why do you go to that store?"

"I like Reb Yudel Krinsky."

She looked at me and was quiet. Then she said,

"Take off your coat, Asher, and I will give you a glass of milk."

The next day, my father flew to Washington and returned home very late at night. When I woke Friday morning, he had already left for his office. In the kitchen over breakfast, my mother said, "You've been going to Reb Yudel Krinsky's store after school?"

"Yes, Mama."

"Why?"

"I like him."

"Why didn't you tell me you were going?"

"I was afraid you would be angry."

She regarded me in silence for a moment. Then she said softly, "I'm sorry I make you afraid of me, my Asher. I don't want to make you afraid of me."

I was quiet.

After a long moment, she said, "Asher, you understand your father is very busy now because of what has happened in Russia."

"Yes." But I wasn't really certain I understood.

"You understand the Russians are hurting Jews."

"Yes, Mama."

"You understand your father is trying to help those Jews."

"Yes, Mama."

"We think there will be a great persecution of Jews in Russia now. Your father is talking about that with important people in the American government."

I was quiet.

"Asher, I don't like your father to be away from home so much. But your father is doing what the Rebbe asks. Would you want your father to say no to the Rebbe?"

"No, Mama."

"Asher, do you understand I have to finish my work in school?"

I hesitated, not knowing how to respond.

"You don't understand."

I was quiet.

"No," my mother said. "Of course you don't under-stand." She was silent a long time. Then she said, "All right, Asher. You may go to Reb Yudel Krinsky's store."

"Thank you, Mama."

"But don't stay too long and come straight home when you leave."

"Yes, Mama."

"And don't make a nuisance of yourself."

"No, Mama."

She looked at me and shook her head sadly. Her eyes were dark. "Please drink your juice," she said quietly. "All the vitamins will go out of it."

It was my father's custom to wake very early on Shabbos morning and go to the mikveh, which was a one-story red-brick building on the corner diagonally across the street from our house. My mother would go every few weeks, but my father went every Friday and Shabbos and sometimes in the middle of the week. I did not go with him then, for it is only necessary to immerse oneself in a ritual bath when one has reached puberty.

My father went to the mikveh that Shabbos morning. It was a cold clear January day. He returned to the apartment with his hair still wet, as always. We started to the synagogue together. On the way, I asked him if he would be traveling to Washington again that week.

"Monday," he said.

"Will the Russians arrest more Jews, Papa?"

"Who knows what the Russians will do?"

"Mama says you'll be traveling a lot now."

"Yes."

"Reb Yudel Krinsky said Stalin killed tens of mil-lions of people."

"Yes," my father said. Then he looked at me and said quietly, "Give my good wishes to Reb Yudel Krin-sky when you see him again."

"Yes, Papa."

Inside the synagogue, my father took his seat at the

table near the Ark and I sat at a table in the rear with some of my classmates. The synagogue was always crowded. It was a large synagogue with paneled walls, chandeliers, tables and benches, a podium near the center of the floor, and an Ark built into the front wall. Off in the corner to the right of the Ark, near a narrow door that led from the synagogue to a small private room, was the cushioned chair on which the Rebbe usually sat, a tallis covering his head so that his face could not be seen. He would come in with his head covered and go out with his head covered; only an edge of his beard would be visible. Sometimes he came in only for those sections of the service that had to be prayed together with the congregation. He prayed without swaying back and forth, with no movement of any kind.

He came into the synagogue that Shabbos about twenty minutes after the start of the service. He seemed particularly still as he prayed. His face was buried in his tallis. He sat in his chair, looking like a small white sacred mountain. I watched him. I saw others watching him. About ten minutes before the end of the service, he rose and left the synagogue through the small door near the Ark.

I said to my father on the way back to the synagogue, "Did the Rebbe pray for the doctors, Papa?"

"I'm sure he did."

"Will you be traveling to Russia now?"

"If a person was born in Russia and then left, it's dangerous for him to travel there."

"But you will travel there, Papa?"

"I don't know, Asher. Right now I think I'll travel into bed. I have a headache."

My father did not attend the Rebbe's talk that afternoon. Instead, he went to bed with a fever.

I saw him lying in his bed, his red beard sticking out over the pale-green blanket.

"Rivkeh, this is foolishness," he said.

"A fever is never foolishness," my mother said.

"It's foolishness. I have to be in Washington Monday."

The talk about foolishness echoed faintly inside me, as if I had heard it before. But I could not remember.

"Asher, please go out," my mother said to me. "Out. Please. One sick man in the house is enough."

"I need two aspirins," my father said.

"You need antibiotics, and I'm calling the doctor as soon as Shabbos is over," my mother said. "We don't want complications. You have Washington Monday and I have a test Monday afternoon. Asher, out I said, out. Please."

The doctor came that night, a cheerful young man with a round face and shell-rimmed glasses. My father had a slight bronchitis. The doctor prescribed antibiotics, liquids, and bed.

When I came into the kitchen the next morning, I found my mother at the table, asleep over her books. She had on the same clothes she had worn the night before.

"Mama," I said.

She did not move. She lay with her head on her arms, almost sprawled on top of her books, breathing softly.

I put my hand on her shoulder and shook her gently.

"Yes," I heard her say, her voice muffled by her arm. "Yes, yes, Yaakov."

I took my hand from her shoulder.

"Yaakov, I will pass the examination," she said, moving her lips against her arm. She talked in Yiddish. "Do not worry yourself, Yaakov."

"Mama," I said loudly.

She came suddenly and sharply awake and sat up straight and stared at me. Her blond wig was awry. She had worn it when the doctor had come in, and had not removed it.

"Mama, are you all right?"

She looked down at her books. Then she looked at the kitchen clock. "I fell asleep at the table." Her eyes were puffed. The side of her face that had rested against her arm was blotched red. "I have to see how your father is."

She rose unsteadily to her feet and went from the kitchen. A few minutes later, she returned. She had removed the wig, changed her clothes, and washed her face.

"How is Papa?"

"Your father is grouchy. He asks you to please go down and buy a *New York Times*. Will you do that?"

"Yes, Mama."

"Without going by way of Kingston Avenue?"

"Yes, Mama."

"And please buy the Yiddish papers, too."

"Yes, Mama. Will Papa be able to go to Washington tomorrow?"

She looked at me. "If the Ribbono Shel Olom wants your father to go to Washington tomorrow, he'll go to Washington."

She spent the day giving my father his medicine, bringing him tea and lemon and honey, studying for her exam, preparing meals, and answering the telephone. Finally, I volunteered to answer the telephone for her. If it was for my father, I said he was sick and could not come to the phone; if it was for my mother, I said she was studying and had asked not to be disturbed. Surprisingly, everyone I talked to about my mother seemed to understand; no one asked her to come to the phone. She was still at the kitchen table when I went to sleep that night.

The next morning, I came into the kitchen and found my mother squeezing orange juice.

"How is Papa feeling?"

"He left half an hour ago."

I stared at her.

"The Ribbono Shel Olom wanted him to go," she said. "Sit down and drink your juice."

Later, she went with me to my school.

"Have a good day, Asher. Give Reb Yudel Krinsky my regards."

"I hope you get a very good mark on your test, Mama."

"Thank you, Asher."

I watched her walk along the parkway, carrying her books.

There were four people in the stationery store when I went there after school that day. I waited patiently. Just as Yudel Krinsky finished with the last customer, two more walked in. Then three more came in. I stood near the cabinet containing the tubes of oil colors and waited.

"Asher," I heard Yudel Krinsky call.

I looked at him between the crowd of customers.

"Asher, in the cabinet next to you. Bring me, please, two tubes of cadmium red light and two tubes of cadmium yellow light. You see them? On the top row."

I saw them. The tubes felt heavy and solid in my hands. I moved between the people and put the tubes on the counter.

"One number-ten bristle brush," I heard the woman next to me say. She spoke in English and had a faint Russian accent.

I looked up. She was in her late fifties and had short gray hair and pale-blue eyes. She wore a light-brown coat and dark-brown galoshes with a fur trim.

Yudel Krinsky went to the glass showcase next to the metal cabinet and returned with a long-handled brush.

"What else?" he asked.

"Rectified turpentine," the woman said.

He placed a white-and-red can on the counter.

"What else?"

"That's all," the woman said. "Thank you."

A few minutes later, the store was empty.

"All day long, people people people," Yudel Krinsky said. "In Russia, we did not use paper the way it is used in America. Here it is used like air." He looked at me. "How is your father feeling?"

"My father flew to Washington."

"He is finished with his bronchitis?"

"Yes." I wondered how he knew my father had had bronchitis.

"When Reb Aryeh Lev is sick, people worry. Now, Asher Lev has a question for me today?"

"Yes."

"Ask. But while you ask you can help me put these boxes on the shelf. Yes?"

"My mama says there will be a great persecution of Jews in Russia now. Do you think the Russians will do that?"

"Not for one minute do I doubt it. Why else would they arrest Jewish doctors in this way?"

"My papa is trying to help."

"Yes," he said. "I know what your father is doing. Give me that other package, Asher. Yes. Thank you."

"If we lived in Russia now, would they be sending my papa to Siberia?"

He held a package in midair and peered at me intently. "A strange question," he murmured.

"Would they?"

"Not for one minute do I doubt it," he said. "Or they would shoot him."

I came out of the store a few minutes later and went home. It was dark and sharply cold. The naked trees moved brokenly in the icy wind.

"Would you like cold milk or hot cocoa?" Mrs. Rackover asked. "It is bitter outside."

"Hot cocoa, please," I said.

She did not say anything to me about Reb Yudel Krinsky.

My mother came home as I was finishing the cocoa. There was snow on her blue coat and blond wig.

"I did well on the test," she said. "All our lives should be as easy as that test."

"From your mouth into God's ears," said Mrs. Rackover in fervent Yiddish.

"We have to celebrate," my mother said. "We'll have a little wine with the fish. Oh, was that an easy test."

"What was it a test in, Mama?"

"You know where Papa keeps the wine, Asher. Please bring a little bottle and put it in the refrigerator."

"What was the test in, Mama?"

"Russian history," my mother said.

About an hour after supper, it began to snow heavily. My mother and I stood at the living-room window, watching for my father.

"I hate this," my mother murmured, staring out the window. "Oh, Ribbono Shel Olom, I hate this. Why do You do this? Tell me why. Who needs it?" Then she spoke in Yiddish. "Yaakov, please be an interceder for me with the Ribbono Shel Olom. Yaakov, do you hear? Yaakov?"

My father returned two hours later, exhausted, snow on his hat, snow on his coat, snow in his beard and eyes. My mother fed him supper and put him to bed. She was at the kitchen table with her books when I fell asleep.

The snow fell through most of the night, then began to freeze in a bitter wind. In the morning, there was ice on the bark of the trees and on the dark metal of the lampposts. The sun shone across the buildings like an exhausted light. I walked to school alone.

Sometime during that morning, the door to our class opened and the mashpia entered the room. We rose respectfully and stood in silence until he took the seat behind the front desk. Our teacher moved to the rear of the room and sat down near a window.

The mashpia spoke to us softly, his eyes half closed.

"Dear children. We spoke last time of the Rebbe's grandfather, may his memory be blessed. We described his years in prison under the Czar. Now, the Rebbe's father, may his memory be blessed, was also in prison, not under the Czar, but under the Bolsheviks. When the Rebbe's grandfather was released from prison, he settled in Ladov. To Ladov came Jews from all over the world who had heard of his terrible suffering. Some of those Jews were great scholars who had opposed him before, but now became his followers. And from Ladov the Rebbe's grandfather sent out emissaries throughout Russia to win Jews to Ladover Hasidus. These emissaries were the arms and legs, the mouth and eyes and ears of the Rebbe's grandfather. Later, when the Rebbe's grandfather, may his memory be a blessing, removed himself from this world, the Rebbe's father also sent out emissaries. Some of these emissaries, dear children, were caught by the Bolsheviks and sent to Siberia, where they perished for the Sanctification of the Name. One of those emissaries was murdered by a Russian peasant the night before the goyische holiday called Easter. Another was caught by secret police teaching Hasidus and was taken to prison and shot. This happened in the Ukraine before the Second World War. Great were the hardships of these emissaries. But the Ribbono Shel Olom remembers their efforts and their suffering. And therefore great is their reward in the world to come."

He talked a few minutes longer, telling us some more stories about past Ladover emissaries. Outside, it began to snow again.

Later, I walked in the snow to Yudel Krinsky's store. I found him behind the counter, sorting paintbrushes. He was alone in the store and was surprised to see me.

"In such a storm you walk to the store? You should go straight home."

I did not want to go home. It was warm in the store and there was that smell of new paper and pencils. I took off my coat and galoshes. Yudel Krinsky waved a brush at me.

"Outside is like Siberia. You are sure you should not go home?"

"I can stay a little while," I said.

"Then help me with the brushes," he said. "A Jew should not only talk, he should also do."

I helped him sort the brushes. Then I helped him stack loose-leaf fillers and boxes of index cards. We talked as we worked. Somewhere in the talking, he began to tell me of his life in Russia. He had lived with his wife and children in a small city in the Ukraine. There were other Ladover Hasidim in the city, and they all worked in a hatpin factory that was managed by a man who had grown up in that city. He permitted them not to come in on Shabbos. Then a Russian was sent to take over the factory. This Russian discovered soon enough that the factory was a place of refuge for Jews who observed the Shabbos. He called a meeting of all the workers, Jews and Gentiles, and influenced the Gentiles to vote against having workers missing from the factory on Shabbos. The Ladover Jews remained with the factory but stayed away on Shabbos, when their places were taken by Russians. The management was satisfied with this arrangement. But in the eyes of the secret police those Jews became enemies of the Soviet state. After a while, ten of the Jewish workers were arrested and sent to Siberia. Yudel Krinsky was one of the ten.

He paused, blinked his large eyes, and scratched his beaklike nose. He glanced around nervously. Then he took a deep breath. He put down the ream of typing paper he held in his hands and without a word went through the curtained doorway to the small room in the back of the store. He was gone a while. I looked out the plate-glass window. It was snowing heavily. I began putting on my galoshes. Yudel Krinsky came out from the rear of the store. He stopped behind the counter and peered through the window at the snow blowing through the street. He shook his head again and began moving about the store, turning off lights.

A few minutes later, we stood outside in the snow. He closed and locked the door, fumbling nervously with the ring of keys.

"Sometimes in Siberia when it snowed, it was colder inside than outside." He paused. "Your father should live and be well," he said. "You and your mother should both live and be well. Be careful going home in the snow, Asher. Snow is an enemy."

I watched him walk away up Kingston Avenue, a small man huddled inside a heavy dark coat and wearing a dark kaskett.

I went quickly along Kingston Avenue and turned in to the parkway. The snow was thick. I could feel the icy surface of last night's snow beneath the snow now on the street. It was slippery and treacherous and I took a long time getting home. Coming up to the apartment house along the parkway, I raised my eyes and looked through the snow at our living-room window. I saw my mother framed in the window, staring down at me.

She met me at the door.

"Where were you?"

I told her.

"Do you know what time it is?"

We had talked about Russia and Siberia, I said. We had—

She wasn't listening. She seemed in a frenzy of rage and panic. "Your father is in Detroit, and you come home almost an hour late. What do you want from me? What are you doing to me, Asher?" She was screaming. "I don't understand. What did I do to you? Tell me, what did I do to you?"

I stared at her, feeling terrified, feeling a dark horror move over me.

"Didn't you realize someone was at home waiting? Didn't it occur to you what it means to wait? I called the school ten minutes ago and there was no answer. Asher, do you know what those ten minutes of waiting were like?" Her voice broke. She took a trembling breath. "Ribbono Shel Olom," she said. "What do You want from me?" She turned suddenly and went along the hallway. "What do You want from me?" I heard her say again. Then I heard the door to her bedroom slam shut.

In the sudden overwhelming silence that filled the apartment, I thought I could hear the sounds of the snow falling through the icy air outside.

I came into my room. I was trembling. I was shivering and trembling. I lay on my bed in my coat and galoshes and could not stop trembling. The snow made pebble sounds against the window of the dark room. Sometimes in Siberia when it snowed, it was colder inside than outside, I heard Yudel Krinsky say. Snow is an enemy, snow is an enemy. Your father should live and be well. You and your mother should both live and be well. I took a deep breath and held it a long time. I held my hands tightly together. I stiffened my body and legs. I could not stop trembling. The apartment was very dark. I heard the door to my parents' bedroom open. Someone came through the hallway and into the living room, moving softly on slippered feet. Then I heard nothing. Then I heard my mother. I heard her voice; it seemed close by in the darkness. She was in the living room. I heard her chanting from the Book of Psalms. She chanted a long time. Then she stopped and there was a long silence. Then I heard her say clearly in the silence, "I cannot do it, Yaakov." She spoke in Yiddish. "Do you hear me, my brother? How can I do it? I am only a little girl. What do you want from me? Ribbono-Shel Olom, what does the world want from me?" Then there was another long silence. Then she began to chant again from the Book of Psalms. I lay there on my bed in my coat and galoshes, listening to my mother chant from the Book of Psalms.

A long while later, she went back into her room. We had no supper that night. I lay on my bed in the darkness; then I fell asleep, still wearing my coat and galoshes. Sometime in the night, I woke from a dream and felt myself smothering. I felt buried in snow and ice, and then woke fully and realized I had slid down into my coat and the lined hood was over my head. I got into pajamas and went to the bathroom. I heard the snow on the frosted window. My father was in Detroit in the snow. The snow blew against the window. I went to my room and got into bed. The darkness was alive with the sounds of the storm-filled night. I had known of my father's trip and had forgotten it in the warmth of Yudel Krinsky's store. I thought of the brushes I had helped Yudel Krinsky sort. Then I thought of the metal cabinet filled with tubes of oil color. I did not understand why I should be thinking of that cabinet. Then I fell asleep.

My mother said to me the next morning over breakfast, "Asher, if you want to continue going to Reb

Yudel Krinsky's store, you will have to remember to return at a reasonable time."

"Yes, Mama."

"And if it snows when you leave school, please come straight home."

"Yes, Mama."

She looked at me soberly. "I lost my temper last night."

I was quiet.

"You frightened me, Asher. But I should not have lost my temper."

"I apologize for what I did, Mama."

"Yes. You frightened me. I'm trying very hard to get used to it, Asher. I'm really trying." She looked at me through the sheen of tears in her eyes. "I wish I hadn't lost my temper. I told myself that the next time it happened I wouldn't be frightened. But I was a failure." She put a napkin to her eyes. Then she said softly, "Drink your juice, my Asher. I'll walk with you to your school."

Later, we came out of the apartment house and walked along the snow-filled parkway and stopped at the path that led to the entrance doors of the school.

She kissed my forehead and said, "Have a good day in school, Asher. I hope you get a fine mark on your arithmetic test."

"Thank you, Mama." The test had been postponed from last week to today. But I had forgotten again to study for it. "Will Papa's plane be able to land today?"

"If the Ribbono Shel Olom wants it to land, it will land."

She turned and started along the parkway. I watched her walk up the street carrying her books.

I failed the arithmetic test.

THREE

During supper on the first Monday in March, the phone rang and my father went to answer it. When he returned, he said in a choked voice, quoting in Hebrew, " 'When your enemy falls, do not rejoice,' " and he told us that Stalin had had a stroke, was paralyzed and unconscious, and was dying.

The following Wednesday, the story was in the newspapers. The official announcement had come out of Russia Tuesday midnight, Eastern Standard Time. I never asked my father how he had learned of Stalin's illness more than a day before the official announcement. He would not have told me.

On my way home from school Thursday afternoon, I saw a car pull up in front of our headquarters building. Six men came out of the car. I recognized one of them; he was in his twenties and he had worked two offices down from my father when my father had been on the first floor of the building. The others looked to be in their fifties or sixties, men with gray beards, dark coats, and dark hats. They went up the steps of the building and disappeared inside.

My father did not come home that night. The next morning, my mother and I heard over the radio that Stalin had died the previous afternoon at 1:50 p.m. Eastern Standard Time.

My mother turned off the radio as the announcer started a commercial. We sat in silence. The refrigerator hummed softly.

" 'So perish the enemies of God,' " my mother quoted softly in Hebrew.

I told my mother about the men I had seen come out of the car the day before.

"Who were they, Mama?"

"Ask your father," she said quietly.

I asked my father later that day. "Ladover from Europe," he said.

Early the next morning, my father went to the mikveh. He returned to the apartment, his hair wet; his sidecurls, which he had not tucked behind his ears, were dripping.

"You will catch pneumonia one day," my mother said, bringing a bath towel into the kitchen. "Please dry yourself."

"Simcha is out," my father said to her. "He's in London."

My mother paled. "When?"

"Yesterday."

"Thank God," my mother said. "Thank God."

"Who is Simcha?" I asked.

"A Jew," my father said. "From Kiev."

I did not ask anything else.

My father went out of the kitchen to put on his tallis, which he always wore under his coat as we walked to the synagogue. On our way to the synagogue, he asked, "Do you know where Vienna is, Asher?"

I did not even know what Vienna was.

"Vienna is the capital city of Austria."

I did not know where Austria was.

"Geography you don't know. Chumash and Rashi you don't know. Mishnayes you don't know. Sometimes I wonder whose son you are, Asher."

"We didn't study Austria, Papa. I don't think we studied Austria."

"And arithmetic you don't know."

"I don't like arithmetic."

"Yes," he said. "I've noticed you don't like arithmetic."

The morning service began a few minutes after we entered the synagogue. I saw my father at the table near the front of the synagogue, his head covered by his tallis. The tables were crowded. With very few exceptions, every adult inside that synagogue had experienced the tyranny of Stalin. People prayed loudly, fervently, swaying back and forth on the benches. There was a momentary pause when the service reached Borchu. Everyone stood, waiting. The narrow door in the corner to the right of the Ark opened slowly and the Rebbe stepped out. His head and face were covered by his tallis. The Rebbe stood near his chair and faced the Ark.

The old man who was leading the service chanted in a loud quavering voice, "Borchu es Adonoi hamevoroch."

The congregation responded almost in a shout, "Boruch Adonoi hamevoroch leolom voed."

The old man repeated, "Boruch Adonoi hamevoroch leolom voed."

The Rebbe turned and sat down in his chair. His movements were very slow. The tallis completely covered his head and face. The congregants took their seats. The service continued. A tremulous crescendo of sound began to fill the synagogue. Men swayed fervently back and forth. Arms gesticulated toward the ceiling and walls. I prayed loudly, swaying, caught up in the intensity of feeling that had taken possession of the service.

The Rebbe sat in his chair, praying. He sat very still, robed in his tallis. He held a prayer book in both hands. He held the prayer book rigidly and turned the pages with slow and deliberate movements of his right hand. He sat like that, very still, praying. His quiet presence began to move out toward the congregants and dominate the large synagogue. Slowly the outward intensity of the service began to diminish. The wild swaying ceased. The loud cries and gesticulations disappeared. A hushed thick tangible concentration of controlled fervor rose from the congregation. I was no longer swaying; I was concentrating on the words of the prayers. The words moved and danced in front of me. I felt the words inside me. "From Egypt you redeemed us, O Lord our God," I prayed, "and from the house of slavery you ransomed us." The words were alive. I felt them alive and moving inside me.

The Rebbe left after the Musaf Kedushoh. A few minutes later, the service ended. I came outside and saw Yudel Krinsky.

"A good Shabbos to you, Asher Lev," he said. He still wore the kaskett. "I have not seen you all week."

"I'll come to see you Monday," I said.

He seemed sad. "The dead do not return to life because a tyrant dies. The Ribbono Shel Olom was late. Stalin should have died thirty years ago." He walked slowly away.

We sat at the Shabbos meal a long time that day. My father sang the zemiros slowly, his eyes closed, his body swaying faintly. My mother and I sang with him. From time to time, he stopped and sat in silence, his hand over his mouth. I saw him give me an occasional glance. After the meal, he left the house and went to the synagogue.

I saw a picture in the *Times* the following day of Stalin lying in his coffin. Behind the coffin were mounds of flowers. I could not take my eyes off the picture. This was the man who had killed tens of millions of people. Now he lay in his mustache and uniform in front of a mountain of flowers, dead, as dead as the millions he had slain, as dead as Yudel Krinsky's wife and children. I could not stop staring at the picture of Stalin dead in his coffin.

I went over to Yudel Krinsky's store that Monday and helped him wait on some customers. We were alone for a few minutes between customers and he said to me, glancing around quickly, "The others who follow him will be just like him. There are many Stalins in Russia."

I helped him stack packages of paper. I was beginning to understand the differences between grades of paper. Often now I could tell the weight and quality of a piece of paper by holding it in my hands.

My mother said to me that night, "No, Asher. I don't think there can be another Stalin now in Russia."

"Reb Yudel Krinsky said there are many Stalins in Russia."

"Yes, your Reb Yudel Krinsky is right, Asher. Russia is full of Stalins. But the time of Stalin in Russia is over for now."

"Mama, does it make a difference for Jews that Stalin is dead?"

"Yes, Asher. I think it makes a difference."

The following Shabbos afternoon, my father went to the synagogue to hear the Rebbe's talk. My mother asked me to come into the living room. She wanted to talk to me, she said. We sat on the sofa. I looked out the window at the winter trees.

"Asher, do you know where Vienna is?" my mother said softly. "We may move to Vienna."

I stared at her and could not respond.

"Your father asked me to tell you. There's a certain work he has to do now, and he can only do it if we live in Vienna."

"What work?" I heard myself ask.

She was silent a moment. Then she said, "It has to do with the Jews in Russia."

"Papa has been doing that here for years."

"This is different work, Asher."

"I don't want to go to Vienna, Mama."

"The Rebbe has told your father that he may ask us to go."

"Why now? Why all of a sudden now?"

"Because Stalin is dead, Asher. Things can be done now that no one could have done before."

"I don't want to go."

"We'll go if your father is asked to go."

"No," I said.

"Asher, please."

"I don't care," I said.

"Asher," my mother said softly. She leaned forward. "Asher." I felt her hands brush across my face in a caress. "My Asher, my baby, I don't know what else to tell you. We'll go if the Rebbe tells us to go. We must help your father. If the Rebbe tells us to go, we'll go."

Later, I lay on my bed in my room and covered my eyes with my hands. I felt tired. I thought of Yudel Krinsky. I saw his bulging eyes glancing nervously around. Stalin should have died thirty years ago, Yudel Krinsky had said. Yes, I thought. Yes, yes, thirty years ago. Not now. Not last week. Thirty years ago or ten years from now. But not last week. I hated him for dying last week.

My father returned home very late that night. The next morning, he flew to Chicago.

I was ill that week. I lay in bed with a sore throat and a fever. By Wednesday, the sore throat was gone but the fever remained. Our doctor came on Thursday, called it a low-grade infection, and left a prescription.

All through that week, my mother went to school. My father returned from Chicago on Monday and spent the remaining days of the week in his office. Each night, they came into my room together. I saw them standing together by my bed, looking down at me. I saw them as through a fog, distorted, my father tall and strong, his features framed by his red hair and long red beard, all of him rigid and shimmering; my mother short and wraithlike, a being of smoky clouds shaped by changing winds. My uncle Yitzchok came into the room one day. He leaned over the bed and gave me a broad smile. I could see his round face and the streaks of gray hair in his beard. He smelled strongly of cigars. "Listen to me," I heard him say. "Listen to your Uncle Yitzchok. Get well and I'll buy your drawings. You hear me, Asher? I'll buy your drawings." I turned my head away. Yudel Krinsky came to see me. His eyes looked around nervously. He scratched his beaked nose and said in his hoarse voice, "The son of Reb Aryeh Lev must get out of bed. Asher and Yudel have to talk some more. And there is paper to stack. Yes, this is cold-pressed paper and this is hot-pressed paper. This is twenty-pound paper and this is forty-pound paper. This is paper for charcoal and this is paper for watercolor. On this canvas board you can use oil color, and on this heavy paper you can use pastels. How do I know these things? I learned. If you want to survive in this world, you have to learn to learn quickly. Vienna? I was only a few hours once in Vienna. Before the war, it was known as a city of cafés and waltzes. It is a city that hates Jews."

I lay in bed with my eyes closed and did not want to leave my room. I thought at one time during that week that a violent snowstorm raged outside; but I was not sure and I did not care. I did not want to leave my room. I did not want to leave my street. I knew the boys in my class and the men in my synagogue; I knew the women on the benches and the owners of the shops. I knew the trees and the buildings and the cracks in the sidewalk; I knew the lampposts and the fireplugs and the shrubs on the lawns. And I was frightened of traveling. I hated taking the subway. I hated taking the bus. I was terrified of taking an airplane, terrified. Vienna. The name conjured up distorted horrors: dark foreign streets, evil shadows, incomprehensible words, menacing laughter at my sidecurls and skullcap. I would not go to Vienna. But what would I say to the Rebbe? I did not know. Maybe the Rebbe would change his mind. Ribbono Shel Olom, help the Rebbe to change his mind. Please, Ribbono Shel Olom. Please.

By Shabbos morning, the fever was gone. But my mother would not permit me to go to the synagogue. I moved slowly about the house in my pajamas and robe, feeling very tired.

Sometime during the afternoon, I asked my mother, "Did Uncle Yitzchok and Reb Yudel Krinsky visit me when I was sick?"

She gave me a tired worried look. "No."

"I must have dreamed it," I said.

That Monday evening, my father came home and told us we would be moving to Vienna next October, immediately after the holidays.

I told Yudel Krinsky the next day, "My papa said we're moving to Vienna after Simchas Torah."

"Ah," he said in his hoarse voice. "That is why you asked about Vienna."

"Do you know about Vienna?"

"Vienna is the center of Europe. Many people and many things move from Western Europe to Eastern Europe through Vienna. And many people and many things move from Eastern Europe to Western Europe through Vienna."

"I don't understand."

"Asher, I was one who came from Eastern Europe to Western Europe through Vienna."

I stared at him.

"They told me it was once a city of happy waltzes. I did not see its happiness. I saw that it hates Jews." He glanced around briefly. "Where are Jews not hated? But somehow one feels Vienna should be different. It is not different. Hand me the box of oil colors, Asher. Thank you. It is not different. This is soft charcoal, Asher. It is good to use on this paper. In Russia, I made hatpins. You see what a man can learn in order to survive? The only charcoal I saw in Russia was in the Jewish houses that were burned by Petlyura and his madmen. Ah, how we felt when we heard Petlyura had been shot in Paris. But you do not know about Petlyura."

"I don't want to go to Vienna."

He looked at me sadly. "I understand," he said.

I said to my mother that evening, "I don't want to go to Vienna."

"I know," my mother said softly.

I said to my father that night, "Why did the Rebbe choose you to go to Vienna?"

"The Rebbe chose me to be head of a new office that is being organized. We are going to teach Ladover Hasidus all over Europe. We are going to open Ladover yeshivos in Paris, Geneva, London, Zurich, Bucharest, Rome, in Sweden and Norway, wherever the Ribbono Shel Olom will give us the strength to go."

"But why do we have to go to Vienna?"

"Because this work can't be done from Brooklyn, Asher."

"But why Vienna, Papa?"

"Because it's the center of Europe. From Vienna, I'll be able to travel all through Europe."

I stared at my father. "You're going to travel in Europe?"

"Of course, Asher."

"I don't want to go to Vienna, Papa."

"Asher."

"I don't want to leave here. I like it here."

"Yes," my father said quietly. "I've noticed you like it here. But we'll go anyway, Asher. And you'll learn to like it there."

I saw my Uncle Yitzchok outside our synagogue after services next Shabbos, and I said to him, "My papa is taking us to Vienna after Simchas Torah."

He smiled down at me and his watery brown eyes crinkled. "I know, I know. What an honor. You should be proud of your papa."

"Uncle Yitzchok, I don't want to go."

"Of course you don't want to go. What little boy wants to leave his neighborhood and his school and his friends and go off to a strange land? But it's for Torah, Asher." His round face beamed at me. "Your papa will be spreading Hasidus. That is what our papa, olov hasholom, did when he traveled for the Rebbe's father. You will get used to Vienna, Asher. I hear it's a nice city. Don't look so unhappy. Listen to your uncle. You should be proud of your father."

I turned away from him.

"Asher," he said.

I turned back.

"I see you all the time in Yudel Krinsky's store. Why don't you come in and say hello sometimes?"

I was quiet.

"Come in and say hello to your uncle sometimes," he said. "Yes, Asher?"

I nodded.

"Asher, not to speak of it on Shabbos, but have you drawn anything lately?"

I shrugged a shoulder.

"Come in and say hello sometimes." He took a step away from me, then looked back. "The Rebbe must think your father is a very great man to have given him such a responsibility." He said it quietly, with a distant look in his eyes. "My little brother is now a great man." He walked slowly off into the crowd in front of the synagogue.

I said to my father during our Shabbos meal that afternoon, "Where will I go to school in Vienna?"

He had just finished singing one of the zemiros. He was holding his head in his hands.

"There is a small yeshiva in Vienna," he said.

"Is it a Ladover yeshiva?"

"No. In a year or two, we'll begin to build a Ladover yeshiva. You will be one of its first students."

"What language do they talk in Vienna?"

"In the yeshiva they talk Yiddish."

"But what language do the people talk?"

"German. And some French."

"I don't know German and French, Papa."

"You'll learn. Now let's sing zemiros."

"I don't want to learn German and French, Papa."

He began to sing softly, his head in his hands. My mother looked down at the top of the table.

"I'm frightened," I said to my father. "I don't want to go away."

"Sha," my father said, interrupting his song. "Everything will be all right, Asher."

I sat there in rigid silence, listening to him sing.

"Will we have to fly to Vienna?" I asked my mother later that day.

"I don't know, Asher."

"I'm frightened of flying, Mama."

She said nothing.

"There won't be anyone for me to talk to in Vienna."

"You'll find someone to talk to."

"Papa said he was going to Vienna to teach Hasidus."

"Yes."

"You said Papa was going to Vienna to help Jews in Russia."

"Yes."

"Which is Papa going to do?"

"Both," my mother said.

"Mama, I don't want to go. I'm afraid to fly. I can't talk German."

"Asher, there are more important reasons for us not to go than whether or not you like to fly or can speak German."

"What reasons, Mama?"

"Reasons," she said. "But it makes no difference, Asher. We'll go anyway."

He came to me that night out of the woods, my mythic ancestor, huge, mountainous, dressed in his dark caftan and fur-trimmed cap, pounding his way through the trees on his Russian master's estate, the earth shaking, the mountains quivering, thunder in his voice. I could not hear what he said. I woke in dread and lay very still, listening to the darkness. I needed to go to the bathroom but I was afraid to leave the bed. I moved down beneath the blanket and slept and then, as if my moment awake had been an intermission between acts of an authored play, saw him again plowing toward me through giant cedars. I woke and went to the bathroom. I stood in the bathroom, shivering. I did not want to go back to my bed. I stood listening to the night, then went through the hallway to the living room. It was dark and hushed and I could hear the sounds of night traffic through the window. I opened the slats of the Venetian blind and peered between them at the street below. It was a clear night. I could not see the moon, but a clear cold blue-white light lay like a ghostly sheen over the parkway and cast the shadows of buildings and trees across the sidewalks. I saw a man walking beneath the trees. He was a man of medium height with a dark beard, a dark coat, and an ordinary dark hat. I saw him walking in the shadows of the trees. Then I did not see him. Then I saw him again, walking slowly beneath the trees. Then he was gone again and I did not know if I was seeing him or not, if I had been asleep before and was awake now, or if I had been awake before and was dreaming now. Then I saw him again, walking slowly, alone; then he entered a shadow and was gone. I do not remember going back to bed. I only remember waking in the morning and staring up at the white ceiling of my room and feeling light and disembodied, as if I were floating on the shadows cast by dark trees beneath a moon.

"Asher," my father said to me at breakfast. "Drink your orange juice."

I was barely listening.

"Asher."

"I dreamed of the Rebbe last night."

I saw them glance at each other.

"I think I dreamed of the Rebbe. I dreamed—I think —He was very loud and there were woods."

"Asher," my mother said. I felt her fingers on my arm. My father put down the orange juice and looked at me.

"It's not a pretty world, Mama."

I saw her lips tremble. Her fingers tightened momentarily on my hand.

"Will you walk with me to school, Mama?"

"Yes," she said.

"I don't want to walk by myself under the trees."

"I'll walk with you, Asher."

The mashpia came into the classroom and spoke to us in a soft voice. I made a point with my dark pencil in the center of a clean page in my Hebrew notebook. About three inches to the right of that point, I made another point. I connected the two points with a single

straight line. The mashpia spoke softly. I made straight
lines and curved lines. The pencil moved as part of my
hand across the page of the Hebrew notebook. The
mashpia waved his hands gently. I made circles and
short choppy lines. The mashpia rose and went slowly
from the room. The teacher sat down behind the desk. I
put down the pencil and closed the notebook. I opened
the notebook and looked at the page. I closed the notebook very quickly. I watched my fingers trembling on
top of the notebook. I put my hands under my thighs. I
could feel them trembling. A while later, I opened the
notebook and looked again at the page. I had drawn a
picture of Stalin dead in his coffin.

FOUR

I drew him dead in his coffin surrounded by flowers. I drew his closed heavy-lidded eyes, his thick straight hair, his walrus mustache. I drew it all from memory into that Hebrew notebook and later that day I drew him again from memory into my English notebook. In the days that followed, I drew him over and over and over again. I drew him empty and hollow; I drew him swollen and bloated. I distorted his face and twisted his eyes. Over and over and over again, I drew him disfigured, ghoulish, a horror of a face in front of that mountain of flowers.

My father went into my room one night that week and found my desk strewn with drawings. There were drawings on the dresser and on the floor. I saw him peering at the drawings on the desk when I came in from the bathroom.

"What is all this?" he asked.

"Drawings."

"Don't be disrespectful to me, Asher. I see they're drawings. You can't study Chumash, but this you have time for."

"Aryeh," my mother called softly. She was standing in the doorway.

"I'm talking to our son, who is an artist again."

"Aryeh," my mother said again.

The two of them went from the room. I sat at my desk in my pajamas. I used one of the charcoal sticks I had bought from Yudel Krinsky earlier that day. Drawing on a sheet of heavy paper in one continuous line, I did the contour of Stalin's face, then his eyes and nose and mustache. Slowly, I shaded the area around his eyes and along the side of his head. I had never used charcoal before. I watched the dead face take on depth. I darkened the area directly beneath the cheekbones and in the ears. I ignored the thick straight hair and the mustache, except for a few quick lines. Now he was a man on the paper, with volume and depth, and he was dead. Then I erased the closed heavy-lidded eyes and redrew them open and staring, eyes wide and dead-staring out onto the world.

I moved back my chair and saw my mother standing behind me. She was looking at the charcoal drawing of Stalin.

"It's a good drawing, Asher," she said softly.

"It isn't pretty."

"No," she said.

I got into bed.

"Your father is worried about your studies, Asher."

I did not say anything.

"Asher, you can't ignore your studies."

"I study, Mama."

"Yes. We see how you study."

"Can I draw you one day, Mama? Yudel Krinsky said he would let me draw him."

"Yes," she said.

"Tomorrow, Mama?"

"No, not tomorrow."

"This week?"

"Not this week. I have tests this week."

"Next week, then."

"All right, Asher. Next week. But not Monday. Monday we are going downtown to be photographed for passports and to fill out papers."

"What are passports?"

She told me.

"I'm not going," I said.

"You'll need to be photographed, Asher."

"I'm not going to Vienna, Mama."

"Asher, please don't be a child."

"Oh, no," I said. "Oh, no. I'm not going to Vienna. I'll stay with Uncle Yitzchok."

"Asher."

"Good night, Mama," I said.

"Don't you want me to hear your Krias Shema?"

"I'll say it to myself," I said.

I asked Yudel Krinsky the next day, "Do you know what a passport is?"

He was posing for me between customers. He kept his head straight but I saw his eyes move in my direction. "Yes," he said. "I know what a passport is."

"My mama and papa want me to get a passport."

"Without a passport, you will not be able to go to Vienna."

"I am not going to Vienna."

"Asher, your father will be doing important things in Vienna."

I did not answer. I was working on his wide sad bulging eyes.

"The Torah says, 'Honor your father and mother,' " Yudel Krinsky said.

"I know. I can read the Torah."

"Asher." He was hurt.

I held up the drawing. He shook his head in amazement. "Such a gift," he murmured. "Your Uncle Yitzchok told me once about this, but I listened the way one always listens to a bragging uncle. But this is a gift, Asher."

"How do I keep the charcoal from rubbing off?"

"Ah," he said. "You use this." He went to a shelf near the display case of drawing material and came back with a spray can. "You can spray it on so. Stand away from the drawing so the spray does not get into your eyes." He pushed the top button and moved the can quickly back and forth across the drawing. The spray was pungent. "Do not breathe it, Asher. Move away." He released the button and looked down at the drawing. He looked at it a long time. "It is a good drawing," he said softly. "The son of Reb Aryeh Lev has a great gift."

"Keep it," I said.

He looked at me.

"Please keep it," I said.

He blinked. "I thank you." He looked down again at the drawing.

Later, I went into my Uncle Yitzchok's jewelry and watch-repair store. It was brightly lighted with ceiling flourescents. The showcases glistened and gleamed. It was a large store and I did not like to go into it because its brightness was cold, like sunlight on distant ice.

My uncle was behind the center showcase. He wore a dark suit and was smoking a cigar. There were two customers in the store being waited on by a young man behind the left row of showcases. To the right of the door was a watchmaker's workbench. A small man with a gray beard sat at the workbench, peering at a watch through an eyepiece. My uncle, the young man, and the watchmaker all wore small dark skullcaps.

"My nephew, the artist," Uncle Yitzchok said, his moist lips smiling around his cigar. "You want to sell me a picture?"

"Can I stay with you when Mama and Papa go to Vienna?"

He stopped smiling and took the cigar out of his mouth. His round fleshy face looked startled. "What are you talking about, Asher?"

"I don't want to go to Vienna."

"I know you don't want to go to Vienna. The whole world knows you don't want to go to Vienna."

"I won't go. Can I stay with you?"

He peered at me in disbelief. He seemed to want to say something but did not know what words to use.

"I told my mama you would let me stay with you."

"You told—" His voice became husky; he cleared his throat noisily. The customers glanced over at him. "Let me think about it," he said. "A thing like this you can't decide on one foot. I'll need to think about it, Asher."

"Uncle Yitzchok, I'll have no place to stay if I can't stay with you. I don't want to go to Boston and stay with Aunt Leah. I want to stay here where I know people."

"Let me think about it, Asher."

I came out of the store into the March night. As I went past the large glittering window of the store, I looked inside and saw my uncle hurriedly dialing the telephone on the counter.

"Asher, why did you talk to your Uncle Yitzchok about living with him?" my father asked me that night.

"I'll need a place to stay, Papa."

"Asher, will you stop this foolishness?"

"It isn't foolishness."

"Stop it," my father said.

"It isn't foolishness."

"Ribbono Shel Olom," my father said. "What are You doing?"

"It's time for you to go to bed, Asher," my mother said softly. "Shall I come with you?"

"Yes, Mama."

She sat looking at the drawings on the desk as I prepared for bed.

"Did you buy the charcoal from Reb Yudel Krinsky?" she asked.

"Yes."

When I lay in the bed, she came over and said to me, "Asher, you're hurting your father."

I did not say anything.

"You shouldn't hurt your father this way."

"I don't care."

"Asher, please, you must not talk like that."

"I don't want to lose it again," I said.

"What?" She stared at me.

"I don't want to lose it again, Mama. I don't care about anyone."

She was silent for a long time. Then she went from the room without saying good night.

That Monday, I would not go with my parents to the passport office. They decided to go another time. It was early, my mother said. There was plenty of time for passports. It was better for me not to miss a day of school, she said.

I went to school. The next day, my father flew to Washington.

On Wednesday night, my mother sat near the window of the living room and I sat a few feet from her on an easy chair, drawing her face with pastels.

"I should be studying for a history test," my mother said.

"Please don't move your head, Mama."

"How do you feel when you draw, Asher? Is it a good feeling?"

I was quiet.

"I've often wondered. It must be a good feeling."

I drew her eyes, the clear brown eyes, and her small lips and straight nose and the delicately boned curves of her cheeks. She seemed small and delicate to me, a fledgling one holds in a hand. Her skin was fair and smooth and smelled of warm perfume and night flowers. I shaded her face delicately with warm earth browns and put only the vaguest of cold viridian on her white neck.

I thought I heard her say, "Why do you draw, Asher?"

I did not reply.

"What does it mean to you, my Asher?" I thought I heard her say. "Because it may hurt us."

Gently, I rubbed an earth red into the shadow beneath the delicate curve of her jaw.

"Asher," I thought I heard her say. "Asher."

"I'm sorry, Mama. What did you ask?"

"It wasn't important," she said after a moment.

I held up the drawing.

She looked at it for a very long time. Then she said, "What are we going to do, Asher?"

I was quiet.

"Ribbono Shel Olom, what are we going to do?"

"I have to put fixative on your picture, Mama."

I could feel her staring at me as I went out of the room.

My father returned from Washington late Thursday night and left for his office early Friday morning. I did not see him until that afternoon, when he came back from his office to prepare for Shabbos.

I was in my room when he came home. A few minutes later, I heard him in the kitchen talking to my mother. Then, suddenly, his voice was loud. He spoke in Yiddish. In recent weeks, he had begun speaking Yiddish as frequently as English. I could not make out what he said. I heard my mother say in English, "Aryeh, the boy." Then their voices lowered. A moment later, I heard them go into their bedroom.

We sat at the Shabbos table that night and ate, and sang zemiros. My father said very little. When he sang, he held his head in his hands and swayed slowly back and forth. My mother and I sang with him.

That was the night I began to realize that something was happening to my eyes. I looked at my father and saw lines and planes I had never seen before. I could feel with my eyes. I could feel my eyes moving across the lines around his eyes and into and over the deep furrows on his forehead. He was thirty-five years old, and there were lines on his face and forehead. I could feel the lines with my eyes and feel, too, the long straight flat bridge of his nose and the clear darkness of his eyes and the strong thick curves of the red eyebrows and the thick red hair of his beard graying a little—I saw the stray gray strands in the tangle of hair below his lips. I could feel lines and points and planes. I could feel texture and color. I saw the Shabbos candles on the table glowing gold and red. I saw my mother small and warm and silken in a lovely Shabbos dress of pale blue and white. I saw my hands white and bony, my fingers long and thin, my face in the mirror above the buffet pale with black eyes and wild red hair. I felt myself flooded with the shapes and textures of the world around me. I closed my eyes. But I could still see that way inside my head. I was seeing with another pair of eyes that had suddenly come awake. I sat still in my chair and felt frightened.

I opened my eyes. My parents were looking at me.

"Are you all right, Asher?" my mother asked.

"Yes."

"You look— Do you have a fever?" She put her hand on my head. I saw her fingers over the top of my eyes. "No," she said, and withdrew her hand.

My father went on singing. I heard him as if from a distance but I could see him sharply, the tiny folds of skin in the outer corners of his eyes, the strong flare of his nostrils, the lines of his lips beneath the untrimmed beard. Then I saw him open his eyes. He may have felt my eyes on him. He opened his eyes and gazed directly into my eyes. His eyes, clear and dark, locked with mine, and for a long moment I felt his strength and sensed the pools from which it nourished—and I looked down at the table.

Then I heard him say quietly, "You made a beautiful drawing of your mother, Asher." He spoke in Yiddish. "A beautiful drawing." He closed his eyes and hummed a slow Ladover melody he had sung to me often years ago in the time before my mother had become ill. Then he opened his eyes again. "Asher, you have a gift. I do not know if it is a gift from the Ribbono Shel Olom or from the Other Side. If it is from the Other Side, then it is foolishness, dangerous foolishness, for it will take you away from Torah and from your people and lead you to think only of yourself. I want to tell you something. Listen to me, my Asher. About twenty-five years ago, all the yeshivos in Russia were closed by the Communists, and the students were scattered in different places in small groups. The only groups who continued to fight against this destruction of Torah by the enemies of Torah were the Ladover and Breslover Hasidim. The Rebbe's father, may he rest in peace, fought to establish yeshivos, went to jail, and almost lost his life before he finally got out of Russia and came to America. Are you listening to me, Asher? During the ten years before the Second World War, Ladover Hasidim ran illegal yeshivos in Russia and helped keep Torah alive. They were small yeshivos, ten students here, twenty students there, forty students somewhere else. Torah remained alive. Your mother recently found an old copy of *Stern* in a library here in New York. *Stern* was a newspaper published in the Ukraine by Jewish Communists who hated the Master of the Universe and His Torah. These Jewish Communists wrote that they had completely destroyed Yiddishkeit in Russia. The only ones standing in the way of their final goal were Ladover and Breslover Hasidim. The Communists themselves wrote this, Asher."

"It's true," my mother murmured. "It's true."

"Now listen to me, Asher. I know you are only a boy, but perhaps you will be able to understand anyway. Someone once asked how it is possible to establish a connection between man and the Master of the Universe. The answer was that man must take the first step. In order for there to be a connection between man and the Master of the Universe, there must first be an opening, a passageway, even a passageway as small as the eye of a needle. But man must make the opening by himself; man must take the beginning step. Then the Master of the Universe will move in, as it were, and widen the passageway. Asher, we have to make passageways to our people in Russia. We have a responsibility to them. We must make passageways for them to move into. They cannot make the opening on their side, so we must make it on our side. Do you understand me, Asher?"

I nodded slowly.

"Jews in Europe are starving for Torah. The Rebbe is sending me to Europe to build centers for Torah. Our people in Russia are starving for words from the outside. The Rebbe is sending me to Europe to make passageways for them. This is more important than anything else. These are Jewish lives, Asher. Nothing is more important in the eyes of the Master of the Universe than a Jewish life. Do you understand me?"

I was quiet. I saw his dark eyes and the strong dream that filled them, and I was quiet.

"Asher," my father said.

"I think Asher understands," my mother said quietly.

"Let Asher say if he understands."

"Yes, Papa."

He was silent a moment, nodding his head. Then he said, "Finish your tea, Asher, and we sing more zemiros."

I said to my mother later, as she sat on the edge of my bed, "I'm also a Jewish life, Mama. I'm also precious in the eyes of the Ribbono Shel Olom."

Her thin hands fluttered over a button on the front of her dress. "Yes," she said faintly.

"Does someone have a responsibility to me?"

She seemed not to know what to say.

"Mama?"

"Taking you to Vienna is not irresponsibility, Asher."

"I don't want to go. I'm afraid to go. Something inside me says I shouldn't go."

"Now you're being a child."

"It says I shouldn't go, Mama."

"Asher, please."

"Can I stay with Aunt Leah in Boston? No, I can't stay in Boston. I have to stay here. I have to stay here on my street, Mama. Why doesn't anyone listen to me?"

She put her hand gently against my face. I saw the white skin and the bony ridges and the rise of the veins. Her fingers were cool. Her dress rustled softly as she moved.

"Everyone is listening," she said. "There would be no problem if no one were listening to you, Asher."

My Uncle Yitzchok and his family joined us for the first Seder of the Passover festival. It was a long respectful Seder, with much singing and words of Torah and telling of stories about the Rebbe and his father. My father sat on large cushions on his chair. He wore a white cotton robe. With his strong body and long red beard and dark eyes, he dominated the room.

I do not remember how it happened, but sometime during the Seder meal my uncle and I were together in my room and he was looking at some of my drawings.

"Yes," he said. "You can draw. Millions of people can draw."

I looked away from him, my face hot.

"Your father doesn't know what to do with you, Asher."

"Can I stay with you? I can work for you in the store. Is there anything I can do in the store?"

"Asher, listen to me. I wish I could tell you this without hurting you. You're behaving like a child. Everyone is saying that you're behaving like a child."

"I can do errands for you, Uncle Yitzchok. It won't cost you much. I'll just need some money for charcoal and paper and things."

"Where do you get your money now, Asher?"

"I save up the candy money Mama gives me."

"For God's sake, Asher, grow up. You're driving your father crazy."

"Can't I stay with you?"

"No, you can't stay with me. Do you think my brother will let you stay with me while he and your mother go off to Europe? What's the matter with you, Asher? You sound like you can't use your head any more."

I may have to stay with Aunt Leah, after all, I thought. But I can't leave my street.

"Let's go back to the Seder," my Uncle Yitzchok said. As we started from the room, he said to me, "Listen, I won't lie to you, Asher. It doesn't change my mind, but I won't lie to you. Millions of people can draw, but I don't think too many of them draw like you."

We had no school during the Passover festival. On the first of the intermediate days of the festival, I walked over to Yudel Krinsky's store and found him behind the counter eating a hard-boiled egg and chewing a matzo. He greeted me soberly.

"Hello, Asher. Everyone is talking about you."

"Were the Ladover and Breslover Hasidim the only groups in Russia who fought for Torah against the Jewish Communists?"

He seemed startled. "Ah," he said, chewing hard and swallowing. He was having trouble getting the matzo down. He coughed. His eyes watered. He took a deep breath and wiped his eyes with the sleeve of his white smock. "At least say hello first, Asher. A man cannot eat hard-boiled eggs and matzos and answer serious questions all at the same time." He chewed and swallowed again. "Now, Asher, what did you ask me?"

I asked it again.

"What is this all of a sudden? Who told you about Jewish Communists?"

"My father."

"Ah," he said. "I understand." He put the remnants of the hard-boiled egg and matzo on the paper he had spread on top of the counter and wiped his hands with a handkerchief. He glanced around. It was early afternoon. We were alone. A bright April sun shone outside. "I do not know if they were the only ones," he said. "But they fought, and not only against Jewish Communists, but against goyische Communists also. Sometimes the Jewish Communists were worse than the goyim. Ask your mother about the Jewish Communists, Asher. She is studying about Russia. Yes, we and the Breslover fought, and they hated us for it and still hate us, those of them Stalin left alive. The secret police would find out about Ladover or Breslover Jews, and they would come to arrest them on Friday night when they were sure the Jews would be home with their families. In Siberia, I met a Breslover Hasid who told me that twenty-nine Breslover Hasidim were arrested in the city of Uman in 1938. They were accused of attempting to organize an underground Trotsky organization with the checks they were receiving from friends in America. You are young, Asher. You cannot begin to understand the stupidity of such an accusation. Breslover Hasidim organizing a Trotsky underground! They were beaten and tortured. One of them was beaten in front of the others in order to force the others to confess to the accusation. They also suffered from hunger, because they would not dirty themselves eating the food they were given. Three of them died in the prison in Uman. The rest were sent to Siberia. I discovered after the war that only three survived. The Breslover who told me this was taken from my camp a few weeks later and I never saw him again. I do not know if he is one of the three. Asher, they hated us and were afraid of us and arrested and killed us whenever they could."

He glanced around quickly. He took a deep breath. He stared gloomily at the matzo on the counter. "I remember when I first met you I was in a grocery store with matzos over my head. In Russia, to obtain matzos we had to turn over the world. People went to prison because of matzos. Ah, it is a strange world, Asher. Sometimes I think the Master of the Universe has another world to take care of, and He neglects this world, God forbid. Would you like a piece of matzo, Asher?"

I did not want any matzo. I came out of the store onto the street. It was a warm day, one of the first warm days after the long winter.

I walked slowly along Brooklyn Parkway beneath the trees. Old women sat on the benches along the islands of the parkway, sunning themselves and gossiping. Soon Passover would be over; soon I would not have Yudel Krinsky to talk to; soon the street would be gone. There was a feeling of the summer coming, of decisions being made, of haste and departure, of light and shade, of brightness and darkness. I saw the sun glinting off the black metal of a fireplug. I saw a gaunt skeletal-faced old lady laughing happily on a bench. I saw a little boy in a skullcap and sidecurls walking along the parkway dragging his metal-braced right leg in a heavy flatfooted limp. I saw a little girl of about three walking with a boy of about seven. They were talking and laughing and holding their hands together and swinging their arms.

The boy wore a skullcap and sidecurls; ritual fringes protruded from beneath his shirt and flapped gaily in the air as he walked. They looked to be brother and sister. How many times had I seen a brother and sister walking like that along Brooklyn Parkway? How many times? Something was happening to my eyes and my head and I did not know how to think or feel about it.

Mrs. Rackover said to me when I came into the apartment, "Where were you? You are more than an hour late for lunch."

"I was walking."

"You were walking. You were driving me crazy. Go wash your hands and I will give you something to eat."

"Where is my mother?"

"Your mother went to the library. Go wash your hands, Asher. I cannot spend half the day giving you lunch."

"They were very beautiful," I said. "Why didn't I see it before?"

"What?" Mrs. Rackover said.

"I wonder if they have a mother and father," I said.

"What is the matter with you, Asher? Are you sick? Do you have a fever?"

"No."

"Go wash your hands. You are driving us all crazy with your pictures and your stubbornness. What kind of Jewish boy behaves this way to a mother and father? You ought to be ashamed of yourself."

Why didn't I ever see it before? I asked myself. Something has happened to my eyes and my head. I looked at my eyes and head in the mirror over the bathroom sink. They looked the same as always, eyes dark and hair red and wild. But something had happened inside them. And I did not think I was frightened now.

I spent the afternoon drawing pictures of the brother and sister I had seen walking together on Brooklyn Parkway. I remembered their thin faces and I drew them walking along the parkway. Then I drew them crossing a country road, walking beneath tall trees, chasing a butterfly. I drew them reading together and talking together. I drew them crossing a street together. I drew them laughing together. The desk and the dresser and the bed were strewn with drawings. Later in the afternoon, I went downstairs and walked along the parkway, but I could not find any girl and boy together who looked to be brother and sister.

I was in my room when my mother returned from the library, her arms laden with books. She put the books on the wall table in the hallway and removed her coat. I called her into my room.

"Look," I said, and pointed to the drawings.

"Not now, Asher."

"Mama, please."

She seemed impatient and glanced quickly through a few of the drawings. Then she sat down on the bed and went through them all slowly. She looked a long time at the drawings of the brother and sister reading together and talking together. She put the drawings down. Her eyes were wide and moist. She went from my room without a word. I heard the door to her bedroom close softly. I waited awhile, then went out to the hallway and looked at the books she had left on the table. They were all on Russia. One of them was a grammar of the Russian language.

My father said to me at the Shabbos table the next night, "You look so unhappy these days, Asher."

"I'm sorry, Papa."

"It bothers you that I am away so much?"

"Yes, Papa."

"It bothered me, too, when my father, may he rest in peace, was away. But I do not know how else the work can be done. To touch a person's heart, you must see a person's face. One cannot reach a soul through a telephone." He stroked his red beard slowly. Then he said in a soft singsong voice, "The early tzaddikim, the ones who were the first disciples of the Ba'al Shem Tov, also used to travel. Some took it upon themselves to go into

exile in order to atone for the sins of Israel and to has-
ten the redemption. Others wandered about looking for
kidnapped Jewish children they could ransom. Others
traveled to the ends of the earth looking for a teacher
whose soul was like their soul and with whom they
could study Torah. And others journeyed from place to
place teaching the words of the Ba'al Shem Tov and
changing people's hearts and souls to Hasidus. My father, olov hasholom, after whom you are named, was a
great scholar. That you know, Asher. An emissary from
the Rebbe's father stayed with my father for a while.
They studied together. A year later, my father moved
his family to Ladov and became an emissary of the
Rebbe's father. The night he was killed, they had been
making plans together. My father was to travel to the
Ukraine to start underground yeshivos. Their heads
were full of plans for Torah. They forgot it was the
night before Easter. The drunken peasant remembered." He paused. His eyes glittered in the light of the
Shabbos candles. Then he continued in that same singsong voice, "When the Rebbe's father was able to come
to America, he brought me and your Uncle Yitzchok
and our mother, may she rest in peace, with him. I was
fourteen then. I remember that journey." He paused
again and hummed a brief passage from one of the zemiros. "Yes," he murmured. "The Rebbe's father felt
something had been left unfinished in the world. Plans
had been made and had been left unfinished. A life had
been lost because of those plans and the plans had been
left unfulfilled." He hummed another verse from the zemiros. Then he stopped and closed his eyes. Then he
said, his eyes still closed, "Sing zemiros with me, Asher.
You, too, Rivkeh. Sing zemiros with me."

Later that night, as I got into bed, my mother asked
me, "Did you understand what your father said to you,
Asher?"

"Yes."

"Do you understand what it means to leave a great
work incomplete?"

"I think so, Mama."

"It's important that you understand that, Asher."

"Why are you studying Russian history, Mama?"

"To help your father in his work."

"Was your brother supposed to go to Europe and do what Papa will be doing?"

"No. Your Uncle Yaakov"—her lips trembled—"was going to teach Russian history in New York University. He was also going to be an adviser in the government."

"The American government?"

"Yes, Asher."

"Will you be an adviser in the American government, Mama?"

"No," she said. "I will not be an adviser in the American government. I will graduate from college in June and go with you and your father to Vienna in October. Are you ready to say your Krias Shema, Asher?"

I said the Krias Shema.

A while later, I sensed them through dim and restless sleep standing by my bed, whispering. I felt a hand straighten my blanket. Then I felt fingers move across my face and forehead in a caress, my father's fingers. Then I felt nothing, but I knew they were standing there in silence. Then they went from the room.

I saw my mythic ancestor again that night, moving in huge strides across the face of the earth, stepping over snow-filled mountains, spanning wide and fertile valleys, journeying, journeying, endlessly journeying. I saw him traverse warm villages and regions of ice and snow. I saw him peer into the windows of secret yeshivos and into the barracks of Siberian camps. "It's colder inside than outside," I thought I heard him say. "And what are you doing with your time, my Asher Lev?" I thought I heard him say. He said it thunderously, and I woke and lay in the darkness. Then I got out of bed and went to my desk and turned on the light. I looked at the drawings of the brother and sister. They seemed a scrawl, an absurd and childish movement of the hand, a small-minded frivolity. There were prisons of stone and wastelands of snow and night. What was a drawing in

the face of the darkness of the Other Side? What was a
pen and paper, what were pastels, in the face of the evil
of the shell? I felt myself suddenly entombed and I
snapped off the light and got back into bed. Even in the
dark, I could see the different kinds of blackness in the
room and the way the slit of pale light between the bottom of the window shade and the window sill played on
the wall near my desk and glinted off the drawings.
What do You want from me? I thought. I'm only a ten-
year-old boy. Ten-year-old boys play in the streets; ten-
year-old boys chase back and forth through the hall-
ways of apartment houses; ten-year-old boys ride up
and down elevators for afternoon entertainment; ten-
year-old boys run after cars along New York Avenue. If
You don't want me to use the gift, why did You give it
to me? Or did it come to me from the Other Side? It
was horrifying to think my gift may have been given to
me by the source of evil and ugliness. How can evil and
ugliness make a gift of beauty? I lay in my bed and
thought a long time about what was wanted from me.
Then I was tired and began to drift off to sleep. I
thought I would see my mythic ancestor again and I
fought to stay awake. But I felt myself moving off. It
was only then that I realized I had violated the Shabbos
by turning on the light to look at my drawings, and by
turning it off again. Then it was a while before I was
able to sleep.

During that Passover, the new Soviet government announced that the doctors arrested under the Stalin re-
gime had been released; the announcement said that the
accusations had all been lies. My father was informed
by telephone that two of the Jewish doctors had been
beaten to death by the police while in prison.

The announcement said that fifteen doctors had been
released. I remembered having heard that nine had been
arrested. I did not ask about the difference in numbers.
I was tired, very tired.

On the Thursday after Passover, I went with my
parents for our passports.

FIVE

I remember drawing a building burning, a large marble building set in a green glade and surrounded by gentle hills. I drew it in pastels and made the marble of the building pale blue and veined with small wandering rivulets of white. There was a golden dome with a trim of purple arabesques; there were tall arched windows, somewhat like the windows of the Ladover building. I drew flames pouring from the windows and swirling around the roof and eating into the marble. My mother asked me what it was, and I said it was the library in Alexandria, the one the Moslems had ordered burned because its books could not be as important as the Koran. Did my mother remember telling me that story? My mother remembered. Why had I drawn such a picture? I didn't know. What did the picture mean to me? I shrugged a shoulder.

I drew a book burning. Then I drew piles of books burning. Then I drew houses burning. Then I drew the Ladover building burning. And my mother was no longer asking me what it all meant.

Sometime during those weeks, my mother took me to our family doctor. He prodded and poked and tapped. What is our Asher Lev drawing these days? Ears are fine. Chest is fine. Have you ever been in the museum? No? An afternoon in a good museum is good for the soul—he used the Hebrew word "neshomoh." You're skinny but healthy. Yes, I'll send you to someone for the eyes. How is your husband? You heard about the doctors? Give my regards to your husband. Tell him this American-born Jewish doctor thinks of him often. Goodbye, Asher. Are you using oils? No? When you use oils, be careful of flake white. It contains lead and can hurt you if it gets into your body. Advice from one artist to another. I paint on Sundays. Goodbye, Asher. Goodbye, Mrs. Lev.

A few days later, I went to an eye doctor. He took a long time. My eyes were fine. I did not need glasses. No, there was absolutely nothing the matter with my eyes. Then I went to another kind of doctor. He was a young doctor with thick glasses and a fixed smile. There were games I had to play and questions I had to answer and drawings I had to make. A few days before, I had seen a large gray cat struck by a car on Kingston Avenue. It had run off into an alleyway dragging the lower half of itself in a queer way and leaving behind drops of glistening blood. I drew that cat for the doctor. I drew the cat under the wheels of the car and I drew the cat as I imagined it later in the alleyway. He stared at those drawings a very long time, without smiling. I do not know what he told my mother, but she was very subdued all the way home from his office. My father was in Montreal that day.

The next day, the boy sitting to my right in class leaned over and whispered in Yiddish, "Asher, what are you doing?"

I heard him but could not understand what he was saying and went on working with the pen.

"Asher," I heard him say, still in a whisper but a little louder than before. "How could you do that?"

I felt the boy sitting behind me lean forward and look over my shoulder. The one sitting at my left looked, too. There were gasps and murmurs of surprise. Then the one sitting in front of me, a thin pimply-faced boy with an endlessly running nose and a high nasal voice, turned around, looked, and said in Yiddish in a voice that could have been heard on the other side of the parkway, "You defiled a holy book! Asher Lev, you desecrated the Name of God! You defiled a Chumash!"

He seemed horrified and looked as if he were witnessing the sudden appearance of a representative of the Other Side. He moved out of his desk and backed away from me.

The class had been studying the Book of Leviticus. The teacher, a young dark-bearded recent graduate of the Ladover yeshiva, had been explaining concepts of holiness. Now, with the sudden invasion of the nasal voice, the class was instantly silent. There was a faint stirring as bodies pivoted and heads focused upon me.

I looked at my hand. I saw the old Waterman fountain pen my father had once given me. On the way out of my room earlier that morning, I had put the pen into one of my pockets. Now I held it in my hand. I had drawn a face with it across an entire printed page of my Chumash. I had drawn the face in thick black ink. It was a bearded face, dark-eyed, dark-haired, vaguely menacing. On top of the face, I had drawn a head of dark hair covered by an ordinary dark hat.

The teacher was standing at my desk looking down at the drawing. He said quietly in Yiddish, "What did you do, Asher?"

I did not know what to say. I could not remember having drawn it.

"What would your father say if he saw this?" the teacher asked softly. He did not seem angry. He looked hurt. His voice was patient and gentle.

I felt hot and suddenly very tired. I wanted to go home and go to bed.

"I am surprised and upset," the teacher said, "that the son of Reb Aryeh Lev should do such a thing. I do not know what to say. Please be so good as not to do it again, Asher. Drawing in a Chumash is a desecration of the Name of God."

"Expecially what he drew," said the boy with the running nose and nasal voice.

The teacher turned to him. "Thank you," he said softly. "But I do not need your help. Now everybody please be so good as to look back into your Chumash and let us continue with our discussion. You, too, Asher, put down your fountain pen and look into your Chumash."

I looked into my Chumash. I stared at the face staring back out at me from the page. I had slanted the eyes somewhat and given the lips beneath the beard a sardonic turn. The Rebbe looked evil; the Rebbe looked threatening; the Rebbe looking out at me from the Chumash seemed about to hurt me. That was the expression he would wear when he decided to hurt me. That was the expression he had worn when he had told my father to go to Vienna. I looked at the framed photograph of the Rebbe on the front wall near the blackboard. The eyes were gray and clear; the face was kind. Only the ordinary dark hat was the same in both pictures. I was frightened at the picture I had drawn. I was especially frightened that I could not remember having drawn it.

I went to Yudel Krinsky's store later that day and found him sorting tubes of oil colors, taking them from their boxes and putting them into the compartments of the metal cabinet near the door.

"Sholom aleichem to the son of Reb Aryeh Lev," Yudel Krinsky said cheerfully. "Put down your books and take off your coat. You can help me sort the brushes." He looked at me closely. "How do you feel, Asher? You do not look very good."

"How do you use these colors?" I asked.

"These? The oil colors? You want to use the oil colors?"

"How do you use them? Is there a special way they are used?"

"Oil colors is an entire Torah, Asher. I know nothing about oil colors."

"Why is it called oil color?"

"They mix the original color with a certain oil. With watercolor, they mix the color with water. That is all I know."

"I put the color on a brush and I paint with it?"

"You paint with it on something like this." He reached behind the counter and came up with a small canvas board. "This is the easy thing to paint on. Others paint on canvas they prepare themselves. But this is even beyond Torah already. That is Gemorra and Tosefos."

"I drew on my Chumash today," I said.

"Ah?"

"I drew the face of the Rebbe on my Chumash and I did not even know I drew it until others saw it."

He glanced around the store, scratched his beaked nose, and sighed.

"I made the Rebbe look like a being from the Other Side."

"Asher!" He was horrified.

"And I did not even know," I said. "I did not even know I was drawing it."

"You should talk to your mother and father," Yudel Krinsky said.

"The doctors said I was all right. There was nothing the matter with me, they said. How could I do something like that if there is nothing the matter with me? How much does oil color cost?"

He told me.

"I do not have enough money. I would need at least three—no, at least five—colors, and I do not have enough money. How much will brushes cost? I will need one or two brushes."

He told me.

"What else will I need? I will need something to clean the brushes. I will need a canvas board. How much will it cost to buy something to clean the brushes —turpentine, yes—and to buy a canvas board?"

He told me.

"I will never have enough money to paint oil colors. How can anyone paint in oil colors if it costs so much money? I do not feel well. I think I will go home now and lie down. Did I tell you I drew the face of the Rebbe in my Chumash today? I told you. Goodbye, goodbye."

It was a warm evening. There was a pale film of light in the sky. Soon it would be summer. And then Rosh

Hashonoh and Yom Kippur. And then October. And then Vienna. So I'll go to Vienna. I can draw in Vienna, too. I'll draw the cafés and the strange streets. I'll learn the language. What is so terrible about going to Vienna? I felt myself trembling. I love this street. Yes. I don't want to go into exile. But I'll draw another street. Streets are all the same. Oh, they're not. They're not the same. I don't know enough about this street to really draw it yet; how can I draw a strange street in a foreign land full of people who hate me? Why should I even want to draw such a street?

I walked beneath the trees looking at the people of the street. The parkway was busy with traffic. People were coming out of the subway tunnels. There were green buds on the trees. The benches were empty. Cats scratched through garbage cans. Car horns blared. It seemed to be getting dark. I thought it had become dark very quickly. There were stars. I took the elevator up to our apartment.

My mother was at the door. Her small face was pale and frightened.

"Asher, do you know what time it is?"

I did not know.

"It's after seven o'clock." Her voice was very high. There was that strange look in her eyes. "Where have you been?"

"Walking."

"Walking? Until after seven o'clock? Asher, what am I going to do with you? I was ready to call the police."

"I'm very tired, Mama. I think I'll go to sleep."

"Don't you want supper? Are you all right, Asher? Are you sick?"

"I'll never have enough for the oil colors. How does anyone buy all he needs?"

She stared at me.

"I didn't know, Mama. Is it wrong if you do something when you don't even know you did it? How could that be wrong?"

She stared at me, open-mouthed. I could feel her looking at me as I went through the hallway to my room. It's a nice street, I was thinking. Why do they want to take it from me?

I put on pajamas and got into bed. My mother came into the room. She was telling me I could not go to sleep without supper. She sounded frightened. I wondered why she was frightened. She hadn't drawn the Rebbe's face in a Chumash. Why was she frightened? She kept pleading with me to get out of bed and eat supper. I was barely listening. After a while, she looked ready to cry. She turned and started from the room. She was almost at the doorway when the phone rang. I heard her hurrying through the hall to the phone. She was talking into the phone. How can I get money to buy the oil colors and the canvas board and the brushes and the turpentine? Maybe I can sell a picture to my Uncle Yitzchok. My mother came back into the room and stood by my bed.

"The mashpia called."

I turned my face to the wall.

"The mashpia asked you to see him in his office tomorrow morning at nine o'clock."

There was a crack in the wall I had not seen before. I liked the way it sent out spidery fingers along the surface of the paint.

"What did you do in school today?" my mother asked.

I closed my eyes. Then I opened my eyes very slightly and peered out through my lashes. There were spidery fingers there, too, moving in and out across my eyes. I liked seeing them that way, moving back and forth and in and out like a concealing fog across my eyes. I was slanting my eyes. Do the Rebbe's eyes see spidery fingers in my picture?

I welcomed the fog and fell asleep.

Almost immediately, as if he had been waiting for the moment of sleep the way ancient guardian armies waited for the blast of warning trumpets, my mythic ancestor thundered through the enshrouding fog, his dark-bearded face trembling with rage. There was the roar of moving earth and the rolling sound of his anger. I could not hear what he was saying but I felt his words push against me. I woke and went to the bathroom. I thought I heard my parents talking in their room. I went back to bed and slept. I woke again in the night, feeling very hungry. How can I get money for the oil colors? I must try the oil colors. I fell back asleep and woke in the morning to the sound of rain on the window.

My father was preparing the orange juice. My mother was at the stove. They looked at me when I came into the kitchen and stopped what they were doing.

"Good morning, Asher," my mother said very quietly.

"The mashpia called me in my office late yesterday," my father said, without preliminaries. "Did you know what you were doing?"

"No, Papa."

"You did it and didn't know you were doing it?"

"Yes."

"How can I believe you?"

"Aryeh," my mother said softly.

He turned to her. "I don't know how to react, Rivkeh. A responsible ten-year-old boy doesn't do such things." He turned back to me. "You will be respectful to the mashpia, you hear?"

"Yes, Papa."

"You will listen carefully to what he has to say and you will apologize."

"Yes, Papa."

"I have a million things on my mind now, and I have to worry about my son drawing the face of the Rebbe in a Chumash. How could you have done such a thing?"

"Aryeh," my mother said.

"To desecrate a Chumash. And to make fun of the Rebbe."

"I was not making fun of the Rebbe," I said.

"What were you doing?"

"I don't know. But I was not making fun of the Rebbe. I don't draw pictures to make fun."

"I wish you would stop drawing. We were done with that foolishness."

"Aryeh," my mother said.

"Aryeh, Aryeh," my father said. "What are you Aryehing me for, Rivkeh? How does it look when my son goes around drawing all day instead of learning? How does it look?"

"Stop calling it foolishness," I said.

They turned slowly to look at me.

"Please don't call it foolishness any more, Papa," I said.

They stared at me and were very quiet. My father's face was going rigid. I saw him swallow. My mother was pale.

"Foolishness is something that's stupid," I said. "Foolishness is something a person shouldn't do. Foolishness is something that brings harm to the world. Foolishness is a waste of time. Please don't ever call it foolishness any more, Papa."

There was a long silence. I heard the rain on the window of the kitchen. The refrigerator suddenly turned itself off, deepening the silence. I felt frightened. I had never talked to my father that way before.

"Asher," my mother said. "You are being disrespectful to your father. Kibud ov, Asher. Remember, kibud ov."

"I'm sorry," I said, and lowered my eyes.

My father stroked his beard and took a deep breath. "Sit down, Asher, and drink your orange juice," he said in a voice tremulous with anger. "There are probably no vitamins left in it by now."

The mashpia's office was at the end of the first-floor corridor of the school building, two doors beyond my classroom. I knocked on the door and heard him say in Yiddish, "Come in." I went inside and closed the door quietly behind me.

It was a narrow office, entirely bare except for a small bookcase filled with books and a small dark wood desk that had on it a notebook and a pencil. Rav Yosef Cutler, the mashpia, sat behind the desk in an ordinary wood chair. He wore a long dark jacket, dark trousers, a white shirt with a crumpled collar, a tall dark skull-cap, and a dark tie. His hands were white. He smiled at me across the closetlike room. "Come in, come in, Asherel. Take off your coat; yes, put it there. Good. Sit down, sit down. Put your books on the desk. Tell me, how is your mother? About your father I have no need to ask. I see your father all the time. But how is your mother? Yes? And how are you, Asherel? You look pale. Your eyes are as red as your hair. Are you feeling well?" He spoke in Yiddish and I responded in Yiddish. With the mashpia, one talked only in Yiddish.

I told him I was feeling well. I was a little tired, I said. My mother had taken me to see three different doctors, I said. I was fine, I said. I was fine.

A narrow window took up most of the wall behind the mashpia. I looked out the window at the maples on the street. It was raining outside on the maples. I saw the branches dripping in the rain. How would I paint that, the rain dripping from the branches, the rain streaking the window, the gray rain filling the world with dismal mist? People walked beneath umbrellas. The asphalt glistened. The bleak sky hovered menacingly over the tops of the buildings. The mashpia was saying something to me, but I was not listening because I saw the clouds moving swiftly and darkly across the buildings and I wondered how I could catch that dark movement, that watery swirl of light and dark grays. I watched the mashpia put his hands on the desk, saw him still talking to me, and thought the street was crying and wondered how I could paint the street crying. I thought I had said something like that to myself before, but I could not remember when or where it might have been. The street is crying, I thought, and I'm sitting here. It's my street and I can't draw it. I want to paint it, I have to paint it while it's crying, and why am I sitting here? They're going to take my street away from me, I thought. Do streets in Vienna cry? Not for Jews, they don't. Ribbono Shel Olom, what are You doing to me?

"Asherel," the mashpia was saying in a strange loud voice. "Asherel."

I came slowly back inside myself from the dripping trees and the dismal street and looked at him with a sense of surprise and shock. He was leaning almost halfway across the desk, his eyes wide with alarm.

"Asherel," he said again. "Are you feeling all right?"

I nodded. "Yes," I heard myself say. I did not recognize my own voice. "Yes. Yes."

"I thought— Asherel, I will call your father and he will take you home."

"No," I said. "Do not call my father."

I said it very loudly. He gave me a startled look. Then, slowly, he sat back in his chair.

There was a long silence. He sat very still, regarding me intently. I watched the rain-made rivulets on the window, the patterned flow of colorless liquid upon colorless glass. It will all die when the rain ends, I thought. But what difference does it make?

Oh, it makes a difference, I thought. And if it doesn't make a difference you will make it make a difference. Yes? No. Perhaps it really doesn't make a difference, after all.

"Asherel, listen to me," the mashpia was saying. "I am talking to you and you are dreaming."

"I am sorry," I heard myself say.

"If you are not ill, be so good as to listen to me."

I took my eyes from the window.

"How shall we start, Asherel? Are you listening to me?"

"Yes."

"Good. You feel all right now, yes?"

"Yes."

"Very good. Asherel, how shall we start? I do not want to, God forbid, hurt you or make you feel bad. I talk to you out of love for you and your dear parents." He paused. "I knew your grandfather in Russia. I was with him and the Rebbe's father the night he was killed. All the Jewish people are one body and one soul, he believed. If one part of the body hurts, the entire body hurts—and the entire body must come to the help of the part that hurts. Are you listening to me, Asher?"

I hurt, I thought. Who is coming to my help? "Yes," I said. "I am listening."

"Good," he said gently, and stroked his dark beard. "Asherel, your father also sees the Jewish people as one body and one soul. When a head hurts in the Ukraine, your father suffers in Brooklyn. When Jews cannot study Torah in Kiev, your father cannot sit still in Brooklyn. Do you understand me, Asherel?"

I nodded. I was looking at the window again. It seemed dark outside. Why was it dark outside in the morning? The rain had stopped. The rivulets were gone from the window. But raindrops were still on the panes, looking frozen against the strange darkness outside.

"Now, how do you think your father feels, Asherel, when his son does not want to study Torah, spends days and nights drawing, and even draws the face of the Rebbe in a Chumash? How should a father feel in such a matter, Asherel?"

I did not know what to say, and so I said nothing. I had the impression I was not expected to respond. But how should I feel? I thought. Will he ask me how I feel? And why is it so dark outside?

"Asherel, my child, understand what I am saying to you. We all know you have a gift. We all know such a gift cannot always be controlled. When my·father, may he rest in peace, was young, he had a gift for carving. When I was young, I had a gift for writing stories. When the Rebbe was young, he had a gift for mathematics. Many people feel they are in possession of a great gift when they are young. But one does not always give in to a gift. One does with a life what is precious not only to one's own self but to one's own people. That is the way our people live, Asherel. Do you understand me?"

I understood. It looked like night outside, black night in the morning.

"Asherel, you have a gift. The gift causes you to think only of yourself and your own feelings. No one would care if these were normal times, Asherel. We do not interpret the second commandment the way others do. But these are not normal times."

When have times ever been normal for Jews? I thought. What is he telling me? To stifle the gift? Does he also believe the gift is from the Other Side? Then it should be stifled even in normal times; what does it have to do with the Jewish people? And if it's not from the Other Side, if it's from the Ribbono Shel Olom, why is it less important than what Papa is doing?

"Do you understand me, Asherel?"

I did not understand but I did not say anything.

"Asherel?"

"Look, it is raining again," I said. I could see the fat drops hurtle through the darkness and explode against the window. How could I ever draw or paint that? I thought. Rain like that from darkness like that exploding as though in midair upon invisible glass. But someone had done it. I've seen pictures of it, of a sky like that, of rain against glass. How did they do it?

"Asherel?" the mashpia was saying gently, patiently.

I took my eyes from the window.

"Were you listening to me?" he asked.

"Yes."

He stroked his dark beard with his white hands and narrowed his eyes. "Asherel," he said softly. "Is it true you did not know you were drawing the face of the Rebbe on the Chumash?"

"Yes."

"How is such a thing possible?"

"I do not know."

"I believe you, Asherel." He sat back in his chair and folded his arms and put a hand across his mouth. I saw him watching me intently, his eyes wide and gentle. He has a little of Yudel Krinsky's eyes, I thought. I could make them a little wider and remove some of the lines and they would be like the eyes of Yudel Krinsky. The shapes are the same. Look at the rain on the window.

The mashpia was saying something, but I did not want to listen to him any more. It's raining in sharp diagonals to the verticals and horizontals of the window. Look at those slashing diagonals. The mashpia was saying something about Vienna but I would not listen. The darkness was gone from the street and I could see the trees beneath the lashing rain. The rain moved in waterfalls across the asphalt. The curbs were flooded with rushing streams of dark water. Oh, if I could paint this, I thought. Ribbono Shel Olom, if I could paint this world, this clean world of rain and patterns on glass, and trees on my street, and people beneath the trees. I would even paint and draw pain and suffering if I could paint and draw the other, too. I would paint the rain as tears and I would paint the rain as waters of purification. What do they want from me? Ribbono Shel Olom, it's Your gift. Why don't You show them it's Your gift?

". . . to Vienna in October?" I heard the mashpia say.

I looked at him blankly.

He sighed. "You were not listening to me, Asherel."

I did not say anything.

"What shall we do with you, Asherel? What shall we do with you?" He shook his head sadly.

Everyone seemed to be asking that now. What shall we do with you, Asher?

"I was asking, Asherel, how do you feel about going with your father and mother to Vienna in October."

"To Vienna in October," I heard myself say. "Yes." I took a breath. "How should I feel? I will go to Vienna. Papa and Mama are going to Vienna. How can I not go?"

He sat there with his arms crossed, one hand over his mouth, and regarded me intently.

"Where would I stay?" I said. "How can a ten-year-old child stay alone? I cannot stay with my Uncle Yitzchok. My father will not allow me to stay. Of course I will go to Vienna with my father and mother in October."

What month is this? I thought. April. May, June, July, August, September, October. Six months. I can draw and paint some of the street in six months. But how will I buy the oil colors? Maybe I can find something in place of oil colors. How can I know what can be in place of oil colors when I don't know anything at all about oil colors?

"Of course I will go to Vienna," I heard myself say again. "Of course I will go to Vienna. My father is going to Vienna to build yeshivos for the Rebbe. How can I not go to Vienna?" Then I was crying. I could not help myself. I was crying. "How?" I said. "How? Ribbono Shel Olom, how?" I sat there crying. "I do not want to go, but I will go," I said. "Ribbono Shel Olom, I am afraid to go away now from my street. It will leave me again and I will never have any of it back. But I will go to Vienna with Papa and Mama. How can I not go? What do they all want from me? How can I not go?"

The mashpia had taken his hand away from his mouth. He was standing now behind the desk. He leaned down and from a drawer in the desk brought out a small bottle of water and a paper cup. He poured some water and handed me the cup.

"Drink, Asherel," he said softly.

I remembered to make the blessing over water, to which he responded with amen. I drank the water and put the cup on the desk. I looked at my hand and found it was trembling. Then I felt all of me trembling. It seemed to me I had spent long hours of my life until then shaking and trembling. I was tired. I wanted to go home and go to bed.

The mashpia said very quietly, "Listen, Asherel, do me a favor. Once when I was in your classroom, I saw you drawing in your notebook. But I did not see the drawing. Make a drawing for me. Here is a clean notebook and a pencil. Make a few drawings for me."

I looked at him and did not know what to say.

"Asherel?" he said softly. "I will leave you alone for a while. Yes? Can you make a few drawings for me?"

I nodded, feeling a pounding inside my head.

"You can take your time, Asherel. If I am not back when you finish, leave the notebook and pencil on the

desk and go back to your classroom. I will ask only that
you turn out the light and close the door." He came
around from behind the desk and stood by the door.
"You may finish the water in the bottle if you wish.
Give my good wishes to your mother."

He went out so quietly I did not hear the door close.

I sat there feeling the pounding inside my head and a
sudden heaviness against my chest. I took a deep
breath. I was able to breathe without difficulty but the
heaviness remained. I did not know what to do. I did
not want to draw. I was tired and I wanted to go home
and go to bed. I stared at the notebook and pencil on
the desk. I should not have said that about going to
Vienna. I should not have cried. The mashpia would tell
my mother and father and they would be upset and
angry, and my father had enough to worry about now. I
stared at the window. It was still raining. The trees
looked forlorn in the rain. I saw the rain dripping off
the buildings and splashing into the dark pools on the
street. I moved my chair closer to the desk and opened
the notebook. Its pages were blank and unlined. I
looked closely at the heavy cover; it was a sketch pad.
The pencil was a soft-leaded Eberhard, a drawing pencil. I stared at the door to the office. It was closed.

I drew a point with the pencil on the first page of the
sketchbook. I drew another point a few inches away. I
connected the two points with a straight line. I drew another straight line, in tension with the first line. I drew a
third, balancing line. Then I was drawing a face. Then I
was drawing faces. Then there were trees and lines of
walking people. I drew faces of children laughing and
crying. I drew the look of the street from the window of
our living room. I drew Yudel Krinsky surrounded by
matzos in the grocery store. I drew the Ladover building. I drew a man walking alone beneath the trees of the
parkway, wearing dark clothes, a dark beard, and an
ordinary dark hat. I drew until the point of the pencil
was gone; then I tore at the wood with my fingernails to
get to the lead. I drew and shaded and sketched and left
blank patches and filled patches, and at one point I

thought I needed something more for a face at a window and I poured some water into the cup and dipped my forefinger into the water and rubbed the wet forefinger across the side of the face beneath the high delicate curve of cheekbone. The shading inside the concave plane of cheek came sharply alive, and there was my mother's face at the window. Then I drew a boy and girl walking together beneath the maples of the parkway. They're brother and sister, I thought, and drew them holding hands, heads close together, faces alike, thin with high cheekbones. Then I drew the Rebbe praying quietly near the Ark, his head covered by his tallis. Then I no longer knew what I was drawing. I was filling the pages with beings and shapes and textures, trying to feel the rain on the windows and on the trees, trying to feel cold and snow, trying to feel darkness and night, and getting none of it on the pages, and finally I threw the pencil down on the desk and slammed the sketchbook shut. I picked up my coat and my books and ran from the room. I was part of the way down the corridor when I remembered I had forgotten to turn off the light. I went back and opened the door and looked inside. The sketchbook lay nakedly on the desk. I turned off the light and closed the door and went down the corridor and out of the school.

I hated what I had drawn in that sketchbook. I should not have done it. Why had he asked me to do it? I hated the drawings. They were lies, stagnant creations done to someone else's demands, and I despised them. I was walking beneath the trees in the rain. I felt the rain on my face and in my eyes. How do you draw rain in someone's eyes? It seemed there was a great deal of rain and I was walking in it endlessly. There was the sound of cars in the rain, and occasionally the sound of aircraft in the clouds overhead, and the dripping of the trees and the lawns soggy, and sometimes a stray wet cat between the pails of garbage in the alleyways. I was going into a huge gray stone building and I remembered none of the drawings had been of my father. Not a single drawing in that sketchbook was of my father. There were huge glass doors bordered in bronze and a marble interior and someone at a counter talking to me, looking at me curiously and pointing up a marble staircase. I climbed the stairs. I saw the rain on the tall rectangular windows. There were long corridors. I wandered through the corridors. I was very hungry and my head hurt. I wandered through the corridors looking closely at the walls. I do not know how long I was there. Someone came over and said something to me and I could not hear him. There was something on a wall I needed to see. He said it again and I felt him staring at me as I went from there down the marble staircase. It was dark outside. The rain had stopped. The air was misty with fog. The fog clung to the vague circles of light around the lampposts. I walked home in that fog. As I came up to the apartment house, I looked up at the living-room window. It was dark. I took the elevator upstairs.

The door to the apartment opened a second after I rang the bell. Mrs. Rackover stood there, gaping at me. Then she ran back through the hallway and picked up the phone.

I went into my room and took off my clothes. Mrs. Rackover was talking excitedly into the phone. I wondered where my mother was. My father was in Washington. I was putting on my pajamas when Mrs. Rackover came into my room. Where had I been? Did I know what time it was? My mother was sick with fear and had gone to bed. They had called the police. She had just called them back to tell them I was home. What was I doing? I was driving everybody crazy.

I was not listening. It intrigued me that I had made no drawings of my father. The mashpia would notice that. But why had I made no drawings of my father?

My mother stood in the doorway. She was in a loose-fitting pale-blue nightgown. Her short dark hair was tangled. She seemed frenzied and there were dark circles around her eyes. I felt myself beginning to cry when I saw her. But I did not cry. I would not cry. She would ask me to make drawings for her.

I said, "There's a statue of Moses right under the roof. Did you ever see that, Mama? A statue of Moses."

"Master of the Universe," Mrs. Rackover breathed. "What is the boy saying?"

My mother looked at me dazedly. She seemed so small, so frail.

"The others all had strange names," I said. "But Moses was there. Moshe Rabbenu was there near the top of the building."

"What building? What building?" Mrs. Rackover said.

"The museum," my mother said in a very small voice.

Mrs. Rackover stared at her in disbelief.

"I liked Robert Henri best of all," I said. "Of all the Americans, he was the best. Am I saying the name right? Henri?" I was pronouncing it "Henry."

"Why didn't you tell me you were going?" my mother said. "Why didn't you call me?"

"I didn't know."

She hugged the nightgown to herself and stared at me.

"I liked Hopper, too," I said. "I liked his sunlight."

"Asher, Asher, what are you doing? You went out of the school in the middle of the day and disappeared. Your father isn't home and you disappeared. What are you doing?"

I was no longer listening. My mother went on talking. She seemed to be talking very loudly. Now Mrs. Rackover was talking. I got into bed. Their talking was very loud. I turned my face to the wall. There was the crack and its spidery tributaries. I had forgotten to draw the crack for the mashpia. I wondered what else I had forgotten to draw besides that and my father. I fell asleep.

The darkness woke me. I felt it upon me in my sleep and I came awake and stared into it, listening. I did not know how long I had slept. The darkness seemed faintly resonant with distant sound. I thought I heard someone singing. The sound faded in and out. I was dreaming. I knew I was dreaming. I could feel my eyes wide open but I knew I must be dreaming that my mother was singing somewhere in the darkness.

My father was in the kitchen when I came in the next morning. His eyes were heavy and tired. My mother was at the stove, her back to me. They looked at me as I sat down at the table. They seemed to be moving very slowly. My father said something to me and I responded. He was preparing our orange juice but moving very slowly.

I heard him say, "You should not have done that, Asher." His voice was without expression.

I said, "I'm sorry, Papa."

"You frightened your mother."

"I won't do it again, Papa."

"You will come home immediately after school."

"Yes, Papa."

"You will not go to Reb Yudel Krinsky's store."

"Yes, Papa."

"You will not go to the museum again without permission."

"Yes, Papa."

My mother turned and watched me. She was very pale and the sockets of her eyes were dark.

"Did you understand what the mashpia said to you?"

"Yes, Papa."

"You are sure you understand?"

"Yes, Papa."

"If you were a genius in mathematics, I would understand. If you were a genius in writing, I would also understand. If you were a genius in Gemorra, I would certainly understand. But a genius in drawing is foolishness, and I will not let it interfere with our lives. Do you understand me, Asher?"

"Yes, Papa." Yes Papa, yes Papa, it's foolishness Papa, yes Papa. "Are you going away again today, Papa?"

"Yes."

There was sunlight on the trees and the parkway looked clean. The cars parked along the inside lanes shone in the sun. I came into the school. The thin pimply-faced boy who sat in front of me stood in the doorway to the classroom with a group of four or five other students. He watched me come up the corridor.

"Here comes the desecrater of sacred books," he said in Yiddish in his loud nasal voice.

The ones near him laughed. The corridor was crowded with students and I saw some of them turn and look at him curiously.

"You want to go inside?" he said to me.

I did not respond.

"Shall we let him inside, this goy, this destroyer of Jewish books?"

I pushed by him and went to my seat. Behind me I heard the one with the nasal voice say something, but I could not make out the words. Those around him burst into laughter.

I came out of school later that day and turned up the parkway and walked to Yudel Krinsky's store. Sometime during the half hour I spent with him, he went into the back of the store. I put five tubes of oil color, a bottle of turpentine, and a bottle of linseed oil into one of my coat pockets. I slipped two bristle brushes into my loose-leaf notebook. Before I left the store, I bought a small canvas board; I had enough money for that. I walked home in the last of the sunlight and saw my mother framed in the window of our living room as I came up to the house.

She did not ask me why I was late. My father was not home.

I put the tubes and bottles and the brushes into a drawer of my desk and slipped the canvas board into the space between the desk and the wall.

In school the next Sunday morning, the thin boy with the nasal voice stood blocking the doorway again. He saw me coming up the corridor. "Here he comes," he said loudly. "Asher Lev, the desecrater of Chumoshim."

The corridor seemed to echo with his words and with the laughter of students.

I went straight home from school; my father was not traveling that day.

The following day, I came into the classroom a moment after the teacher arrived. The pimply-faced boy was seated at his desk. He leered at me as I passed him.

The mashpia came into the room during the day and spoke to us about the verse "And you shall love your neighbor as yourself." From time to time during the talk, he glanced at me. He wants to see if I am drawing or listening, I thought. I kept my eyes on him but was drawing inside my head and moving my forefinger carefully and slowly across a small portion of the surface of my desk. Then the mashpia left.

On the street after school, the thin boy said to me loudly, "You did not desecrate a Chumash today, Asher Lev. How come?"

"Leave him alone," someone else said.

I walked away from them and spent the next hour and a half in the museum.

There was no one in the window of the apartment as I came up the street. Mrs. Rackover opened the door. She said, "Supper is waiting for you," and went up the hallway into the kitchen.

I ate supper with my mother. She did not say anything to me about being late. My father was in Detroit.

At breakfast the next morning, I said, "Is Papa coming home from Detroit today?"

"Yes."

"When?"

"In the early afternoon."

I came home immediately after school.

The next morning, I asked my father, "Are you going away today, Papa?"

My mother gave me an uneasy look.

"I don't have to travel anywhere until a week from next Tuesday," my father said. "We have meetings until then."

My days passed slowly. The thin boy stopped bothering me. I came straight home from school every day. I returned home one Monday and thought my desk had been moved: the canvas board was not quite where I had placed it; the drawer with the oil tubes seemed to have been hurriedly gone through. But I could not be certain.

It was May. I could see leaves on the trees. From the window of my living room, the maples along the parkway seemed young and delicate, fragile with spring growth. I sketched and drew them. I watched the growing of the leaves and drew the twists and turns of their branches against the sky. I was drawing my street, and inside me was the fearful awareness that I would soon lose it and have nothing I loved that I could draw.

That month, my father began to help my mother with her study of Russian. I would hear them together in the nights after I had gone to bed and the lights were out in my room. He was helping her memorize the meanings of words and the conjugations of verbs. He corrected her pronunciation. Sometimes I would hear them laughing.

On Tuesday in the second week of May, my father flew to Washington. He would not return until Thursday. I spent Tuesday and Wednesday afternoon in the museum.

That Thursday afternoon, a Washington–New York airliner came down in the East River on its approach to LaGuardia Airport. The fifty-seven people aboard were killed. We heard the news over the kitchen radio during supper. My mother froze in her chair until the flight number was announced. Then she took a series of small gulping breaths and sat very still, her eyes flat and dead.

"Mama," I called out.

She shuddered, and looked at me. After a moment, she said very quietly, "I wonder if artists also travel a lot, Asher."

Dimly, then, I began to sense what my father's journeys demanded of her. "Have a safe journey, Aryeh," she would always say to him at the start of one of his trips. I had always thought that to be a simple formula for departure. Now I began to hear the muted tonalities within the words.

We were together for a while after supper in our living room. I sat on the sofa, watching her gaze out the window at the street. I had begun in recent weeks to be conscious of the lines and planes not only of her face but of her body as well. It seemed astonishing to me that so small a frame could have borne me and not at all surprising that it appeared incapable of bearing once again. She seemed sad and bowed, as if an enormous heaviness had been thrust upon her. Outside, there was still sunlight on the tops of the buildings and trees. A faint glow fell upon the upper part of our window. Reflecting downward, the glow was caught by the contour of her delicately boned features, giving them a pale golden luminosity. She seemed very beautiful to me then, in all her sadness and frailty and tenacious strength. I looked at her, holding the picture of her in my mind. I closed my eyes and, starting with the top of her forehead, began to draw her from memory inside my head. When I grew uncertain over a line, I opened my eyes and memorized the line and closed my eyes and continued drawing. I had the lines of her face and body fixed in my mind before the twilight turned to night.

I said to her before I fell asleep that night, "Why do you let Papa travel so much?"

"Let him?" She did not understand.

"Why don't you ask Papa to stop?"

"It's your father's life, Asher. How can I ask him to stop?"

My father returned from Washington late that night. It had been a good trip and he was in a jubilant mood at breakfast the following morning. He and my mother talked about the Russian desk in the State Department, but I did not understand what they said. After breakfast, the three of us walked together along the parkway. It was a warm blue day. My father continued to talk about his Washington trip. I could not remember when I had last seen him so happy. I looked at the morning sunlight on the leaves of the trees. My mother and father were talking earnestly together. Then they were laughing. I watched them talking and laughing. My father went into the Ladover building to his office and my mother went along the parkway with her books. I came into my school. Immediately after school I went home.

My father returned from his office a few minutes after my mother came back from college. I heard them talking quietly together in the kitchen. Then they went into their bedroom. They were in the bedroom a very long time.

Something had happened to my father between the time he had gone into his office and the time he had returned home. At the Shabbos table that evening, he was subdued. He kept glancing at me throughout the meal. Often he seemed on the threshold of anger. He was sullen. He kept rubbing the side of his face. He sang zemiros with an intensity I had not heard from him since my mother's illness. At one point during the meal, after a long silence in which he had sat staring moodily down at the table, he slowly raised his head and began to sing his father's melody to Yoh Ribbon Olom. I heard the long sustained note with which he held the first word, and I felt a shiver move through me. All the months of my mother's illness returned, all the pain and fear. My mother put her face in her hands. "Yoh Ribbon Olom," my father sang. God, Master of the Universe, You are the King, the King of all kings. I found myself clutching my fork as if I were readying a weapon in my defense.

I asked my mother, before I fell asleep, "What happened today, Mama?"

She told me to say the Krias Shema, and went from my room.

My father walked alone to the synagogue the next morning. When I came in, I saw him at his table, his tallis over his head.

That morning, the Rebbe came into the synagogue at Borchu, then took his chair near the Ark. I prayed intently. After a while, I began to feel eyes upon me. But I would not look up. I felt eyes still upon me. I glanced through the synagogue. It was crowded. I scanned the area near the Ark and saw the Rebbe looking at me. He was looking at me across the expanse of the entire synagogue. I could see his dark eyes looking at me from below the fringe of the tallis that covered his head. I felt as if he were standing directly before me. I stared down at my prayer book. My face burned. My heart beat fiercely. After a long moment, I looked up. The Rebbe sat very still, praying. I could not see his face.

My father was silent all through the Shabbos meal. He went back to the synagogue as soon as we were done eating. He had things on his mind, my mother told me. She was tired, she said. She went into her bedroom.

That night, my parents went over to my Uncle Yitzchok's house and I remained alone in the apartment. I wandered through the silent rooms. Then I took the tubes of oil colors out of my drawer and set the canvas board on my chair. I stood there, staring at the tubes and the brushes and the canvas. I wanted to paint but felt my mind and hands paralyzed. I could not touch the tubes of oil. I cringed at the thought of handling the brushes. I had stolen. I felt myself filled with horror. The gift had caused me to steal. I hated the gift. But I wanted to do the painting. I stood there unable to move. Finally, I went from the room and stood in front of our living-room window, staring down at the stream of night movement on the parkway and wishing I had never touched a pencil or a crayon, or met Yudel Krinsky, or seen a tube of oil color. The gift was making me ill and causing everyone around me to suffer—and I hated it, despised it, wanted to burn and destroy it, felt toward it a mountainous rage. I was suddenly very tired. A wearying darkness moved across my eyes. I returned to my room and put away the oil colors and the brushes and the canvas board. I lay in my bed. The apartment was dark. I heard my father singing Yoh Ribbon Olom. I saw my mother standing in front of the living-room window. I was painting my mother in front of the window but the colors would not come off the brush. The canvas remained white. I tried to put color onto the canvas but it remained clean and white. I hated it clean and white. I hurled the brush at it. The color splattered on the walls and floor. But the canvas remained clean and white.

I fell asleep. Afterward it seemed to me I had slept a very long time.

I remember going to Yudel Krinsky's store that Monday and waiting for him to turn his back to me for a moment so I could slip the tubes and brushes back into place. I remember the mashpia talking to me in his office and asking me why I really did not want to go to Vienna. I remember talking and talking and finally saying I couldn't talk any more and telling him about the canvas that wouldn't take paint; as hard as I tried, it just wouldn't take paint. I remember my father's tormented look and the deepening darkness around my mother's eyes. I remember someone asking me if I wanted to have a private talk with the Rebbe and that I screamed no, I hated the Rebbe, he was stealing my street from me, and then ran away and found myself beneath the trees of the parkway, looking at the dots of light made by the sun as it came through the leaves. I remember subdued conversations between my parents, the distant whispering of people in the synagogue, and the way my classmates shied away from me in school.

Later, in the summer, I walked with my mother along the lake near our bungalow and she explained to me again and again the three choices the Rebbe had given my father. He could decide not to go to Europe and continue his present work in the United States; or he could go to Europe with my mother and leave me with my Uncle Yitzchok and his family; or he could go alone, leave my mother and me in America, and return periodically to be with us. The mashpia, my teachers, and the Rebbe had decided that I could not go to Vienna. That was what the Rebbe had told my father the Friday after his return from Washington. That was what my father and mother had gone to discuss with my Uncle Yitzchok that Saturday night.

"We decided to leave you with your Uncle Yitz-chok," my mother explained patiently over and over again that summer. "Then we came home and found you and saw we could not give your Uncle Yitzchok such a responsibility. Do you understand, my Asher? Do you understand what we're doing?"

I walked with my mother and listened and did not understand. I drew very little that summer. The fatigue seemed overwhelming and relentless. I was unable to hold a pencil for too long. I slept a great deal. I kept telling my mother I understood.

But I really began to understand it the night in the airport that October when my father held me very close to him and kissed me. I felt his beard and lips on my cheek and smelled his warmth and strength. "Be well, Asher," he murmured in Yiddish. "Only be well. Everything will be all right, my son. We are doing the work of the Master of the Universe."

Then he went off with my mother, and they talked alone for a few minutes.

"Have a safe journey, my husband," I heard my mother say. She was crying. My father waved at me. I saw him go through the glass doors, limping slightly, carrying his attaché case and a copy of the *New York Times*. Then he disappeared into the crowd of passengers.

"Have a safe journey, my husband," my mother kept saying as we stood near the doors. "Have a safe journey, my husband."

*Book
Two*

SIX

That was an autumn of cold winds that stripped the leaves from the trees and blew them in clouds through the street. I would wake from dreams and hear the leaves against my window. On Shabbos afternoon, I would stand at the window of our living room and watch the trees rain leaves and the leaves swirl back and forth at the whim of traffic and wind. By November, the trees were almost bare. Solitary leaves clung to the branches as tenacious reminders of life. They fell and the trees stood naked on the street. It rained and the leaves lay rotting in the gutters. It snowed and the leaves were gone.

I missed my father. He wrote often. In the weeks immediately after his departure, his letters came to us from Vienna. In January, we received letters from Zurich and Geneva. In February, we received letters from Paris. In March, we received letters from Bucharest. Then he wrote us again from Vienna; he missed us, he said; the work was difficult and endless, he said, but he had faith that the Ribbono Shel Olom would help him; he looked forward to being with us and with the Rebbe for Passover.

I did not understand how much I truly missed him until the first Shabbos he was gone. My mother and I were alone in the apartment—my Uncle Yitzchok's wife was ill and could not have us in their home—and the absence of my father's zemiros was like an emptiness gouged out of the Shabbos by the Other Side.

Strangers called us on the phone. They were people

who had been in Europe, had come across my father in this or that city, and had promised to call his family when they returned to America. Some were businessmen. One was a professor who called us from Boston. Another was a physician who called us from Montreal. Twice we received calls from people in Washington, D.C. My father was well; he sent us his love; he was working hard and traveling a great deal. One of the callers from Washington wished us a happy Hanukkah and pronounced "Hanukkah" in a way that left me reasonably certain he was not a Jew.

Sometimes at night, when I had said the Krias Shema and my mother was gone from my room, I would lie awake and try to imagine where my father was and what he was doing. I would see him journeying from city to city, limping through terminals, his face with its dark eyes and red beard framed in the windows of planes and trains as he sped across mountains and valleys, journeying to teach Torah and Hasidus, journeying to meetings about the Jews of Russia, journeying, endlessly journeying, as my mythic ancestor had once journeyed. I would think of him lonely and alone in the hostile enormity of Europe and feel horror at what I had done. I would say to myself then that all I needed to do was tell my mother, "I want to go to Vienna, Mama. I don't want to be away from Papa." That was all I needed to do. I would resolve to do it. First thing in the morning, I would do it. I would tell my mother at breakfast, "I want to go to Vienna, Mama. I don't want to be away from Papa." But I could not do it.

I wished my father had not had to go to Europe. I wished the Ribbono Shel Olom could have arranged matters differently for my father. I missed him. In missing him, I began to draw him in all the places on the street I had never drawn him before.

I remembered him walking Sunday mornings beneath the trees, reading the copy of the *New York Times* he had just bought, the thick paper held flat in his arms as one might hold a child. Sometimes I walked with him and marveled that he could read and avoid the trees and fireplugs and the cracks and juts in the sidewalk; or I watched him from the window of our living room and saw him coming toward the house, his hat tilted on the back of his head, his red beard a counterpoint to the darkness of his clothes.

I said to him once, walking back with him from the candy store on a Sunday morning, "Does my papa read the whole newspaper? Look how big it is."

He smiled and said, "I read the news and the magazine and the section on books."

"Does my mama read the same parts as my papa?"

"Yes."

"Is there a part on drawing?" I asked. I was four years old then.

"Yes. I don't read that part."

"When I learn to read, I will read the part on drawing. I like drawing."

"Yes," he said. "I've noticed."

I asked him once, "Papa, if you only read those parts of the newspaper, why must we buy the whole newspaper?"

"That's the way it's sold, Asher."

"Does anyone read the whole newspaper?"

"Yes. But most people read what interests them."

"What is this part called, Papa?" I could not quite make out the words. I was six at the time.

"Sports," he said.

"You don't read sports, Papa?"

"It's a foolish waste of precious time," he said. Then he added in Yiddish, "It comes from the Other Side, Asher. Boxing, football. . . . People are hurt. It must come from the Other Side."

I drew him sitting on the parkway bench in front of our apartment house. In the spring and early summer, and sometimes in the beginning weeks of autumn, he would sit on that bench with my mother on a festival afternoon. They would talk quietly together and I would scamper about. I was a child then and never really understood what they were saying. But I remembered their faces and gestures, the lowered eyes, the smiles, the light brushing of fingers across an arm or shoulder. I remembered those moments on that bench, and now I drew them.

And I drew, too, the way my father once looked at a bird lying on its side against the curb near our house. It was Shabbos and we were on our way back from the synagogue.

"Is it dead, Papa?" I was six and could not bring myself to look at it.

"Yes," I heard him say in a sad and distant way.

"Why did it die?"

"Everything that lives must die."

"Everything?"

"Yes."

"You, too, Papa? And Mama?"

"Yes."

"And me?"

"Yes," he said. Then he added in Yiddish, "But may it be only after you live a long and good life, my Asher."

I couldn't grasp it. I forced myself to look at the bird. Everything alive would one day be as still as that bird?

"Why?" I asked.

"That's the way the Ribbono Shel Olom made His world, Asher."

"Why?"

"So life would be precious, Asher. Something that is yours forever is never precious."

"I'm frightened, Papa."

"Come. We'll go home and have our Shabbos meal and sing zemiros to the Ribbono Shel Olom."

Sometimes on a festival afternoon, my father and I would climb the stairs to the top floor of our apartment house. Then we would go up the last flight of stairs and my father would push open the huge metal door and we would step out onto the roof. We would stand near the clotheslines and the brick chimney and stare out across the tops of trees and the roofs of houses at the distant sky and smoky haze of the city. We could barely see the trees of Prospect Park for the tall buildings, and we could not see the lake at all. But the traffic noise floated up to us muted by distance, and the wind felt cool and clean. There was the feeling of being away from the world, alone away from the world, and near the sky, somehow nearer even to the Ribbono Shel Olom.

"It's only a taste," my father said once, looking out across the buildings and trees. "But remember, Asher, some tastes remain a long time on the tongue. A taste of the Ribbono Shel Olom. . . ."

I was seven at the time. Now I remembered, and I drew that memory of my father on the roof.

I drew him walking along the street with his friends, talking, arguing, gesticulating. I drew him raging at me once when I ran across the wide center lane of the parkway without waiting for the light to change. I drew him walking with my mother, tall, bending toward her as she spoke. I drew him in all the small and quiet ways I had never thought to draw him before. And it seemed to me that I was closer to him during those early months of his absence than at any other time of my life.

The same week my father left for Vienna, my mother bought a small wooden table, placed it to the left of our living-room window, and made that her desk. The kitchen was too closed in, she said. She wanted to be able to look out the window.

A few days later, she bought a little bookcase and put it near the table. The room remained our living room; but it also became her study.

My father's chair at the head of our living-room table remained unoccupied, as did his chair in our kitchen. But I thought it might not be wrong for my mother to use my father's desk in their bedroom, and I asked her about it.

"It belongs to your father," she said.

She had graduated from college and was working for a master's degree now in Russian affairs. The kitchen was deserted, except for meals. The living room became the room in which we lived.

She missed my father. I would sit with her sometimes in the evening and watch her studying, and I would see her put down her pen and raise her eyes to the window and look out at the street and the sky. Her warm brown eyes would be misty; her face wore a remembering look. I would think then, I want to go to Vienna, Mama. I don't want to be away from Papa. But I could never bring myself to say it.

She said to me one Shabbos afternoon, "My brother Yaakov, olov hasholom, used to tell me how Jews in Europe traveled and were away from their families for months. But I didn't think it would happen in America."

I'm sorry, I wanted to say. I'm sorry. I couldn't help it, Mama. I'm sorry. But I remained silent.

"You miss Papa?" she asked me softly.

"Yes."

"I miss him, too," she said. "Very much." Then she added in Yiddish, "He is traveling for the Rebbe." She gazed out the window. "He should live and be well. He should have safe journeys."

I drew her sitting at the table studying. I drew her gazing sadly out the window. She developed a habit in those weeks of chewing on her pencils, and I drew her with pencils in her mouth.

"I used to do that when I was a little girl in school," she said, gazing at a drawing of her with a pencil in her mouth. "I'll have to break that habit, Asher. There are germs on pencils."

But she could not break the habit and in the end she gave up trying.

She began to talk about her brother during those months. On our walks together to the synagogue or to my school, she would mention him when something she said or did touched memories concealed beneath time and pain. Her parents had died when she was young. There had been her sister Leah, eight years older than my mother; and her brother, Yaakov, three years older than my mother. They had gone to live with their father's sister, now also dead. Yaakov had been mother and father to little Rivkeh. "It's hard to lose a mother and father the first time. Then to lose them again a second time. . . ."

Yaakov had been thin and delicately built, a male counterpart of my mother. It had been impossible not to recognize them immediately as brother and sister. He had been a brilliant student in the Ladover yeshiva. The Rebbe himself had chosen him to become a student of Russian affairs, to become an adviser to the Rebbe, to travel, to—

"Why did the Ribbono Shel Olom kill Uncle Yaakov?" I asked my mother once.

"Why? I don't know why. Do we understand the ways of everything in this world? We have to have faith that the Ribbono Shel Olom is good and knows what He is doing."

She said it through tears.

The bookcase that stood next to her new desk in the living room was a small dark-wood three-shelf case about four feet high and three feet wide. By December, it was almost entirely filled with new books. I glanced at some of the titles one Shabbos afternoon: *History of the Jews in Russia and Poland,* by Simon Dubnov; *The Foreign Policy of Soviet Russia,* by Max Beloff; *Law and Social Change in the USSR,* by John N. Hazard; *The Jews in the Soviet Union,* by Solomon Schwartz; *The Bolshevik Revolution,* by E. H. Carr. There were two books on the Soviet secret police that I tried to read; but I could understand neither of them.

In the middle of December, she bought another bookcase, a duplicate of the first. It, too, began to fill rapidly with books on Russia. She was doing a great deal of writing. Papers for her courses, she said. For graduate school, one had to write many papers. I was not sure I understood. What was the paper she was writing now? I asked. It had to do with the murder of the Russian Yiddish writers and the doctors' plot, she said. Did I remember the doctors' plot? Yes, I remem-

bered the doctors' plot. I remembered the murder of the
Russian Yiddish writers, too, I said.

She was typing her papers now, and I would at first
not be able to fall asleep for the noise of the typewriter.
But I grew accustomed to it quickly enough after three
bad nights; she insisted I learn to fall asleep with the
typewriter going; she did not have the time to indulge
my need for quiet sliding into sleep. So I would fall
asleep to the rhythm and clack of her typewriter. Sometimes I woke in the early morning and found her at her
desk, asleep over her books near the typewriter, the
pale sunlight shining on her face through the open slats
of the window blind. I would take a pad and pencil and
draw her then, draw her asleep over her books, her face
cradled in her arms, all of her at rest like a child. I drew
those moments of her asleep at her desk because they
served me as balance for those moments when she
would stand by the window staring at the street, seeing
neither the trees nor the traffic nor the people of the
parkway but my father on a different street, in different
traffic, with different people. Those moments when I
saw her at the window like that were the most difficult
for me to bear, for I understood clearly that I was the
cause of her unhappiness. I drew those moments, too,
but I needed her moments of rest and peace to help
stave off my own moments of darkness and doubt.

I drew endlessly all those weeks after my father's departure. I drew while I walked; I drew while I ate; I
drew while I sat in class; I drew in Yudel Krinsky's
store; I drew in the museum. Once I woke in the morning and found I had drawn on the wall near my bed a
picture in red crayon of my mythic ancestor. To this
day, I do not know how I did that picture.

In the last week of December, my mother brought
home a wooden box. A gift, she said to me; purchased
from Reb Yudel Krinsky. For no reason; just a gift because she loved me. The box contained twelve tubes of
oil colors, half a dozen bristle brushes of different sizes,
a bottle of turpentine, a bottle of linseed oil, a palette

knife, and a palette. She had also bought me a small easel and half a dozen small-sized stretched canvases.

On the night of December 26, 1953, when Shabbos was over, I spread some of my father's old copies of the Sunday *Times* on the floor of my room, set up the easel, and squeezed some red, yellow, and blue hues onto the palette. Then I put some white on the palette. I dabbed a narrow brush into the red and tapped it lightly against a sheet of newspaper on the floor. The red hue left marks across the newsprint, bright red against black and white. I looked at the red line on the newspaper; it had come off the brush. I ran the brush against the newspaper, feeling the play of oil against the paper, watching the hue come off and streak, testing how long a streak it made. Then I put some yellow on another brush and ran it into the red on the newspaper. I ran yellow and red together. I ran blue and red together. I ran yellow and blue together. I outlined a face on the newspaper and painted it in orange and green, using turpentine and linseed oil to dilute the colors, molding with the colors, trying to get the planes and forms. I loved the oil and turpentine odors. I tried painting a face on a white canvas board but it did not work; I could not do the molding. My mother sat on my bed watching me for a long time. Then she left. A few minutes later, I heard her begin typing in the living room. I continued working on the face and finished it but did not do it well. It's an exercise, I said to myself. It's cardboard, not even canvas. But I did not sleep much that night.

The next night, I painted my first oil on canvas, a picture of my mother looking out the window of our living room. It was as if I had been painting in oils all my life.

My mother came into my room one night in January and sat on my bed. I was doing an oil on canvas of Yudel Krinsky surrounded by stacks of matzos in the grocery store. She watched me for a while, then said quietly, "It's a lovely painting, Asher."

"Thank you, Mama."

"May I interrupt you?" she asked.

I stopped my work.

"Your father wrote asking about school."

I looked away from her at the painting. The square shapes of the boxes of matzos intrigued me.

"Asher, look at me. What should I tell your father?"

"I'm trying, Mama."

"Your teacher says you're not trying. The mashpia says you're not trying. What should I tell your father?"

"I don't care."

"Asher."

What if I tilt some of those squares? I thought. Won't that make it more interesting?

"Asher, I have to tell your father something. What will I tell your father? I will have to tell him the truth. Asher, what do you do in school? Isn't there anything you like?"

"Yes," I said. Suppose I tilted one row of boxes one way and another row of boxes another way. What would happen?

"But you can't do that all day and all night, Asher. You can't go through school not learning."

"I'm learning, Mama."

"I don't know what to do with you," she said. She got up off the bed and went from the room.

I'll try it, I thought. And maybe I'll tilt Yudel Krinsky's body a little in different directions, too. That might make it really interesting.

I scraped off the paint and started again.

I sat in the last row of seats in my classroom drawing in my Hebrew notebook. The teacher, a middle-aged man with a round face and black beard, said from across the room, "What are you doing, Asher Lev?"

I felt my face go hot. I put down the pen.

He came toward me up the center aisle of the classroom. Everyone watched intently. He stopped in front of my desk.

"What were you doing?"

I removed my hand from the notebook. I had drawn his face, giving his eyes the stern and serious expression they always wore.

He looked at my drawing. Then he looked at me.

"When will you grow up, Asher Lev?" he said sadly. "You are eleven years old."

I did not say anything.

"At least you did not draw in a Chumash," he said.

Someone in the room snickered.

The teacher turned and stared at the class. "I do not need you to help me. It is enough that I have to say it." He looked at me again. "Try to grow up, Asher Lev. It is already time. You do not do your father honor with such behavior."

The mashpia said to me one day in the last week of January, "You are not learning, Asherel. Your teacher does not know what to do with you."

"I am trying."

He sighed. We were in his office. Outside, there was winter sunlight on the bare trees.

"Your father wrote to me," he said. "Your father is very upset. He asks me to speak to you."

I was quiet.

"Can I help you in any way, Asherel?"

I did not know what to say.

"If I thought it would be different if your father was home, I would immediately tell the Rebbe."

I stared at him.

"But it would not be different." He was silent a moment. "No, it would not be different. Give your mother my very good wishes for her health, Asherel."

My Uncle Yitzchok came over to the apartment one Shabbos afternoon on the way to the Rebbe's talk. We sat in the living room. My father had written to him about my studies, he said. Not to speak of it on Shabbos, he said, but what was I doing with all my time and why wasn't I studying?

My mother stared uncomfortably at the carpet. I looked out the window at the snow melting on the trees.

"Listen," my uncle said to me, "you can't spend your life drawing. Once in a while, it's fine. As a hobby. But you can't stop learning Torah, Asher. How will it look if I have a nephew who can't even study a page of Gemorra? You want to draw, go ahead and draw. I'll even buy some of your drawings. But draw once in a while. What kind of boy spends his whole life drawing? It kills the brain."

I did not respond.

"Listen to your uncle. I'll write and tell your father that I talked to you and that you'll really try. All right?"

"Yes," I said.

He left to go to the Rebbe's Shabbos afternoon talk.

"What do they all want from me?" I said to my mother.

"They want you to study Torah. A boy your age should be studying Torah."

I went into my room and stood by the window, staring out at the melting snow. I did not hate studying. I had no strength for it. My drawing needed all my strength. Couldn't they see that? What did they all want from me?

I came into Yudel Krinsky's store one day in February.

"You are a scandal," he said to me in his hoarse voice. "The world knows you are not studying Torah." He fixed his bulging eyes on me. "Your father journeys through Europe bringing Jews back to Torah, and here his own son refuses to study Torah. Asher, you are a scandal."

I told him I wanted one tube of cobalt blue and one large tube of titanium white. My mother was giving me money now for the things I needed.

He put the tubes into a paper bag. "A son should not

hurt his father," he said sadly. "Especially a father like Reb Aryeh Lev."

Mrs. Rackover all but stopped talking to me. She walked around in a permanent sullen rage over what she called the stink of paint in the apartment. She would leave altogether, she once yelled at me, if it were not for her feeling of respect toward my father. What kind of Jewish child was I? My father was giving his life for Torah and Hasidus, and I was wasting my life with paint. Goyim behaved this way toward their fathers, not Jews. She kept scrubbing the floor of my room. She left the window open for hours. So my father should not be greeted by the stink of paint when he came home for Pesach, she said.

I was encountering my father everywhere I went. I was hearing about my father from everyone I talked to. He was more in my life now than he had been before his journey.

Early in the afternoon of the third Friday in March, my mother and I went to the Parkway Museum. It was Purim and I was off from school. It was also the day before Shabbos. We wanted to save time. Rather than walk, we took the subway.

An old woman sat in the seat across the aisle from us. Her clothes were ragged and fitted her badly. She wore a kerchief over her hair. Her eyes were sunken and watery; her face was deeply lined. I took out my pad and pencil and sketched her quickly, trying to anticipate the lurching motions of the train. It was a brief ride to the museum from where we lived. I was almost done by the time we arrived at our stop.

I showed the sketch to my mother.

"Yes," she said. "But what did you do to her eyes?"

I had seen the old woman's eyes as pools of brimming dark water and had drawn them that way. "I wanted to show she was sad."

My mother looked closely at the drawing. "Yes," she said quietly. "I understand."

We came up out of the subway station onto the parkway. It was a windy day, but there was sunlight on the street and we knew the winter was gone.

The museum was a large marble and whitestone building fronted by tall trees and a deep spread of rolling lawn. It dominated the area in which it stood, massive, glistening in the sunlight. All along the front of the building directly below the roof were deep niches; set into those niches were statues of great men. One of the statues was of Moses. He stood there near the top of the building, huge, the folds of his robe spilling from him in a rich cascade of marble. It was good going into a museum with a statue of Moses. I wondered if there were any other statues of great Jews anywhere in the world. I took my mother's hand as we walked quickly toward the building.

"I was here with my brother once," she said, "to see an exhibit of Jewish manuscripts. I've never seen any of the paintings. We never thought it was important."

We came through the glass doors into the stone and marble interior. I was not interested in the teepees and canoes and Indians on the first floor. We went up the wide marble staircase to the galleries. I held my mother's hand. I saw with mild surprise that my head now reached to her shoulders. I had grown in the last months and had not known it.

There were very few people in the galleries. I went along slowly with my mother, looking at the paintings. Uniformed guards stood near the entrances to the galleries. They looked at us curiously as we went by.

We came into a large room with paintings in ornate frames. Some of the paint in the paintings seemed to be gold.

"These are the ones, Mama," I said quietly.

She looked at the paintings. I saw her eyes scan the room slowly. She sighed and shook her head.

"I'll explain this to you outside, Asher."

"Why not here, Mama?"

She did not respond. "Where are the others you couldn't understand, Asher?"

We went to another gallery.

"I like the way he paints the water and the gardens. But why does he paint so many like that?" I pointed to a row of paintings on the wall. "Look how he paints them like that over and over again, Mama."

Bright pink spots appeared on my mother's cheeks. I saw her look instinctively away from the paintings, then slowly look back. Looking at her flushed cheeks, I was suddenly reminded of the way she used to look when I was a child and we went together on winter walks beneath the trees of the parkway. But she seemed embarrassed now and very uncomfortable.

"Some artists think it is very beautiful to paint this way."

" Is it against the Torah?"

"You'll have to ask your father, Asher. I think it is, yes."

"Can it be against the Torah to paint something beautiful?"

"I don't know. You'll have to ask your father, Asher. But I think it's against the Torah to paint women the way this artist paints them. The Torah asks us to practice modesty." She used the Hebrew word "tzenius" for modesty.

"Lots of painters paint this way, Mama."

"Yes," she said. "I know. What else did you want to ask me, Asher? I'm embarrassed standing here in front of these paintings. Let's move away, please."

I took her through many galleries to a room filled with paintings that bewildered me. They did not seem to be paintings at all but huge canvases smeared and blotched with wild and random streaks of color.

"Are these paintings, Mama?"

"There are those who think these are paintings, yes."

"What do they mean?"

"I don't know, Asher."

"How can they be paintings if they don't show anything?"

"I don't know what to tell you. I don't know very much about art, Asher." She peered into the adjoining gallery. "Do you understand those paintings?" she asked.

"I see a Jewish man and a fish with wings and a girl surrounded by flowers and candles. It's by Chagall, the Jewish painter."

"Do you understand the one on the opposite wall, Asher?"

"I see the front and side of a woman's face. The woman is sitting by a window. She's wearing a hat with a flower and is holding a cat in her hand. It's by Picasso. I like Picasso very much, Mama. But there are things by him I don't understand." I gazed at the paintings in the room where we stood. "I don't understand these at all. Not any of them."

"We ought to go back, Asher. It's getting late and I have to make Shabbos."

"How can I understand these paintings, Mama?"

"I don't know, Asher. I wish you would worry half as much about understanding your schoolwork as you do about these paintings. Let's go home. It's not summer, and Shabbos will be here soon."

We came out of the museum and crossed the street to the subway tunnel. Standing on the station platform waiting for the train, I asked my mother, "Can you explain those paintings to me, Mama?"

"The first ones we saw?"

"Yes."

"They were about a man called Jesus."

Next to us on the platform stood an old man with a gray beard and a dark hat and coat. He was reading a Yiddish newspaper. He looked up from the newspaper and stared at my mother.

I felt my mother's fingers on my arm. We moved away from the old man.

"I know about Jesus," I said. "Jesus is the God of the goyim."

"Jesus was a Jew who lived in Eretz Yisroel at the time of the Romans. The Romans killed him. That was the way Romans executed people. They hung them from those big poles, the way you saw in the paintings."

"Were many Jews killed by the Romans?"

"Thousands. Tens of thousands."

"Why did the Romans kill Jesus?"

"He said he was the moshiach. They thought he would make a revolution against them."

"Was he the moshiach, Mama?"

"No. He was not the moshiach. The moshiach has not yet come, Asher. Look how much suffering there is in the world. Would there be so much suffering if the moshiach had really come?"

"Why are there so many paintings about him if he wasn't the moshiach?"

"The goyim believe he was the moshiach. The goyim believe he was the son of the Ribbono Shel Olom. They make paintings of him because he is holy to them."

"What does that mean, the son of the Ribbono Shel Olom?"

"I don't begin to understand it," my mother said. She was silent a moment, staring moodily at the tracks. Then she said, "Where your painting has brought me, Asher. To Jesus." She shook her head.

The train roared out of the darkness into the station. Our car was crowded. I stood next to my mother, holding tightly to a pole and swaying with the motions of the car. A film of perspiration covered my mother's forehead and upper lip. She was silent all the way home.

Late that night, she came into my room and sat down on my bed. A while earlier, she had heard me say the Krias Shema and had gone from the room. Now she sat on my bed and I felt her against my legs in the darkness.

"Are you awake, Asher?"

"Yes, Mama."

"I can't sleep. I was thinking of your father."

"I missed Papa's zemiros tonight."

She stirred faintly on the bed.

"I especially miss Papa on Shabbos."

"Yes," she said. "I also miss your father especially on Shabbos."

"Papa would be very angry if he knew about the museum."

"He would be very angry."

"Will you tell him?"

"Of course I'll tell him."

I was quiet.

"Asher, would you go to the museum if I told you not to?"

I did not say anything.

"Asher?"

"I don't know, Mama. Please don't tell me not to."

I heard her sigh. "I wish I knew what to do," she said. "I hope the Ribbono Shel Olom will help me not to hurt your father. Look where it's taken us, Asher. Your painting. It's taken us to Jesus. And to the way they paint women. Painting is for goyim, Asher. Jews don't draw and paint."

"Chagall is a Jew."

"Religious Jews, Asher. Torah Jews. Such Jews don't draw and paint. What would the Rebbe say if he knew we were in the museum? God forbid the Rebbe should find out."

I didn't know what the Rebbe would say. It frightened me to think that the Rebbe might be angry.

"I wish I knew what to do," my mother murmured. "I wish your father was home."

The next Monday, I went alone to the museum after school and spent an hour copying paintings of Jesus into my sketchbook. I noticed two guards watching me and whispering to each other. People went by and stared curiously. A short big-chested man looked at me, looked at my sketchbook, then scowled and walked stiffly away. I worked slowly and carefully, copying with a pencil into the sketchbook. It was only later, on my way home, that it occurred to me how strange it must have been to see a red-haired boy in a black skullcap and dangling earlocks standing in a museum and copying paintings about Jesus.

I showed the drawings to my mother. "I'm teaching myself to draw better this way, Mama."

She was horrified. "Do you know how much Jewish blood has been spilled because of him, Asher? How could you spend your precious time doing this?"

"But I needed to, Mama."

"There are other paintings you can copy, Asher."

"But I needed the expression, Mama. I couldn't find that expression anywhere else."

She stared intently at the drawings. Then she sighed and shook her head. She seemed not to know what to say.

Two days later, I went back to the museum and copied paintings of women without clothes. I drew them slowly, following the contours with care. I found it difficult to do. I returned the next day and the day after. I did not show any of those drawings to my mother.

For the rest of March and through the first week of April, I went to that museum every chance I had. By the second week of April, I was able to draw many of the figures in the paintings from memory.

My mother was busy preparing the apartment for Passover and at the same time writing a dissertation for her master's degree. She knew I was going regularly to the museum. But she said nothing more to me about it.

Late in the night of the second Sunday in April, I felt someone moving about near my bed and heard whispered voices. I knew it was a dream about my mythic ancestor. I lay in the bed with my eyes closed and waited for him to appear. The voices ceased. My ancestor did not appear. I went on sleeping. The next morning, I came into the kitchen and found my father at the table with an orange in his hand.

He had lost a lot of weight. He looked weary and gaunt. He did not greet me. He ordered me to sit down.

My mother looked small and pale. He knew about the oil-color set. He knew about the visits to the museum. He had seen the sketchbook filled with drawings of Jesus and nudes. He had spent half a year of his life creating yeshivos and teaching Torah and Hasidus all over Europe. Then he had returned to America and had discovered that his own home was now inhabited by pagans. He was in an uncontrollable rage. I had never before seen him in such a rage. Even years ago, when he had once talked on the telephone about how Russians treated Jews, there had not been this quality of relentless and lashing fury to his anger. My drawings had touched something fundamental to his being. He kept talking about my drawings of "that man." He would not pronounce the name. Did I know how much Jewish blood had been spilled because of that man? Did I know how many Jews had been killed in the name of that man during the Crusades? Did I know that the reason Hitler had been able to slaughter six million Jews without too much complaint from the world was that for two thousand years the world had been taught that Jews, not Romans, had killed that man? Did I know that his father, olov hasholom, my grandfather, had been murdered by a Russian peasant who was celebrating a holiday having to do with that man? And the other drawings, the drawings of women and girls—didn't I know that the body was the gift of the Ribbono Shel Olom; that the Torah forbade us to treat it without modesty; that such drawings were vile, that they followed in the ways of the goyim; that Jews, Torah Jews, would never think of drawing such things? The body was a private and sacred domain. To display that privacy in a painting was disgusting. And look what all the time I wasted drawing had done to my schoolwork. I acted as if I weren't going to school at all. What was the matter with me? Where had I been born? Whose son was I? What had I been learning all these years? How could I have done such things? Why wasn't I studying? Did I want him to regret all the work he had done in Europe? Did I want to destroy the task he had chosen for himself? Did I want to shame him? Did I want to shame myself?

Day after day, this went on. He did not talk to me any more; he shouted. In the night, I heard him shouting at my mother. They began to fight regularly.

"Why does Papa yell at you?" I asked my mother one night toward the end of that week. We were in the living room together. She was at her desk. My father was at a meeting with the Rebbe.

"Your father is upset."

"But he yells at you. Why does he have to yell at you? He never yelled at you like that before."

"He gave me a responsibility."

"What responsibility, Mama?"

"To raise you."

"Papa is yelling at you because he doesn't think you're raising me?"

"Your father came home and saw your drawings and your school marks and was very upset."

"What was Papa yelling last night?"

"He was upset that I bought you oil colors."

"Why?"

"Your father thinks I'm encouraging your foolishness. I told your father I bought you oil colors because I hoped you would thank me by studying harder in school."

"You didn't tell me that, Mama."

"I know."

"Mama?"

"Yes, Asher."

"Why did you buy me the oil colors?"

"So you shouldn't steal them again from Reb Yudel Krinsky."

I felt my face go very hot.

"I have at least two more hours of work left, Asher. Please go to your room. Draw if you want. But don't draw Jesus or any of the other things. I can't talk to you any more now. Please."

My father said to me at the kitchen table the next

morning, "Asher, stop drawing with your fork on the napkin, and eat."

I put the fork back into the plate of eggs in front of me. I was thinking that the coffee in my mother's cup might make a good color to wash across a face I had drawn the night before. I felt something on my hand, something very hard and tight, and I looked down and saw my father's fingers clenched around my wrist. I stared in astonishment at the fingers, saw the bones jut out from beneath the flesh, saw the ridges of the knuckles, then felt the pain move up swiftly through my arm. He was squeezing the wrist of my right arm; his face, pale within its frame of red beard, was contorted with rage. I cried out. My mother shouted something. Above the noise of her shout, I heard something clatter to the table. The fork. I had without thinking begun to use the fork again as a drawing instrument. My mother shouted something again. I began to cry. My father released my hand. My wrist throbbed. I could not stop crying. My mother continued to shout. My father stood at the table, his face pale, all of him quivering with rage.

They were screaming at each other, my mother and father. They were screaming at each other and I sat there listening, wanting to run away but not daring to move, feeling the pain and the fear and knowing that it was because of me and not knowing what I could do about any of it. I stared at my wrist. It looked blotched. I could see the marks of my father's fingers on the skin. I flexed it slowly. Nothing seemed broken.

". . . ignored by my own son," my father was shouting. "Kibud ov. Where is kibud ov? I will not bring up such a son."

I started to say something. My mother interrupted. Her face was white with anger.

"Please," I said. "Papa. Please."

They ignored me. My mother said something in Russian. My father replied in Russian.

"Papa, please," I said, raising my voice. "Papa, please!"

They both looked at me.

"Please don't be angry at me, Papa. I can't help it."

They looked at each other. Then they looked again at me.

"An animal can't help it," my father said. "A human being can always help it."

"I can't help it, Papa," I said.

"A man has a will," my father said. "Do you understand me, Asher? The Ribbono Shel Olom gave every man a will. Every man is responsible for what he does, because he has a will and by that will he directs his life. There is no such thing as a man who can't help it. Only a sick man can't help it."

"Aryeh," my mother said. "Aryeh." I barely heard her. Her voice was almost inaudible. She was talking to the surface of the table.

"I have a will, Papa. It makes me want to draw."

"That's an evil will. You must fight that will. That will comes from the Other Side."

"I can't fight it, Papa."

"You will fight it. You will not waste your life with goyische foolishness. No, it isn't foolishness any more. It's worse than foolishness. You bring drawings of that man into the house. You bring drawings of girls without clothes into the house. What next? Next you will become a goy. Better you should not have been born."

My mother gasped.

"Listen to me," my father said. He was speaking suddenly in Yiddish. "I am killing myself for the Ribbono Shel Olom. I have broken up my family for the Ribbono Shel Olom. I do not see my wife for months because of my work for the Ribbono Shel Olom. I came home for Pesach to be with my family, to be with the Rebbe, to rest. And what do I find? You know what I find. And what do I hear? I hear my son telling me he cannot stop drawing pictures of naked women and that man. Listen to me, Asher. This will stop. You will fight it. Or I will force you to return to Vienna with me after the summer. Better you should stay in Vienna and be a little crazy than you should stay in New York and become a goy."

"Ribbono Shel Olom," my mother breathed. "Aryeh, please."

"We must fight against the Other Side, Rivkeh," my father shouted in Yiddish. "We must fight against it! Otherwise it will destroy the world."

All through that day, I kept hearing my father's words. We must fight against it. Otherwise it will destroy the world. The words echoed throughout the apartment as we went through the final preparations for Passover, cleaning, repapering shelves, stacking the Passover foods. We must fight against it, I heard my father say. We must fight against it. In the afternoon, when I was no longer needed in the kitchen, I went into my room and drew my father angry, drew a picture of him in reds and browns, angry and shouting. It was a good picture. I put it into my desk beneath a pile of books.

He seemed to forget his anger that night and we sat at the Shabbos table. We sang zemiros. He told us of his travels and his work. There would be Ladover yeshivos one day in all the great cities of Europe, he said. But it would take time. And patience. And faith in the Ribbono Shel Olom. He was gentle, docile, apologetic, especially toward my mother. I saw him glancing at her repeatedly during the meal. Finally, she smiled at him. He began to sing a joyous Ladover tune. We joined him and the three of us sang together.

When I woke in the morning, I found he had already left for the mikveh. My mother was in the kitchen. Her face wore a radiant look. I had a glass of milk and waited for my father to return so we could go to the synagogue together. I waited a long time. He was clearly not returning from the mikveh to the apartment. I went to the synagogue alone and found him at his usual place, with his tallis covering his head. He had either forgotten about me or had chosen not to go with me to the synagogue. I did not talk about it with him.

We spent the first Seder at my Uncle Yitzchok's house. The table was crowded. I remember that when

we were reading the section about the four sons my father looked up at the mention of the evil son and
glanced at me. It was an involuntary gesture; I saw he
regretted it immediately and looked away. I felt a shiver
of dread run through me. My father regarded me as an
evil son. I do not remember anything about the rest of
that Seder.

Nor do I remember anything about the Seder on the
following night, which we celebrated alone in our own
apartment. I recall only that I drank too much wine and
became a little ill and was put to bed feeling hot and
sweaty and faintly nauseated. I lay beneath the blanket
and felt the taste of the wine on my tongue and the
throbbing inside my head. I opened my eyes and the
nausea moved through me and I thought I would be
sick. I closed my eyes quickly and was rocking back and
forth in the bed, slowly rocking back and forth, feeling
very hot and sweaty, feeling the sweat on my face and
in the hollows of my eyes. Behind my eyes was one of
the nudes I had copied. I felt my eyes begin to move
across the contours. I was drawing with my eyes inside
myself, copying the painting slowly, very slowly, and
feeling the contours with my eyes. I stopped and let my
eyes rest. My eyes rested a long time in the dark soft-
ness of the picture. Then I felt them begin to move
again across the rise and fall of the contours, across the
warm light and dark colors. I felt the colors and the
lines. I felt the forms. I felt light and shade and color
and shape. I felt the picture move inside myself, slowly,
in a gentle spin. Then it began to whirl and suddenly it
was white, color and shape all fusing into brilliant white
light, and I felt the picture spinning wildly, all white
light quivering and spinning crazily inside my head, and
I opened my eyes and was very frightened. I was bathed
in sweat. My hands were wet. I lay in bed, terrified. It *is*
the Other Side, I told myself. It *is* the Other Side. But I
can't help it. I lay in bed and stared into the darkness
and listened to the strange new pounding of my heart.

My mother said to me during the first of the intermediate days of Passover, "You shouldn't be so frightened when your father and I quarrel."

"I hate it."

"People who love each other sometimes quarrel, Asher."

"I hate to hear Papa shouting at you."

"Your father is a little frightened. So he shouts at the person closest to him. My brother, olov hasholom, used to shout at me."

"Why is Papa frightened?"

"He has many responsibilities. And he sees you aren't learning. He thinks you will become a goy. He doesn't want to go back to Vienna. But he also doesn't want to remain here and stop his work in Europe. Are you listening, Asher?"

"Mama, can I go to the museum this week?"

She sighed softly. "Wait until after your father leaves," she said.

I woke one night later in the week and heard them quarreling in their bedroom. The words were muffled but the sounds were loud. I lay in the darkness. Stop it, I thought. Stop it. Please stop it. I heard his voice and I thought of my mother in the bedroom with him. Ribbono Shel Olom, stop it. Maybe I can go to Vienna now. I'll tell him in the morning that I'll go. But I felt sudden terror and knew I could not tell him. The quarreling ended abruptly. I listened to the silence. My window was slightly open. The shade scraped softly against the sill.

In the morning after my father left the apartment, I said to my mother, "I heard you fighting last night, Mama."

She looked upset and embarrassed.

"I don't like Papa when he shouts at you. Why was he shouting at you?"

"Your father wanted me to promise I would not let you go to the museum." She shook her head sadly. "I can't promise the impossible."

"I don't like Papa when he's like this."

"I'm not sure your father is wrong, Asher."

I stared at her.

"I'm not sure," she said.

I went to the museum later that day. I wanted to look again at one of the Picassos. On the way to the Picasso, I stopped at one of the paintings of Jesus. I did not copy the painting; I merely looked at it. My eyes moved across it. The wounds intrigued me. How had he made the wounds so real? Had there really been wounds like that? I wondered what it felt like having wounds like that.

I returned home late in the afternoon. My mother did not ask me where I had been.

I remember little else about that Passover, save the quality of menacing darkness that seeped into everything we said and did inside that apartment. All my life, I had loved that festival. It had meant for me warmth and love, the end of winter and the coming of grass and summer sun. Now it was choked with bitterness and fear. My father dominated the apartment on the nights when he was there, and dominated it, too, on the days when he was not. The small kitchen echoed his anger. I lay awake in the nights and heard his shouts even when the apartment was silent and the only sound in my room was the soft scraping of the window shade against the sill.

He seemed a different person. He was in his mid-thirties now, but his red hair had begun to gray. There were weblike lines around his eyes and deep wedges along his forehead and on the bridge between his eyes. He had never been a happy person; but there had always been some moments when he had been light-hearted and frivolous. That was all gone now. He carried himself erect; he was tall and strong. But he carried, too, a burden he had brought back with him from Europe, the burden of the years it would take him to realize his dream.

He had his own dream. He needed all his strength for that dream. Interference drained his strength. He would fight interference. It was clear enough that he now regarded me as a serious interference.

He said very little to me during the last two days of the festival. He spent most of his time in the synagogue. In the apartment, he read a Hasidic book and talked with my mother. There was another loud quarrel the night after Passover. It took me out of deep sleep and was over even before I came fully awake. But I was awake enough to feel a sense of fear at his presence and, together with the fear, a sense of sudden anger at my helplessness.

I was not unhappy to hear my mother wish him a safe journey two days after Passover and see him go off to his waiting aircraft, limping slightly, his black attaché case and a copy of the *New York Times* in his hands.

I chose two subjects, the two I knew concerned him most: Talmud and Bible. I began to study those two subjects. I read and memorized. I did not stop drawing, but I did not draw as often as I had earlier. Whenever I felt unable to study, I remembered the quarrels and my mother's pale features, and I studied. I studied only what I thought the teacher wanted me to know for class and for tests. I continued going to the museum, but less frequently than before. I continued copying paintings of Jesus and nudes, and other subjects as well.

My mother saw me studying and said nothing. My teacher smiled triumphantly. The mashpia blessed me. At the end of May, my mother told me she had written to my father about the improvement in my schoolwork.

My father wrote habitually two or three times a week. By the end of the first week in June, ten days had passed without mail from him. By the end of the second week, there was still no mail, and my mother was showing signs of concern. She called the Rebbe's office and was told they, too, had not heard from my father and that she should have faith in the Master of the Universe, everything would be all right. By the middle of the fourth week, my mother seemed ill; her face was sallow; there was darkness around her eyes; when I talked to her, she did not hear me. She did not get out of bed on Thursday. Mrs. Rackover came early, gave me breakfast, and sent me off to school.

Late that night, I heard my mother in the living room, chanting from the Book of Psalms. I came quietly into the room and saw her standing by the window. The room was dark. She stood by the window staring out into the street and chanting Psalms by heart. Then she stopped. She moved forward slightly, inclined her head, and rested her forehead against the windowpane. "Yaakov, do not let anything happen to Aryeh," she said softly in Yiddish. "Yaakov, are you listening? This is your sister. Do not let anything happen to my Aryeh. Are you listening to me, Yaakov? Please. Yaakov. Please."

I went back to my room. I did not sleep that night.

The next day, Friday, was the final day of my school year. My mother was unable to get out of bed and would not eat all day. I spent that Shabbos with my Uncle Yitzchok and his family. My uncle tried hard not to let me see his fear, and failed.

Early Monday morning, the phone rang. My mother answered it. I heard her talking in Yiddish. It was a brief conversation.

I stood next to her in our hallway.

"The Rebbe's office called. Your father is in Vienna."

"Where was he all that time?"

"They only told me that he was safe in Vienna."

"He would have written if he had been in Vienna all that time."

"Yes."

"He was in Russia," I said.

"Get dressed," she said. "It's a beautiful day outside. We'll go somewhere. Where do you want to go, Asher? Let's go to Prospect Park. We'll go to Prospect Park and take food for a picnic and we'll even go rowing. You can draw me rowing. But don't draw me if I fall backward off the seat. Then we'll go to the museum. Yes," she said, "we'll go to the museum."

We spent the summer in the bungalow colony in the Berkshires. I painted and drew and studied Talmud and Bible. My mother read and worked on the last section of her master's dissertation. She was in her early thirties now, and she seemed particularly lovely that summer, rowing with me along the lake, walking with me beneath the pines, watching a summer rain with me from the porch of our bungalow. I drew her over and over again that summer.

My father spent the summer in Vienna. He returned a week before Rosh Hashonoh. His dark eyes glittered with achievement. It had been a good summer. Ladover yeshivos were opening in Vienna and Paris. Yes, it had been an excellent summer. He said nothing to me about my studies.

I remember that Rosh Hashonoh. I remember the sounding of the shofar, the congregation standing, a sea of heads covered with prayer shawls, the Rebbe at the podium, the shofar at his lips. He wore a long white garment over his dark clothes. On the podium lay the white sacks filled with pieces of paper containing prayers the people wished the Rebbe to say for them. He sounded the shofar over the prayers. The sounds pierced the silence. Over and over, he sounded the shofar. I remember that day because I saw my father look up from his prayer book and stare at me across the synagogue. He stared at me through almost the entire sounding of the shofar. It occurred to me later that one of the prayers in those sacks had contained my name.

He asked me during Succos if I thought I would want to come to Vienna the following year. But now I did not want to be any place where he was, for he had set himself up as an adversary to me and I feared going with him. He could not force me now to go to Vienna; my schoolwork was good. I had the feeling he regretted the improvement in my grades.

He left for Vienna toward the end of October, two days after Simchas Torah.

The following summer, my mother went to Europe. She told me in the last week of June that she missed my father very much; five days later she sailed to Le Havre. She had her master's degree now and was working on her doctorate. From time to time throughout the year, she had gone to the Ladover building; for meetings with the Rebbe's staff, she had said in answer to my questions.

I lived with my Uncle Yitzchok all that summer. I drew and painted and spent a lot of time in Yudel Krinsky's store. He was married now. He no longer wore the kaskett. I ran errands for him. Occasionally I ran errands for my Uncle Yitzchok.

That was the summer three new Ladover families moved into the big apartment house across the street from my Uncle Yitzchok's home, all of them from Russia. I would watch them from the stoop of my uncle's house—shy, hesitant, bewildered, glancing fearfully at whoever came near them. There was a boy my age in one of the families. I saw him on the street one day in front of his apartment house. I went over to him. He was shorter and thinner than I and had wide eyes and long dangling earlocks.

"How are you?" I said in Yiddish.

He looked at me suspiciously.

"Welcome to Brooklyn."

He started to turn away.

"My name is Asher Lev."

He stopped and gazed at me intently, his eyes narrow. I saw him glance quickly around.

"The son of Reb Aryeh Lev?" he said in a quiet voice.

"Yes."

"How do I know you are the son of Reb Aryeh Lev?"

"Everyone does."

"Yes? Everyone?" He glanced around again. "What do you want?"

"Where are you from in Russia?"

He looked at me again out of narrowed eyes. "Tashkent."

"Did you meet my father in Russia?"

His lip stiffened.

"How did my father get you out?"

"Who said your father got us out? Who said that?" He seemed suddenly frightened. "I never said that."

"I thought he might have helped to get you out."

"Listen, what do you want from me? Ask your father."

"My father is in Europe."

"Listen," he said in a thin tight voice. "In Russia, there are Jews with beards and earlocks who spy for the government. What do you want from me? If your father will not tell you, how can I tell you? I do not know anything."

He turned and walked quickly away and disappeared into the apartment house. I did not speak to him again.

SEVEN

The mashpia called me into his office. The Rebbe wanted to meet with me, he said. The Rebbe met with all the yeshiva students who were about to become bnai mitzvah, he said. The Rebbe especially wanted to meet with me alone; he gave quiet and resonant emphasis to the word *yechidus*—alone.

A week before my meeting with the Rebbe, I began going to the office of the mashpia every day after school. We studied Torah and Hasidus. The mashpia was preparing me for my meeting with the Rebbe.

We studied about three kinds of Jews in the world: the rosho, the one who sins and has evil thoughts, whose efforts to live a good life are an endless struggle —most of us are in that category, the mashpia said sadly; the benoni, the one whose acts are without fault but who cannot control his thinking—very few achieve that high level, the mashpia said; and the tzaddik—a tzaddik can only be born, the mashpia said. It is the greatest gift of the Ribbono Shel Olom; yes, a tzaddik can only be born. Only tzaddikim have control over their hearts; the mashpia said, quoting the Midrash.

We studied the meaning of the verse in Deuteronomy, "But the thing is very near to you, in your mouth and in your heart, that you may do it." What does the word *very* come to teach us? That the person whose understanding in the knowledge of the Master of the Universe is limited, who cannot comprehend the greatness of the blessed Being Without End, who cannot produce awe and love of God in his mind and understanding—such a person can nevertheless come to fear and love God through the observance of all the commandments of the Torah, for the commandments are *very* near to all Jews.

We studied the meaning of the verse in Proverbs "The candle of God is the soul of man." The souls of Jews are like the flame of a candle, the mashpia said. The flame burns upward; it seeks to be parted from the wick in order to unite with its source above, in the universal element of fire. Similarly, the soul of the Jew yearns to separate itself and depart from the body in order to unite with the Master of the Universe, even though this means that nothing will remain of its former nature as a distinct and separate entity. It is in the nature of the Jewish soul to desire this union with the Being Without End, unlike the souls of the Gentiles, which are derived from the Other Side and which strive to remain independent beings and entities.

We studied about the sitra achra, the Other Side, the realm of darkness and evil given life by God not out of His true desire but in the manner of one who reluctantly throws something over his shoulder to an enemy, thereby making it possible for God to punish the wicked who help the sitra achra and reward the righteous who subjugate it.

I did not understand many of the things that we studied, especially his explanations of the verse in Proverbs and his account of the difference between Jewish and Gentile souls. But he was a patient teacher and I enjoyed the hours I spent with him. I did not draw or paint that week.

My father was home the January night of my meeting with the Rebbe. He said to me in Yiddish as I was putting on my coat, "Remember with whom you will be speaking."

He seemed tense and apprehensive. My mother looked proud.

It was a cold night. I walked quickly along the parkway. A winter wind blew through the street; I heard it in the bare trees overhead. The sky was clear and dark, jeweled with cold and distant stars.

I came into the Ladover building and walked up the stairway to the second floor. I had been told to go to the room at the end of the corridor to my right. The corridor was carpeted. Bright lights burned inside ceiling fixtures. I came to the room and opened the door.

It was a large waiting room with white walls, a single window in the wall to my right, and a heavy wooden door in the wall across from the window. There was a desk beneath the window and chairs along the walls. On the wall opposite the doorway where I stood was a framed photograph of the Rebbe. Rav Mendel Dorochoff sat behind the desk. He wore dark clothes and a tall dark skullcap. He was the Rebbe's gabbai, the chief of staff, the one who arranged the Rebbe's meetings and could speak in the name of the Rebbe with the same authority as the Rebbe.

The only other person in the room was a tall heavy-shouldered man in a dark winter coat and baggy brown trousers. His face was ruddy and deeply lined. He had a white walrus mustache and a thick shock of flowing white hair. His hands were huge, and he wore a dark beret. He was writing in a small pad he held in his left hand. He glanced up at me as I entered, smiled vaguely, and resumed writing in the pad. I could not remember ever having seen him before.

I went over to the desk. Rav Dorochoff looked up.

"Good evening, Asher Lev," he said in Yiddish. He had a deep nasal voice and sharp gray eyes. He was in his late forties, but his beard was coal black, as was the hair beneath the skullcap. "Your mother is well?"

I nodded.

"You have no tongue?" he said, looking at me.

I found my voice. "My mother is well, thank you." I spoke in Yiddish.

Out of the corner of my eyes I saw the man in the

beret smile faintly. I could not tell if he was smiling over my lost voice or over something he had written in his pad.

"Sit down," Rav Dorochoff said. "The Rebbe will see you soon."

I sat down two chairs to the right of the man in the beret. Rav Dorochoff sat behind the desk reading sheets of paper filled with Hebrew or Yiddish typing. I sat very still in the chair. It was a hard wooden chair with a straight back. The man next to me flipped a page in his pad and continued writing. An aircraft passed overhead. The man shook his head, flipped another page, and went on writing. He held the pad in his hand close to his chest. I looked closely at the pad and saw he was not writing but drawing. I looked away and sat very still, facing the door set into the wall opposite the window and the desk. It was a heavy wooden door, stained walnut. Gentle arabesques of thin dark metal played along its surface. Long triangular wedges of metal hinged the door to its frame. I felt eyes on my face. I felt them moving across my chest. I kept staring at the door. I felt the eyes leave my face for a moment; then I felt them again. I glanced at the man in the beret. He looked back at me. He had pale-blue eyes. He smiled vaguely through the thick walrus mustache, then looked down again at his pad. I glanced over at Rav Dorochoff. He sat at the desk, reading. The room was very still. The man in the beret flipped the page of his pad and went on drawing.

The door opposite me opened soundlessly. A woman stepped nimbly into the room and closed the door behind her. She was tall and slim and well dressed. She went quickly through the room and shut the door.

Rav Dorochoff got up from behind his desk, motioned me to follow him, crossed the room, and opened the heavy wooden door. He stepped back and waved me across the threshold. The door closed soundlessly behind me.

The room was large. It contained a single glass-enclosed bookcase, a large walnut-stained desk, and three chairs near the desk. The walls were white and bare. The desk was bare. Lights burned in a small glass chandelier overhead. A tall Gothic window, its uppermost section open, took up much of the wall to the left of the desk.

Behind the desk sat the Rebbe. He wore a dark caftan and an ordinary dark hat. A dark cord girdled the caftan. His face was pale. He seemed more a presence than a man.

"Asher Lev," he said, raising his hand slightly, then letting it rest again on the desk. "Sit down, Asher Lev." He spoke in Yiddish. His voice was soft. "How is your mother?"

I started to respond. I felt the words deep in my throat. I could not get the words out of my throat. I swallowed hard and took a deep breath. I saw the Rebbe looking at me.

"Thank you, Rebbe," I heard myself say in Yiddish. "My mother is well." I was sitting in one of the chairs near the desk but could not remember how I had got there.

"Asher Lev," the Rebbe said softly, "I wanted to see you and to give you my blessings for your bar mitzvah."

"Thank you, Rebbe."

"Asher," the Rebbe said. "How are you feeling?"

"I am well, Rebbe."

"I remember when you were born. I remember your bris."

I was quiet.

"You will become a bar mitzvah this Shabbos."

"Yes, Rebbe."

He looked at me. "I remember your father's father. I bless you in the name of your grandfather. May you have a life of Torah and commandments."

"Thank you, Rebbe."

"Asher."

"Yes, Rebbe."

"A life should be lived for the sake of heaven. One man is not better than another because he is a doctor while the other is a shoemaker. One man is not better than another because he is a lawyer while the other is a painter. A life is measured by how it is lived for the sake of heaven. Do you understand me, Asher Lev?"

"Yes, Rebbe."

"But there are those who do not understand this."

I was quiet.

"There are those you love and who love you who do not accept this. Asher, to honor your father is one of the Ten Commandments."

"Yes, Rebbe."

"I give you my blessings, Asher Lev son of Reb Aryeh Lev."

His right hand made a slight waving gesture. I got to my feet. I felt dazed and bewildered.

"Good night, Asher Lev."

"Good night, Rebbe."

I went from the room and closed the heavy door behind me. It closed soundlessly without effort.

I started through the waiting room. The man in the beret stood up. He went quickly past me, opened the heavy door, stepped inside, and closed it. A vague odor trailed behind him, the odor of earth and oil and paint. I saw a folded piece of paper on the chair I had occupied earlier. I stopped and picked it up and unfolded it. It was a pencil drawing, a photographic likeness of my face made with an exquisite economy of line and without light and shade. The lower right-hand corner of the drawing contained a signature: Jacob Kahn. Below the signature was the date: 1-10-56.

I sat down on the chair and stared at the drawing. Rav Dorochoff was behind his desk, reading. He seemed not to know I was there. I folded the drawing and put it carefully into a pocket. I took out my small sketchbook and, with a ball-point pen, drew in one continuous line the face of Jacob Kahn. In the lower right-hand corner of the drawing I signed my name: Asher Lev. Below the signature I wrote the date: 26 Teveth 5716. I left the drawing on the chair Jacob Kahn had occupied and went over to Rav Dorochoff.

"Good night," I said.

He looked up at me. "Good night, Asher Lev. Mazel tov." He paused, and added, "May you bring joy to your parents."

"Thank you."

I went from the room. I walked quickly down the stairs. I could hear voices. There were people still working in some of the offices on the street floor. I came out onto the stone porch. The night wind bathed my face. I sat on the rail of the porch and looked at the parkway. I sat there a very long time, remembering other times I had sat on that porch.

A man came out of the building, stopped for a moment in the doorway, and walked over to me. I got off the rail.

"My name is Jacob Kahn," he said. He had a strong voice and he spoke with a vague Russian accent.

"My name is Asher Lev," I said.

We shook hands. He had a powerful grip. I felt my hand swallowed by his.

"Thank you for your drawing," he said.

"Thank you for yours."

"Do you have any idea at all what you are getting into?"

"No."

"Become a carpenter. Become a shoemaker."

I was quiet.

"Become a street cleaner."

I did not respond.

He sighed. "You are crazy," he said. "We are all crazy. I know your father. He will become my enemy."

I said nothing.

"Why should I make your father my enemy? Why? Tell me why."

I did not respond.

He sighed again. "Our Rebbe is very clever. If it isn't me, it will be someone else. Yes? He prefers to take a chance with me."

I was quiet.

"Of course, yes. The Rebbe is clever. I will watch you. We have a clever Rebbe." He drew his hand out of his coat pocket. "This is yours." It was the sketchbook I had once filled for the mashpia.

"Thank you." I put the sketchbook into my pocket.

"Now," he said. "We begin. I do not like to start new relationships in the winter. It is not in my nature to do that. Also there is a sculpture I must finish and I will not have time for you now. You will call me in the middle of March. I am in the telephone book." He stopped and peered at me intently. "You will call?"

"Yes," I heard myself say.

"You understand that I am not what you call a Torah Jew. I am a great admirer of the Rebbe's. My father was a follower of the Rebbe's father. But I am not a religious Jew. You understand that?"

"I understand."

"Good. Now, between today and the middle of March is a long time. You will do something for me in that time. You will take a journey to the Museum of Modern Art, you will go up to the second floor, and you will look at a painting called *Guernica,* by Picasso. You will study this painting. You will memorize this painting. You will do whatever you feel you have to do in order to master this painting. Then you will call me in March, and we will meet, and talk, and work. Do you understand?"

"Yes."

"It is in my nature to be blunt and honest. I shall ask you a question. You are entering the world of goyim, Asher Lev. Do you know that?"

"Yes."

"It is not only goyim. It is Christian goyim."

"Yes."

"You should better become a wagon driver," he said, using the Yiddish term. "You should better become a water carrier."

I said nothing.

"All right," he said. "The Rebbe asked me to make it clear to you. I have made it clear to you. It is time to go home."

We went together down the stairs and along the walk to the street.

"Tell me," he said. "Have you been to the Parkway Museum?"

"Yes."

"Have you seen my paintings?"

"Yes."

He waited.

"I didn't understand them," I said.

I thought I heard him sigh. He had his big hands deep in the pockets of his coat. He shrugged his shoulders. The night wind blew against his lined face.

"You are only thirteen years old," he said. "Yet it disturbs me to hear you say that. You will call me in March. Which way are you walking?"

"Toward New York Avenue."

"I go the other way. Good night, Asher Lev."

We shook hands. He went on up the parkway.

I walked home quickly beneath the stars and the trees.

Neither my father nor my mother appeared surprised by what I told them. My father would not look at me as I talked. He seemed to cringe in pain. My mother wavered apprehensively between my father's pain and my dazed joy and seemed not to know what to say.

"I'm not reconciled to this, Rivkeh," my father said with bitterness in his voice. He was talking to my mother as if I were not in the room. "I can't reconcile myself to such a decision."

"Aryeh," my mother said quietly. "It's the Rebbe's decision."

"Only because everyone is afraid the boy will break and go his own way. Why should everyone be afraid the boy will break away? Why? He is my son. I want to raise my son in my own way."

My mother was silent. Her eyes were dark.

"I am not reconciled," my father said. "I will spend my life traveling for the Rebbe, and my son will spend his life painting pictures. How can I reconcile myself to this, Rivkeh? Tell me. How? There will be trouble from this. When a son goes so far away from a father, there can only be trouble."

"I don't want there to be trouble between us, Papa," I said.

He looked at me and slowly rubbed the side of his face. I had a sudden memory of the way his beard used to feel against my cheek when I had been very young. "Asher, I know you don't want trouble. I am not accusing you, God forbid, of being an evil person. But there is something inside you I don't understand. It will bring trouble. Look at the trouble it has already brought. I don't know what you are. You are my own son, and I don't know what you are. I am ashamed of my own son."

"Aryeh," my mother said softly. She seemed about to cry.

My father closed his eyes. He kept his eyes closed a long time. He said softly, "There are many things in this world I do not understand, Rivkeh. But this—this is the biggest mystery of all. And I can't reconcile myself to it."

My father carried his burden of pain all through the celebration of my bar mitzvah. People knew of the Rebbe's decision. No one dared question it. For the Rebbe was the tzaddik and spoke as representative of the Master of the Universe. His seeing was not as the seeing of others; his acts were not as the acts of others. My father's right to shape my life had been taken from him by the same being who gave his own life meaning— the Rebbe. At the same time, no one knew how to react to the decision, for they could see my father's pain. I had become alien to him. In some incomprehensible manner, a cosmic error had been made. The line of inheritance had been perverted. A demonic force had thrust itself into centuries of transmitted responsibility. He could not bear its presence. And he no longer knew how to engage it in battle. So he walked in pain and shame all through the Shabbos of my bar mitzvah and all through the following day when relatives and friends sang and danced their joy. And he carried that pain and shame with him through the glass doors of the waiting room and into the aircraft that took him back to Europe in the third week of January.

Our school day on Sunday ended at one o'clock in the afternoon. On the last Sunday in January, my mother took me by subway to the Museum of Modern Art in Manhattan. The following Sunday, my mother went with me again. She bought me a large reproduction of *Guernica*. I studied the reproduction during the week, then went alone to the museum the following Sunday. I went every Sunday for the rest of February and the first two weeks of March. At the end of the second week of March, I called Jacob Kahn.

EIGHT

"This is Asher Lev," I said into the telephone.

"Hello, Asher Lev."

"It's the middle of March," I said.

"You saw *Guernica*?"

"Yes."

"How many times did you see it?"

I told him.

"You studied *Guernica*?"

"Yes."

"What else did you do?"

"I drew each section of it at least twice."

"What else?"

"I can draw it from memory."

"What else?"

"I studied the drawings he made before and after he painted it."

"Come to my studio this Sunday in the afternoon." He gave me an upper Manhattan address. "Can you come?"

"I can come at two o'clock."

"You will stay until dinner. We do not keep kosher. I will see you Sunday."

"Yes."

"Asher Lev."

"Yes."

"You are familiar with the story about the massacre of the innocents?"

"No."

190

"Then you will read about it, please, for Sunday. You will find it in the New Testament, the Book of Matthew, chapter two, verse sixteen."

I did not say anything.

"The New Testament," he said. "The Bible of the goyim."

"Yes."

"You will find it and read it."

"Yes," I said.

"You are familiar with the painting *Massacre of the Innocents,* by Guido Reni?"

"No."

"You will go to the library and find a reproduction of it and study it. If you cannot find Guido Reni's *Massacre of the Innocents,* then find Poussin's. But study one of them at least. Do you understand?"

"Yes."

"I will see you Sunday at two o'clock."

"Yes. Goodbye."

"Goodbye, Asher Lev."

I went to the library after school the next day and read the passage in the New Testament about King Herod ordering his soldiers to kill all the children of Bethlehem who were two years old and younger, after having been told that a child had been born who would become king of the Jews. It felt strange holding and reading a copy of the Christian Bible. I could not understand what the story had to do with *Guernica.*

I found a small reproduction of *Massacre of the Innocents,* by Guido Reni, in a thick volume of the history of art. I looked at it closely. I had my reproduction of *Guernica* with me. I opened it and compared the two pictures. The faces of the women in the Reni painting intrigued me, especially that of the woman in the upper left of the picture. I found the Poussin painting in another volume and studied it carefully. After a while, I closed the books and went out of the library.

It was dark and cold. I took the subway home. My mother had a class on Thursday nights. Mrs. Rackover gave me supper. I went into my room and thought about *Guernica*. Mrs. Rackover came in to say she was leaving. I heard the apartment door close behind her.

I was alone in the apartment. I sat at my desk and looked at the reproduction of *Guernica*, which I had put on the wall near my bed. The city of Guernica had been destroyed by the German air force in 1937, during the Spanish Civil War. Picasso had painted the mural for the Spanish Pavilion of the International Exhibition in Paris that year. I knew that painting by heart and could draw it in my mind. I had dreamed about the bull and the horse. I had drawn the screaming pain-filled faces of the women in my notebooks during classes. I had put the anguished women with the dead child into the back of an English exam book, and had gotten it back with a written remark from the teacher about this being an English, not an art, examination; he gave me a D on the test. I did not understand what *Guernica* had to do with the Christian Bible; I did not understand what it had to do with the *Massacre of the Innocents*. I felt upset and uncomfortable at having read from the Christian Bible. I thought of my father. I thought of the mashpia. I wondered if the Rebbe really knew what Jacob Kahn was doing. I felt vaguely unclean.

I had some homework. I started working on it, quickly, perfunctorily. In the middle of an algebra problem, I found myself drawing from memory the head of one of the screaming women in Guido Reni's *Massacre of the Innocents*. I looked at the head. Then I went back to the algebra problem.

I heard the apartment door open and close. My mother was home. She came into my room a moment later, carrying a book.

"There was no mail from your father?" she asked.

"No."

"Did you have supper?"

"Yes."

"What's the matter?"

"Nothing."

"Are you all right? Do you have a fever?"

"No."

She glanced at the notebook with the algebra problem and the Reni head.

"Her child was massacred," I said.

She looked startled.

I told her about the painting. Then I told her about the account of the massacre in the Christian Bible.

"I didn't like reading from that book. I saw where it said Jews killed Jesus. I feel guilty reading the Bible of the goyim."

She gazed at the head in the notebook and did not respond.

"Why did he ask me to read that?"

"When you see him Sunday, ask him. Do you want something to drink before going to sleep?"

"No, Mama."

"Have you had milk today?"

"Yes."

"I brought you this book. You said to me once that you liked the paintings of Robert Henri. A professor in the art department gave me this for you to read." She put the book on my desk. "Good night, Asher. Don't stay up late."

"You told the professor about me?"

"I said my son is interested in art and likes Robert Henri. He told me to tell you to read this book. He also told me that Jacob Kahn is one of the greatest artists alive today. He worked with Picasso in Paris before the First World War. He was a little astonished that you're being taught by Jacob Kahn." She smiled wryly. "Everyone seems astonished by that. Good night, Asher. I have a meeting early in the morning with the Rebbe's staff. Khrushchev's speech about Stalin also has everyone astonished."

She went from the room. A moment later, I heard her moving about in the kitchen.

I looked at the book she had put down on my desk. It was called *The Art Spirit*. I finished my homework quickly.

In bed, I leafed idly through the book, reading passages at random. I liked this man. I liked the warm and honest way he wrote. I lay in bed leafing through the book, and I read:

If you want to know how to do a thing you must first have a complete desire to do that thing. Then go to kindred spirits—others who have wanted to do that thing—and study their ways and means, learn from their successes and failures and add your quota. Thus you may acquire from the experience of the race. And with this technical knowledge you may go forward, expressing through the play of forms the music that is in you and which is very personal to you.

I was not sure I understood what the phrase "the play of forms" meant. I continued reading, skipping the passages on technique which I was determined to read later.

I read:

He should be careful of the influence of those with whom he consorts, and he runs a great risk in becoming a member of a large society, for large bodies tend toward the leveling of individuality to a common consent, the forming and adherence to a creed.

I read:

You can do anything you want to do. What is rare is this actual wanting to do a specific thing: wanting it so much that you are practically blind to all other things, that nothing else will satisfy you.

I read:

An artist has got to get acquainted with himself just as much as he can. It is no easy job, for it is not a present-day habit of humanity.

I read:

... every great artist is a man who has freed himself from his family, his nation, his race. Every man who has shown the world the way to beauty, to true culture, has been a rebel, a "universal" without patriotism, without home, who has found his people everywhere.

I read that again. Then I read:

The artist should have a powerful will. He should be powerfully possessed by one idea. He should be intoxicated with the idea of the thing he wants to express.

I began to read the book from the beginning, slowly. I woke in the night and found the book in my hands and the reading light on. I turned off the light, and slept.

In the morning, my mother said, "You didn't sleep last night."

"It's a good book, Mama."

"Sit down and have your breakfast, Asher."

"Did you read the book?"

"I looked through it quickly on the subway."

"Did you read what he said about an artist having to free himself?"

"No. I don't remember that."

I told it to her. "I don't think I want to free myself that way," I said.

"In what way do you want to free yourself, Asher?"

"I don't know."

"Eat your breakfast," she said softly, "and I'll walk with you to school. I have the meeting to go to."

There was no mail from my father that day. Nor was there any mail from him the next day, which was Shabbos.

My mother and I were in the living room late that Saturday night when the phone rang. I went to answer it.

"Asher Lev?" It was Jacob Kahn.

"Yes."

"Bring all the drawings you made of *Guernica*. Bring other drawings, too. Any you want."

"I'll bring them."

"You know how to travel?"

"Yes."

"I will see you tomorrow at two o'clock."

My mother was at her desk, reading.

"No," she said when I told her about the phone call. "I think I ought to go with you the first time."

"I want to go alone."

"Asher, it's easier to get lost on the New York subway than it is to walk from here to your yeshiva."

But I insisted, and in the end she consented. I would go alone. I was to be back by seven o'clock. If I could not be back by seven, I was to call her.

I stayed up late that night, drawing sections of *Guernica* from memory. I spent a long time thinking about the faces of the women in the Reni and Poussin paintings and about the story of the massacre in the Christian Bible. My mother was still at her desk when I finally went to bed.

I had an algebra test the next day that I had forgotten to study for; I did not do well. I came out of the school building at one o'clock and went quickly to the subway. It was a cold cloudy March day. I had left my books in school and carried with me only the sketchbook filled with my *Guernica* drawings and another sketchbook filled with drawings of my street. The subway was not crowded. I watched carefully for the stations where I needed to change trains. I noticed that the farther I traveled from Brooklyn, the more frequently I was stared at. In my dark-blue winter coat and hat, and with my thin pale features and red hair and dangling earlocks, I was not exactly a typical New Yorker. At one point in the journey, during a particularly long ride between stations, I opened my *Guernica* sketchbook and began leafing through the drawings. I saw the eyes in the round face of the elderly woman sitting next to me slowly grow wide with astonishment. I closed the sketchbook and looked out the window near my seat. We were in underground darkness outside the window and I could see only my reflection. I spent the rest of the journey looking at my reflection in that dark window of the train.

I got out at the Ninety-sixth Street and Broadway stop. The wide street was crowded with people and traffic. I walked some blocks along Broadway and turned down a street toward the Hudson River. I found the address he had given me. It was an old gray brick loft building. I had to press a button outside the metal-and-glass front door. An old man with white hair and rheumy eyes opened the door.

"Yes?" he said. He had a hoarse voice.

"Jacob Kahn," I said.

He looked at me out of the rheumy eyes, waiting.

"My name is Asher Lev," I said.

He nodded and stepped aside to let me in. He pointed to a book on a stand near the door.

"Sign," he said. "And sign out when you leave. Building regulations. Fifth floor for Mr. Kahn."

He shuffled off toward the elevator. I followed. It was a slow, lumbering elevator.

"You one of them artist fellers?" he asked.

"Which?"

"They come in and out all the time." He peered at me closely out of his wet eyes. "You don't look like one of them," he said. His hoarse voice had begun to remind me vaguely of Yudel Krinsky.

The elevator lurched to a halt. He pulled open the metal door.

"Mr. Kahn's place is the last door on the right. You need the elevator when you're through, you push this button here and I'll come up."

He pulled the metal door shut. The noisy whine of the elevator faded quickly. I walked down the corridor. It was dimly lighted and smelled vaguely of strong disinfectant cleanser. I stopped outside the door to Jacob Kahn's studio and waited. I was sweating heavily, and I removed my hat and coat; I left my skullcap on. I heard voices inside. I recognized Jacob Kahn's voice; the other was the voice of a woman. I stood there hesitating. I stood there a long time. I looked at my wrist watch; it was a little past two o'clock. I knocked softly on the door. The voices did not stop. I rang the bell. The voices ceased abruptly and I heard footsteps. The door was opened and Jacob Kahn stood there, broad-shouldered, white-haired, wearing paint-smeared dungarees and a plaid shirt with the sleeves rolled up to the elbows. A cigarette stuck out from beneath his walrus mustache. With the sleeves of his shirt rolled up, I could see the muscles of his arms; they were powerful arms, and they looked sculpted from stone.

"Come in, Asher Lev," he said. "Come in. Anna, the prodigy is here." I felt his fingers grasp my arm. He took my coat and hat and tossed them somewhere. He pushed the door shut with a swift movement of his leg. "Welcome, Asher Lev," he said, smiling down at me. "It is good to see you here. Anna, where are you? Ah, here. Anna, this is my Asher Lev. Asher Lev, this is my Anna Schaeffer."

A woman had materialized suddenly from behind an enormous canvas. She was of medium height, matronly, with an oval face, sharp blue eyes, and short silvery hair. She wore a dark-blue wool dress and a long necklace of white beads. She offered me her hand. I hesitated. Jacob Kahn moved adroitly toward her, took the offered hand in his left hand, lifted my hand in his right hand, and joined our two hands together. I felt the woman's palm and fingers against my skin. Her flesh was warm and dry.

"To the future," Jacob Kahn said solemnly. "To the beginning of good things. We are assembled to celebrate our glory, if I may paraphrase Apollinaire. Anna, it is not polite to stare."

She was staring at my skullcap. I saw her eyes on the skullcap, then I saw them move slowly across my head and face to my sidecurls. They remained fixed on my sidecurls.

"Anna," Jacob Kahn said softly. He removed the cigarette from his mouth and flicked ashes onto the bare wooden floor.

"You did not tell me," the woman said to him, her eyes still on my sidecurls. "You are a tricky old man."

"Are you upset with me that I did not tell you?"

"Yes, I am upset. You are tricky and nasty." She did not sound upset.

"He is a prodigy, Anna. A prodigy in payos."

"Payos?" She was still staring at me.

"The hair you are gaping at. The earlocks."

"Payos," she said. "Payos. And a skullcap. And dark clothes. And a prodigy." She looked at Jacob Kahn. "You are a mean, tricky, and nasty old man. You are not being nice to an old woman, Jacob Kahn."

"On the contrary, my Anna. I am being very nice. I am being enormously nice. It is against my nature not to be nice. I introduce the boy to you without advance preparation. All the disadvantages are his. All the advantages are yours. Could I be nicer?"

"Yes," she said. "You could bring me a drink." Then she turned to him and said something in French. He laughed, stepped carefully between two huge canvases, and disappeared.

She turned back to me slowly and smiled. "Come over here with me, Asher Lev. Let us stand where there is more light."

I followed behind her, treading carefully between the sculptures and easels and canvases and worktables that were the heavy traffic of that room. We stood near a wall of windows. The sky, filled with clouds that gave off gray light, seemed to border upon the windows. Beyond low rooftops and trees and a strip of highway, I could see the dark waters of the Hudson and the New Jersey shoreline.

"Let me look at you in the light," she said. I saw her blue eyes moving across me. "You have Chagall's pale face. Do you suffer fainting spells?"

"No."

"I asked Jacob which of the three he thought you might become."

"The three?"

"Modigliani, Soutine, and Pascin. Pascin's name was originally Pincas. Have you heard of those three? They were Jews."

"I've seen some of their paintings."

"They were dedicated people. You have not been beaten for drawing, have you?"

"No."

"Soutine was severely beaten when he was young. When he was your age, I believe. You are thirteen? Yes. He was quite severely beaten. Orthodox Jews do not care much for painting, I understand. You are what is called a Hasid?"

I nodded.

"Your parents do not mind your drawing and painting?"

I was quiet.

She smiled faintly. "May I ask you what your father does?"

I told her. She seemed surprised.

"How very interesting," she murmured. "Why aren't you and your mother with your father in Europe?"

I told her that, too, briefly.

She looked at me intently. Then she looked out the window, her eyes narrow in the gray light. A barge moved slowly across the dark surface of the water.

"Are you very religious?" she asked quietly, still looking out the window.

"I'm an observant Jew."

"What does that mean, specifically?"

I did not know what to say.

She looked at me. "Do you believe in a special way? Do you behave in a special way?"

"I believe in God and the Torah He gave to the Jewish people. I pray three times a day. I eat only kosher food. I observe Shabbos—the Sabbath—and festivals and holy days. We don't travel or work on the Sabbath and festivals and holy days. I believe the Rebbe is a gift to us by God to help lead us in our lives. I believe—"

"The Rebbe?" she said.

"The Rebbe is the leader of our group."

"Ah," she murmured. "Yes. The man in Brooklyn Jacob goes to visit all these years. Yes. Go on."

"I believe it is man's task to make life holy. I believe—"

"Asher Lev," she said softly, "Asher Lev."

"Yes?"

"Asher Lev, you are entering the wrong world," she said.

I was quiet.

"Asher Lev, this world will destroy you. Art is not for people who want to make the world holy. You will be like a nun in a bro— in a—theater for burlesque. Do you understand me, Asher Lev? If you want to make the world holy, stay in Brooklyn."

I did not respond. There was a long silence.

She stood peering gloomily out the window. "He does not take students, you know. He has never had students in America. He had students in Europe. When Hitler came, the students were not kind." She was silent a moment. Then she looked at me. "You will not hurt him," she said. "Many have hurt him. He is like a monk. There are so many things he does not understand."

I did not know what to say. I shook my head.

She smiled. "I am a possessive woman. I worry about my painters and sculptors. Where are your drawings, Asher Lev? Jacob said you were bringing drawings."

I handed her my sketchbooks. She placed them on one of the worktables near the wall of windows, opened one, and began slowly, very slowly, turning the pages. I watched her for a while. Her face was expressionless. She looked to be in her sixties, but I could not be certain. I wondered where Jacob Kahn was. I could not hear anyone else in the studio. I watched her slowly turning the pages of the sketchbook. Then I moved away from her. She did not seem to notice me. I began to walk about the room.

It was an enormous room. The walls were huge. High overhead was a large skylight set in a slanted roof. One of its windows was open. Gray light fell across bronze and stone and wood sculptures that stood scattered

202 / *Chaim Potok*

about the floor, and across huge canvases that leaned against the walls and smaller canvases set in easels. There were worktables everywhere, some cluttered with tubes of paint and various sizes of brushes and small rollers, others laden with chisels and mallets. There was dust and paint on the floor and walls, on the worktables and easels; I thought I could even see flecks of paint on the ceiling overhead. I felt tiny, surrounded by the enormity of the room and the creations it contained.

I heard someone behind me and turned. It was Anna Schaeffer. I had the feeling she had been watching me for some time. I saw her looking at two huge bronze sculptures directly before me.

"I never weary of looking at those," she said. "I plead with him every week to let me take them. There are museums that want them. But he parts with very little now. He says he wants in his old age to be surrounded by the work of his hands. Here are your sketchbooks. You are, bluntly put, magnificent. Ingres would have been proud. You have a sense of line that can only be a gift. Do your people believe drawing is a gift from God? Even though they despise drawing? No doubt they believe it is a gift of Satan. Yes? In any event, your drawings of *Guernica* are astonishing. You even remembered to put in the dripping of the paint. The others are drawings of your street, yes? They are quite exquisite. Who is this man whom you draw so often?"

"Yudel Krinsky." I told her about him.

"And this woman?"

"My mother."

"And this man?"

"My father."

She looked closely at the drawing of my father. She nodded slowly to herself.

"And this?"

"Someone I dream about. An ancestor."

"Asher Lev, are you really thirteen years old?"

"Yes."

"Why not?" she murmured. "Why not? Goya was

twelve. Picasso was nine. Why not? It could happen in Brooklyn to a boy with payos." She looked around. "Where is he? Jacob," she called. "Jacob."

He came out of the dimness behind tall sculptures set in a far corner of the studio. He carried a glass in his hand and was smoking a cigarette. He walked quickly toward us, smiling, and gave her the glass.

"You have become acquainted?" he said to the two of us.

"Yes," Anna Schaeffer said soberly. "We have become acquainted." She sipped from the glass and left a lipstick stain on its rim. "Whenever you tell me, Jacob. Anytime you feel he is ready." She sipped again from her glass.

"It will be five years," Jacob Kahn said to her. "Millions of people can draw. Art is whether or not there is a scream in him wanting to get out in a special way."

"Or a laugh," she said. "Picasso laughs, too."

"Or a laugh," he said.

Millions of people can draw. My Uncle Yitzchok had said that to me once. Millions of people can draw. When had he said that?

Jacob Kahn turned to me and held out his hand, indicating the sketchbooks. I gave them to him and he went through them quickly, then returned them to me. He looked at me in silence. He seemed sad.

"Listen to me, Asher Lev. You can become a portrait painter. You can paint calendars for matzo companies. You can paint Rosh Hashonoh greeting cards. What do you need this for?"

I did not say anything. Anna Schaeffer sipped quietly from her drink, her eyes fixed upon Jacob Kahn.

"Do you understand what this is?" Jacob Kahn asked me, his strong voice rising. "Do you begin to understand what you are going to be doing to yourself? You understand now what Picasso did, yes? Even Picasso, the pagan, had to do this. At times, there is no other way. Do you understand me, Asher Lev? This is not a toy. This is not a child scrawling on a wall. This is a tradition; it is a religion, Asher Lev. You are entering a religion called painting. It has its fanatics and its rebels. And I will force you to master it. Do you hear me? No one will listen to what you have to say unless they are convinced you have mastered it. Only one who has mastered a tradition has a right to attempt to add to it or to rebel against it. Do you understand me, Asher Lev?"

I nodded slowly.

"Asher Lev, it is a tradition of goyim and pagans. Its values are goyisch and pagan. Its concepts are goyisch and pagan. Its way of life is goyisch and pagan. In the entire history of European art, there has not been a single religious Jew who was a great painter. Think carefully of what you are doing before you make your decision. I say this not only for the Rebbe but for myself as well. I do not want to spend time with you, Asher Lev, and then have you tell me you made a mistake. Do you understand?"

"Jacob," the woman said softly. "You are frightening the boy."

"It is my intention to frighten him out of his wits. I want him to go back to Brooklyn and remain a nice Jewish boy. What does he need this for, Anna?"

"What did you need it for, Jacob?"

"I know what I went through," he said.

"Excuse us a moment, Asher," the woman said to me. She took Jacob Kahn's arm. They moved off toward the windows. I stood alone amidst the sculptures and canvases. I could hear them talking softly, but I could not make out the words. I stood there surrounded by lines and shapes in metal and stone: tall poignant sculptures of mothers and children; exquisite female heads; delicately turning torsos of men and women; black stone fists jutting like sudden screams from unpolished stone bases; entwined lovers; huge birds as in a fantasist's dream; beasts from a private mythology; and shapes without representational form, exquisitely molded liquid motion in polished bronze. None of the canvases contained representational forms. They shim-

mered and vibrated with subtle harmonies and sudden
complementaries textured with sand and plaster and, in
one huge canvas, with small slivers of blue glass embed-
ded in an impasto of swirling orange. They were powerful paintings of color and texture—his subject was color
and texture—and I felt their sensuousness move against
me, and I was uncomfortable and a little afraid. I closed
my eyes. I opened my eyes, and there was the flood of
color again, a surge of sensuous power, raw, elemental,
as when lengthy darkness is abruptly replaced by a sudden pouring in of sunlight. I had seen his canvases in
the museum; they had not affected me this way. None
of them had had this quality of raw sensuousness.

An easel stood a few feet away to my left. There was
a painting on it, similar to but smaller in size than the
others. I looked at it closely and saw it was dry. I removed it and put it against the edge of an untouched
canvas. A row of small white stretched canvases stood
against a wall. I picked up a canvas and put it on the
easel. There were tubes of oil colors on the adjoining
table, along with brushes and turpentine. I painted
hands and a face onto the canvas. I worked swiftly,
doing the mouth and eyes and mustache and hair, then
moving colors through the space behind the head. Set
back from the head I painted an easel with a canvas and
a face on the canvas. I made the face pale and the earlocks red. I omitted painting pupils into the eyes. The
eyes stared blankly from the canvas within the canvas. I
put the brushes on the table and stepped back, and
moved heavily into Jacob Kahn. I felt his powerful
hands on my shoulders, holding me so I would not fall.
I felt him holding me, almost in an embrace. Then he
released me.

He was looking at the canvas.

"Anna has scolded me severely for my bluntness," he
said quietly, looking at the canvas. "It is my nature to
be blunt." He put his large hands into the pockets of his
dungarees and stood very straight, still looking at the
canvas. "I do not know what to say to you, Asher Lev. I

am moved by your trust. But you see better at thirteen than I did at eighteen. When you are eighteen, perhaps you will see better than I did at twenty-five."

"At twenty-five, you had been through two pogroms," the woman said to him.

He looked at her. "The eye inside a man is not improved by pogroms."

"You underestimate yourself, Jacob."

"No," he said. "I know about eyes. I have lived and worked with some of the best eyes of our century. You have seen the drawings of his street. That is an eye drawing, Anna. Hands alone do not draw this way."

"First you frighten him too much. Now you praise him too much. You are an impossible man, Jacob Kahn."

"No," he said. "It is not Jacob Kahn who is impossible." He turned abruptly to me. "Listen, Asher Lev. I cannot teach you too much more about how to see. I will teach you some tricks. Then you will throw the tricks away and invent your own. I will teach you composition. I will teach you how to create tension. I will teach you how to handle rage in color and line. You draw with too much love. No man can love as much as you and survive as an artist. You will become sentimental. And sentimentalism is death to art. Do you understand what I am saying? No, of course not. How can you understand that? You are thirteen years old. I must remember that you are only thirteen years old."

"Jacob," the woman said. "I must go."

"Wait. I want you to hear what I have to say."

"I will miss my flight."

"You will not miss your flight. It is not yet four o'clock. Listen to what I say to the boy. He will be as much yours as mine." He turned to me. "Asher Lev, I will give you five years of my time. If at the end of those five years you are not ready for Anna, we are finished and it will all have been a waste. If, however, you are ready for Anna, I will make suggestions as to how we are to proceed. I want you to understand something. It is not in my nature to begin a relationship with a lie. I am not doing this as a favor to the Rebbe. I have respect for the Rebbe, but I have passion for my art. The Rebbe asked me to guide you and to keep you from evil ways. Those were his words. I do not know what evil is when it comes to art. I only know what is good art and what is bad art. Those were my words to the Rebbe. The Rebbe trusts me and will rely on my honest heart. Those were the Rebbe's answering words to my remarks. I will not teach you on the basis of that trust. Artists should not be trusted. If an artist is not deceitful every so often in the cause of his art, then he is a poor artist. Those were my remarks to the Rebbe. Still, he trusts me. So be it. He trusts me. But it is of no real consequence to me whether the Rebbe does or does not trust me. I am taking you on not as a favor to the Rebbe but because you have greatness. I am selfish. All artists are selfish and self-centered. I am taking you on because I will derive pleasure in molding your greatness, just as I derive pleasure in molding clay and marble. For five years, I will sculpt you and bring out of you what is already inside you. I will work with your faults and flaws and genius, as Michelangelo worked with the flaws and power of the marble that became his *David*. Are you listening to me, Asher Lev? Do you hear me, Anna? I am seventy-two years old. I do not have five years to give to anything that is less than a marble for a *David*." He looked at the woman. "Do you have anything you wish to say, Anna?"

"Yes," the woman said. "I have a plane to catch to London."

"Go catch your plane. Give Oskar my good wishes. Tell him I will be in London in June for his retrospective. Tell him prune juice is good for old age if used in moderation."

"You are an impossible old man," the woman said. "Do not let him frighten you, Asher Lev. I have a stake in you. Your art will one day make you famous and me and you rich."

"You are already rich," Jacob Kahn said.

"It can never hurt to become richer."

"Go catch your plane. There are men here with work to do."

"I wish you luck, Asher Lev. Everything else you already have." She offered me her hand. I took it without hesitation. "Goodbye, Asher Lev." Her grip was warm and firm.

Jacob Kahn took her to the door. They talked quietly for a moment. Then he opened the door for her and walked with her along the hallway to the elevator. They continued talking quietly. The elevator came and she stepped inside. Then she was gone and Jacob Kahn was back in the studio. He closed the door softly behind him and stood there, his hands jammed into his dungaree pockets, looking at me.

"She is a great woman," he said quietly. "She found me in Paris when I was starving. You are fortunate. I do not think you will ever starve." He moved away from the door and came slowly toward me. "You have a gift, Asher Lev. You have a responsibility." He stopped in front of me. "Do you know what that responsibility is?"

I did not say anything.

"Tell me what you think that responsibility is," he said.

I was quiet. I did not know what to say.

"Do you feel you are responsible to anyone? To anything?"

"To my people," I said hesitantly.

"What people?"

"To Jews."

"To Jews," he echoed. "Why do you think you are responsible to Jews?"

"All Jews are responsible one for the other," I said, quoting the statement from the Talmud my father had years ago quoted to me.

"As an artist you are responsible to Jews?" He seemed angry. "Listen to me, Asher Lev. As an artist you are responsible to no one and to nothing, except to yourself and to the truth as you see it. Do you understand? An artist is responsible to his art. Anything else is propaganda. Anything else is what the Communists in

Russia call art. I will teach you responsibility to art. Let your Ladover Hasidim teach you responsibility to Jews. Do you understand? Yes. I think you understand. You did not do what you did to your family without understanding that. It is not weakness to feel guilty at having done it. But the guilt should not interfere with your art. Use the guilt to make better art. Now come with me to this canvas. I am going to teach you that painting is not storytelling. If you want to tell stories, become either an illustrator or a writer. If you want to be a painter, you will learn to use line and color and shape and texture to create paintings, not stories. Now look at this canvas and tell me what you see."

We spent the rest of the afternoon talking about line and color and shape and texture. Then he watched me make a pen-and-ink drawing of a little boy and a girl walking hand in hand along my street. Then I watched him make a pen-and-ink drawing of a row of low houses around a small cobblestone square. One of the houses was very dilapidated. Narrow winding streets led away from the square. There were trees and benches in the square and old dark metal lampposts.

"This is my street," he said. "It is called Place Émile-Goudeau. When I lived in this old building here, the street used to be called Rue Ravignan. It may still be called that today. I have not been back in a very long time. Do you see this old building? We called it the Bateau Lavoir. Max Jacob named it. You have never heard of Max Jacob? He was a poet. He was a Jew who became a Catholic out of conviction. But the Nazis killed him anyway. Picasso lived here. God, how poor we were. And how hard we worked. We changed the eyes of the world. This is my street, Asher Lev. The street where I was born does not exist. It is a park now in Kiev. But this street is where I was truly born." He was silent a long time, his shoulders bowed as he sat over the drawing. "The things we talked about," he murmured. "Who will ever know of the things we talked about?" He was silent again. Then he raised his head and looked at me, his eyes very narrow. "I wondered a long time who would ever know of the things we talked about." He was silent once again. He resumed drawing. He drew a room with a window facing a sloping hill and rooftops. He drew a short man painting strange faces and figures onto a huge canvas. He drew a tall man painting square and rectangular objects onto a small canvas. He drew himself carving sharp wedges into a block of stone. He seemed lost in his drawing. I sat and watched him work. His huge hand grasped the pen and gave life to the lines that flowed from it. I saw his street alive, saw its shops, its cafés, its poverty, its bitter winters, its artists. I do not remember how many drawings of that street he made that day. But before he was done I felt the street as part of my own parkway, its trees and benches and lampposts part of what I saw each day as I gazed through the window of my living room onto the world I wanted to create anew with line and color and texture and shape.

Later, as we stood at the door, he said to me, "You will come every Sunday afternoon, yes? We will work and talk. Can you come next Sunday afternoon?"

I told him I could not come because next Sunday was two days before Passover and my father would be home. I would not want to come again until my father left, I said.

"Your father knows about us, Asher."

I did not want to hurt my father unnecessarily, I said. I would wait until after he left.

"I understand. But I am disappointed. You will bring more drawings with you next time. And bring an oil painting. A new painting, one you will make between now and next time. Remember what we talked about. Do not paint me a story. Paint me a painting. Goodbye, Asher Lev. Have a good Pesach."

I walked along the dim empty corridor to the elevator. The building seemed to echo faintly. A short man painting a huge canvas and, nearby, a tall man painting a small canvas. I heard the whine of the elevator. Bateau Lavoir. Laundry Boat; like the laundry boats on the Seine. It was built on the side of a hill and you came in on the street floor, as you would onto the deck of a ship, and went down its dark corridors and stairways to the rooms below. Named by Max Jacob, a Jew who became a Catholic and died as a Jew. The elevator door opened. I stepped inside. The door closed. I felt the elevator start down.

"You been there a long time," the old man with the rheumy eyes said.

I barely heard him.

"Four hours," he said in his hoarse voice.

I looked at my watch. It was almost six o'clock.

"You studying to be a painter?"

I nodded.

He looked at me closely and shook his head. The elevator stopped. He opened the door.

"Sign out in the book there," he said, and shuffled off toward a room near the end of the elevator corridor.

I put "5:52" in the out column next to my name. I noticed the signature directly above mine: Anna Schaeffer. I stared at it for a moment. Then I put on my hat and coat and came out of the building. The door closed shut behind me.

A cold wind blew through the street. I stood alongside the metal-and-glass door of the building and prayed the afternoon service. Then I took the subway home. I was back a few minutes before seven.

The apartment was dark. On the kitchen table I found a note from my mother. My supper was on a plate in the refrigerator. My mother was at an emergency meeting with the Rebbe's staff. She did not know when she would be back.

I ate supper alone in the silent apartment. Then I went to the living room and looked out the window at the street. "This is my street," I heard Jacob Kahn say. "This street is where I was truly born." I stood at the window and stared out at the trees and lampposts and rushing cars. I saw rushing cars and small shops and outdoor cafés and old lampposts. I saw cobblestones and the cement of our sidewalk. I saw the wide parkway and the benches. I saw people walking beneath the bare trees. I saw my mother walking beneath the bare trees. She was walking very quickly. Coming toward the house, she looked up and saw me in the window and made a gesture of greeting. I was at the door to the apartment when she came out of the elevator. I helped her take off her coat. She was pale. I followed her into the kitchen. She put the kettle on the stove.

"How was your day with Jacob Kahn?" she asked.

"Very good. Mama?"

"Will you be able to learn a lot from him?"

"Yes. Mama, is anything wrong?"

"Yes," she said. "Your father will not be home for Pesach."

I stared at her.

"No one knows where your father is," she said.

"Papa isn't in Europe?"

"No one knows."

"The Rebbe knows."

"The Rebbe told me to have faith in the Ribbono Shel Olom."

"The Rebbe doesn't know where Papa is?"

"The Rebbe didn't tell me whether he does or doesn't know. He only told me to have faith in the Ribbono Shel Olom."

"Papa's in Russia," I said.

My mother said nothing.

"He's in Russia," I said, feeling cold with horror.

My mother did not respond. Her face was sallow. Her hands trembled faintly as she poured boiling water from the kettle into a cup.

"Do you have homework?"

"Yes."

"Go do your homework, Asher. I have to prepare for my classes tomorrow."

"When will Papa be home?"

"No one knows."

"He won't be home until Rosh Hashonoh?"

"No one knows."

"Mama—"

"Go and do your homework, Asher. Please. Please."

I left her sitting at the table over her cup of coffee. I could not do my homework. I lay in my bed and thought of my father in Russia. I saw him at secret meetings of Ladover Hasidim, conveying the Rebbe's words of hope and faith. "The Rebbe remembers you," I kept hearing him say. "The Rebbe blesses you. The Rebbe asks you not to forget the Master of the Universe. The Rebbe has you always in his mind and heart." I saw him journeying through small mud-caked towns and large stone-and-steel cities, meeting two Hasidim here, ten Hasidim there, teaching, praying, urging that faith not be abandoned despite the dark and awesome power of the sitra achra. I saw him establishing yeshivos in basements and cellars. I saw him watched by the thousand eyes of secret police. I saw him arrested and beaten and sent to—

I slept and had horror-filled dreams. The next morning, my mother looked as if she had not slept at all.

We heard nothing more about my father the rest of that week. Everyone in school seemed to know he was missing, though no one said anything openly to me. Teachers left me alone. Classmates became kind. The mashpia called me into his office and talked to me about the need to have faith in the Ribbono Shel Olom. Mrs. Rackover moved about the apartment in gentle silence. My Uncle Yitzchok invited us to his Seder and my mother accepted. Yudel Krinsky sighed repeatedly as he filled a small box with the tubes of oil colors I had bought, then told me he was adding three brushes at no cost—a Pesach gift, he said in his hoarse voice. He seemed deeply sad and fearful.

I spent late Thursday afternoon in the library, looking at a color reproduction of Michelangelo's *David*. The next Sunday afternoon, I came out of my school and walked to the subway and journeyed again to Jacob Kahn.

NINE

A week after Passover, my father cabled us from Vienna. He was well; a letter would follow.

The letter came a few days later. It was written in Yiddish. He hoped we were well and had had a good Pesach. He had had an unusual and very satisfying Pesach. He missed us and looked forward to being with us and with the Rebbe after the summer. Did my mother think she might possibly be able to come to Vienna for July and August?

Early in June, Jacob Kahn flew to London and was away for five days. He and the artist whose retrospective he had gone to see had been close friends for five decades. He told me when he returned that the artist had barely managed to escape from Prague in the late thirties after discovering that his name was on a Gestapo list for arrest and execution without trial. His art was considered degenerate.

"Art is a danger to some people," he said. "Picasso used to say art is subversive."

Did he enjoy the retrospective? I asked.

"I did not go to enjoy it. His art is not enjoyable. He is not Matisse. But he is a great artist and the retrospective did him full justice."

Had the artist been happy? I asked.

No, the artist had not been happy. He had been tormented over what to do next. What kind of silly question had I asked? Had I ever known of a great artist who was happy?

"Rubens," I said.

He stared gloomily out the tall windows of the studio. Perhaps, he said. Anything was possible with the Baroque.

In the last week of June, my mother left by ship for Le Havre and I moved into my Uncle Yitzchok's house.

Jacob Kahn told me he often spent his summers in Provincetown. But he had sculptures to complete. So he would be in New York all that summer. I spent the month of July traveling back and forth by subway between my Uncle Yitzchok's house and Jacob Kahn's studio. I traveled there two or three times a week. I had my mother's permission to go to Jacob Kahn as often as he would want to see me; I needed only to tell my uncle or aunt that I was going and when I expected to be back.

It was a stifling month, oppressive with humid heat that remained through the nights. The asphalt of the streets softened in the heat. Subway ceiling fans blew the heat through the trains. I walked the streets drenched in sweat; I rode the subway drenched in sweat; I drew and painted drenched in sweat. I watched Jacob Kahn work stripped to the waist on a block of marble. I began painting stripped to the waist. My Uncle Yitzchok walked into my room one evening and found me painting stripped to the waist and let me know he thought it indecent to be dressed like that. He had a responsibility to my parents; I was to cover my body and wear my ritual fringes. I painted and drew in the house wearing an undershirt and my ritual fringes. In Jacob Kahn's studio, I painted stripped to the waist.

He said to me one day in the second week of July, "Asher Lev, there are two ways of painting the world. In the whole history of art, there are only these two ways. One is the way of Greece and Africa, which sees the world as a geometric design. The other is the way of Persia and India and China, which sees the world as a flower. Ingres, Cézanne, Picasso paint the world as geometry. Van Gogh, Renoir, Kandinsky, Chagall paint the world as a flower. I am a geometrician. I sculpt cylinders, cubes, triangles, and cones. The world is structure, and structure to me is geometry. I sculpt geometry. I see the world as hard-edged, filled with lines and angles. And I see it as wild and raging and hideous, and only occasionally beautiful. The world fills me with disgust more often than it fills me with joy. Are you listening to me, Asher Lev? The world is a terrible place. I do not sculpt and paint to make the world sacred. I sculpt and paint to give permanence to my feelings about how terrible this world truly is. Nothing is real to me except my own feelings; nothing is true except my own feelings as I see them all around me in my sculptures and paintings. I know these feelings are true, because if they were not true they would make art that is as terrible as the world. You do not understand me yet, Asher Lev. My little Hasid. My sanctifier of the world. My half-naked painter with dangling payos and a paint-smeared skullcap. One day you will understand about the truth of feelings."

He said to me two days later, "What are you painting?"

I said, "A classmate."

"Do you hate him?"

I was quiet.

"You hate him and are afraid to paint your hatred. Yes?"

I did not say anything.

"It is a false painting. It reeks of cowardice and indecision. In art, cowardice and indecision can be seen in every stroke of a brush. If you hate him, paint your hatred or do not paint him at all. One must not paint everything one feels. But once you decide to paint something, you must paint the truth or you will paint green rot. This boy in your class—he mistreats you?"

I nodded.

"He is mean to you? He laughs at you?"

I nodded.

"These marks on his face—they are pimples?"

I nodded.

"And you hate him?"

I nodded.

"Then paint him the way you feel about him. Use your lines and colors and shapes to make your statement simply and clearly. Do you understand?"

He came over to me later and peered at the canvas. He nodded slowly. "It is an excellent painting." He looked at me soberly. "I would not like to be hated by you, Asher Lev."

He said to me the next day, "Have you heard from your parents?"

I told him that I had received a letter that morning from my mother. They were well. My father was very busy. My mother was able to help him from time to time in his work. They missed me and sent me their love.

"What work does your mother help your father with?"

"Work."

"What work?"

"It has to do with Russian Jews," I said.

He regarded me out of suddenly narrowed eyes.

"My father has connections with Jews in Russia. My mother is getting her doctorate in Russian affairs. She helps him in some way. I don't know how."

He was quiet. His tall powerful half-naked body seemed strangely rigid. Then he said very softly, "Your parents are good people. Your father is a brave man. Finish your work, Asher Lev. It is almost time for you to go home."

The following week, the third week of July, we went to the Metropolitan Museum of Art. We walked through centuries of Byzantine and Western crucifixions. He showed me the development of structure and form and expression, and the handling of pictorial space. I saw crucifixions all the way home and dreamed of crucifixions all through the night.

I told him the next day that I did not think I wanted to see any more crucifixions. He became angry.

"Asher Lev, you want to go off into a corner somewhere and paint little rabbis in long beards? Then go away and do not waste my time. Go paint your little rabbis. No one will pay any attention to you. I am not telling you to paint crucifixions. I am telling you that you must understand what a crucifixion is in art if you want to be a great artist. The crucifixion must be available to you as a form. Do you understand? No, I see you do not understand. In any case, we will see more crucifixions and more resurrections and more nativities and more Greek and Roman gods and more scenes of war and love—because that is the world of art, Asher Lev. And we will see more naked women, and you will learn the reason for the differences between the naked women of Titian and those of Rubens. This is the world you want to make sacred. You had better learn it well first before you begin."

We went to the Metropolitan Museum of Art every day that week. People stared at us as we walked through the vast galleries—a tall white-haired mustached man explaining crucifixions and nudes to a short white-faced red-haired boy with dangling earlocks and a skullcap.

He insisted that I come to him early Sunday morning in the fourth week of July. I came out of my Uncle Yitzchok's house a few minutes after eight o'clock. The air was warm and humid. A hazy sun shone through the trees. The city seemed deserted. I waited a long time for a subway. I got to Jacob Kahn's studio a little before ten o'clock. He opened the door, and I saw a girl standing in the sunlight that came through the wall of windows. She looked to be in her early twenties, had short raven hair and dark eyes, and was beautiful in a dark and somber way. She wore a brightly colored summer dress and she regarded me curiously as I came into the studio.

Jacob Kahn led me to a far corner.

"I have asked the girl to pose for you today," he said.

I looked at him.

"She is an excellent model and you will draw her in the nude."

I felt myself beginning to sweat heavily and did not know what to say.

"I want you to see the contours and the rhythms with your own eyes. It is not enough to copy Titian and Ingres and Renoir."

I did not say anything. I was trembling inside. I felt a choking heaviness in my throat and chest.

"Asher Lev, listen to me." He was talking gently but with tense insistence. "The human body is a glory of structure and form. When an artist draws or paints or sculpts it, he is a battleground between intelligence and emotion, between his rational side and his sensual side. You do understand that. Yes. I see you do. The manner in which certain artists have resolved that battle has created some of the greatest masterpieces of art. You must learn to understand this battle."

I looked over at the girl. She was gazing out the tall windows at the rooftops and the wide line of river beyond.

"Asher Lev, the Rebbe told me never to permit you to draw this way. I have chosen to disregard the Rebbe. The nude is a form of art I want you to master. To attempt to achieve greatness in art without mastering this art form is like attempting to be a great Hasidic teacher without knowledge of the Kabbalah."

I did not say anything. The girl's face was luminous in the sunlight. I thought of Vermeer. There was a long heavy silence.

"I will send her away," Jacob Kahn said finally.

"I'll try," I said.

He gazed at me intently. "I do not want to hurt you, Asher Lev."

"I'll try," I said again, feeling the choking tightness in my throat.

"Very well," he said. "Come with me."

I followed him through the studio to the wall of windows. I had a sudden powerful numbing vision of my mythic ancestor. I thought of the Rebbe. I thought of the mashpia. I found myself in front of the windows near the girl, listening to Jacob Kahn.

"You will begin with simple line drawings in charcoal. I want only the flow of the line. I want no chiaroscuro."

He spoke briefly to the girl. She went behind a screen. I set my pad on an easel. She came out from behind the screen and sat on a chair. Sunlight fell across her face and shoulders and breasts and thighs. She sat with one leg crossed over the other, her head slightly back. I saw the sunlight on her skin. She was very beautiful. I did not even know her name. I saw the flowing curve of the breasts. I saw the line of shoulders and hip and thigh and leg. I drew her carefully. My arm felt nerveless, drained of its strength. I felt sweat in my armpits and along my back. My face dripped sweat. Jacob Kahn stood behind me, watching. I finished the drawing. It was very bad. I felt ashamed. I took a deep breath and moved to a clean sheet of paper and began again. The girl sat very still, bathed in sunlight. I looked at her and worked carefully, translating her body into lines, making choices, each curve, each subtle change in the flow of her flesh, necessitating an interpreting choice of line. I started a third drawing. Jacob Kahn signaled to her. She changed her pose, sitting forward on the chair, her face in her hands, her breasts suddenly pendulous. I drew her that way twice. She changed her pose again, sitting with one leg up on the chair, clasping the leg to herself with her arms, her chin resting on her knee, her thighs open. I drew her that way and then drew her again in two more poses before it was time for lunch. I ate the sandwich my aunt had packed for me. Jacob Kahn and the girl went out for lunch and returned in less than half an hour. I spent all the rest of that day drawing the girl. She left shortly before five o'clock.

Jacob Kahn piled my drawings one on top of the other on a table. He held up the first drawing. Then he held up the last drawing.

"You see?" he said quietly.

I saw.

"And it is only in one day. A great eye learns to see quickly. We will do this again next Sunday. Yes?"

I nodded.

"Do not look so sad, Asher Lev. You are not defiled. You have only made some pictures of a beautiful girl. Beautiful pictures of a beautiful girl. Is that cause for defilement?"

I did not respond.

He looked at me and shook his head. "Perhaps yeshiva boys in payos should not be artists. Go home and take a shower and go to sleep, Asher Lev. You have had a long day."

I went home in a daze. I felt drained, suspended; I felt hot and irritated and unclean. I could not sleep. I saw the girl. I saw her body and the flow of her lines. I drew her in the darkness of the room. I drew her with my eyes, letting my eyes move slowly across her. I drew her slowly until there was again the sudden light and I was able to sleep.

I drew her again the following Sunday, and it was easier. I drew her again the Sunday after that, and it was easier still.

I had been traveling to Jacob Kahn's studio on Sundays and Tuesdays, and sometimes on Thursdays. Now I began to go almost every day. A few times, he was not there and I worked alone. On occasion in the late afternoons, artists would come in, men whose paintings I had seen in reproductions and in the Museum of Modern Art. I would listen to them talking with Jacob Kahn. It was during those late-afternoon conversations that I learned about the Social Realists and Regionalists of the Depression decade; about the Federal Art Project; about the mottoes "Paint Proletarian" and "Paint American"; about Stuart Davis's attack against the Regionalist John Steuart Curry; about the group called the American Abstract Artists and their rejection of Impressionism, Expressionism, and Surrealism; about Neoplasticism and Abstract Cubism and Russian Constructivism; about gesture painters and color-field painters; about Abstract Expressionism. I painted and listened. I understood some of it and remembered most of it. Once the introductions and curious glances were over, they did not seem to care about my skullcap and earlocks. They only seemed to care about my painting.

My parents returned to the United States by boat on the first Sunday of September. I did not see Jacob Kahn again until the middle of October.

I barely recognized my father. He was gaunt. He limped badly. His eyes were tired. His beard was turning gray. He was nearly forty, but he looked to be sixty. I cried inside myself when I first saw him.

He came into my room two days before Rosh Hashonoh and stood leaning against the wall near the doorway. I had turned the room into a small studio. An easel stood near the window. There were reproductions of great paintings all over the walls. My father stood near Andrea del Sarto's *Sculptor* and Raphael's *School of Athens*. I had been working on a canvas when he had come in. I stopped and put down my brushes.

"Please sit down, Papa."

But he stood near the doorway and would not come further into the room. He was in his own home, but my room had become alien ground to him.

He said wearily in Yiddish, "I have not even had a chance yet to talk with my son. How are you, Asher?"

"I am feeling well, Papa."

"You look well. You look—happy." He gazed slowly around the room at the reproductions on the walls, at the clutter of drawings on my desk and dresser and bed, at the canvases stacked beneath the window and along the wall near the closet. "You have been busy," he murmured.

I was quiet.

He looked at me. "Jacob Kahn is a good teacher?"

"Yes."

"I have known Jacob Kahn for a long time. He was

one of those the Rebbe helped bring from Paris before the Germans came. He is a good person."

"Are you well, Papa?"

"Yes. But I am tired."

"You've lost weight."

"I have worked hard. But we are succeeding now. It was nearly creation out of nothing. Now there is something. In Paris and Rome and Vienna and Geneva, there is now something." He looked at me sadly. "All this material, Asher. The paper and the paints and the easel. All this you bought with the money you made doing errands for your Uncle Yitzchok and Reb Yudel Krinsky?"

"Mama helped. Jacob Kahn helped."

He nodded slowly. Then he said, "I am not reconciled, Asher. I am unable to accept what you are doing. I have told the Rebbe I am not reconciled."

I was quiet.

"It is not possible for me to accept this." He moved his arm in a weary gesture, indicating the reproductions on the walls, the canvases near the window, the drawings on the desk. "This is not what I wanted from my son. In this matter, I do not care what the Rebbe tells me. You are my son, not the son of the Rebbe. I am not reconciled. Asher, do you intend to go to college?"

"I think so. Yes."

"You will continue to study with Jacob Kahn?"

"Yes."

"You will not be able to come to Europe?"

"No."

He nodded slowly. "The Ribbono Shel Olom is sometimes unkind. What would it have hurt Him to have kept the sitra achra away from you? What? Do not forget your people, Asher. That is all I ask of you. That is all that is left for me to ask of you."

I was quiet. There was a long silence. He turned and started from the room.

"Papa."

He looked at me.

"Were you in Russia, Papa?"

He blinked and stiffened. He said very quietly, "Sometimes there are questions that should not be asked, Asher. I also have questions I do not ask." I saw him looking at the drawings on my desk. I followed his eyes. He was looking at one of the drawings I had made of the nude model in Jacob Kahn's studio. I had signed and dated the drawing. The date stood out clearly beneath the signature. "Good night, Asher." He went quietly from the room.

My mother said to me one day during Succos, "Asher, do you think you could move in with your Uncle Yitzchok if I went with your father to Europe?"

I stared at her and was afraid.

"Your father needs me. I was here when you needed me. Now your father needs me."

"This year?"

"No. Next year."

"I don't want to live a whole year with Uncle Yitzchok."

"Why?"

"I don't want to talk about it."

"We'll talk about it," she said. "You are not the only member of this family with special needs."

My father returned to Europe in the second week of October and I resumed my journeys to Jacob Kahn's studio.

I came into the kitchen one night in November and found my mother staring at the table.

"Mama?"

She looked up at me.

"Is something wrong, Mama?"

"No. I was—remembering." Her voice sounded strange.

"Remembering?"

"Yes."

"What?"

"Just—remembering."

Another night, I found her standing alongside her table in the living room, gazing out the window at the dark street. The table was piled high with her books and papers.

"Mama?"

She did not respond.

"Mama?"

"Yes, Aryeh," she said softly. "Of course. I'm coming."

"Mama, are you all right?"

She turned then, startled. "Asher," she murmured. "Asher." She seemed small and frail and I thought she had been crying.

One Shabbos night in December, we sat together at the dinner table and after a pause during zemiros she began to hum my father's melody to Yoh Ribbon Olom. Her eyes were closed. She hummed softly. I had the feeling she was not aware of what she was doing. She opened her eyes and smiled faintly. Then she looked quickly around. She seemed surprised to find herself with me. She began another melody. I joined her and we sang together.

She said to me a few nights later, "You're out so late, Asher. What do you do in the library so late?"

"I study."

"For school?"

"No. For Jacob Kahn."

She looked at me in surprise.

"Art history. Reproductions. It's very important, Mama."

"Can't you bring the books home, Asher?"

"A lot of them are reference books, Mama."

"It's very lonely here at night, Asher."

At breakfast one morning in January, my mother said to me, "I finished my dissertation, Asher. The university is asking me about my plans for next year. Shall I tell them I'll be in New York?"

"Yes," I said. "Yes."

She sighed softly and was quiet.

I heard her in the living room late that night talking

to herself in strained whispers. I had wakened from a dream about my mythic ancestor. I had not dreamed about him for a while now. He had made up for his absence. My heart pounded from the dream. I felt the blood in my head. I lay rigid in my bed, and then heard my mother in the living room. She was whispering words I could not understand. Then I recognized the sounds of the words. She was whispering in Russian. I lay in my bed and did not know if I was more terrified by the dream or by my mother's whispers. After a while, she stopped. I heard her slippered feet come through the hall. Then she went into her room.

I could not sleep. I turned on the light and went to the bathroom. I came back to the room and sat at the desk and could not draw. I went back to my bed. Faint light framed my window by the time I was able to sleep.

Jacob Kahn watched me work on a painting in his studio that Sunday afternoon, and after a while he said angrily, "What are you doing? Stop it. You are making a mess. Where is the unity of form? The colors do not hold together. Wipe it out and start again."

I put the brushes down.

"What is the matter with you today? Are you ill?"

"No."

He looked at the canvas. "What were you painting?"

"My mother."

He looked at me. "You are not ready yet to move away from representational form. You think such painting is a joke?"

I felt my face go hot. "No," I heard myself say. "I never thought it was a joke."

"I'm sorry," he said quickly. "That was a foolish thing to ask. I apologize. Now, pick up your brushes and start again. You are making a painting. I do not care what your painting is about. First it must be a painting. Straighten out your feelings inside yourself and make a painting. Or go home and take a shower and go to sleep."

I wiped the face from the canvas. But I could not do anything else. I could not even paint a line.

"I don't know what I want to say. I don't know how I feel."

"Go home, Asher Lev. We all have impossible days."

My mother said to me sometime during the week, "Asher, why don't you want to live with your Uncle Yitzchok?"

"I don't."

"Why?"

"I just don't."

"You're not being nice," she said. "You're behaving like a child."

"A summer is all right. But not a whole year."

"Once you would have been delighted for our permission to live with your Uncle Yitzchok."

I did not say anything.

"I have to make a decision in the next few weeks, Asher. The university has begun hiring staff for the coming year."

"I don't want to be alone, Mama."

"I know," she said. "But it may be time for you to concern yourself with what others want, Asher. You are not the only person with needs in this world."

I could not sleep that night. The next night, I slept and dreamed of my mythic ancestor, who came thundering through dark primal forests of tall moist trees, shouting at me in a voice that splintered the words into long slivers of metal. I woke and remained awake the rest of the night.

The next morning, I fell asleep over my Gemorra in class and was awakened by the teacher's heavy hand on my shoulder. He was a short round man with a dark beard and glittering dark eyes and he was considerably less indulgent toward me than my other teachers had been.

"Rembrandt sleeps," I heard him say in Yiddish. "The whole world must hold its breath while Rembrandt sleeps."

Soft laughter moved through the classroom. Eyes fastened upon the teacher. I had been the butt of their laughter for years now; I was still unaccustomed to it.

The teacher glared down at me. "Listen, Rembrandt Lev." There was loud laughter. "In my class, no one sleeps. You have to sleep, go home. In my class, we study Torah. We do not study how to sleep. If you fall asleep in my class, I will make life bitter for you. Do I make myself clear? Are my words simple enough for you to understand? If you fall asleep and make people say sha sha, I will make your life bitter like gall gall."

There was a slowly widening ripple of laughter as the explanation of the play on the name Chagall was whispered through the room. The teacher turned and walked up the aisle to his desk.

That was the day someone slipped a note into my Gemorra during the lunch recess. I found it when I returned to my desk. It was written in ink on white paper and printed in block letters:

> *Modigliani, Pascin, and Soutine*
> *Worked in ochres and ultramarine.*
> *Soutine lived in strife;*
> *Pascin took his life;*
> *And Modigliani used drugs for cuisine.*

I looked up from my seat in the back row of the room. I felt the blood in my face and head. I looked carefully through the room. The teacher's voice droned dully over a passage of Gemorra. A few seats in front of me to my right, I saw a student's head begin slowly to turn in my direction. I looked quickly down at the poem. Out of the corner of my eye I watched the smile spread quickly across the pimply face. I could also hear the high piercing voice: "Here comes Asher Picasso Lev, the destroyer of Torah. Make way for goy Lev. Hey, Asher, do you draw dirty pictures, too? Draw a dirty picture for the mashpia. Draw me, Asher Lev. No, draw me, Asher Lev. Draw me. Draw me."

I folded the note and put it into one of my pockets. I could see the block letters and the words. Soutine lived in strife; Pascin took his life. . . . I saw those words all

the rest of that day in school and was still seeing them
that night as I lay in my bed trying to fall asleep.

The next day, there was another note in my Gemorra:

> *Asher Lev*
> *Won't go to Heav;*
> *To Hell he'll go*
> *Far down below.*

That night, I found myself seated at my desk, shaking
with rage. I sat in front of a blank sheet of drawing
paper and felt the rage like a wild torrent inside me. I
had never felt such rage before; I wanted to kill him, to
beat him and smash him and kill him, so I would never
again have to see his pimply face or hear his piercing
voice. I drew a line on the paper. Then I drew circles
and points and whorls. I drew more lines. I looked at
the paper. It was meaningless and absurd and very bad.
I threw it away.

My mother said to me on Saturday night, "I will be
back late. Don't wait up for me."

"Is the meeting about Russian Jews, Mama?"

"Yes."

"Are you going to talk to the Rebbe about next
year?"

"Yes."

"I don't want you to go away, Mama."

"I know what you don't want. Good night, Asher."

I worked a long time on a canvas in Jacob Kahn's
studio the next day. I avoided recognizable forms. He
came over to me and peered at the canvas.

"It is interesting," he said. "But it is a failure."

I put my brushes down.

"Your feelings about your mother are producing terrible art. Paint still-lifes for a while. Do some self-por-
traits. You are making a mess with these other efforts."

He was merciless over failure. The subway ride back
home that night was a torment.

The next day, I found another copy of the first poem

in my Gemorra: "Modigliani, Pascin, and Soutine . . ." And two days later I found: "Asher Lev/Won't go to Heav. . . ."

My mother was at a meeting that night and I was alone in the apartment. I wandered through the silent rooms, stopping for a moment to gaze through the living-room window at the parkway outside. The street had begun to feel quietly hostile to me, as if resentful of my journeys away from it and of the alien skills I brought back each time I returned. The metal lampposts felt cold to my eyes; the light they cast seemed filled with darkening mists. The trees swayed in a winter wind, their naked branches black in the night and strangely insubstantial. I saw it then, quite suddenly, and knew what I would do. One second there had been nothing, and then there was the idea. I did not understand what had happened to bring on the idea. I went away from the window and came into my room. Sitting at my desk, I drew with a pen, working slowly, calmly, and with ease, the segment from Michelangelo's Last Judgment of the boat beached on the Styx and Charon striking at his doomed passengers with an oar, forcing them onto the shores of torment and hell. I drew much of it from memory, but I wanted to be as accurate as I could, so I checked it repeatedly against a reproduction in a book I had purchased on Michelangelo. I drew the writhing twisting tormented bodies spilling from the boat. I drew the terror on the faces of the dead and the damned. I made all the faces his face, pimply, scrawny —eyes bulging, mouths open, shrieking in horror. I exaggerated the talons and painted ears of Charon; I darkened his face, bringing out the whites of his raging eyes. I folded the drawing and went to bed.

The next day, on my way out of the classroom for the noon recess, I slipped the drawing into his Gemorra. I saw the sudden stiffening of his shoulders when he found it. I saw him stare at it. I saw him turn to look at me, then stop. He crumpled the drawing. But he did not throw it away. He put it into a pocket.

That night, I drew a segment from the Last Judgment

of a man being pulled headlong into hell by serpentine demons. I drew his face on the man and put the drawing into his Gemorra the next day.

He said nothing to me about the drawings. But he began to avoid me. His thin face would fill with dread whenever he caught me looking at him. I had the feeling he regarded me now as evil and malevolent, as a demonic and contaminating spawn of the Other Side.

I did not attempt another painting of my mother that Sunday. Instead I did a painting of the boy in my class at the moment he saw the first drawing I had slipped into his Gemorra. Jacob Kahn called the painting evil and excellent.

Two days later, my mother told me she would be going to Europe at the end of June and would remain there throughout the coming year. I was to live with my Uncle Yitzchok, or I could come with her to Europe and live in Vienna.

"Asher, look at me," she said, in response to my pleas. "How many of me do you see?"

I did not answer.

"You see only one. There is only one of me. I can be in only one place at a time. Your father needs me. Do you understand? And I want to spend the year with your father. I don't want to talk about it any more. The Rebbe approved of the decision. Your father will remain in Europe and I will join him at the end of June."

"Papa will not come back for Pesach?"

"No."

She became angry when I continued to plead that she stay. Pink spots colored her high cheekbones. Her voice became strident. She called me a child. She said that half a dozen children would not have made more demands on her than I had. Now it was time for my father. He needed her. Did I understand that? He needed her. He was exhausted from his work and he wanted her to be with him. If I wanted her, too, I would have to come to Vienna.

She stormed angrily from the room.

I talked to Jacob Kahn.

"Yes," he said. "I know all about it. Your mother called me."

"I don't want to live with my uncle."

"Why not?"

"He's loud and fat and rich."

"There is nothing wrong with being rich. It is the rich who buy paintings. It is when you are bought by the rich that you will know you are a successful artist."

"He's a boor."

"You will have to grow accustomed to it. The world will indulge you just so long, Asher Lev. Then it will stop. You will simply have to grow accustomed to that truth."

The mashpia called me into his office during the first week of April. The Rebbe wanted to see me, alone.

For the second time in my life, I climbed the flight of stairs in the Ladover building and went along the hallway to the waiting room. This time, the room was crowded. I was there almost an hour before Rav Mendel Dorochoff took me into the Rebbe's office.

The Rebbe sat quietly behind the bare desk. His eyes were dark. Outside the arched window, the street glittered in the April night.

"Sit down, Asher. There, yes, sit down. It has been a while since I have seen you. But I have been kept informed. Yes. They tell me the world will hear of you one day as an artist."

I was quiet.

"I have you in my mind and heart, Asher Lev. I pray to the Master of the Universe that the world will one day also hear of you as a Jew. Do you understand my words? Jacob Kahn will make of you an artist. But only you will make of yourself a Jew."

I was quiet.

There was a long silence. The street throbbed faintly beneath its dark canvas of night.

"Asher Lev."

"Yes, Rebbe."

"Your mother has told you of my decision."

"Yes, Rebbe."

"It is necessary for your father and mother to be together now. For your father's health and for your father's work. You will live with your uncle and continue to study with Jacob Kahn."

"Yes, Rebbe."

"You will behave toward your uncle and aunt as you would toward your father and mother. They have accepted the responsibility of caring for you."

"Yes, Rebbe."

Outside the window, the street vibrated softly, menacingly, in the black night.

"Asher Lev."

"Yes, Rebbe."

"You are entering the world of the Other Side. Be careful. I knew your grandfather. I knew your mother before you were born. I remember you as a child. I remember your mother's illness. Your family is very precious to me. I have looked upon you as a son. I have you and your parents constantly in my mind and heart. Be careful of the Other Side, Asher Lev."

"Yes, Rebbe."

"I give you my blessings and my good wishes for a kosher and joyous Pesach."

I went quickly along the hallway and down the stairs and out into the dark street. It was cold. The street was cold. I saw a cobblestone square and a dilapidated building and trees. I saw a young man drawing figures in the dust of the square, using a stick and drawing in one continuous line the contours of hens and horses and birds. Steep narrow streets led from the square. The square was warm. Sunlight fell across the trees and the old building and the young man gazing at the hens and horses and birds in the dust out of burning dark eyes.

My street was cold now in the April night. I felt it cold against my face as I turned in to the apartment house where I lived. I felt it cold all through the first two days of Passover. Then I journeyed to galleries in Manhattan and was on streets filled with color and form. My father was not home. I had no school until the end of the festival. I used the intermediate days of the festival to wander along streets warmer than my own.

I wandered into Anna Schaeffer's gallery. It was a large modern gallery, taking up the entire fourth floor of a tall building in the Seventies along Madison Avenue. I came out of the elevator and saw her sitting behind an ornate intricately carved desk at the far end of the gallery to my left. She saw me and motioned me over to her. She seemed delighted.

The gallery was crowded. There was a sculpture show that had received excellent notices and was attracting a great deal of attention. There were people at the desk. But she talked to me alone in a back room stacked with canvases and sculptures. Yes, she knew exactly how I was getting along. Did I know Jacob Kahn was having a show in late October? I didn't know. Did I know he would be spending the summer in Provincetown, painting, and that he would take me with him? I didn't know.

She stared at me. "You are Asher Lev?"

"Yes."

"You are the student of Jacob Kahn?"

"Yes."

"What do you do in the studio?"

"I paint."

"You do not talk to each other?"

"We talk."

"He is a wicked old man. He is waiting to surprise you. Do not let on I said a word. Promise."

I promised.

She came with me to the elevator.

"One day, you will have your own show here, Asher Lev. Then you will be famous and we will be rich. Do not forget to act surprised when that wicked old man tells you."

He told me two weeks later. I acted surprised.

The days grew warm. The street remained cold. My mother had begun the preparations for her journey. She purchased clothes. She shipped part of her library to an address in Vienna. She rented our apartment to a family that had recently arrived from Russia. She attended meetings with the Rebbe's staff. She defended her dissertation and received her doctorate. She seemed filled with new energy. She did everything quickly, radiantly. Sometimes I would hear her singing to herself. She seemed fulfilled.

One day, movers came and took away the small table in the living room that had been her desk. She had decided to ship that as well to the address in Vienna. It had good memories, she said. She wanted to be near that table. I stared at the empty space in the living room where it had stood, and it seemed a chasm now lay across the floor and wall near the window.

I wandered the cold street. In Jacob Kahn's studio, I began to paint my memories of my early years on that street. I painted my mother young, with myself in her arms. I painted her holding me. I painted her walking with me. I painted us together on a parkway bench. I painted us standing against tall buildings. I painted us walking through Prospect Park. I painted us in a dreamlike green land with distant hills and pale clouds in a deep-blue sky. Week after week, I painted my mother and myself together, though I did not always give the mother and the child our faces. Jacob Kahn watched me in silence. One Sunday in June, he stood behind me as I worked on a huge canvas of a mother and child seated on a mound of grass beneath tall leafy trees. I heard him say softly, "Asher Lev, do you have any idea what you are doing?"

I told him I was painting a mother and her child.

He said nothing more to me about those paintings.

On the last Thursday in June, my mother and I took a cab to a dock in Manhattan. I held her to me. I was as tall as she now. She cried. The cabin was narrow. I held her to me and felt her small and frail in my arms.

"Have a safe journey, Mama," I said.

Later, I stood on the dock and watched the huge ship pull away. I took a cab back to my street. I stood outside the building, looking up at the window of our living room. Then I walked slowly beneath the cold trees to my Uncle Yitzchok's house.

*Book
Three*

TEN

That summer I lived in a house on the edge of sand dunes. My room was a low-ceilinged attic with a window that looked out on the dunes and the beach and the ocean. In the early morning, I could see the sun on the water and the silver foaming of the surf. The sun rose through the morning mist and burned the mist away, and then was golden on the beach and white on the Cape Cod houses a few hundred yards on up the dunes, where dark scrub brush grew in the sandy earth. Gulls wheeled and called above the water and the sand, their wings stark white in the sun. I watched the gulls from the window of my room and from the porch of the house, and I painted them over and over again, using watercolors or washes of oils; painted their soarings into the sun, their wings in the wind, their wide diving circles over the surface of the waves. Often I did not paint at all, but sat on the porch listening and watching, feeling the salt wind on my face, hearing the surf and the cries of the gulls.

"An artist needs time to do nothing but sit around and think and let ideas come to him," Jacob Kahn said to me one afternoon on that porch after I had sat on a chair for hours, gazing at the sunlight on the water and the sand and the houses farther up along the dunes. "Gertrude Stein said that once. She was an impossible human being. But she was wise."

"Now I understand the sunlight in paintings by Hopper."

He gazed at the houses along the dunes. "Yes," he

said. "That is Hopper's white sunlight. One day, you will understand the sunlight in Monet and Van Gogh and Cézanne."

Often in the early mornings, I came out of the house and walked across the dunes to the beach. The dunes were cool then from the night. I wore sandals and shorts and a shirt and had on my tefillin. Those mornings, the beach was my synagogue and the waves and gulls were audience to my prayers. I stood on the beach and felt wind-blown sprays of ocean on my face, and I prayed. And sometimes the words seemed more appropriate to this beach than to the synagogue on my street.

One morning, I finished praying and came back across the dunes and found Jacob Kahn on the porch.

"I was watching you," he said quietly. "I used to pray once. Do you talk to God when you pray?"

"Yes."

"I have lost that faculty. I cannot pray. I talk to God through my sculpture and painting."

"That's also prayer."

He smiled faintly, the morning sun on his face. "The Rebbe said precisely that. You are following the party line, Asher Lev. But we know it is not the same thing, don't we?"

Sometimes in the mornings, I came out onto the porch and saw him walking with his wife across the dunes. She was a shy quiet woman with short white hair and soft brown eyes. Her name was Tanya and she spoke English with a heavy Russian accent. She loved to sit on the porch reading books in Russian and in French. I would watch them walking together across the dunes. She came to below his shoulders in height and often he would bend toward her as they talked. I would watch them together and then turn my eyes away and stare out across the waves at the distant joining of water and sky.

I would not eat food that was not kosher, so they brought a table and chair and a portable electric stove and refrigerator into my room and I prepared my own food. Mostly, I ate canned foods and hard-boiled eggs and raw vegetables. On occasion, as I sat at the table eating, I wondered how my father had managed to eat during all his years of travel.

After breakfast, Jacob Kahn and I would set up our easels at the edge of the dunes and paint. He taught me how the Impressionists had painted light and what Cézanne had done with color and form. Once a sailboat came close to the shore and was circled by the gulls. Using washes of oils, he showed me how John Marin might have painted that. I had seen Marin's watercolors in museums. Now I began to understand their lines of tension, their fluidity and power.

I began to understand, too, though only with difficulty, why and how he painted as he did. The canvas was a two-dimensional field, he said. Any attempt to convert it to an object of three dimensions was an illusion and a falsehood. The only honest way to paint today was either to represent objects that were recognizable, and at the same time integral to the two-dimensional nature of the canvas, or to do away with objects entirely and create paintings of color and texture and form, paintings that translated the volumes and voids in nature into fields of color, paintings in which the solids were flattened and the voids were filled and the planes were organized into what Hans Hofmann called "complexes." I watched him paint and began to understand what he meant. But I could not paint that way myself. I needed hands and faces and eyes, though for a while now I had not needed them to be three-dimensional.

"You are too religious to be an Abstract Expressionist," he said to me one morning. "We are ill at ease in the universe. We are rebellious and individualistic. We welcome accidents in painting. You are emotional and sensual but you are also rational. That is your Ladover background. It is not in my nature to urge a person to give up his background and culture in order to become a painter. That is because it is not in my nature to be a fool. A man's painting either reflects his culture or is a comment upon it, or it is merely decoration or photography. You do not have to be an Abstract Expressionist in order to be a great painter. In any event, by the time you reach your twenties Abstract Expressionism may be gone as an important movement in American painting. Though I do not think so. I think people will paint this way for a thousand years."

Toward noon, with the sun hot and glaring overhead, we would bring our easels and paints into the house and cross the dunes to the beach. We would swim in the cold ocean water. I learned to swim that summer with the help of Jacob Kahn. He was a powerful swimmer. I would stand on the beach and watch him swimming off in the distance, his arms flashing in the sunlight. He had bronzed quickly in the sun; I had burned. Part of my first week in that house I spent realizing how fair-skinned I really was.

Sometimes, standing on that beach, I would remember the beach along the lake in the Berkshires where my mother and I had walked years ago. It seemed another world now, just as my street seemed another world, cold and distant from the warmth of dunes and summer sun. I wondered where my mother was and what she was doing. When the wondering edged into pain, I came off the beach into the water and swam beneath the sun and the wheeling gulls.

In the afternoons, we went off by ourselves and painted alone. I painted in my room or outside on the porch. He painted in his studio, a huge room that took up most of the interior of the house. It had tall windows and was always filled with light. He was painting large canvases and they lay stacked against one of the walls. I had helped him stretch those canvases, setting up a platform with horses and plywood, placing the stretchers on top of the plywood, rolling the canvas onto the stretchers and cutting it and tacking it, fighting wrinkles and dangerous tightness. It had taken us almost a week to stretch those canvases. Now he was filling them with color and form.

I painted the dunes and the beach and the vast sweep of ocean beyond. I painted the gulls and the sun and the pale-blue arc of the sky. I painted my mother on a lakefront. I painted my father eating an indistinct meal at an indistinct table near a window overlooking vague gabled buildings and blurred lights.

One afternoon, I painted a portrait of myself in my fisherman's cap, with my long red earlocks and the tufts of red hair on my cheeks and chin and my eyes dark but flecked with tiny spots of light. I looked at the portrait and I tucked my earlocks behind my ears.

In the evenings, Jacob Kahn and I often walked along Commercial Street. He looked at me that evening when I came down after my private supper and said nothing. We drove to the Chrysler Museum in his new Buick. Inside one of the rooms, he spent twenty minutes explaining the structure of a huge Picasso to me. Then we came out into the night and walked along Commercial Street. It was crowded with traffic and people.

"This is a street I like," he said. "But in five years it will be for tourists. Still, it is a good street."

He wore dungarees and a light shirt and sandals. People greeted him repeatedly as we went along the street. He took me into some of the galleries. The owners all knew him. He introduced me to everyone who spoke to him.

In one of the galleries on Commercial Street, we stood in front of a series of canvases and he said to me, "I do not like geometric abstraction. It has no contact with our time. It is not in touch with what is human in man. Mondrian is a great artist. But he cannot express the feeling that is necessary in a painting if I am to care for it."

A man came over to us, tall and tanned, with dark hair and pale-blue eyes. They shook hands. The man was an artist. He had a show in a nearby gallery. Had Jacob Kahn seen it? No? He ought to see it. Who's the boy? Asher Lev? Nice to meet you, kid. Had Jacob Kahn heard the word that the heavy money would probably be in Tokyo in five to ten years? That was the word. The whole art world was going to shift to Tokyo. That was where the next center of art would be. New York was through. He himself was thinking of moving to Tokyo in a year or two. Nice to meet you, Jack. Nice to meet you, kid. Catch the show if you can. He went out of the gallery into the crowded street.

"Every trade has them," Jacob Kahn said. "They are called whores."

We walked along the street in the warm night. There was the salt smell of the ocean and the dark star-filled sky and the odors of broiling fish and meat from the open-air restaurants. We walked together a long time. Then we drove home.

We stood on the porch of the house and looked across the dunes to the ocean. We could hear the distant thunder of the surf along the shore.

"Asher Lev," Jacob Kahn said softly. "Do not become a whore."

I stared at him. His face was indistinct in the dark night.

"It is not likely that you will starve as an artist. It is also not likely that you will become very rich. Anna tends to be optimistic with her artists. In any event, poor or rich, do not become a whore."

I told him I had no intention of becoming a whore.

"No? You are already on the way, Asher Lev. I would not object if you did that to your payos out of conviction. But you did it out of shame and cowardice. That is the beginning of artistic whoring."

I felt my throat thicken. "My father wears his payos behind his ears. Some Ladover Hasidim do not even wear payos. They aren't that important to us."

"Asher Lev, an artist who deceives himself is a fraud and a whore. You did that because you were ashamed. You did that because wearing payos did not fit your idea of an artist. Asher Lev, an artist is a person first. He is an individual. If there is no person, there is no artist. It is of no importance to me whether you wear your payos behind your ears or whether you cut off your hair entirely and go around bald. I am not a defender of payos. Great artists will not give a damn about your payos; they will only give a damn about your art. The artists who will care about your payos are not worth caring about. You want to cut off your payos, go ahead. But do not do it because you think it will make you more acceptable as an artist. Good night, Asher Lev. Tomorrow morning, I will begin to teach you what Kandinsky tried to accomplish. I will also show you why Abstract Expressionists are indebted to Chaim Soutine." He peered at me intently in the darkness. "Asher Lev, did I upset you?"

"Yes."

"Good. I spoke bluntly. It is not in my nature to be circumspect about important matters."

I was quiet.

"Good night, Asher Lev."

He went into the house.

I stood alone on the porch and stared out across the sands at the water and the night. There was a wind now from the ocean, cool and damp against my face. The porch ran the length of the house and was screened off from the outside. The darkness throbbed softly with the earth life of an ocean shore. I heard the tapping of insects upon the screen. A mosquito buzzed nearby, strangely loud in the pulsing night. Distant laughter floated toward me, borne by the night wind. I felt hot, and I shivered. And I was ashamed.

We did not talk again about my earlocks. I left them as they had been, loose and long against the sides of my face.

Nor did we talk about how we spent Shabbos. I would not paint on Shabbos. I spent Shabbos mornings praying and reviewing the Torah reading. I spent Shabbos afternoons studying a book on Hasidus I had brought with me. Jacob Kahn spent Shabbos mornings on the beach with his wife and Shabbos afternoons painting.

On Tisha b'Av, I read the Book of Lamentations aloud to myself in my room. I fasted and would not paint. I sat on the porch in the afternoon, watching the sun on the sand. Tanya Kahn sat nearby, reading. She looked up at one point and in her heavy accent said quietly, "When will you be able to eat, Asher?"

"After dark."

"You are skin and bones. You should not starve yourself."

I did not respond.

"My younger brother was very religious. Like you. Everyone admired him. But the Nazis killed him anyway. It did not do him much good to be so religious."

She went back to her reading. I sat gazing across the dunes at the rushing surf.

Jacob Kahn came out onto the porch from the house. He brought with him the odors of turpentine and oil colors. He wore shorts and sandals, and there was paint on his arms and chest and white hair and on the shorts and sandals. He looked somber.

"That went well. I am satisfied. I will hate it in the morning but now I am satisfied. My little Hasid is still fasting?"

I nodded.

"I will wash up and we will take a walk. Do you have strength for a walk?"

"Yes."

He went back into the house and came out a few minutes later, wearing clean shorts and a light shirt.

"There is paint on your mustache," his wife said.

"Yes? We will let it remain for a while. A testament to a day of good work. Come, Asher."

We left his wife on the porch reading, and started across the dunes. The sand was hot. I felt it shifting and sliding beneath my sandals, felt it on my feet and between my toes. Along the edge of the beach lay scattered remnants of the night: beer cans, bits of paper, a prophylactic. Jacob Kahn left his sandals on the beach and walked along the surf and I walked beside him, keeping my feet out of the water. The sun burned overhead; I felt it burning my face and arms.

"You are fasting for the destruction of the Temple?" Jacob Kahn said.

"Yes."

"And for the death of the six million?"

"I've been thinking of the six million. Yes."

"My father used to fast. I could never understand the point to it. I fasted a few times when I was young. But when I came to Paris I stopped because it meant nothing to me. It meant nothing to me when I lived in Berlin in the twenties and again in Paris in the thirties. I have had long discussions with the Rebbe about fasting. I have lost the faculty of appreciating such an act of faith." He stopped walking and stared out across the ocean. "Sometimes I think all the water is blood. It is a strange feeling." He was silent. The wind blew through his white hair. I saw the flecks of paint on his face, luminous in the sun. He crouched down along the edge of the surf where the sand was moist but untouched now by the encroaching film of water. His hands gathered sand into a small mound. I watched his fingers begin to work on the moist sand. "It pleases me that you have chosen not to abandon things that are meaningful to you. I do not have many things that are meaningful to me. Except my doubts and my fears. And my art." His fingers were shaping the sand, working swiftly, molding. I saw a face come to life. I saw eyes and a nose and lips. It was his own face. He was sculpting a self-portrait out of the sand along the edge of the foaming surf. The sightless eyes stared out across the water. He rose slowly to his feet and gazed down at the face. "I would like not to die too soon. There are many things I still want to do. I would like to live beyond eighty. Monet did it. Renoir did it. Picasso will do it. Nothing will stop that Spanish genius from reaching eighty. I will bet even Chagall will do it. In Paris, we sometimes thought Chagall would not reach forty. Yes, I would like to live beyond eighty." He looked at me and shook his head. "Asher Lev, sometimes I find your presence a little— upsetting. You carry with you too much of my own past. Come. Walk with me along the beach. We will look at your Hopper sunlight on the houses. You will contemplate God and I will contemplate futility." He smiled wryly. "I do not enjoy myself when I am like this. But there is nothing to be done. It is in my nature to be this way from time to time."

We walked along the surf and then on up across the hot dunes. We walked in silence, and overhead the gulls circled and called in the hot afternoon sky. We came through the scrub brush and looked at the sunlight on the houses.

"I cannot do it," I heard him say. "No one can do it." He gazed wide-eyed at the blinding sunlight. "Even Monet could not do it. And he had the greatest eye of all." He turned and stared back down across the dunes at the beach and the distant mound of moist sand that wore his face. "My blood-offering," he murmured. "But it will not help."

We walked back to the house.

He went to bed early that night and in the morning he would not rise.

"He is in a mood," his wife said calmly. "Once in a while, he has a mood."

She would not let me see him.

I painted alone on the porch of the house. I painted his face in the sand with the surf tearing at it.

His wife came out onto the porch and gazed at the painting.

"Once in a while, he remembers the sculptures he left behind in Paris when we ran from the Nazis. They melted it all down. Ten years of sculpture." She looked at me. "You are very good. A good painter and a good person. Be careful. The world is not nice to good people."

She sat down on a chair and opened a book.

He would not come out of his room all that day.

The next morning, a car pulled up to the house and a tall brown-haired man stepped out and came toward the porch. Tanya Kahn greeted him and introduced us. He looked at the painting I was working on, then looked at me. I knew his name; I had seen his paintings in museums. He went into the house.

Four more painters came over that day, one of them from as far away as Woods Hole. The others were all in Provincetown for the summer. I knew their names.

Shortly before noon the next day, a cab stopped at

the house and Anna Schaeffer hurried inside. She greeted me briefly and went off with Tanya Kahn. They were gone a long time. The cab waited near the house.

I stood on the porch watching the gulls. Had there been birds on the trees along my street? Had I ever seen them wheeling and circling? I could not remember.

Behind me, a door opened and closed softly. I turned.

"Are you having a good summer?" Anna Schaeffer asked.

"Yes."

"I am glad."

"Will he be all right?"

"Yes. It passes. But it is unpleasant while he has it. He is like a light that is dying. It takes a few days. You are doing good work this summer?"

"I think so."

"Jacob Kahn reports to me that he is satisfied. Now I must take that cab back to Hyannis and see if there is a flight to New York. Goodbye, Asher Lev. Be especially kind to your teacher. He is filled with memories of unpleasant things these days."

She went off in the cab. Tanya Kahn came onto the porch.

"He is better. Anna has a way of helping him." She sat down on a chair and opened her book. "He has always come out of it. Of course, there is the chance he may not. One learns to live with fear."

He came out onto the porch that evening and watched the sky grow dark. Then he went inside. Later, as I passed his studio on the way to my room, I saw he had turned on a set of floodlights and was painting, stripped to the waist, a huge canvas toned in a wash of burnt sienna. He was painting in a frenzy, filling the surface with crimson and black forms. I watched him for a while, then went up to my room.

In the morning, we painted together. We did not talk about the past three days. When we went down to the beach before noon to swim, I saw him staring at the sand beyond the curving line of surf. The sand was damp and smooth. He went into the water and swam a long time far away from the shore. Then he came out of the water and stood next to me, dripping, his white hair wild and wet, droplets of water clinging to his mustache.

"I will make it past eighty," he said, "if I can keep from thinking too much about the past. That was a good swim for an impossible old man of seventy-three."

We walked back together across the dunes to the house.

The following week, I received a letter from my mother. She was well. My father was working very hard. She urged me to take care of myself and not to forget that I was a Jew. She sent her good wishes to Jacob Kahn.

The letter was postmarked Zurich. The previous letters I had received from her had been postmarked Vienna, Paris, and Bucharest.

Often that summer, I lay in my bed trying to sleep and found myself thinking of my parents. I would see them gazing out train windows at misty hills and dark mountains and tiny villages set in green valleys. I would see them on the boulevards of great cities, walking together, my father tall and bearded, dressed in his neat dark clothes, my mother short, slight, her eyes warm and alive to the sounds around her, the two of them together, my father's head inclined toward her, listening to her words. I wondered what they talked about during all those days of travel. Russian Jews? The yeshivos my father was bringing to life? Their strange son? My father's certainty of the trouble I would one day bring upon them? I would lie awake in the night, seeing them together, and finally I would sleep, and sometimes there would be dreams.

One day in the third week of August, Jacob Kahn took me to Hyannis and we spent part of the day visiting galleries. Two days later, we drove to Boston to see a Cubist exhibit. All the way back in the car, Jacob Kahn talked about the exhibit and about the Cubists he had known in Paris before the First World War.

"We changed the eyes of the world, Asher Lev. Picasso and Braque with painting and Jacob Kahn with sculpture. Picasso was frightening. We met and talked, all of us, and thought of this or that idea. Picasso would go back to his studio and in a few hours he had it all worked out on a canvas. He is a genius. He can use up a lifetime of ideas of an ordinary good painter in a few weeks. People used to hide their canvases from him. There is something demonic about such a gift, Asher Lev. Demonic or divine, I do not know which. Giotto, Michelangelo, Picasso. It will be three hundred years before the world assimilates what has happened to art as a result of Picasso and the Cubists." He smiled delightedly. "Ah, the stories I can tell."

"You are an old gossip," his wife said, looking up. She had been sitting beside him on the front seat, reading.

"Yes," he said. "I love gossip. It is one of my more delicious weaknesses."

A few days later, he drove me to the Provincetown docks and let me out. I wandered along the waterfront, sketching the boats and the gulls and the boys diving and swimming. I watched them diving and swimming and I sketched their young bodies in the sunlight. Then I stopped sketching for a while and stood at the end of a long wooden pier and watched them in the water, swimming smoothly with the liquid ease of fish. I envied them their freedom. I went from the pier and walked slowly along the streets of the town, narrow crowded streets filled with cafés and restaurants and souvenir shops. I came into a small aquarium and watched sharks swim about behind thick glass. I sketched the twisting of their bodies and the hideousness of their mouths. People gathered around me, and there were murmurs of awe. Here is my gift, I thought. Publicly displayed. I drew without hesitation. I thought I heard someone applaud; I could not be certain. I saw a young boy of about eight leaning forward, watching. I signed one of the drawings, dated it, tore it from the sketchbook, and gave it to him. His eyes went wide. There was a soft ripple of laughter and approval.

I came out into the sunlight and walked the streets.
Sometime during the walking, I saw myself in the window of a restaurant and stared indifferently at my face
and realized my sidecurls were behind my ears. I turned
away and continued along the street. I went up a side
street and sketched the faces of old women on the
porches of small wooden houses. I sketched the faces of
old men, wrinkled leathery faces, the faces of fishermen
who knew intimately a kind of universe far from the
street where I had grown up. Here on a street of Provincetown fishing families, I sketched people I had never
known before but with whom I felt a strange kinship.
We all lived together on the same quicksilvery water
and sand. I sketched their faces and gave some of the
sketches away and was rewarded with grateful smiles.

Later that day, Jacob Kahn picked me up in front of
the gallery where we had met the man he had called a
whore. He looked at my face.

"You had a good day?" he asked quietly.

I showed him the sketches. He glanced through them
and nodded.

"You had a good day," he said.

"I am going to be an artist," I said. "I am going to be
a great artist."

"You have been an artist for a long time, Asher
Lev."

We drove together through the town.

Early one morning at the end of August, a truck
came up to the house. We loaded the paintings of the
summer into the back and closed and locked the doors.
We stood on the porch and watched the truck drive off.

"He is a careful driver," Jacob Kahn said. "I have
used him before."

I did not say anything.

Later, we swam together and then I sat at the edge of
the line of surf and made a sculpture of my face out of
wet sand. Jacob Kahn watched me.

"It is very good," he said when I was done.

We swam again, and when we came out of the water
the face had crumbled into a pile of soggy sand, dis-

solved by the surf. We stared at it and I looked at Jacob Kahn.

"No," he said. "I will not be ill again. I will never make it to eighty if I indulge myself too much with that illness."

But I saw that face of sand in my sleep that night, and I woke and went to the window and stared out at the dunes and thought I heard soft mocking laughter float toward me from the dark water beyond.

Two days later, we drove back to New York and my summer of water and sand came to an end.

ELEVEN

I was attending the Ladover yeshiva high school. I asked to see the registrar.

He was a short thin man with a dark beard and a bald head. He wore rimless spectacles and a small dark skullcap. He looked up from behind his neat desk.

"Yes?"

"I did not ask to take French."

"And?"

"Someone put French on my class card."

"Yes?"

"I do not want to take French. What do I need with French?"

He adjusted the spectacles delicately on the bridge of his thin nose. "Asher Lev, you will take French. You will take four years of French. And you will earn for yourself excellent marks in French. The Rebbe specifically requested that we make certain you study French."

I stared at him.

"Is there anything else?"

"No."

"Then good day, Asher Lev."

On Rosh Hashonoh, I sat in the synagogue and prayed. The prayer shawls and white garments flooded the synagogue with light; there was white light everywhere, on the chairs and benches, near the podium where the reader chanted the prayers, near the Ark where the Rebbe sat praying, quietly, alone, faintly lu-

254

minous against the dark wood of the wall. We stood, and the Rebbe sounded the shofar. The sounds filled the large synagogue, the air vibrating invisibly as the piercing notes caught up with one another and echoed from distant corners. I looked at the bundle of prayers on the podium in front of the Rebbe. Somewhere in those bundles, there were prayers for my mother and father and for Jacob Kahn. I hoped the Ribbono Shel Olom would listen more seriously to my prayers for my parents and Jacob Kahn than He had to my father's prayers for me.

On Yom Kippur, I wept when I remembered my father's weeping over the martyrdom of the ten sages. On Succos, I marched in the synagogue procession with the lulov and esrog my uncle had purchased for me. On Simchas Torah, I danced with a Torah scroll—and there on the edge of the crowd of thousands that always came to watch our joy on that day was Jacob Kahn. I pulled him into the line and we held the Torah together and danced. His small dark skullcap was as awkward on his head as was the grasp of his fingers upon the Torah. But we held it together and we danced.

I continued going to him on Sunday afternoons. I continued painting and drawing, and now I did some sculpting, too. I studied Gemorra. I studied Hasidus. I studied French.

The opening of Jacob Kahn's show took place on a Sunday afternoon in late October. It was a lavish black-tie affair with drinks and food. The gallery was crowded. The sculptures had been carefully positioned along the floor and walls. In form and line and texture, in the way they utilized the space within and around them, they were clear and awesome indicators of a powerful and visionary aesthetic. He had transformed forever the nature of sculpting as Picasso had transformed forever the nature of painting.

One of the sculptures consisted of two heads facing in the same direction. One head was Jacob Kahn's; the other was mine. They were identical to the heads we had sculpted out of wet sand along the edge of the clutching surf. Now they were in bronze. The small red label on the base of the sculpture indicated it had already been purchased.

I moved through the gallery, listening. It seemed an intelligent crowd. I heard much talk about Picasso and Cubism and Henry Moore. Most of the painters I had met over the months in his studio were there. At one point during the afternoon, I found myself next to Anna Schaeffer. She wore a gown and her face was flushed with excitement.

"It is a grand success," she cried exuberantly. "You have no idea what I went through to get him to agree to a show. You will not give me such trouble, Asher Lev, will you? I could not take such heartache from both of you. Look. Look around. It is a magnificent day."

She turned to greet someone and I moved away. I saw Jacob Kahn near a wall, dressed in a dark suit and dark bow tie, surrounded by a dense crowd, and looking stiff and uncomfortable. His wife stood beside him, smiling and talking calmly to a woman in diamonds but looking as if she would rather be reading one of her Russian or French books. Somehow I managed to make my way up to them.

"Asher," Tanya Kahn said. "You are looking fine."

"Congratulations," I said. "It's a great show."

"Yes?" Jacob Kahn said.

"You don't think so?"

"I wish I had Picasso's gall and could stay away from these things. They destroy me. A few more of these and I will never make it to eighty."

"You will make it to ninety," Tanya Kahn said calmly.

"I wish I had that Spaniard's gall. Instead I have a Jewish heart. I would not want to hurt Anna."

"I like the two heads," I said.

He looked at me.

"Very much."

"I like them, too," he said.

"Who bought them?"

He shrugged and would not respond.

I moved through the crowd and stood next to Anna Schaeffer.

"I saw you with Jacob," she said. "Is he suffering terribly?"

"He says he is."

"Poor man. He does this to please me. He wishes he had Picasso's contempt for such things. Yes. How I know that old man."

"Who bought the two heads?"

"Which?"

I told her.

"Ah," she said.

"Who bought them?"

She told me. I stared at her. She smiled faintly.

"They are among his collectors. They have a number of his pieces. It is a beautiful sculpture. He made it when he returned after the summer." She looked at me. "He has developed an affection for you, Asher Lev."

I did not say anything.

When I left the gallery later that afternoon, it was still crowded. On the subway ride home, I thought about the sculpture of the two heads and wondered where they would put it. In a library? In a garden? In a living room? What would the eyes stare at? Ornate drapery? Marble? Books in leather bindings? Rare flowers? It was a queer feeling to know that a likeness of my head would soon be in the home of one of the wealthiest families in America.

The reviews of the show were uniformly appreciative and filled with praise. I read in one of the newspapers that the entire show had sold out at the opening. The next time I saw Jacob Kahn, I congratulated him on that. He looked bereaved.

The weeks went by. I continued traveling to Jacob Kahn. The room in which I lived became crowded with drawings and canvases.

My uncle came into the room, one night early in December, and stood in the doorway watching me work on a painting of my memory of Mrs. Rackover. She had gone to live with a married daughter in Detroit after my

mother left for Europe, and had died of a heart attack
on a downtown Detroit street in late November while
shopping for a gift for a new grandson. He stood in the
doorway a long time, watching me paint. Then he
cleared his throat softly.

"Am I disturbing you?"

"No."

"It is a good painting."

"Thank you."

"Asher. Goldie and I were talking. Look at your
room. It is crowded and small."

"It's a room."

"We will fix up the attic for you."

I stopped painting and looked at him.

"It is a whole floor. No one uses it. We will fix it up
and you will have more room."

Carpenters came. Painters came. A month later, the
whole family—my uncle, my aunt, their four children—
helped me move upstairs. When it was done, my uncle
surveyed the attic, chewed thoughtfully on his cigar,
and said, "Now you are a painter. When someone
writes the history of Asher Lev, he will say his uncle
fixed him up with his first real studio. *This* is a studio.
Not the closets you had until now. It will take you five
years to fill up this studio."

I did a painting of him and his family and gave it to
them for Hanukkah. He framed it and put it on a wall
of the living room. He called it his "authentic Lev" and
kept talking about the fortune it would be worth one
day.

The attic room was large, with a high sloping roof
and a tall window that looked out onto an old maple. I
could barely see the street through the thick tangle of
branches.

I worked and slept in that room. I did not think it
would take me five years to fill it.

Between semesters, Jacob Kahn took me by train to a
Van Gogh exhibit at the Philadelphia Museum of Art.
We talked about the Post-Impressionists and the Nabis

and the Fauves. We talked about Gauguin and Matisse and Vlaminck. We came back in a snowstorm that delayed the train and got us into New York more than two hours late. I called my uncle from the station. He answered the telephone and I heard his voice tremble. He was relieved to hear from me and grateful that I had thought to call.

Early in February, Jacob Kahn sent a plaster piece out for casting in bronze. When it came back, I saw it was a sculpture of the two of us dancing with a Torah. I had not seen him sculpt it. He put it in a corner of the studio. One day, I looked for it and it was no longer there.

"Tanya likes it," he said. "I took it home."

I asked him once if they had any children. They had had a daughter, he said. She had died of influenza in Paris at the age of four.

He came to the Ladover farbrengen in the second week of February. We were commemorating the day that the Rebbe's father removed himself from this world. The synagogue was filled with thousands of people. The men sat at the tables. The students stood on benches around the walls. There were benches along the area in front of the Ark. Elders and guests of honor sat on those benches. I saw two Jewish novelists on one of those benches. And I saw Jacob Kahn, thick-shouldered, the dark beret covering his white hair. The Rebbe sat on a cushioned chair at a table in front of a microphone. He wore a dark caftan and an ordinary dark hat. He spoke for a few minutes in Yiddish about the need for a true Torah education for Jewish children. He quoted from the Gemorra and the Midrash and the Zohar. The huge crowd was hushed, listening. His words came clearly through the microphone. Those same words were being translated by telephonic hookup to every Ladover community in the world—to England, France, Germany, Italy, Switzerland, Holland, Denmark, Norway, Sweden, Austria, Israel, South America, North Africa, Australia, Canada, Mexico, and perhaps elsewhere as well. I wondered if my parents were now listening to the Rebbe. It was a suddenly warm feeling to think that the three of us might be listening to the Rebbe together.

When the Rebbe was done talking, someone began a song. There was rhythmic singing. Little paper cups of vodka were held up to be blessed by a nod of the Rebbe's head before being drunk. Then the singing stopped and the Rebbe spoke again—about the importance of the sanctity of the Jewish family. There was more singing. I looked up at the benches behind the Rebbe and saw that Jacob Kahn was no longer there. A moment later, I felt a tug at my sleeve.

"Come outside with me, Asher," Jacob Kahn said.

I followed behind him as he moved slowly through the dense crowd.

Outside on the street, the air was cold and sharp with the feeling of coming snow. We stood on the sidewalk away from the crowd near the doors. There were two police cars at the curb and four patrolmen on the sidewalk in front of the building.

"Fifteen years ago, there was nothing here," Jacob Kahn said, gazing at the synagogue and at the headquarters building alongside it. "The house was here. I think a doctor or a dentist owned it. But none of this was here." He gestured toward the crowd. "He is a good man, our Rebbe." He looked at me. "I will be going to Europe for a month. I was called two days ago and thought I would tell you tonight rather than telephone. I leave tomorrow night."

I shivered in the wind.

"In Zurich, they are planning a retrospective for a good friend. They are asking for advice. That will take a week. Then I will go to Italy. There is some marble I want to look at."

I was quiet.

"Asher Lev, it will only be for a month. Your world has not come to an end because Jacob Kahn is going on a trip. You may use the studio anytime you wish. There is a new piece of wood I had brought in today that you might want to use."

I did not say anything.

"It is not in my nature to make long farewells. Good-bye, Asher Lev." He shook my hand and walked away quickly beneath the winter trees.

I did not go back inside. I walked home and went to bed.

I took the subway to his studio the following Sunday afternoon. But I found the silent enormity of the room intolerable. After an hour, I closed it up and went home.

I did not return to his studio. Instead I worked in my attic room. I painted him swimming in the ocean. I painted him sculpting in the sand. I painted him walking with his wife. I painted the two of us painting together at the edge of the dunes. I painted him painting a huge canvas stripped to the waist. The room began to look cluttered with drawings and canvases. No, I would not need five years to fill this room.

He returned in March, one month after he had gone. He called me. It had been a fine trip. Italy especially had been admirable. Italy was always admirable. Especially Florence.

"I met your parents in Zurich. They are well and send you their love. You know they will be back for Pesach. Will I see you Sunday?"

"Yes."

"You will have to see Florence one day, Asher Lev. There are people I will send you to. It is a gift, that city."

I went to him the following Sunday. He looked well and was exuberant. "I am always exuberant after Italy. It is the marble." We worked together and soon it was as if he had not been away at all.

My parents arrived by ship on the last day of March. They moved into my uncle's house and lived in the room I had occupied before being transferred to the attic. My father looked rested. He had put on weight and had almost completely lost his limp. Looking at him during those weeks, I often wondered if I, too, would be gray in my early forties. But he seemed once again strong and it was clear that he had really needed my mother.

We said very little to one another. He was uneasy in my presence. There was between us now a permanent high wall of uncertainty and hostility.

My uncle made an effort to pierce that wall the first night my parents were back. He brought my father upstairs to the attic. I was at my desk, reading.

They stood in the doorway, looking around at the clutter of drawings and canvases.

"I will have to buy him a house," my uncle said, speaking in Yiddish and chewing on a cigar. "Look how he is filling the attic."

My father's face was dark. I could see the anger in his eyes. "You are encouraging him." He spoke as if I were not in the room.

"I am doing what I think is right."

"You give him money for his paint. I did not ask you to give him money."

"Aryeh, do you want your son to steal?"

My father looked at him. I could see his lips tighten beneath his graying beard.

"Listen to me, Aryeh. Listen to your brother. Reconcile yourself to your son."

My father said nothing.

"He is a good boy. He cannot help what he does."

"Only an animal cannot help what he does."

"Aryeh—"

My father turned and went from the room.

There was a heavy silence. My uncle sighed and shook his head. "He is a stubborn man, your father. It is both a weakness and a strength to be so stubborn."

Sometime during the intermediate days of Passover, I walked with my mother along the parkway near our apartment house. She looked young and lovely. But her eyes were sad.

"Jacob Kahn told us in Zurich that you had a fine summer."

"Yes."

"He succeeded in angering your father."

I was quiet. We walked beneath the trees.

"It is impossible to talk to your father about you. Hopelessly impossible." She looked at me and her eyes were moist. "It hurts me to be caught between my husband and my son."

I did not know what to say. We walked on and came to the apartment house and stood on the street, looking up at the window of the living room. The Venetian blind had been raised. We could see the houses and the street reflected in the glass of the window.

"We think we may give up the apartment," my mother said. "We don't know how long we'll be in Europe. It doesn't seem to make much sense to keep it."

We turned and started back to my uncle's house.

"Asher, come with us to Europe."

"No."

"We miss you. I miss you. There are great art schools in Vienna."

"No."

"Asher—"

"He'll try to take it away from me. No."

She stared.

"No," I said. "No."

"All right, Asher."

"I'm worse than an animal. I'm—"

"Asher, please."

"He won't take it away from me."

"All right. All right. Hush. All right."

She took my hand. I felt her slender fingers cool and strong against my skin. We walked back together beneath the young spring trees.

My uncle urged them not to give up the apartment. Had the Rebbe told my father his position in Europe was permanent? No, the Rebbe had not said that. Then they should keep the apartment. Did they know how difficult it was to acquire a rent-controlled apartment these days?

They left for Europe by ship in the third week of April and I went back to Jacob Kahn.

"Yes," Jacob Kahn said when I told him of my parents' visit. "I am afraid I have made an enemy of your father."

"Why does he hate me? I don't understand."

"He thinks you are wasting your life. He thinks you have betrayed him. It is not pleasant for a man like your father to see his son painting nudes and the other things you paint. It is for him at best a frivolity and at worst a desecration. You and your father are two different natures. There is nothing to be done about it, Asher Lev."

"The Rebbe isn't angry. Why isn't the Rebbe angry?"

"The Rebbe is a very wise man. And he is of a different nature than your father."

"I don't understand."

"Do not try to understand. Become a great artist. That is the only way to justify what you are doing to everyone's life."

I painted and studied and brooded about my parents. Jacob Kahn's words haunted me: "That is the only way to justify what you are doing to everyone's life." I did not understand what he meant. I did not feel I had to justify anything. I had not willfully hurt anyone. What did I have to justify? I did not want to paint in order to justify anything; I wanted to paint because I wanted to paint. I wanted to paint the same way my father wanted to travel and work for the Rebbe. My father worked for Torah. I worked for—what? How could I explain it? For beauty? No. Many of the pictures I painted were not beautiful. For what, then? For a truth I did not know how to put into words. For a truth I could only bring to life by means of color and line and texture and form.

And so I painted and studied and began once again

to see my thunderous mythic ancestor. I saw other things as well: the prophylactic on the Provincetown beach, the nudes I had drawn and painted, the girls waiting along Manhattan side streets, certain books in stores, certain magazines on newsstands. I painted in a frenzy of fierce and restless energy; and slowly the room filled with my work. One day in June, I put a wet and finished canvas near my attic window. I looked outside and could not see the street for the thick new leaves of the tree.

I spent that summer in Provincetown with Jacob and Tanya Kahn. It was a calm and beautiful summer. I met some of his artist friends. They spent long nights talking. I sat and listened.

I sat and listened the following summer, too, and sometime toward the end of the summer I began to join in the talk. There were things I wanted to say. I said them, and they sat and listened, and we talked.

Those were lovely summers. Only once in both summers did Jacob Kahn indulge his illness, and then only briefly.

My parents returned to America for the holidays after that last Provincetown summer. My mother began urging me to spend the following summer in Vienna. But I was afraid a summer in Vienna would extend itself into one or two years in Europe. I had come to enjoy living with my aunt and uncle and their noisy brood of children. I did not want to live with my father. So I refused.

That was a bleak holiday for me. My aunt and uncle joined my mother in her insistence that I go to Vienna. My father remained aloof, not seeming to care whether I went or not. Jacob Kahn was campaigning around the country for John Kennedy. Hitler had taught him to take an interest in politics, he had said to me after Kennedy's nomination. He was going to organize a nation-wide artists-for-Kennedy group. "People will listen to a seventy-five-year-old man," he said. "They will think I possess wisdom." I did not see him all during the campaign.

I relented to their pleas. I would go to Vienna.

"You were right to do that," Jacob Kahn said when I saw him again after the election.

"Why?"

"They are your parents. You should be with your parents."

"Why?"

He looked at me sharply. "You do not want to go?"

"No."

"Why did you agree?"

"They all piled on me."

"You have been piled on before, Asher Lev."

"I wish you had been around."

"Learn to stand on your own feet, Asher Lev. Even if I live to eighty, I will not be here forever."

"I don't want to live with my father."

"Then change your mind."

"No."

"Then do something. But do not brood in my studio. Brood in your attic. Here we think and we work. We do not indulge ourselves in brooding."

"I'll brood in my algebra class. It's as good a place as any for brooding. Maybe I'll brood in my physics class."

"You are developing an interesting sense of humor, Asher Lev."

He said to me one day in December, "I think John Kennedy will be a great President. I like the people he is surrounding himself with."

But I was not interested in politics and cared little about Kennedy and his people. I shrugged and continued painting.

He stood behind me one afternoon and watched me paint. He was silent a long time. Then he said, "Asher Lev, what are you doing?"

I explained it to him. He looked at me. Then he looked at the canvas.

"Yes," he said very quietly. "I understand."

He went off to his own work. But from time to time

throughout the rest of that afternoon I saw him glancing at me in a strange and curious way.

The winter weeks passed with leaden heaviness. I did not want them to pass at all. I dreaded the oncoming summer.

There was still coldness in the air the first day of Passover. I spent all the intermediate days in galleries and museums. On one of those days, Jacob Kahn accompanied me to the Museum of Modern Art and I discovered something about two of the Picassos that I had not noticed on previous trips. I pointed it out to Jacob Kahn, and he stared at the paintings and nodded slowly and gave me that strange and curious look again.

Early one May afternoon, I took a subway to a Jewish museum in Manhattan. I saw Torah crowns, Torah pointers, Torah covers, spice boxes, illuminated manuscripts. Some were fine pieces of work. But there was no art. It was all crafts and unmoving. I felt vaguely betrayed.

On the last Tuesday in June, my uncle drove me to Idlewild Airport and put me on a plane for Vienna.

I became ill on the plane. I was ill during the stopover in London. I was ill on the flight from London to Vienna. In Vienna, I lay in a strange bed in a strange room and saw my mother's face through dark fog. Somewhere along the edge of the fog, I sensed my father's rage. I heard strange voices in languages I could not recognize. I heard Yiddish and French and what sounded like Russian. Food poisoning, someone said. Virus, someone said. Nervous shock, someone said. I heard my father shouting. I sat in front of an open window that looked across a dark river to old gabled buildings. It was raining. Rain came in the open window and collected in puddles on the wooden floor. I saw Yudel Krinsky. What was Yudel Krinsky doing in Vienna? Hello, Reb Yudel Krinsky. Vienna is a city of waltzes and cafés, Yudel Krinsky whispered. Vienna is a city that hates Jews. It rained on the river and the gabled houses. I saw sand and a vast ocean in the rain. I saw dunes and white sunlight on shingled houses. Someone had me by the arm. I heard my mother and father. There was a quarrel. It swirled poisonously around me. I felt its rage and hate. A man with a beard led me gently into a silver bird and sat with me through clouds.

My uncle met me at the airport and took me home. It was the end of the third week of July. I lay in bed three days, then began wandering around the house. I did a painting of a dark river in rain.

In the second week of August, my uncle put me on a bus to Provincetown. Jacob Kahn met me at the station. He looked bronzed and his hair and walrus mustache were sharply white in the brilliant sunlight.

"Well, Asher Lev," he said gently. "The climate of Vienna did not agree with you. Welcome."

I went home with him. We painted and swam and walked in the surf. We looked at the Hopper sunlight on the houses along the dunes.

Tanya Kahn showed me a small sculpture he had made in July and had had bronzed by a caster outside of Wellfleet. It was a sculpture of me wearing shorts, a sports shirt, sandals, and my fisherman's cap. He had placed my sidecurls behind my ears.

"He missed you," Tanya Kahn said.

The registrar called me into his office.

"Asher Lev, you are planning to go to college?"

"Yes."

"To which college?"

"Brooklyn."

He adjusted the rimless spectacles on the bridge of his thin nose and peered at me. "Your parents know of your plans?"

"Yes."

"They approve?"

"My mother approves. My mother wants me to go to college."

He did not ask me about my father. Instead he said, "What will you study in college?"

"I do not know."

"Whatever you study, one of your courses will be Russian."

I looked at him.

"The Russian language."

"No," I said.

"The Rebbe has expressly asked—"

"No."

"Do not be disrespectful, Asher Lev."

"No," I said. "No."

He peered at me narrowly through the rimless spectacles. "Very well. Good day, Asher Lev."

Outside on the street, the trees wore dead leaves. I shivered in the November wind.

Rav Mendel Dorochoff asked to see me. I climbed the stairway of the headquarters building late one evening and walked along the corridor to the waiting room. The room was empty save for Rav Dorochoff, who sat behind the desk, gaunt, dark-bearded.

"Sit down, Asher Lev," he said.

I took the chair he offered me.

"Your parents are well?"

"My mother is well."

He looked at me from behind his desk. After a moment, he said, "Asher Lev, you are going to college?"

"Yes."

"You will continue to attend the yeshiva while you are in college?"

"Yes."

"Asher Lev, we feel it will be of help if you studied the Russian language in college."

"I am not interested in the Russian language. I do not care about the Russian language."

"Asher Lev, remember to whom you are speaking."

"Leave me alone," I said.

"Asher—"

"Leave me alone. One is enough. Leave me alone. Please."

"I am speaking for the Rebbe, Asher Lev."

"Please," I said. "Please please please."

He was silent for a long time. Then he dismissed me with an abrupt gesture of his hand.

There was snow on the street. A bitter wind blew along the parkway.

I was told that the Rebbe wanted to see me. I climbed the stairway on trembling legs and came into the waiting room. Rav Mendel Dorochoff took me into the Rebbe's office and left, closing the heavy wooden door.

The Rebbe sat behind his desk. He looked at me from across the room. He seemed garbed in light.

"Asher Lev," I heard him say softly. "Come here. Come here."

I went up to him. I felt his eyes on my face.

"You look tired, my Asher. Sit here beside me. Here."

I sat in a chair alongside his desk.

He gazed at me somberly. "How are you feeling, Asher?"

"I am well, Rebbe."

"How you have grown. And your beard. But you are thin. You are too thin. Jacob Kahn tells me you work very hard."

I was quiet.

"He has been a good teacher?"

"Yes."

"He is a good person. He is not an observer of the commandments. But he is a good person."

I did not say anything.

"I hear from your parents that they are well."

"Yes."

"The letters from your mother—they are often sad."

I was quiet.

"Asher, Asher," the Rebbe said softly. "This world has not been kind to you."

I sat very still. He shook his head slowly.

" 'Everything is in the hands of heaven, except the fear of heaven,' " he quoted. "What can I tell you, my

Asher? I do not know what the Master of the Universe has waiting for us. Certain things are given, and it is for man to use them to bring goodness into the world. The Master of the Universe gives us glimpses, only glimpses. It is for us to open our eyes wide."

I was quiet.

"Asher Lev. My Asher Lev. Jacob Kahn tells me you have greatness. He tells me you will soon be ready to show yourself to the world. His words are for me a glimpse, a light. I say to myself Asher Lev will be a great artist. He will travel about the world in search of ideas and people. Great artists make the entire world their home. You have already begun to travel. And I say to myself there are great museums in Europe. There are great museums in Russia. You know of the Hermitage in Leningrad and the museum in Moscow. Russia is a rich land in art and you will one day wish to travel there. That is for me a glimpse, my Asher. I am trying to open my eyes wide and to see. I will tell you what my father, may he rest in peace, once told me. Seeds must be sown everywhere. Only some will bear fruit. But there would not be the fruit from the few had the many not been sown. Do you understand, my Asher?"

I nodded slowly.

"Yes," he said. "I am certain you understand. I wish you a long and healthy life, my son. I give you my blessings for greatness in the world of art and greatness in the world of your people."

I walked back to my uncle's house in the ice and snow of the January streets.

That spring, I flew to Chicago with Jacob Kahn to see a Brancusi exhibit at the Art Institute. That summer, I drove to Provincetown with Jacob and Tanya Kahn and lived in my world of water and sand. That fall, I entered college and registered for a class in Russian.

I painted. I attended college and studied Russian. I attended the yeshiva and studied Gemorra and Hasidus.

I traveled to Manhattan galleries and saw the beginnings of a mocking art which I disliked. Jacob Kahn called it nihilism. He despised it. He regarded it as an undisciplined destruction of aesthetic values. Duchamp was to blame for this, he said bitterly. I began to understand what it meant to have once been a revolutionary in art and then to become, in turn, the target of a new revolution. "Sometimes I think it is not wise to grow too old," Jacob Kahn said to me one windy afternoon as we walked together along Madison Avenue. "But I am not aware that we are given a choice in this matter."

He brought me into Anna Schaeffer's gallery. She was behind her desk and she smiled delightedly when she saw us.

"My young prodigy and my impossible old man," she said, taking my hand. Jacob Kahn kissed her cheek. There were paintings on the walls. The forms and muted colors intrigued me.

"He is a splendid painter," Anna Schaeffer said to me. "A Viennese. He loves to paint chairs. He is another of my impossible old men. Go and look at them."

I wandered through the gallery. Anna Schaeffer and Jacob Kahn were talking quietly. I came back to them.

"He's very good," I said.

"Yes," Anna Schaeffer said. "And he sells well."

"I knew him in Paris," Jacob Kahn said. "He sold well in Paris, too."

"That is where your pictures will hang in the spring," Anna Schaeffer said to me, pointing to the walls.

I stared at her and felt a shock move through me.

"I would have done it this year," she said. "But this old man would not let me."

"He is still a boy this year," Jacob Kahn said. "A boy should not rush to make his soul naked."

"I think you will be the youngest artist ever to have a one-man show in a Madison Avenue gallery," Anna Schaeffer said. "I may bill you as 'Asher Lev, Brooklyn Prodigy.'" She laughed softly. "Look at his face, Jacob."

"I am looking. I would like to sculpt that expression.

But I do not happen to be carrying a block of marble on me."

Outside, we walked together on the windy street.

"You are happy, yes?" Jacob Kahn said.

I nodded and did not know what to say.

"Be happy," he said. "Be happy. These are the good times. Be happy, Asher Lev. Later you will understand how truly good these times have been."

My uncle and aunt were delighted when I told them. Yudel Krinsky was delighted. "The colors you paint with you bought here, yes? I am happy for you, Asher Lev."

I wrote my mother. She wrote me back saying she was very happy. Yes, she had informed my father. They would probably return from Europe sometime during the summer, she wrote. My father's work was coming to an end. Would I inform my aunt and uncle, and would I ask them to inform the tenants in the apartment?

I lived that year in a fever of expectation. The winter seemed unusually mild. Jacob Kahn came to the house one day and, from the stacks of canvases piled against the walls, selected the ones for the show.

"It will take your uncle five years to scrape the paint from your room," he said. "You have learned all my bad habits." He looked at me. "Yes, we will show the two nudes, Asher Lev. They are important to your development. We are not playing games. You will enter in truth or you will not enter at all."

A truck came one afternoon while I was in school and took away the paintings he had chosen.

The weeks went by. One April afternoon, I came into Anna Schaeffer's gallery and watched as they put up the paintings. I did not like how some of the canvases had been hung.

"Artists should paint and not hang," Anna Schaeffer said. "Your colleagues have destroyed the frame and soon they will destroy the wall. Go away, Asher Lev. Go home and paint. I was hanging canvases before you were born."

I walked the wind-blown streets of Manhattan. She

had said "your colleagues." I walked the streets and tasted the golden sun that lay across the city.

To this day, I do not know all the details that went into the preparation of that show. Anna Schaeffer sent out the announcements, contacted some of her collectors privately, and prepared the catalogue. A week before the opening, I learned that it had all amounted to a great deal of money.

"Who is paying for it?" I asked Jacob Kahn.

"You are."

I stared at him.

"She will take it from your sales. She has a great affection for you. But she is a businesswoman."

"Does she also get a percentage of each sale?"

"Thirty percent. Do not look at me like that. What do you think she means when she talks about becoming rich off your work? She has become rich off mine. But we are fortunate. Some galleries take forty and fifty percent."

"What if I don't sell?"

"She is gambling. Gamblers sometimes lose."

She did not lose. But she did not win, either. The opening was a moderate success. Some of her collectors came. Some of my classmates came. Some critics came. Yudel Krinsky came. Rav Mendel Dorochoff came, looked, and walked out. My uncle and aunt were there. People sauntered in off the streets. It was a warm day in early May and the streets were crowded. There were drinks and food, non-kosher food. She was in the art business, not in the religious-catering business, Anna Schaeffer had said. This was not a bar mitzvah but an art show. I did not eat.

The sharpest memory I have of that show, a memory that was reinforced by the two other shows she gave me before I left for Europe and that returns to haunt me more and more frequently these days, is the memory of standing in that gallery and seeing the faces of my world on its walls—paintings of my people and my street, paintings of my mother and me walking together, paintings of Yudel Krinsky and Mrs. Rackover, paintings of old ladies on the parkway benches—all of the years of my life summed up on the walls of a gallery, and then seeing some of the empty spaces when the show was over: Yudel Krinsky was gone; Mrs. Rackover was gone; my mother and I were gone; some of the old ladies on the park benches were gone.

"We are not rich," Anna Schaeffer said to me when it was done and the walls were bare. "But we are not poor, either. The critics were kind."

The critics who had noticed me had commented on my extreme youth and been very kind, with the exception of one who dismissed me as a fraud and described me as glutted with banality, sentimentality, and "a menacing affinity for Picassoid forms." Jacob Kahn liked that phrase. He went around quoting it for weeks. "Anna, did you know our prodigy has a menacing affinity for Picassoid forms?" Anna Schaeffer was not amused.

I wrote my mother about the show. She wrote me back expressing her joy. They would not return that summer, she added. My father's work was not yet done. She asked me to call the tenants in the apartment and inform them that they would not have to move out. I spent the summer in Provincetown with Jacob and Tanya Kahn.

Jacob Kahn was in Paris visiting a retrospective given for an old friend from his Berlin days when President Kennedy was assassinated. He returned to America a few days after the funeral, locked himself in his studio, and painted. I saw the canvas when it was done. It radiated his anguish.

He said to me once during those days of pain, "This will be a new dark age. I remember Germany. But where can I run to now? I think I will not enjoy reaching eighty." Later Tanya Kahn called and said he was not well. Yes, he was indulging himself again. No, she had no idea how long it would last.

It took almost a week. When I saw him again, he would not talk about it.

My second show took place the following spring. The

critics were very kind, except for our friend of the Picassoid forms, who had other things to say this time.

"We are not rich yet," Anna Schaeffer said. "But I am beginning to feel optimistic."

"You are a greedy old woman," Jacob Kahn said.

"A greedy rich old woman," Anna Schaeffer said.

In July, I went with Jacob and Tanya Kahn to Provincetown. My parents returned from Europe in the middle of August. My father's work was done. He had been reassigned to an office next to Rav Mendel Dorochoff on the second floor of the Ladover building.

My parents moved back into our old apartment and when I returned from Provincetown I moved into my old room. I could not paint in that room because it was too small. There was a brief family meeting with my aunt and uncle and my parents. My father's suggestion resolved the difficulty. I lived with my parents and painted in my uncle's house.

TWELVE

They had lived years without me. Now they possessed a language of shared experience in which I was nonexistent. Often they would slip into the shorthand of private signs and notations that form the speech of people who have been together intimately for great lengths of time. There were smiles about the train system from Vienna to Zurich, expressions of wonder at the cleanliness of Switzerland, grimaces over the traffic in Paris. There was quiet laughter over incidents with coal stoves, the leaking roofs, and windows that rattled in high winds. "How do you know about that window?" I heard my mother say delightedly once to my father. "You didn't stand there waiting for me. I stood there waiting for you." "I know about that window, Rivkeh," I heard my father say. "The concierge said the window had been rattling since the days of Napoleon. It was an anti-French window, the concierge said." And they laughed.

It sounded strange to hear them laughing about my mother's habit of waiting at windows. They talked to each other with ease and assurance and knowing intimacy. Often I felt they were together now as they had been before I was born.

My father was in his middle forties. There was vigor and dignity about his gray hair and clear dark eyes and thickset shoulders. His limp was barely noticeable. He walked surrounded with the sense of his achievement in Europe. And when I watched people come up to him in the synagogue I saw by the manner in which they addressed him that his success was the common knowledge of our entire community.

My mother had lost her thinness. I had not thought her capable of putting on weight. But her body had filled, and though the thin lines of her face had remained and the cheekbones were still high, I could now feel the flesh on her once delicately boned fingers. Her eyes glowed; she seemed luminous; her years with my father had returned her to her young world of hope and fulfilled dreams. And on occasion I would hear between her and my father words with private meanings and see them exchange bedroom glances.

My father's attitude to my work had undergone a quiet change. He lived now upon a mountain of achievement that gave him the strength to be indifferent about my art and no longer to see it as a threat. He regarded me as if from a distance and disliked me without rage.

He came into my room one night, a few weeks after we had settled back into the apartment, and said, "Asher, your mother showed me some of the articles written about you. Are those art magazines important?"

"If you're an artist, they're important."

"What does the expression 'Picassoid forms' mean?"

"The shapes that Picasso creates in his art."

"I didn't like what that man wrote."

"I didn't either, Papa."

"It was strange to see your name attacked with such cruelty. Were you upset?"

"Yes."

"He was very cruel."

"We have different views about art."

"Goyim take art very seriously, Asher."

"So do many Jews."

We regarded each other for a moment. Then he said, "I'm glad the critics like what you do, Asher. I'm glad you didn't shame us."

My mother asked me the next morning as we walked together along the parkway, "When will your next show be, Asher?"

"A year from January."

"Will there be paintings of nudes?"

"Yes."

She was silent.

"Why, Mama?"

"Your father wants to see it. But he won't go if there are nudes."

We took our separate trains. She traveled to New York University, where she taught Russian affairs. I traveled to Brooklyn College, where I majored in sociology and studied Russian. I had decided to major in sociology. It was a safe subject and would not interfere with my painting.

She came into my room that night as I was reading an article in a French art magazine about a recent Picasso exhibition in Paris, and said, "Asher, may I interrupt you?"

I put down the magazine.

"Asher, your father asked me to talk to you." She looked uncomfortable. "Do you know the Zalkowitz family?"

"No."

"They live on President Street near your Uncle Yitzchok. Reb Zalkowitz is in the Diamond Exchange in Manhattan."

I said nothing. She seemed very uncomfortable.

"They have a daughter," she said.

I stared at her. Then I laughed, suddenly and loudly.

"Asher. Please." She looked hurt. Pink spots appeared on her high cheeks. She turned and went from the room.

I stopped laughing. After a moment, I found myself trembling with dread.

My father said to me in the kitchen the next morning, "Reb Zalkowitz is a fine and generous man."

"I'm sure he is."

"Asher, isn't it time?" He said it gently.

"No," I said. "No."

He was quiet a moment. Then he said, "Drink your juice, Asher. All the vitamins will go out of it."

I sat in the living room with my mother one night in November. My father was at a staff meeting. It was raining outside. I could hear the rain thudding heavily against the window. My mother was at her table alongside the window, bent over a pile of student papers. She wore glasses now for her reading.

I saw her look up and gaze out the window. The blind had been drawn but the slats were partly open and we could see through them to the glitter of lights in the wet street below.

"In Paris when it used to rain, it was the worst time of the year," she murmured. She looked at me and smiled. "I've waited at the windows of almost half the cities of the world for your father. I'm used to it now. What are you reading?"

I told her. She looked back out the window.

"He was a great writer," she murmured. "Stalin killed him, too. And he wasn't a Jew." She looked at me again. "Where did you get the book?"

"One of my professors."

She nodded. "Asher, when you were very young your father used to worry that you were retarded because you weren't learning to read and write as quickly as others. I used to tell him you would learn well only those things that interested you. What is the other book you have there?"

"It's about the Russian Constructivists. Russian artists."

"Asher?"

"Yes, Mama."

"Asher, I don't want to interfere in your work. But your father asked me to talk to you."

I looked at her and waited.

"I'm embarrassed to ask you again, Asher."

Still I waited.

"Asher, will you have paintings of nudes in your next exhibition?"

"I don't know, Mama. The next exhibition is more than a year away."

She was silent. Then she said, "I want you and your

father to be friends, Asher. Please. That means a great deal to me."

My father came into my room the following night and said, "I asked the Rebbe why he insisted that you study French and Russian. He said he thought it would be helpful to you."

"It has been."

"Yes? How?"

"There are good books about art in French and Russian."

His face stiffened.

He said to me the next morning at breakfast, "Asher, were you planning to go anywhere special next summer?"

"I haven't been planning anything yet for next summer."

"Your mother and I thought you might spend a week or two with us in the Berkshires."

"I think I'll be painting all summer. I have the show in January."

"The show," he murmured, rubbing the side of his face. "The show."

"Aryeh," my mother said gently. "Please."

He said to me one evening, in the course of a long conversation, "Asher, when a painter thinks of a painting is it the same thing as when a writer thinks of a book?"

"Yes, with some painters. They're literary painters. I think that's bad painting."

"How do you paint, Asher?"

"I paint my feelings. I paint how I see and feel about the world. I express my feelings in shapes and colors and lines. But I paint a painting, not a story."

"You paint your feelings?"

"Yes."

"Sometimes feelings are dangerous, Asher. Sometimes they are from the sitra achra."

I looked at him.

"Sometimes feelings should be concealed and not let out in the open."

"Some people can't conceal their feelings, Papa."

"Who?"

"Some people."

"Such people can be dangerous, Asher."

"Yes."

"I'm trying to understand you, Asher. But it's very difficult."

I said to Jacob Kahn, "How do you explain a man who has a master's degree in political science, has traveled through half the world, has lived in Europe for years, and doesn't understand the first thing about painting?"

"Asher Lev, there are professors of art who do not understand the first thing about painting."

"I'm talking about my father."

"I know whom you are talking about. Why should your father understand painting? From a yeshiva education you expect a man to understand painting? From a yeshiva education you get a case of aesthetic blindness."

"I have a yeshiva education."

"Asher Lev, you took from your yeshiva only the things that didn't interfere with your art. You are a freak. They could not give you a case of aesthetic blindness. They would have had to kill you to do that."

"My father has a college education and a master's in political science."

"So? He has a master's in political science. So? Asher Lev, I know your father. I have talked with him about art. He will appreciate a pretty calendar picture of Abraham and the angels or Rebecca at the well. But he would not want his son to dedicate his life to making such pictures. He certainly would not want his son to dedicate his life to making the kind of pictures his son is actually making. I personally am acquainted with two professors of history, one professor of Talmud, a mathematician, two professors of Bible, a politician, and the president of a great corporation who are afflicted with aesthetic blindness and feel the same way as your father. Why are you so surprised about your father? Please. I am tired of talking about your father. I would like you to keep your problems with your father out of my studio. You make a fog in the air with those problems. Now, you were explaining to me what you did in this painting. Tell me again about your concept of unity and shape."

Between terms, I flew to Chicago with Jacob Kahn for a Matisse exhibition. My father came into my room the night I returned and said, "You didn't tell me you would fly to Chicago today."

"I didn't think it mattered."

"You didn't think it mattered? A trip to Chicago doesn't matter?"

"I'm not a child, Papa."

"It has nothing to do with your being a child. I might have had a message for you to deliver."

I stared at him.

"There are Ladover in Chicago. I might have wanted you to take something for me."

I did not understand what he was saying.

"Asher, was it worth a trip to Chicago to see that man's paintings?"

"Matisse is one of the greatest painters of the century, Papa."

"It's expensive to fly to Chicago to see paintings."

"I have the money, Papa."

"I know you have the money, Asher."

"I'm spending it on things that are important to me."

"It won't hurt you to do something on your trips that is important to us. Next time you travel, please let me know."

A week later, I told him about a trip I would be taking to Minneapolis for a Giacometti exhibit. He had never heard of Giacometti. He gave me an envelope containing a letter from the Rebbe. The plane landed in a snowstorm. A man walked quickly over to me as I came out of the jet passenger tunnel. He wore a dark-brown coat and a dark-brown hat and looked to be in his late twenties. He had a black beard and spoke unaccented English.

"Excuse me. Are you Asher Lev?"

"Yes."

He told me his name. I handed him the envelope. He put it into an inside pocket. "I'd offer you a lift, but I'm not going into town." He walked away quickly.

"Were there any problems?" my father asked when I returned.

"No."

"Did he give you a message for me?"

"No."

"Did he say anything?"

"No. What was in the letter, Papa?"

"A message from the Rebbe."

"What kind of a message?"

"The man you met is the head of our yeshiva in Minneapolis. His wife is ill. The Rebbe sent her a blessing. The Rebbe likes such things to be delivered personally."

During the spring vacation, I traveled with Jacob Kahn to a Braque exhibition in Boston. We were met at the airport by a tall thin man with a dark beard and a dark suit and hat.

"Asher Lev?" He spoke with a New England accent.

"Yes."

He told me his name. I gave him an envelope and he walked away.

Jacob Kahn smiled and shook his head. "Asher Lev, I wondered how long it would be."

"The Rebbe believes in the personal touch."

"It is part of his greatness. We have a clever Rebbe."

"How is it he doesn't have you delivering messages?"

"I never tell them my travel plans. You think I have nothing else to do but be part of the Rebbe's private courier service? Come, let us go see Braque. I may have watched him do some of the paintings they are showing."

My mother said to me early in May, "Where will you spend the summer, Asher?"

"In Provincetown."

"Your father and I will be in the Berkshires."

I was quiet.

"Can you spend some time with us this summer, Asher?"

"I need all my time for painting, Mama."

"Two weeks, Asher."

"Would Papa let me paint?"

"I don't know."

"I need every minute, Mama."

"Your father is trying very hard to understand you, Asher. It would help if we could all be together this summer."

I said nothing.

"Asher," she said. "Asher. You have no idea what it's like to be standing between you and your father."

I spent the summer in Provincetown with Jacob and Tanya Kahn and returned with paintings and a tan and without my sidecurls. My father said nothing to me about the sidecurls. In a curious way, he seemed almost relieved. He himself wore sidecurls because his father had worn them. He had never made much of an issue about them with me. Now he seemed relieved by my tacit indication that the sidecurls were as far as I intended to go, for I had retained my beard and the ritual fringes beneath my shirt.

My mother said to me during one of our morning walks to the subway, "I'm ashamed to ask you again, Asher."

"I don't know yet, Mama."

"Why do there have to be nudes? There are so many other great paintings you have."

"They're important to me as an artist."

"I understand why others paint nudes. But I don't understand why you must paint nudes and exhibit the paintings."

"I paint and exhibit them for the same reason others paint and exhibit them."

"You'll hurt your father, Asher. He won't come."

I was quiet.

"I wish you wouldn't do it, Asher."

"I may have to, Mama."

"Why will you have to?"

"I'm an artist, Mama."

"I don't understand," she said. "I only understand that you'll hurt your father."

Jacob Kahn and Anna Schaeffer came over to my uncle's house one evening to help me choose the paintings. They chose almost everything I had. I hesitated over the nudes.

"What is wrong?" Jacob Kahn said.

"Nothing."

"Our artist has become shy, Anna."

"Our artist cannot afford to be shy, Jacob. Our artist is an important figure in the art world. Our artist is an important investment. Our artist is being given a very big show. There are artists in this world twice his age who would cut off their painting arms for such a show. We will ignore our artist's shyness and take the nudes. You understand we are taking them merely to exploit you, Asher Lev. It is only an accident that they happen to be magnificent paintings."

I let them take the nudes.

The show was in January. It lasted three weeks. My parents did not come. When it was over, I stared at the walls and was sick with a new dread.

"My God, they're swallowing up my world faster than I can paint it. They even took my fishermen."

Jacob Kahn said nothing.

"What am I going to do?"

Anna Schaeffer said soberly, "Jacob, walk with him."

"What am I going to do?" I had never felt such emptiness and horror and dread. "I don't want to repeat myself."

Jacob Kahn took me outside. We walked along Madison Avenue. It was a cold windy day. The streets were filled with old snow.

"Your parents did not come," Jacob Kahn said.

"No."

"That was the business with the nudes."

"Yes."

"Asher Lev, you have been too good a student." He

was silent a moment. The wind blew against his white hair and mustache and dark beret and against the raised collar of his coat. "But you were right to let Anna have the nudes. They are fine works. Even our friend of the Picassoid forms thought they were fine."

I looked at him and was quiet.

"Our friend of the Picassoid forms now thinks you have surpassed your master. It is in the nature of critics to be fickle."

I said nothing. The cold wind stung my eyes.

"There are distinct disadvantages to reaching eighty," Jacob Kahn said, talking into the wind and not looking at me. "But it is better to reach it than not to reach it. I think I will try for ninety. That old Spaniard is going to make ninety. Why not this old Jew? But even if I make it I will probably be disappointed." He was quiet. We walked together along the winter street. Then he stopped and turned to me. "You will have to find other worlds, Asher Lev. I told you once about the happy years. There will never again be such years. You understand now, you will always have to find new worlds or you will die as an artist. Here is your subway." He held out his hand. "Goodbye, Asher Lev." He turned and walked away.

I called Tanya Kahn the next day. Jacob Kahn was ill, she said. No, she did not know how long it would last this time. I called her a few days later. He was still not well, she said.

Anna Schaeffer told me during a phone conversation the following day that Jacob Kahn had requested an exhibition of his paintings and sculptures for the fall and was working furiously in his studio.

"The master is jealous of the apprentice," she said into the phone. "It is good for artists to be jealous. It is especially good for Anna Schaeffer."

That Friday night, I sat with my parents at our dining-room table. We were between courses and had just finished singing one of the Shabbos zemiros. My father sat with his eyes closed. There was a long silence. My mother said quietly, "Will you have another exhibition soon, Asher?" She used the word "exhibition" because my father did not like the word "show."

"Not for a while. Not for another two years, probably."

"Why so long?"

"It isn't long, Mama. I can't keep grinding out paintings. I have to think of what I want to do next."

My father opened his eyes. "Paint more naked women," he said.

"Aryeh," my mother said. "Please."

I felt the blood in my face. My father tugged slowly at his beard.

"Asher, do you know what it's like to have people I have worked with for years come over and ask me why my son paints naked women?" He spoke quietly and with pain in his voice.

"They aren't naked women, Papa. They're nudes."

His dark eyes brooded. He rubbed the side of his face. "This isn't Shabbos talk," he said. "We shouldn't be talking about these things at a Shabbos table."

"I'll bring in the dessert," my mother said.

"There's a difference between naked women and nudes, Papa."

My father looked at me intently. He turned to my mother. "Rivkeh, did you know that there's a difference between a naked woman and a nude?" Pink spots appeared on my mother's high cheekbones. She did not reply. My father turned to me. "Asher, I'm a reasonably intelligent man. Tell me what the difference is between a naked woman and a nude."

"A naked woman is a woman without clothes. A nude is an artist's personal vision of a body without clothes."

"Is such a personal vision important in your art?"

"That's what art is, Papa. It's a person's private vision expressed in aesthetic forms."

His dark eyes narrowed. My mother glanced at him, then looked at me.

"Yes," he said. "I understand. But why do you have to have personal visions about naked women, Asher?

I've seen your paintings. I don't understand your style of painting, but at least I didn't find them offensive. Why do you have to paint and display to the public things that are offensive?"

"They aren't offensive to people who understand art."

"They're offensive to people like me, Asher. I'm asking you why you have to paint that way."

"Because I'm an artist."

"Asher, look at me. I'm not a fool. I speak to senators and governors. I sit behind a desk that helps the Rebbe to run almost half the Ladover machinery in the world. I have a bachelor's and a master's in political science. Explain it to me so that I can understand it. Why do *you* have to paint and display nudes?"

"Because I'm part of a tradition, Papa. Mastery of the art form of the nude is very important to that tradition. Every important artist who ever lived drew or painted the nude."

"Art is a tradition."

"Yes."

"I understand. But why is the nude so important in this tradition?"

"Because it has always been part of that tradition."

"Who began it?"

"The Greeks."

"Ah," he said. "The Greeks. Our old friends, the Greeks. All right, Asher. I can understand a little better now why you paint nudes. Why do you display them?"

"I don't want to sit in a room painting for myself. I want to communicate what I do. And I want critics to know I can do it."

"Even if it offends people?"

"Everything offends someone."

"Even if it offends your father?"

I did not respond.

"There is such a matter as respect for your father. That's also a tradition."

"I respect you, Papa. But I can't respect your aesthetic blindness."

"Aesthetic blindness? Do you hear, Rivkeh? Aesthetic blindness." My mother looked slowly from my father to me, then back to my father. "An interesting concept. Aesthetic blindness. And what about moral blindness, Asher?"

"I'm not hurting anybody, Papa."

"One day you will, Asher. This will lead you to the sitra achra."

"No."

"Asher, if you had a choice between aesthetic blindness and moral blindness, which would you choose?"

I said nothing.

"I'm warning you, Asher. One day you'll hurt someone with this kind of attitude. And then you'll be doing the work of the sitra achra."

You're hurting me now with your attitude, I thought. But I remained silent.

"I'll bring in the dessert," my mother said quietly.

"Not yet, Rivkeh. Let's sing some more zemiros first. Nudes and Greeks are not Shabbos talk. Let's sing zemiros and bring the Shabbos back to the table."

He said to me a few days later, "I've been reading what the critics are writing about your last exhibition. I pride myself that I understand the English language. But I don't understand what your critics are talking about."

"It's a technical language, Papa. Doesn't political science have a technical language?"

He asked me to explain some of the concepts. We talked for a long time about the two-dimensional surface of the canvas, about illusion, depth, planar structure, points, areas, lines, dispersive and progressive shapes, surface control, color separation, values, contrasts, accents, matrix. I began to lose him somewhere around planar structure, and by surface control it was hopeless. He listened attentively to what I was saying. But there was nothing in his intellectual or emotional equipment to which he could connect my words. He possessed no frames of reference for such concepts. He could not even ask intelligent questions. My world of aesthetics was as bewildering to him as his insatiable need for travel was to me.

We spent days discussing those concepts and came slowly to understand how futile it all was. He stopped talking to me about my painting. In the weeks that followed, he began to react to my presence in the apartment with a brooding silence.

My mother said to me one day in April, "Is Jacob Kahn well?"

"As far as I know, yes."

"You haven't been going to see him."

"No."

"Will you see him again soon?"

"I don't know."

She looked at me. I thought I heard her sigh.

I was in the living room one night that week when I heard my father's voice come from their bedroom. "I've tried, Rivkeh. But it's impossible. What do you want from me?"

I stared out the window at the street. There were young leaves on the trees. But the street seemed colder and darker now than it had ever been before. I turned away from the window and from the bleak parkway below.

Florence is a gift, Jacob Kahn had said.

In the first week of May, my father flew to Chicago for the Rebbe. It was his first lengthy trip since he and my mother had returned from Europe. Ten days later, he flew to Denver.

My mother stood gazing out the window of the living room. "You know, I thought I had gotten used to it. How many windows have I waited at? But I'm not used to it at all."

"Mama?"

"Yes, Asher."

"I want to go to Europe this summer. After I graduate."

She turned slowly from the window to look at me. Her face was pale and her eyes were dark.

"To Europe?" she said softly.

"I think it's very important to me that I go to Europe now."

She turned back to the window and was silent a long time. Then she said very quietly, "It's strange, Asher, how a person can do something for half a lifetime and still not get used to it. I thought I was used to it. But I was fooling myself."

I talked to my father when he returned from Denver very late that night.

"It's a fine idea." He seemed elated. "Where will you go?"

"To Florence."

"We can give you the names of people to see in Florence. It's a fine idea. Isn't it a fine idea, Rivkeh?"

"Yes."

"I thought I would also go to Rome and Paris."

"We can give you the names of people in Rome and Paris, too. Remember the Levis in Rome, Rivkeh?"

"Yes."

"Remember they took us to that hill and the man there tried to sell us statues because he thought I was Greek Orthodox?"

"I remember."

"I'll make a list of all the places where you can eat without worry. And I'll give you the names of people you can call. Europe is something I happen to know about. Isn't that right, Rivkeh?"

"Yes, Aryeh."

Florence is a gift, Jacob Kahn had said.

THIRTEEN

I remember the river and the shadows of the bridges on the dark surface of the water. The river ran dark even in sunlight, except along its deep banks where the reflections of the stone walls and houses were the color of summer sand and rippled faintly in the lazy flow of water. In a little more than a year, that river would rage and flood the city and destroy things so precious to me that I would weep into the silent mornings of Paris. But that summer the river was gentle, a dark cool benign presence beneath the hot Florence sun, and I would cross it in the morning to enter the old city and cross it again in the evenings to return to the room where I lived.

The room was on the third floor of a four-story hotel that stood along the southern bank of the river. It had a bed, a chair, a table, and a washroom. The window looked across the river and the city to the hill villages and mountains beyond. In the early mornings, with the city still cool from the night, I would come from the hotel and walk along narrow streets to the house of an old woman whose name my father had given me. There, in a room filled with the furniture of a time long before I was born, I would eat the breakfast she prepared for me. She was in her seventies, a widow, from a Leghorn family dating back five hundred years. During the war, she had been concealed in the hills by Florentines and Sienèse. Her husband had been killed in the German retreat. Now she lived alone with her furniture and her memories and an Italian translation of the Book of

Psalms which she was forever reading. I ate her breakfasts and suppers. Lunch consisted of iced tea or a Coke from a paper cup in a shop or café in the city.

After breakfast, I would walk across a stone bridge into the old city and go through shaded narrow streets heavy with tourists and traffic and lined with shops. All through the month of July, I walked the streets of that city. From a Berlitz grammar, I taught myself tourist Italian. Walking through Renaissance streets and squares, feeling against my feet the stone stairways and battlements of the Palazzo Vecchio and the Bargello, feeling against my face the cool damp faintly musty interiors of the Santa Croce and the Santa Trinità, gazing at the fresco of the *Last Judgment* on the Duomo and at the chancel beneath the huge dome where one Medici was wounded and another was killed—walking and tasting the sudden sun and shade of its streets, the dimness of its churches, the wealth of its galleries, the echoing savagery of its palaces and squares, I learned of the city's beauty and blood, of the Ghibellines and Guelphs, of the Pitti, the Strozzi, the Pazzi and the Medici, of Savonarola, of Dante and Machiavelli, of Giotto and da Vinci and Raphael and Michelangelo. Florence was a gift.

In the late afternoons, I would go back across the river along the covered Ponte Vecchio and gaze into the gold- and silversmith shops and watch the faces of merchants and shoppers and feel the coolness of the air beneath the roof of the bridge. I would walk the narrow streets to the house of the old woman and eat my supper and return to my room on the third floor of the hotel. From the window, I would watch the evening and the night come slowly across the city; watch the golden hue of the sun over the hills; watch the hills change hues and go slowly misty and soft; watch the darkness come into the sky and the lights of the city come to life in the slow falling of night. Those hours by that window in the evenings were of a loveliness I have never again felt in my life—hours in a Renaissance city lived by a man born in a Brooklyn street, a man wearing a red beard and ritual fringes and a fisherman's cap.

I went to the Piazza del Duomo often in those weeks to see the Michelangelo *Pietà* and the Vasari fresco and the Ghiberti East Doors of the baptistery. I carried my sketchbook and drawing pencils wherever I went, but I remember that the first time I saw the Michelangelo *Pietà* in the Duomo I could not draw it. It was the fifth day of July. I stared at its Romanesque and Gothic contours, at the twisted arm and bent head, at the circle formed by Jesus and the two Marys, at the vertical of Nicodemus—I stared at the geometry of the stone and felt the stone luminous with strange suffering and sorrow. I was an observant Jew, yet that block of stone moved through me like a cry, like the call of seagulls over morning surf, like—like the echoing blasts of the shofar sounded by the Rebbe. I do not mean to blaspheme. My frames of reference have been formed by the life I have lived. I do not know how a devout Christian reacts to that *Pietà*. I was only able to relate it to elements in my own lived past. I stared at it. I walked slowly around it. I do not remember how long I was there that first time. When I came back out into the brightness of the crowded square, I was astonished to discover that my eyes were wet.

I returned the next day and studied it again. Then I began to draw it. I drew its rhomboid contour. I drew each of its four people separately. I drew the heads separately. I drew the twisted arm. People stood behind me, watching. A long time later, I stopped drawing and walked back through the cool interior of the cathedral and out into the hot sun-flooded square.

In the square, between the cathedral and the baptistery, there was a traffic safety zone, a small island surrounded by a river of buses and cars. Often a man would stand in that safety zone feeding the pigeons of the square. He was an old man with a lined face and shrunken gums. He wore torn baggy trousers and a long-sleeved shirt. He stood in the island with his arms outstretched, palms turned upward. There was birdseed in his palms and the pigeons flocked to him, using him as they would a telephone pole or a tree, sitting on his arms and shoulders and waiting for a chance at the seed. He stood very still, smiling toothlessly, and tourists would snap his picture and drop a coin into the small cardboard box at his feet.

I came out of the Duomo that day after having spent hours drawing the *Pietà,* and there was the man with the pigeons on his arms. I watched him for a while, then opened my sketchbook and began to draw him. He reminded me vaguely of the fishermen of Provincetown. I felt people watching. I drew him quickly. "Hey, he's good," I heard someone say. When I was done, I closed the sketchbook and walked away.

I returned to the Duomo the following day, but the man with the pigeons was not there. I went into the cathedral and was there the rest of the morning, drawing the *Pietà.* When I came out of the cathedral, the square was hot with sunlight, and the man was there again, his arms covered with pigeons. I watched him for a while, then had some iced tea and began walking through the streets.

I walked to the Accademia. It was a long walk and I stopped often on the way and drew the people and the streets of the city. Inside the Accademia, I walked slowly through the long tapestry-lined hall to the *David.* I stared at it and after a moment I walked away and leaned against a wall.

I did not draw it. I leaned against the wall and looked at it, then walked close to it and looked at it, then walked slowly around it. It stood bathed in the sunlight that poured down upon it through the dome overhead, a white marble giant that dominated the space around it and was its own frozen dimension. I looked and I did not draw, and finally I came away and went into the street.

I began to walk quickly. I came to a narrow street and rested for a while in the shade of stone houses. The street was crowded. I felt tired. I walked a while longer, then took a cab back to my room. I lay down on the bed in my clothes and slept. After about an hour, I woke feeling hot and faintly dizzy. I washed my face in cold water and went back outside. I walked across the Ponte Vecchio and wandered about the city. I went past the Uffizi and found it had closed at four o'clock. It was almost six. I went quickly back across the bridge to the house of the old woman. She served me supper, then sat in an old leather chair reading from her Book of Psalms. I watched her for a while, then did a rapid drawing of her. She did not see me.

The next day, I drew her again. I drew her looking younger this time, sitting with the Book of Psalms on her lap. In my room, I looked closely at the drawing and found it vaguely resembled my mother. I stared at the drawing, then tore it from my sketchbook and threw it away.

The following morning, I returned to the Accademia and stood for more than an hour drawing the *David*. I drew the head, with the eyes that reflected the decision to enter the arena of power; I drew the huge veined hands that would soon kill; I drew the shouldered sling being lifted in preparation for the delivery of death. The little man with the broken nose had created this sculpture in an act of awesome rebellion against his tradition and his teacher. Other *David*s I had seen were small in size and represented David after the battle. This *David* was a giant and represented the decision to enter the battle. The little Italian had effected a spatial and temporal shift that had changed the course of art.

I spent almost the entire morning in the Accademia drawing the *David*. Then I walked to the Duomo. The man with the pigeons was in the square. I drew the bent head of the *Pietà*. I spent the afternoon in the Uffizi.

That night, my mythic ancestor returned after a lengthy absence. But he was less thunderous than he had ever been before and did not wake me from my sleep.

One evening in the last week of July, I came into the house of the old woman and found a man waiting for me. He wore dark trousers, a white open-collar short-sleeved shirt, and a dark hat. He was tall and thin and black-bearded and looked to be in his thirties.

"Asher Lev?"

"Yes."

"Your father told me how to reach you." He spoke in Yiddish and had a deep nasal voice. "I am Dov Lieberman."

"Hello, Dov Lieberman."

We shook hands. His palm was moist.

"You are leaving for Rome the day after tomorrow?" he asked.

"Yes."

"By train?"

"Yes."

"What train?"

I told him.

"I wonder if I might ask a favor." He produced a small white envelope. "Someone will meet you at the station."

"What is it?"

"A letter."

"There is no mail service in Italy?"

He smiled. "It is sometimes untrustworthy."

I took the envelope. He thanked me.

"You are a Ladover?" I asked.

"Yes."

"There are other Ladover in Florence?"

"Not yet. I only arrived two days ago from Rome."

"Where are you from originally?"

"Leningrad."

We shook hands again and he left.

I spent the next morning in the Duomo with the *Pietà*. In the early afternoon, I took a cab to the synagogue; it seemed an exquisite part of the loveliness of the city. I spent the rest of the afternoon in the Uffizi, then had supper and returned to my room.

That night, I sat at the window and looked out at the lights of the city and found I could not stop thinking of the *Pietà* and the *David*. The next day, on the swiftly moving train to Rome, I drew the *Pietà* from memory, and discovered that the woman supporting the twisted arm of the crucified Jesus bore a faint resemblance to my mother. I stared at the drawing in horror, and destroyed it.

A bearded man in a dark suit and hat met me in the Rome station. He was short and looked to be in his early forties.

"Asher Lev?"

"Yes."

"Sholom aleichem."

We shook hands. He told me his name. I handed him the envelope.

"You are staying here long?" He spoke in Yiddish.

"A week."

"If you have time, come and visit." He gave me his name and phone number. "I will show you the yeshiva your father built. You know where you may eat?"

"Yes."

"Call me if you have time. Goodbye."

He disappeared into the crowd inside the huge terminal.

I spent the week touring Rome. The city seemed glutted with tourists. I saw the Arch of Titus and the Colosseum. I saw the stone ruins of the Forum and the stone monuments of the new city. I saw the towering Baroque magnificence of St. Peter's. What had Jacob Kahn once said about the Baroque? I could not remember. The Sistine Chapel seemed a multilingual mob scene. But I looked at the ceiling and the walls, and the noise faded. There, in the *Last Judgment*, was the hell I had once drawn in an act of vengeance. How long ago had that been? I could not remember.

I called him on my last day in Rome. He came in an old Fiat to my hotel and took me on a long ride through narrow streets and old neighborhoods.

"How old is the yeshiva?" I asked him.

"Five years."

"How many students do you have?"

"One hundred and eight."

"How many students did you have five years ago?"

"Seventeen."

I looked at him.

"Your father did it. It was creation out of nothing."

Somewhere on a crowded side street in the middle of the city, he showed me a four-story building with a beige-colored façade. Inside were classrooms, offices, a small social hall, and a synagogue.

"Six years ago, it was a hotel."

"Who raised the money to buy it?"

"Your father. I helped when I came."

"You are not originally from Rome."

"No."

"From where are you?"

"Kiev."

"Do you have anything you want me to deliver in Paris? I am flying to Paris tomorrow."

"No. Thank you. I have nothing." We stood outside on the crowded street, looking up at the yeshiva building. "Your father did it all," the man said. "He is a remarkable person, your father."

I flew to Paris the next morning. During the flight, I drew the *Pietà* again from memory, and omitted the figure of the man behind the dead Jesus. I could not understand why I felt the need to remove that figure. I stared curiously at the drawing and found its structure distasteful. I tore it up. I was strangely tired. I took a cab from the airport to the hotel, checked in, and lay down on the bed.

I woke in the night in the dark room and felt myself entombed in suffocating dread. I was bathed in sweat. I groped for the light. The sudden brightness hurt my eyes. I sat on the edge of the bed and realized I had fallen asleep in my clothes. I got into pajamas and washed and went back to my bed. I was immediately asleep.

He came then, smashing through the tall forests, looking mountainous with anger. I saw him push apart the giant trees and come bearing down upon me, dark-bearded and dark-visaged, thundering his rage. I felt myself screaming in my sleep and I came awake and stared into the darkness and, for a long moment of horror, thought I had gone blind. Then I saw the faint slits of light around the curtains of the window and I got out of the bed and went to the bathroom. I could not sleep. I pulled aside the curtains and peered through the window. I saw mist and gray morning light and tall ghostly spires in the distance. I stood by the window and watched the morning move slowly into the sky and across the Paris streets.

I had slept almost half a day and a full night. But I was still tired. I dressed and prayed the morning service and came out of the hotel. I went up the side street to the Boulevard des Italiens and walked slowly along the boulevard to the restaurant where my father had told me I could eat. During breakfast, I drew on the tablecloth the contour of the Duomo *Pietà* with the vertical figure eliminated. I made the two side figures into bearded males, giving them the same robes as those worn by the Marys. I looked at the drawing. The dread was gone. I had no strength left for fighting. I would have to let it lead me now or there would be deeper and deeper layers of the wearying darkness. And I dreaded that darkness more than I did anything I might do with canvas and paint. I finished my breakfast, left the drawing on the tablecloth, and came out onto the boulevard. It was still cool. The street was crowded now with people and traffic. I returned to the hotel.

There was a message for me with a name and a telephone number. I made the call from my room, then left the hotel and walked up the Avenue de l'Opéra to the Louvre.

At five that afternoon, I stood at the bookstand near the Pont des Arts and watched the thick flow of cars along the Quai du Louvre. It was hot and the sky was pale blue and hazy. Boats moved up and down the Seine. Over to the right, the towers and spire of Nôtre Dame jutted mistily into the sky.

A small Peugeot disengaged itself from the stream of traffic and stopped at the curb. Brakes screeched and horns sounded. The man in the car motioned to me frantically. I saw a gendarme start toward the car. I climbed inside. The car pulled away quickly and rejoined the traffic. The gendarme stood at the curb, pointing to his head with a finger.

"Sholom aleichem," the man said. "Avraham Cutler." He was the administrative head of the yeshiva my father had established in Paris.

"Aleichem sholom. My name is Asher Lev."

"Welcome to Paris, Asher Lev." He spoke in Yiddish. "Your father gave you something for me?"

I handed him an envelope. He was in his forties, of average height, portly, and wore a dark suit, white shirt, and dark hat. He had pale-blue eyes and a dark beard. He put the envelope into a pocket.

"How is your father?" he asked.

"He is well, thank you."

"You know my father?"

"Of course. The mashpia."

"I have not seen him in over a year. How does he look?"

"Very well."

"We are driving to the yeshiva. We have about an hour until dinner. Is there any place you would like to go first?"

"Is Montmartre too far out of our way?"

"Where in Montmartre?"

I told him.

"It is only a little out of the way. We have time. What is this place?"

"The old studio of Picasso."

"Ah," he said, nodding. "I understand."

We drove through wide tree-lined boulevards and narrow side streets and over a sprawling cemetery.

"Montmartre," he said. He looked at me and smiled. "A Ladover makes a pilgrimage to the Bateau Lavoir. Interesting."

He lost his way and we had to ask for directions. His French was fluent. We drove through winding streets, then up a steep hill. At the top of the hill, he pulled the car over to the curb and turned off the motor.

"There," he said, and pointed. "Place Émile-Goudeau."

I crossed into the small cobblestone square and looked at the dilapidated building. It was only one story high on this side of the hill, old, flaked with peeling white paint. It had a scarred dark-green wooden door and gray-framed windows. On one side of it stood a three-story hotel. On the other side was a stone house partly concealed behind a tall tree and a wooden fence. A dark metal fountain with four female figures stood in the square. Pigeons and stray dogs moved lazily about the cobblestones. I stood in the square and with the blunt end of a pencil drew into the dust alongside a bench the contour of my mother's profile. I did not know why I felt the need to do that. I got back into the car and we drove away. A few years later, that building would be gutted by fire and only the side I had faced would remain. But that day it seemed the building would be around at least as long as the little Spanish man who had once painted inside it.

"You are doing more paintings?" Avraham Cutler asked.

"I am thinking about it."

"What does the Rebbe say about your paintings?"

"I have never asked him."

He looked at me and smiled knowingly. "Our Rebbe is a wise man."

We drove to a cream-colored four-story stone building on a wide tree-lined boulevard. He parked the car on the street and we came inside. I saw classrooms, offices, a dining room, a social hall, and a small gym.

"The social hall converts to a synagogue," he said.

"How many students do you have?"

"One hundred seventy-nine. They are all over sixteen. They live and eat here. Six years ago, there was nothing. This was an apartment house. You are welcome to eat here with us whenever you wish. We have a room, too, if you should need it."

"I have a room."

"Your father said you would be in Paris three weeks."

"I am not sure."

He looked at me.

"I may stay longer," I said.

"In that case, you are certainly welcome to live and eat with us."

I ate with them that evening. The dining room was crowded and noisy. The yeshiva ran all through the year and was not affected by the summer. I was introduced over and over again as Asher Lev, son of Reb Aryeh Lev. They all knew my father.

Later, he drove me back to my hotel.

"You are visiting the museums?"

"Yes."

"It is a beautiful city. Where did you learn your French?"

I told him. He smiled knowingly. "Yes," he said. "The Rebbe is a very wise man."

He called me the next morning. A Ladover was coming in from Israel on his way to the Rebbe and would be giving a lecture in the yeshiva on Wednesday night. Was I interested in attending? I was interested.

The lecturer was tall and thin, with a pale-blond beard and delicate hands. I introduced myself to him after the lecture.

"Ah," he murmured. "The painter."

"You know my father?"

"Who does not know Reb Aryeh Lev?"

I produced a white envelope. "Could you give this to him?"

"Of course." He put the envelope into a pocket. "You are working on more pictures?"

"Yes."

The following week, someone left a letter for me with Avraham Cutler. I went down to the yeshiva by cab and picked it up. It was from my parents. They did not understand why I wanted to remain in Europe, but they respected my wishes. I was not a child. My father gave me his blessings.

A few days later, I received a letter at the hotel from my mother. She missed me. She wished I had not felt it necessary to remain in Europe. She wished me all that I wished for myself, and informed me that my father was once again traveling regularly for the Rebbe.

I rented a three-room furnished apartment two blocks from the yeshiva and converted one of the rooms to a studio. I discovered an art-supply store on a nearby boulevard and asked Avraham Cutler to help me haul canvases and paints and an easel to the apartment.

"You are settling in for ten years?" he said, puffing up the narrow wooden stairs under a load of canvas stretchers.

"For one or two."

"In that case, you should meet some of our families. It is not healthy to be always alone."

The apartment was on the top floor of a five-floor walk-up. I could see the roofs and chimneys of the adjoining buildings. The windows of the apartment were huge, extending almost from floor to ceiling. They were covered with curtains and drapes.

By the first of September of that year, I had begun a new painting—the old man with the pigeons in the Piazza del Duomo. I wrote Anna Schaeffer to let her know I was alive and well and working in Paris. She wrote me back immediately. Now I was a real painter, she said. Asher Lev in Paris. It had a ring to it. Asher Lev in Paris. I should stay away from cafés and night life and paint pictures that would make us rich. I should stay away from the artists of the New School of Paris; they were timid bores. I should paint and paint and make her happy and rich. She did not mention Jacob Kahn.

Four weeks later, on a day when I could feel the cold of the fall begin to settle into the city, I received a package from her in the mail. I opened it and saw a new dark-blue beret. There was a card: "From an impossi-

ble old lady to an impossible young man. Affectionate-
ly, Anna."

I put the beret into a drawer and continued to wear
my fisherman's cap.

I remember the winter rain and the way it washed
across the roofs of the houses and stained the beige fa-
çades of the walls. The house stood near the head of a
steep narrow cobblestone street, and from the windows
of the apartment I could see the rain flow in swift rivulets along the stone curbs, then follow the turn of the
curbs into the wide boulevard below. It was cold in the
rain but I did not have to walk in it often. I lived and
painted in the apartment; I ate in the yeshiva's dining
room, prayed in its synagogue, and attended an occasional lecture on Hasidus. Sometimes, gazing out the
window at one of the blue windless days of winter, I
would feel the need to leave the apartment. Then I
would walk beneath the chestnut trees of the city's boulevards or take the Métro to the Louvre or to the Jeu de
Paume near the Place de la Concorde. I did not stay
away from the artists of the New School of Paris, as
some call it; and I did not find them to be bores.

I had stretched my own canvases. They stood stacked
against a wall of the room I had turned into a studio. In
the early morning, I would pray and eat breakfast in the
yeshiva, then go back along the boulevard and up the
steep street to the house. There would be schoolchildren
on the street then and men pulling away from the curb
in little cars and shopkeepers opening their stores. I
would climb the narrow stairs to my apartment and
come into the studio and stare at the white canvases
against the wall.

Weeks passed and became months. It rained. The
skies were dark often now. Few people walked the narrow street. The canvases remained bare.

Away from my world, alone in an apartment that offered me neither memories nor roots, I began to find old
and distant memories of my own, long buried by pain

and time and slowly brought to the surface now by the sight of waiting white canvases and by the winter emptiness of the small Parisian street. It was time now for that. I had painted my visible street until there was nothing left of it for me to put onto canvas. Now I would have to paint the street that could not be seen.

I remembered my mythic ancestor. He had never been too difficult to bring to memory. But now I could recall tales told to a wondering child about a Jew who had made a Russian nobleman rich by tending his estates. The nobleman was a despotic goy, a degenerate whose debaucheries grew wilder as he grew wealthier. The Jew, my mythic ancestor, made him wealthier. Serfs were on occasion slain by that nobleman during his long hours of drunken insanity, and once houses were set on fire by a wildly thrown torch and a village was burned. You see how a goy behaves, went the whispered word to the child. A Jew does not behave this way. But the Jew had made him wealthy, wondered the child. Is not the Jew also somehow to blame? The child had never given voice to that question. Now the man who had once been the child asked it again and wondered if the giving and the goodness and the journeys of that mythic ancestor might have been acts born in the memories of screams and burning flesh. A balance had to be given the world; the demonic had to be reshaped into meaning. Had a dream-haunted Jew spent the rest of his life sculpting form out of the horror of his private night?

I did not know. But I sensed it as truth.

I began to paint my mythic ancestor. Over and over again, I painted him now, in his wealth and his journeys, in the midst of fire and death and dreams, a weary Jew traveling to balance the world.

I remembered my grandfather, the scholar, the recluse, the dweller in the study halls of synagogues and academies of learning. What had transformed him from recluse and scholar to emissary for the Rebbe's father? Had the encounter with the journeying Ladover Hasid brought back to memory the journeys of his ancestor? I wondered how a journeying ancestor could suddenly transform a recluse into a journeying Hasid. Had something inarticulate been handed down from generation to generation that came to life in each individual at a time most appropriate to him?

I did not know. But I sensed it as truth.

I painted my grandfather. Over and over again, I painted him now, seated in dusty rooms with sacred books, traveling across endless Russian steppes, dead on a dark street with an axe in his skull, his journey incomplete.

Outside my window, there was snow. A cold wind blew through the boulevards and stripped the last dead leaves from the trees.

I remembered my father during my mother's illness. He had been as torn by her illness as by his inability to journey for the Rebbe. I had never been able to understand that torment. Now I wondered if journeying meant to him more than a way of bringing God into the world. Was journeying an unknowing act of atonement? In the dim past, a village had burned to the ground and people had died. The Gemorra teaches us that a man who slays another man slays not only one individual but all the children and children's children that individual might have brought into life. Traditions are born by the power of an initial thrust that hurls acts and ideas across the centuries. Had the death by fire of those individuals been such a thrust? Was my ancestor's act of atonement to extend through all the generations of our family line? Had he unwittingly transmitted the need for such an act to his children; had they transmitted it to their children?

I did not know. But I sensed it as truth.

I remembered my mother and the long quiet conversations between her and my father when I had been a child. Surely she had sensed the depth of his feelings about his journeys. She, too, had told me stories about my mythic ancestor. Had she somehow dimly perceived the true nature of my ancestor's journey? Then, perceiving it, had she joined her brother's incompleted task to my father's beginning journeys and thereby, without being fully aware of what she was doing, made possible the continuation of the line of atonement? Had I, with my need to give meaning to paper and canvas rather than to people and events, interrupted an act of eternal atonement?

I did not know.

Now I thought of my mother and began to sense something of her years of anguish. Standing between two different ways of giving meaning to the world, and at the same time possessed by her own fears and memories, she had moved now toward me, now toward my father, keeping both worlds of meaning alive, nourishing with her tiny being, and despite her torments, both me and my father. Paint pretty pictures, Asher, she had said. Make the world pretty. Show me your good drawings, Asher. Why have you stopped drawing? She had kept the gift alive during the dead years; and she had kept herself alive by picking up her dead brother's work and had kept my father alive by enabling him to resume his journeys. Trapped between two realms of meaning, she had straddled both realms, quietly feeding and nourishing them both, and herself as well. I could only dimly perceive such an awesome act of will. But I could begin to feel her torment now as she waited by our living-room window for both her husband and her son. What did she think of as she stood by the window? Of the phone call that had informed my father of her brother's death? Would she wait now in dread all the rest of her life, now for me, now for my father, now for us both—as she had once waited for me to return from a museum, as she had once waited for my father to return in a snowstorm? And I could understand her torment now; I could see her waiting endlessly with the fear that someone she loved would be brought to her dead. I could feel her anguish.

Then I found I could no longer paint and I walked the winter streets of the city and felt its coldness. There was snow and rain and the city lay bleak and spent beneath the dark skies. I wandered through museums and galleries. I walked the winding streets of Montmartre and peered through the misty windows of its shops and restaurants. I walked up the mountain of steps to the Sacré-Coeur and wandered through its awesome dimness. I remember that during all this walking and wandering letters went back and forth between me and my parents and between me and Anna Schaeffer. My father had fallen and hurt his leg, but was well now. Jacob Kahn's show had been very well received. My uncle was fine. Yudel Krinsky was fine. It was all vague. Even the walking and wandering was vague. I could not paint.

The rains ended. There were days of blue and warming air. One day, I sat in a café over a warm Coke around the corner from the Sacré-Coeur and found myself drawing the contour of the Duomo *Pietà* on the red tablecloth. I looked at it and paid for the Coke and returned to the apartment.

I sat at my table in the apartment and drew the *Pietà* again, leaving the faces blank. I drew it a third time and made the two Marys into bearded males and made the central figure into one of the Marys. Then I drew the central figure of Jesus, alone, head bent and arm twisted, alone, unsupported. Then I left the apartment and went down the narrow stairs and came out onto the street. I walked beneath the trees of the boulevard and was astonished to discover tiny green buds on the branches. Was the winter gone? Was it spring?

I returned to the apartment and sat at the table and thought of the *David* and its spatial and temporal shift. I looked at the painting of the old man with the pigeons that stood against a wall. And it was then that it came, though I think it had been coming for a long time and I had been choking it and hoping it would die. But it does not die. It kills you first. I knew there would be no other way to do it. No one says you have to paint ultimate anguish and torment. But if you are driven to paint it, you have no other way.

The preliminary drawings came easily then. After a while, I put them away. It was Passover, and I rested.

On a warm spring day, with the sun streaming through

the tall windows and leaves now on the chestnut trees of the boulevard, I started the painting. I sketched it in charcoal on the huge canvas, drawing the long vertical of the center strip of wood in the living-room window of our Brooklyn apartment and the slanted horizontal of the bottom of our Venetian blind as it used to lie stuck a little below the top frame. I drew my mother behind those two lines, her right hand resting upon the upper right side of the window, her left hand against the frame over her head, her eyes directly behind the vertical line but burning through it. I drew the houses of our street and the slanting lines of the blind and the verticals and horizontals of near and distant telephone poles. Then I went away from it and came back the next day and re-worked some of the geometry of its forms. Then I painted it—in ochres and grays, in dark smoky alizarins, in tones of Prussian and cobalt blue. I worked a long time on my mother's eyes and face. I had used a siccative. The paint dried quickly. I took the canvas down and put it against a wall. I felt vaguely unclean, as if I had betrayed a friend.

The following day, I put a fresh canvas on the easel. It was a small canvas and I thought I would fill it quickly. But I found I could not paint. I stood and stared at the canvas. I put the charcoal stick away and tried to do a drawing on paper. I could not draw. I came out of the house and walked down the cobblestone street to the boulevard. Girls in summer dresses walked beneath the trees. I returned to the apartment and looked at the blank canvas. I found I was sweating. I felt the sweat on my forehead and back. I removed the clean canvas from the easel and put the large canvas of my mother in its place. Then I looked a very long time at the painting and knew it was incomplete. It was a good painting but it was incomplete. The telephone poles were only distant reminders of the brutal reality of a crucifix. The painting did not say fully what I had wanted to say; it did not reflect fully the anguish and torment I had wanted to put into it. Within myself, a warning voice spoke soundlessly of fraud.

I had brought something incomplete into the world. Now I felt its incompleteness. "Can you understand what it means for something to be incomplete?" my mother had once asked me. I understood, I understood.

I turned away from the painting and walked to the yeshiva. I had supper and prayed the evening service. I returned to the apartment. Children played on the cobblestone street below my window. I stared at the painting and felt cold with dread. Then I went to bed and lay awake in the darkness, listening to the sounds of the street through my open window: a quarrel, a distant cough, a passing car, the cry of a child—all of it filtered through my feeling of cold dread. I slept very little. In the morning, I woke and prayed and knew what had to be done.

Yes, I could have decided not to do it. Who would have known? Would it have made a difference to anyone in the world that I had felt a sense of incompleteness about a painting? Who would have cared about my silent cry of fraud? Only Jacob Kahn, and perhaps one or two others, might have sensed its incompleteness. And even they could never have known how incomplete it truly was, for by itself it was a good painting. Only I would have known.

But it would have made me a whore to leave it incomplete. It would have made it easier to leave future work incomplete. It would have made it more and more difficult to draw upon that additional aching surge of effort that is always the difference between integrity and deceit in a created work. I would not be the whore to my own existence. Can you understand that? I would not be the whore to my own existence.

I stretched a canvas identical in size to the painting now on the easel. I put the painting against a wall and put the fresh canvas in its place. With charcoal, I drew the frame of the living-room window of our Brooklyn apartment. I drew the strip of wood that divided the window and the slanting bottom of the Venetian blind a few inches from the top of the window. On top—not behind this time, but on top—of the window I drew my

mother in her housecoat, with her arms extended along
the horizontal of the blind, her wrists tied to it with the
cords of the blind, her legs tied at the ankles to the vertical of the inner frame with another section of the cord
of the blind. I arched her body and twisted her head. I
drew my father standing to her right, dressed in a hat
and coat and carrying an attaché case. I drew myself
standing to her left, dressed in paint-spattered clothes
and a fisherman's cap and holding a palette and a long
spearlike brush. I exaggerated the size of the palette and
balanced it by exaggerating the size of my father's attaché case. We were looking at my mother and at each
other. I split my mother's head into balanced segments,
one looking at me, one looking at my father, one looking upward. The torment, the tearing anguish I felt in
her, I put into her mouth, into the twisting curve of her
head, the arching of her slight body, the clenching of
her small fists, the taut downward pointing of her thin
legs. I sprayed fixative on the charcoal and began to put
on the colors, working with the same range of hues I
had utilized in the previous painting—ochres, grays, ali-
zarin, Prussian and cobalt blue—and adding tones of
burnt sienna and cadmium red medium for my hair and
beard. I painted swiftly in a strange nerveless frenzy of
energy. For all the pain you suffered, my mama. For all
the torment of your past and future years, my mama.
For all the anguish this picture of pain will cause you.
For the unspeakable mystery that brings good fathers
and sons into the world and lets a mother watch them
tear at each other's throats. For the Master of the Universe, whose suffering world I do not comprehend. For
dreams of horror, for nights of waiting, for memories of
death, for the love I have for you, for all the things I remember, and for all the things I should remember but
have forgotten, for all these I created this painting—an
observant Jew working on a crucifixion because there
was no aesthetic mold in his own religious tradition into
which he could pour a painting of ultimate anguish and
torment.

I do not remember how long it took me to do that

painting. But on a day of summer rain that cooled the streets and ran in streams across my window, the painting was finally completed. I looked at it and saw it was a good painting. I left it on the easel and went to the yeshiva in the rain and had supper and prayed. Then I walked through the streets of the city and felt the rain on my face and remembered how I had once watched the rain of another street through windows that seemed so distant now and that I suddenly wanted to see once again.

A few days later, I thought I would destroy the paintings. I had done them; that was enough. They did not have to remain alive. But I could not destroy them. I began to paint in a delirium of unceasing energy. All through that summer, I painted my hidden memories of our street. Sometime during that summer, Avraham Cutler introduced me to a family and I returned the greetings of a girl with short dark-brown hair and brown eyes. Later, there were more greetings. Someone once said that there are things about which one ought to write a great deal or nothing at all. About those greetings, I choose to write nothing at all.

Looking old and elegant and rich, Anna Schaeffer showed up at the apartment one fall day on one of her European talent hunts.

She gazed a long time at the two large paintings.

"They are crucifixions," she said very quietly.

I said nothing.

"Asher Lev," she murmured. "Asher Lev." That was all she seemed able to say. She stared at the paintings. A long time later, she looked at me and said, "They are both great paintings." Then she added, "This one is truer than the other," and pointed to the second of the two canvases.

I was quiet.

She looked again at the paintings. Then she said, "What will you do now?"

"I don't know."

"Will you come back to America for the show?"

"Yes."

We were quiet then, gazing together at the paintings.

"How is Jacob Kahn?" I said.

"He is working to reach ninety." After a moment, she said, "Where is the beret I sent you?"

"In a drawer."

"You should wear it."

"No."

"All right," she said gently. "Now, please, you will go outside and take a very long walk."

We shook hands. I walked for hours through narrow streets and along wide boulevards. When I returned, the paintings were gone. I looked out the window of the room that was my studio, and I wept.

She wrote me a few weeks later and told me that all the paintings had arrived safely. She had scheduled the show for February. Would I object if she called the two large paintings *Brooklyn Crucifixion I* and *Brooklyn Crucifixion II*? She needed titles for the catalogue. I wrote back saying the titles were appropriate.

The weeks passed. The leaves fell from the trees. The city turned cold and dark. I walked the streets. I returned to the Bateau Lavoir. I visited galleries and museums. I spent hours with the girl and her family. I wandered about with a sense of dread and oncoming horror.

In the last week of January, I flew to New York and arrived at night in a snowstorm five days before the opening of my show.

FOURTEEN

I had given my parents only vague information about my travel plans, for I had not wanted my mother to be concerned or to meet me at the airport. I took a cab to the house. Standing on the street in the snow, I looked up at our living-room window. It was dark.

I rode the elevator to the third floor and let myself into our apartment. I went through the apartment, turning on lights—the hallway, the living room, the kitchen, my parents' bedroom, my own room. The beds were covered with spreads. The refrigerator hummed softly. The apartment was neat and clean and faintly resonant with its own silence.

I brought my bag into my room. I went out into the hallway and opened the closet. My father's black leather bag always stood on the top shelf when he was not traveling. Now it was gone. I hung up my coat and put my fisherman's cap on the shelf. There were empty wooden clothes hangers on the rod. I brushed against them. They made soft clicking sounds in the silence.

I came back into my room and stood near the doorway. The room looked very small now. A closet, my Uncle Yitzchok had once called it. The paint-it-yourself chair and desk and dresser seemed almost toys. I unpacked and put away my clothes. I wondered where my mother was. At a staff meeting with the Rebbe? Visiting friends? I stood at my window and looked out at the falling snow. It drifted thickly downward across the dark houses of the street. I saw the snow-covered garbage cans in the back yard below. I stood at the window

a long time, watching the snow. Then I turned and
looked slowly around my room—the small chair and
desk and dresser; the wooden bed, with its green-and-
brown cotton spread; the wine-colored linoleum on the
floor. The room had been painted since I had left it a
year and a half ago. The holes made by tacks that had
once held reproductions were now filled. The walls were
smooth and white and bare. They glistened in the overhead light set in the same frosted-glass ceiling fixture
that had always hung from the ceiling. Had I really
lived so much of my life in this tiny room?

I looked at my watch. It was almost eleven-thirty. I
remembered I had left the lights burning in my parents'
bedroom. I went along the hallway and past the kitchen
and came into their room. The large double bed stood
against the wall to my right, covered with its pale-blue
woolen spread. My father's dark-wood desk was against
the wall to my left. It was cluttered with his papers and
books and with old copies of *Time* and *Newsweek*. A
few framed needleworks of flowers and birds hung from
the white walls. On top of my mother's dark-wood
dresser were photographs of her sister Leah's family.
There were no photographs on my father's dresser. The
dark floral rug had been recently cleaned; it gave off a
faint acrid odor. I smelled the odor of the rug. I looked
at the bed and remembered the odor of my mother's illness. I remembered her lying beneath the green quilt,
looking shrunken and dead. Here are the birds and
flowers, Mama. I made the world pretty, Mama. I'm
making my mama well. I had once thought that there
was power in a drawing, that the lines and shapes came
through my hand from the Master of the Universe, that
a drawing could better the world, make it pretty, make
my mother happy, make her well. Aren't you well now,
Mama? I'll make more birds and flowers for you,
Mama. I had thought the power came in the night from
the Master of the Universe through the angels that
guarded me in my sleep. May Michael be at my right
hand; Gabriel at my left; before me, Uriel; behind me,
Raphael. I looked at the double bed and thought I saw

my father there, his red beard sticking over the top of the green quilt. I turned off the lights and came into the kitchen. I stared at the table. It was clean. I thought I saw it covered with books. But it was clean and bare. There was no milk in the refrigerator. I turned off the light and went through the hallway into the living room.

There was my mother's desk against the wall near the window. There were the bookcases near the desk. There was the window covered with the Venetian blind. There was my mother standing at the window, gazing out at the street. There was my mother on top of the window, her hands bound to the bottom of the raised blind, her legs bound to the middle strip of wood that divided the window into its two tall rectangles. There was my father; there was—

I turned off the lights and went through the hallway to my room. I sat on my bed and felt the coldness inside myself and the pounding of the blood in my head. I looked at my watch. It was almost midnight. After a moment, I got off the bed and went to the phone stand in the hallway. I looked up the number and dialed. The ringing went on a long time before it was answered.

"Yes? Yes?" His voice was sleepy and annoyed.

"Rav Dorochoff?"

"Yes? Who is this?" He spoke in Yiddish.

"Asher Lev."

There was silence.

"Rav Dorochoff?"

"Asher Lev," he said, no longer sleepy. "You surprised me. From where are you calling?"

"The apartment."

"You are home?"

"Yes. I am sorry to disturb you so late at night. Where are my parents?"

"Ah," he said. "Yes. Your parents did not tell me you were coming home today."

"They did not know."

"Your parents are at the University of Chicago."

I was quiet.

"Asher?"

"Yes."

"There is a conference on religion and campus problems. Your parents are participating. They are returning tomorrow."

"Thank you," I said.

"Asher Lev, welcome back." He said it warmly. "The Rebbe will be pleased to learn that you have returned."

I hung up the phone and stood in the hallway staring at the white walls. Then I went into my room and got into pajamas. I looked at the section of wall near my pillow where I had once unknowingly drawn my mythic ancestor. The drawing was painted over, gone. I turned off the lights and lay in bed. The bed felt small and uncomfortable. Let me lie down in peace and let me rise up again in peace. Let not my thoughts trouble me, nor evil dreams, nor evil fancies, but let my rest be perfect before Thee.

I did not sleep well. Once I woke in the night and thought I heard my mother singing a Yiddish melody in a strange soft voice.

I came out of the apartment house very early the following morning. The air was gray and cold. The street lights were still on. The snow had stopped falling during the night. Sections of the parkway were solidly drifted over. I walked carefully in paths made by others who had gone before me. The parkway was silent, ghostly, a bleak landscape of buried cars and dark houses and weary snow-laden trees.

I walked to the synagogue and took part in the early service. After the service, some men came over to me and greeted me warmly. Welcome, Asher Lev. Welcome. How was I? Where had I been? How was it in Europe? You look thin. Have you lost weight? Welcome, Asher Lev. Welcome.

I heard someone call my name. I turned and saw Rav Yosef Cutler, the mashpia. He was a little stooped now, and his long dark beard had begun to gray. He shook my hand. His hand was white and dry. Welcome, welcome. He coughed. His voice rasped. How was I feeling? When had I returned? He kept shaking my hand. He looked really happy tō see me.

I handed him a sealed white envelope from his son Avraham in Paris.

"How is my son?" he asked eagerly. He coughed again. "A cold," he said. "A bad cold."

"He is well."

"I have not seen him in a very long time. We hope that for Pesach he will come to America to be with us and the Rebbe. He was helpful to you?"

I thought of Avraham Cutler helping me up five flights of stairs laden with art materials. "Yes."

"I am glad."

I thought, Some of those materials are in the crucifixions.

"You will stay for a while?" the mashpia asked.

"Yes."

He coughed again. He waited a moment, breathing deeply, then said, "Perhaps you will come to the office and we will talk. I would like to know what is happening to my Asherel."

He bundled himself into his long dark coat and went out into the street, his shoulders a little bowed. I watched him go out the doors of the synagogue. He had grown old so quickly.

I put on my galoshes and coat and fisherman's cap and left the synagogue. I bought milk and rolls and eggs in a grocery store. Snowplows were moving through the parkway now, cutting wide lanes for the morning traffic. I went back to the apartment and made myself breakfast. I washed and dried the dishes and put them away. I went into the living room and looked out the window at the parkway. The street was struggling into life, slowly shaking off its entombing snow.

The phone rang. I went quickly into the hallway and picked up the receiver.

"Mr. Asher Lev?" the operator said. "Long distance calling."

"Yes, my name is Asher Lev."

"One moment. Go ahead, please."

"Asher?" It was my mother. Her voice was faintly tremulous.

"Mama?" I felt my heart pounding.

"Asher, you're home. We thought you were coming Thursday. Rav Dorochoff called us this morning. How are you, Asher?"

"I'm fine, Mama."

"Why didn't you tell us when you were coming? Are you all right? Did you have breakfast?"

"Yes, Mama."

"It's good to hear your voice, Asher. Wait. Your father wants to talk to you."

There was a momentary pause.

"Asher?" His voice was deep and strong.

"Yes, Papa."

"Welcome, welcome, Asher. I apologize for the confusion. We thought you wrote and said you would be home right before the exhibition. I apologize, Asher. Are you well?"

"Yes, Papa."

"We're flying back late this afternoon. Has the snow stopped in New York?"

"Yes."

"We'll see you, God willing, in the evening. It's good to talk to you, Asher. Goodbye."

"Goodbye, Papa."

"Goodbye, Asher," my mother said into the phone.

"Goodbye, Mama."

I hung up the phone. I stared at the phone. I stood there and stared at the phone. Then I found myself trembling. I leaned against the wall and could not stop trembling. I put on my galoshes and coat and cap and went out of the apartment into the cold snow-filled street.

It was a little after nine in the morning. The parkway was choked now with slow-moving struggling rush-hour traffic. There was a cold wind. It blew the powdery surface of the snow against the houses and cars. I felt the snow on my face and in my eyes. I walked, and thought of my parents. I felt the wind through my coat. My

beard was encrusted with snow. Where was I? What
corner was this? I had come to a corner that looked familiar despite the hills of snow that had changed its appearance. The street sign was covered with snow. I
turned up the street. Solitary figures walked the street
along a narrow path cut into tall drifts. I saw a man
with a shovel. He wore a dark coat and galoshes and a
cap with earmuffs. He pushed the shovel through the
snow, bent, lifted, threw snow into the street, and
pushed the shovel again. I came up to him. He did not
see me. His wide eyes were wet with cold and exertion.
His beaked nose was red. His gray beard was stiff with
frozen snow.

"Sholom aleichem, Reb Yudel Krinsky," I said.

He stopped and turned slightly and peered at me. He
stood very still for a moment, peering at me intently.
Then his mouth fell open and his eyes blinked and he
let the shovel fall to the snow.

"Asher Lev," he said in his hoarse voice. "Asher
Lev." He shook my hand. He embraced me. I felt his
cold wet face and his frozen beard against my cheek.

"Welcome, Asher Lev. Welcome, welcome. You
were away so long. How long was it? Come inside the
store where it is warm. It is good to see you again.
Come, come inside. What a surprise. On such a bitter
cold day to find Asher Lev."

The store had not changed. It was warm and smelled
of clean paper and new pencils. The metal stand with
the oil colors was still there near the door. I looked
around slowly. It was like returning to a warm dry shel-
tering cave.

He made us some coffee and we talked. He had a
daughter now. Yes, the Master of the Universe had
been good to him. And they were expecting another
child soon. Perhaps a boy this time. He seemed more
tired than I had ever remembered him being before. His
voice was very hoarse and his eyes blinked wearily. Do
we really all grow old so quickly? There is so little time.

Later, I came outside with him and took the shovel

from his hands and cleared the snow from the sidewalk in front of the store. He thanked me.

"The bones are growing old," he said into the wind. "I am surprised the bones are still with me after the years in Siberia. Today is a little like Siberia. It is good to see you again, Asher Lev. You have made my day happy."

He went back into the store. I walked up the street toward the parkway and went past a large store window. I looked inside and found myself staring directly at my uncle, who was standing behind a counter staring back at me. His round fleshy face took on a look of enormous astonishment. I saw him start around the counter toward the door.

He had grown fat. He wore a dark suit and a white shirt and dark tie. His gray hair was covered with a small dark skullcap. He smelled vaguely of cigars. He embraced me and could not stop telling me how glad he was to see I was back. There were two salesmen in the store. They watched us and smiled warmly. What a shame my parents were not yet back from Chicago, my uncle said. Where was I eating tonight? Had I made any more good paintings? Did I think he should see the exhibition? When was the opening? Sunday? Were there any paintings of naked women? He would go if there were no paintings of naked women. There were no naked women, I said. What could I tell him? To stay away? He would want to know why. Because you will see crucifixions, Uncle Yitzchok. You will see strange crucifixions painted by a Ladover Hasid who prays three times a day and believes in the Ribbono Shel Olom and loves his parents and the Rebbe. There were no naked women this time, I said.

It was almost ten-thirty when I got back to the apartment. I called the gallery and asked for Anna Schaeffer. She came on the phone immediately.

"Hello, Asher Lev," she said. "How is my Brooklyn prodigy?"

"Fine."

"Fine? Only fine?"

"On a day like today, fine is a good thing to be."

"Where are you now?"

"In Brooklyn."

"Come to the gallery."

"Today?"

"Yes. We have business together."

"Are the pictures hung?"

"We will begin to hang them tomorrow."

"I was thinking about the crucifixions."

"Yes? What were you thinking?"

"I was—thinking."

"The crucifixions have been sold, Asher Lev."

"Sold?" I felt a coldness move through me.

"Yes."

"To whom?"

She told me.

I leaned heavily against the wall.

"We will open with much of the show sold, Asher Lev. My Brazilian industrialist has been in to see me. The Munich nightclub owner is coming Sunday afternoon. There will be a splendid opening this Sunday with many red labels already on pictures."

I said nothing.

"Hello," she said. "Are you still there?"

"Yes."

"You have nothing to say?"

"I'll see you this afternoon if the subways are running."

"Good," she said.

"Anna, are you still using 'Brooklyn prodigy' in your publicity?"

"This will be the last time."

"I never liked it."

"The very last time," she said.

"How is Jacob Kahn?"

"He has had major surgery on his stomach. But he is recovering. Still, there are days when he is not certain he will reach ninety. Come at about three o'clock, Asher. Yes? I will have time to talk to you."

I hung up the phone and went into my room and lay on the bed. I felt tired. I lay very still, trying to look into the week. It seemed a bleak menacing tunnel. I thought I would get off the bed then and go to the desk and do a drawing. But I was tired and found I could not get up. I lay in bed with my eyes closed and thought of the dark tunnel of the coming days. Then I thought of Jacob Kahn, and again I wondered: Do we all get old and sick so quickly? Then there is almost no time left at all. Suddenly I was very tired. A moment later, I fell asleep.

He came to me then, my mythic ancestor, through the tall moist trees of his Russian master's forest, old, bent with grief, his hand trembling on the cane that supported his wasted frame. His beard was white and wild and his eyes were ash gray in the dark hollow sockets of his head. He opened his mouth to speak. His lips were parched and his teeth were black. Do you hear the pain carried on the wind? It is the cry of wasted lives. Who dares add to that cry? Who dares drain the world of its light? My Asher, my precious Asher, will you and I walk together now through the centuries? He smiled sadly and beckoned to me and disappeared into the trees.

I woke in a trembling sweat and felt hot and dizzy. I lay still on the bed. When I woke again, it was close to two o'clock. I had some coffee and came outside. I felt the air as an icy shock on my burning face. I took the subway to Manhattan.

I remember the train was cold and damp and filthy with wet dirt. People stared sullenly at the blackened floors, looking defeated by the snow-choked day. I remember a blind man playing an accordion and tapping his way through the train. I stared at my reflection in the train window. Come, journey with me through the centuries, my eyes said. One learns to walk decades. I remember the coins clinking in the blind man's metal cup. I gave him a coin. Thank you, sir. God bless you, sir. I looked at myself in the window. Red hair, dark eyes, red beard, fisherman's cap. We will journey through the centuries. Will you need a cane, Asher Lev?

I got off the train and climbed the stairs to the street. It was cold and wet and gray. A bitter wind blew against the tall buildings. I walked along Madison Avenue, peering into the windows of galleries. Pop art. Zombie art. Garish. Cold. Non-art. Duchamp's *Fountain* overflowing onto the world. I came off the street and took the elevator to the fourth floor. There was Anna Schaeffer, dressed in a dark-blue woolen dress, white beads, earrings, her face powdered and old and elegant. She came toward me exultingly, holding out both her hands. She kissed my cheek.

"Asher Lev, welcome, welcome. Give me your coat. You look pale. It is a bad day for a subway ride. Can I give you a coffee? John, a coffee in a paper cup, black with no sugar. We are packing away Rader's pieces. It was a fine show. Come into the back away from the madness, and we will talk."

The gallery floor was crowded with packing crates. Sculptures were being carefully crated. Some of my canvases were already out, standing against the walls. I did not see the crucifixions.

We sat in a small back room near tall deep wooden cases stacked with canvases and talked about the cost of putting together the show, the prices she had placed on each canvas, the canvases that had been sold, prospective buyers, new collectors she had found, federal taxes, city taxes, taxes for this, and taxes for that. I would need a tax lawyer. She knew someone. I was not listening, she said. I had better listen. Was I feeling well?

"Where are the crucifixions?" I asked.

She pointed to a wooden case.

"Where will they hang?"

On the wall before the turn to the elevator. The last paintings one will see. The climax.

"I'm worried, Anna."

"I know you are worried. But I cannot afford to indulge your worry, Asher Lev. You are now an event."

"Those paintings are going to hurt people."

"Yes? So? *Olympia* hurt people. *Le Déjeuner sur*

l'Herbe hurt people. The Impressionists hurt people. Cézanne hurt people. Picasso hurt people. What do you want me to do, Asher Lev?"

"These are people I love."

"Asher Lev, you had better pay attention to this matter of taxes and forget for now about hurting people. Indulge your Jewish sentimentality when you return to Brooklyn."

We talked for almost an hour. I tried to listen as she explained things. But it was difficult. On the wall before the turn to the elevator. I saw my mother and father moving toward that wall.

We were done. I got up to leave.

"Is Jacob Kahn home?"

"Yes."

"Is he permitted visitors?"

"Yes."

"Does he know I'm back?"

"Yes. He has seen the transparencies."

I waited.

She smiled. "He says you are a great artist. He says the crucifixions are masterpieces. He says the second crucifixion is greater than the first. Will you go to see him?"

"Yes."

"You will find he is changed. Let me walk with you to the elevator. Yes, you will find he is changed. No, I do not want you here when we hang the pictures. Yes, we will be working late Saturday night. Yes, you may bring your parents Saturday night. No, we are not serving kosher food at the opening. Anything else? Goodbye, Asher Lev. Be careful in the snow. Brooklyn does not produce an abundance of painter prodigies."

I rode back home in a cold crowded subway. The ride seemed interminable. I came out of the subway station. The parkway was dark. I walked beneath the trees. The snow had frozen to ice along the branches and trunks. The ice glistened coldly in the light of the lampposts. There was a sharp wind. I looked up as I came to the apartment house and saw my mother framed in the

living-room window, looking down at me. I waved to
her. She waved back and went away from the window. I
took the elevator up. She was waiting for me at the elevator door.

She embraced me and held me to her tightly and
cried. She was so small and slight. I felt her thin lips on
my cheek. Her eyes were wet. She could not stop crying. How was I feeling? Why was I so pale? Oh, it was
good to see me. They had missed me. They had thought
of taking a trip to Europe in the summer to see me.
"Let me look at you, my Asher. Let me look at you, my
son. Why are your eyes so red? Come inside. Your father will be home soon. He went to make a report to the
Rebbe on the Chicago trip." Did I know what was taking place on campuses today all over the country?
Chaos. Nihilism. The generation of the Flood. And so
many young Jews were involved. Their parents had not
taught them Torah. Now their heads were filled with the
ideas of the sitra achra. "Why are you so pale, Asher?
Is it the snow? You're unaccustomed to so much snow,
yes?"

Yes.

"Why didn't you tell us when you were coming? You
didn't want to worry us?"

Yes.

"Would you like something hot to drink? Coffee?"

Yes.

"Did you make a lot of good paintings in Paris?"

Yes.

"It's a lovely city, Paris, yes?"

Yes.

"Your father built a beautiful yeshiva in Paris."

Yes.

"Will there be any nudes in your exhibition, Asher?"

No.

"Then your father will be able to come."

I said nothing.

"Asher?"

I said nothing.

"Your father can come?"

Yes, I said. Papa can come. Of course he can come. There are no nudes. Certainly he can come.

I saw her give me a strange look. "Drink your coffee, Asher. Your hands are so cold. I worry when I see you so pale and so cold." She sat next to me at the kitchen table, her delicately boned hands clasped together near the pot of coffee she had prepared. She watched me drink. She could not stop talking—about me, about my father's new work with college students, about her teaching. She talked and talked in her soft voice. I was barely listening. I saw the wall in the gallery before the turn to the elevator. I saw my mother and father moving toward that wall. I saw my mythic ancestor. Come with me, my precious Asher. You and I will walk together now through the centuries, each of us for our separate deeds that unbalanced the world.

I heard the apartment door open and close. Then I heard my father's deep voice. "Rivkeh? Asher is home?" Then he was in the kitchen doorway, still in his dark coat, his narrow-brimmed hat tilted on the back of his head. I stood and felt his strong arms around me and his beard against my face. His beard was cold. There was the clean cold odor of the outside on his coat. "Asher," he murmured. "How good it is to see you again. Let me look at you. How pale you are. Isn't he pale, Rivkeh?" Then he took off his coat and hat and put on his small dark velvet skullcap. The three of us sat at the table, drinking coffee and talking. They talked of their work for Russian Jews, for Jews on college campuses, for Ladover communities in this and that country. I talked of Florence and Rome and Paris. They are nice yeshivos, aren't they? my father asked. Yes, I said. Creation out of nothing, my father said. Yes, I said. Ah, those years when I was alone in Europe. I never thought I would survive those years. Let me look at you again, Asher. We see the advertisements for your exhibition in the *Times*. A major exhibition. My little Asher. A major exhibition. It's difficult for your father to hate something the world seems to value so much. Perhaps your father was wrong. Perhaps

330 / *Chaim Potok*

such a gift is not from the sitra achra. Why are you so pale? Are you well? There will be no nudes at this exhibition. I spoke to your Uncle Yitzchok on the phone before and he said he saw you and you told him there would be no nudes. Then your mother and I will come. No, Saturday night there is an important meeting with the Rebbe. We will come Sunday. We will see the crowds that come to see our son's paintings.

We sat and talked into the night. From time to time, I saw my mother give me a strange look. I do not remember what time we went to bed. I could not sleep. I stared into the darkness of my room. Ribbono Shel Olom, what am I going to do? Journey with me, came the whisper from the tangle of primal trees. We must give a balance to the world.

My father left for his office very early the following morning. My mother served me breakfast. She seemed to want to tell me something but to be too embarrassed to say it. Finally, she said, "Your father asked me to talk to you, Asher."

I looked at her.

"We know the girl's family, Asher."

I said nothing.

"We met them in Paris. It's a fine family, Asher. Your father asked me to tell you that he would give you his blessing."

"All right, Mama."

Bright pink spots appeared on her high cheekbones. "I mention it because your father asked me to, Asher."

"Fine, Mama."

"Do you want more coffee?"

"No, thanks."

"Are you all right? Why are you so pale?"

"I'm tired."

"Is anything wrong?"

"No. Nothing is wrong."

"With the exhibit? With anything?"

"No, Mama."

She looked at me. Her eyes were troubled. After a

moment, she said, "Will you walk with me to the subway, Asher? I have a class this morning."

We walked together along the snow-filled parkway. It was a blue cold windless day. She took the subway to her school. I took the subway to Ninety-sixth Street and Broadway and got off and walked down toward Riverside Drive. I came into a whitestone building with a marble entrance hall and took the elevator to the sixth floor. Tanya Kahn let me in. Her short white hair was in disarray and her eyes were tired. Her face was pale and drawn. She held a Russian book in her hand. The apartment smelled strongly of medicine. On a pedestal near the door stood the small sculpture Jacob Kahn had once made of the two of us dancing with a Torah. Tanya Kahn led me into the bedroom and went out.

Jacob Kahn lay beneath a red quilt on a large double bed. His eyes were closed. His cheeks were sunken. The skin of his face and hands was sickly pale. His thick mane of hair was stark white against the white of the pillow. I looked at him and thought I could not go near him. Here are the birds and flowers, Mama. I'm making my mama well. I came up to the bed. He stirred and opened his eyes. He smiled faintly. I saw his lips move beneath the mustache.

"Asher Lev," he said wearily. "Asher Lev. This is another of my dreams."

"No," I said.

"It is really Asher Lev?"

"Yes."

"I dream a lot now. It is my present major preoccupation." He offered me his hand. The fingers felt dry and brittle. "How have you been, Asher?"

"Good. How are you?"

"They say that what remains of me is in excellent condition." He smiled tiredly. "I believe no one. But do not tell Tanya I said it."

"You'll make a hundred," I said.

"You think so? I do not think it would be worthwhile. The world is not a pleasant place."

No, I thought. No. It's not a pretty world.

"Asher Lev."

"Yes."

"Your crucifixions are great works."

"Thank you."

"The second completes the first. Without the second, the first would not be complete."

I was quiet.

"They are culminations. You will now have to begin something new. You do not want to repeat yourself."

"No."

"I sculpted a *David*. I am proud."

I said nothing.

He turned his head and gazed out the bedroom window at the sun and sky. "I created a new *David*," he murmured. "A breathing *David*." He turned and looked at me. "You liked Florence?"

"Yes."

"A gift?"

"Yes."

"A gift," he murmured. He looked again at the sun and the sky framed in his window. "I used to think the gift was a blessing." He was quiet a moment. "Be a great painter, Asher Lev." He was still looking out the window at the sun and the sky. "That will be the only justification for all the pain your art will cause. Now I am very tired. I think I will sleep a little and return to my present major preoccupation. I wish you good luck, Asher Lev." He closed his eyes and was silent. The walrus mustache stirred faintly with his slow breathing.

I asked Tanya Kahn, "What do the doctors say?"

"They are optimistic."

"Is he able to draw or paint?"

"No. Perhaps in a few weeks."

"Goodbye," I said. "I wish him a complete recovery."

"Thank you. Goodbye, Asher Lev. Good luck with your show."

I rode the elevator downstairs and came out into the winter sunlight and took the subway home.

I remember our meal that Friday night. "Sing zemiros with me, Asher," my father kept saying. "It's
good to have you home." The three of us sang together.
At one point during the meal, he put his head back and
closed his eyes and began to sing his father's melody to
Yoh Ribbon Olom—not in pain this time, but in quiet
exultation. His son was home; his wife was well and at
his side; his work in Europe had been a miraculous creation out of nothing; now new work lay ahead with
Jewish students on tumultuous college campuses. At the
meeting Saturday night, they would discuss opening Ladover study centers at some of the major universities in
the country. New work, new creativity, new journeys
for my father. He sang and his eyes glowed, and my
mother and I sang with him.

I did not know what to do. I could not sleep. In the
synagogue that Shabbos morning, I prayed for a mira-
cle, for an idea, for anything that might help me. The
Rebbe joined the service at Borchu, then sat on his
chair near the Ark, his face concealed by his prayer
shawl. Rebbe, help me. Please. Help me. All right. Yes.
I'll tell my father. I'll sit down and talk to him. This afternoon. Papa, listen. I felt Mama's lonely torment. I
wanted to paint Mama's torment. I wanted it to be a
painting, a great painting, because I love painting as
you love traveling. I work with oils and brushes and
canvas as you work with events and deeds and people.
There is nothing in the Jewish tradition that could have
served me as an aesthetic mold for such a painting. I
had to go to— I had to use a— Do you understand,
Papa? Why are you looking at me like that, Papa? It
isn't the sitra achra, Papa. It's your son. There was no
other way, no other aesthetic mold— He would not
begin to understand. He would hear the word "crucifixion." He would see the crucifix looming monstrously
before his eyes. He would see rivers of Jewish blood.
He would— Rebbe, help me. "Sing zemiros with me,
Asher," my father kept saying later during the Shabbos
afternoon meal. "Rivkeh, Asher, sing zemiros to the
Ribbono Shel Olom."

I went with him back to the synagogue after the meal. We sat together at his table near the Ark and listened to the Rebbe's talk. Later, when Shabbos was over, we walked home together beneath the trees of the parkway. It was cold and dark. There were patches of ice along the street from the snow that had fallen earlier in the week. My father walked with care, limping slightly.

"Asher," I heard him say.

"Yes, Papa."

"You're quiet today. Are you worried about tomorrow?"

"Yes."

"It's an important day for you."

"Yes."

"Wherever I travel now, there is always someone who knows your name. 'Are you the father of Asher Lev, the painter?' they ask me. It's a very strange feeling. Asher Lev, the painter."

I was quiet. The wind blew coldly through the street.

"Is it a strange feeling to be famous?" he asked.

"I'm not famous, Papa."

"It's a strange feeling to me to hear my son called Asher Lev, the painter. When I grew up, a painter was someone who painted the walls and floors of our house. People ask me what you are, and I can't bring myself to tell them you're a painter. I say you're an important artist. Tell me, is it proper to ask how much people pay for your paintings?"

"The small ones sell for about three thousand dollars."

"Three thousand dollars?" He looked astounded. "So much money for a painting?"

I did not respond. We walked carefully over a tall frozen snowdrift.

"Three thousand dollars," he murmured. "Who pays so much money for paintings?"

"They pay more, Papa."

"Who?"

"Collectors. People who buy paintings because they love them or because they want to invest in them."

"Invest?"

"Paintings go up in value if an artist's reputation gets better."

"Yours have gone up in value?"

"Yes."

"Who are these investors, Asher?"

"Rich people, mostly."

"You're painting for the rich?"

"The rich can afford to buy many oil paintings, Papa. Also, museums."

"You've sold paintings to museums, Asher?"

"Yes."

He stopped and stared at me. "You didn't tell me."

"It happened this week."

"Which museum?"

I told him.

His mouth fell open. "In Manhattan? Here?"

"Yes."

"What are they paintings of?"

"They're—paintings."

"We'll see them tomorrow?"

"Yes."

"A museum," he murmured, beginning to walk again. "My son in a museum." He seemed unable to believe it. Almost despite himself, his dark eyes glittered with pride.

My mother was astonished and proud when he told her. "What paintings are they, Asher?" she asked.

"Paintings."

"Of what, Asher?"

"We'll see them tomorrow, Rivkeh," my father said. "Come, we have a meeting to attend."

I saw my mother give me that strange troubled look.

They left for the staff meeting with the Rebbe. I called the gallery and told Anna Schaeffer I would not be coming over tonight with my parents. Yes, tomorrow. Of course I would be on time for the meeting with her West Coast representative. Yes, I would be nice to her Munich night-club owner. Good night. Good night.

I hung up the phone. I roamed the apartment, feeling cold with dread. I should have destroyed them. Who needs them? What good are they going to do the world? I had painted them; wasn't that enough? No, it wasn't enough. They had to be moved into the public arena. You communicate in a public arena; everything else is puerile and cowardly. I could not sleep. I lay awake hours in the dark. I heard my parents come in. It was almost two o'clock in the morning. They sat in the kitchen, drinking coffee and talking softly. I thought I heard the word "museum." They went into their bedroom. I remained awake. There was faint gray light along the rim of my window. Is it morning already? Is it Sunday? What happened to the night? I don't want the night to end. There was sunlight on the window. Inside myself was a darkness of death.

I dressed and prayed and came into the kitchen. My mother stood near the stove. My father was at the counter, making orange juice. His small dark velvet skullcap was pushed forward on his head. He looked at me and smiled. Just in time for your juice, he said, and handed me a glass. I sat at the table. My head felt dull. There was grayness along the edge of my vision. Drink your juice, Asher, I heard my father say. All the vitamins will go out of it. I glanced up and saw my mother looking at me. She served breakfast. Her face was pale. She knew there was something in that gallery I was afraid to have them see. Mama, it's a crucifixion. I made our living-room window into a crucifixion and I put you on it to show the world my feelings about your waiting, your fears, your anguish. Do you understand, Mama? But why didn't you draw the pretty birds, Asher? And the flowers, Asher, why didn't you draw the flowers?

My father went into the living room and sat on the sofa, surrounded by the Sunday *Times* and back issues of *Time* and *Newsweek*. My mother came into the room after a while, glanced through the *Times,* and sat down at her desk near the window. I sat on an easy chair and watched them. The Venetian blind had been raised. Sunlight streamed into the room, touching my parents, the furniture, the rug, the walls with a faintly shimmering luminosity, with the warm golden light of the Rembrandt world. I sat there a long time, very still, watching them. Then I rose quietly and went to my room. I had to be in the gallery at one. The opening was at three. I dressed quickly, feeling a leaden heaviness in my arms and legs.

My parents embraced me. They would come between three and four, my father said. Good luck, good luck, my mother said softly. Success, my Asher. She would not look directly into my eyes.

I came out of the apartment house. The air was cold and sharp with winter wind. I took a cab to the gallery. The elevator brought me to the fourth floor. I came out of the elevator and started toward the rear of the gallery. Then I stopped and stood very still and found I was unable to move.

The gallery was a huge hall-like room, with off-white walls, a deep gold-colored carpet, ornamented ashtrays, plush chairs, and concealed and recessed lights. The wall opposite the elevator ran the entire length of the gallery. This wall turned at a right angle and became a wall about half the length, then turned once again and became a wall about one-fourth the length, of the wall opposite the elevator. This last segment of wall then turned at another right angle and led to the elevator. To the left of the elevator, where Anna Schaeffer's desk normally stood, there was now a bar and a long smorgasbord table. Later, there would be bartenders, waiters, and a quartet playing soft music. I had seen the gallery filled with many different kinds of paintings and sculptures. I had seen it in various states of disarray both before and after shows. I had seen my own works on its walls. I had not thought it capable of too many more surprises for me. Now I stood near the elevator door and stared at the paintings that hung on the gallery's walls, and I could not move.

I had not seen those paintings since the fall. There on

338 / *Chaim Potok*

the walls, hung with exquisite taste, were the shapes and
forms of the invisible world of my street—my mythic
ancestor, my grandfather, wandering, journeying—
painting after painting hung so that the effect was subtly
cumulative, so that the sense of color and line and texture and shape mounted and heightened. The canvases
vibrated. I had not even myself been aware of their
power. I came slowly away from the elevator and followed the walls, looking at the titles—*Village Burning,
Young Man Journeying I, Young Man Journeying II,
Old Man Journeying, Scholar-Saint, Scholar Journeying
I, Scholar Journeying II, Village Death,* and the others;
there were about sixty in all. I looked at the titles and
the paintings and it was as if I had not done them. I
came to the end of the short wall and turned and caught
my breath. She had placed the crucifixions on the wall
opposite where I stood, before the turn to the elevator.
They dominated the wall. I stared at them and felt them
leap across the entire length of the gallery and clutch at
me. I had not imagined them to be so powerful. I
should have muted them. They could not be left so raw
and powerful. I felt myself sweating. I felt the long
clutching grasp of the canvases and myself sweating and
saw my mother tied to the vertical and horizontal lines
of the painting and saw my father and mother looking
at the painting. Then I turned away, terrified before
such an act of creation. Master of the Universe, I did
not mean to attempt to emulate Your power, Your abil-
ity to create out of nothing. I only wanted to make a
few good paintings. Master of the Universe, forgive me.
Please. Forgive me. I turned my back to the paintings
and closed my eyes, for I could no longer endure seeing
the works of my own hands and knowing the pain those
works would soon inflict upon people I loved.

I heard a soft voice behind me and turned and saw
Anna Schaeffer. She wore a pale-blue satin dress and
jewels. There was a diamond tiara in her silver hair. She
looked regal.

"What do you think?" she asked. "Isn't it a splendid
show?"

I told her the paintings had been beautifully hung. But didn't she think the crucifixions were too raw? Didn't she think I had overdone the play of color and texture? Perhaps she had some oils in the back somewhere. There was still time.

"Asher Lev," she murmured. "My Asher Lev. Come, there is someone you must meet. There have been interesting developments."

We went into the back room. She introduced me to her West Coast representative, a portly middle-aged man with a warm laugh and a double chin. Herbert has succeeded in interesting two West Coast collectors in your work, she said. They are bidding against each other. Do you realize what this means? She sounded exultant. Tell him what it means, Herbert. He told me what it meant. I was not listening. I felt cold. Someone brought me black coffee in a paper cup. Yes, the small ones may now go into five figures, someone was saying. Hello, hello, my dear Schiller, hello, how are you? Yes, this is Mr. Lev. Mr. Schiller of Munich. Yes, yes. Splendid. Of course. We will talk afterward. But there are West Coast people who are interested. Yes, of course, we understand. You spoke first. My dear Schiller, my word is sacred. By all means, look around. Yes. And try the smorgasbord. It is splendid. Do you want another coffee, Asher? You are being a very good boy. No, it is not three yet. Yes, we had to let them start coming in. They were blocking the downstairs hallway. You should come out now and mix with the crowd, Asher Lev. Yes, there is a crowd. She radiated. She looked elegant and regal and elated. A fine crowd. Ah, here is the dear man from the *Times*. Hello, hello. So good to see you. The gallery was jammed. I could barely see the paintings for the people. The bar was very busy. The quartet played soft Viennese music. Vienna is a city of waltzes, Asher Lev. But it is a city that hates Jews. Who had told me that? Yudel Krinsky. I did not see my parents. I saw elegant dresses and jewelry and dignified men in dark suits. Anna Schaeffer selected her people carefully for these openings and always invited more people than she

expected would attend. Now it seemed they were all attending. The elevator door opened, disgorging more
people. It looked like a theater crowd. My mythic ancestor, my grandfather, my mother on a cross—and
Viennese music, a thriving bar, a rapidly vanishing
smorgasbord, subdued conversation, "ooh"s and "aah"s
over the paintings, awed stares at the crucifixions. The
colors, look at how he worked the colors. But isn't he
an Orthodox Jew? One of those—what do you call
them—Hasids? How could he paint that? Who's the
woman? Christ, look at the agony on her face. Christ,
he's good. Ah, Mr. Lev, a pleasure, an honor. What
marvelous paintings. Splendid show, Lev. Splendid. I
did not see my parents. The elevator door opened once
again. There they were, caught in the flood of people
that poured into the gallery; my father in his dark coat
and suit and his dark narrow-brimmed hat tipped back
on his head; my mother in a small dark-brown hat and a
dark-brown coat with a fur trim. People swirled past
them. They gazed around, looking bewildered. I made
my way through the thick crowd. Great show, Lev.
Great. Damn good, those crucifixions. First-rate. Papa.
Mama. Here. Here. I came between them and took
their arms. What a crowd, Asher, my father said. All
for your paintings? My mother seemed unable to speak.
She looked very pale and her eyes were dark. I saw her
trying to look at the paintings. But they were blocked
by the crowd near the walls. Anna Schaeffer came over.
How do you do? A pleasure and a privilege to meet the
parents of Asher Lev. Yes, they all came to see your
son's work. Indeed, he is a great painter. I understand
you travel a great deal, Mr. Lev. In my work, one travels a great deal, too. Excuse me, it seems there is something I must attend to. A pleasure to have met you
both. She smiled graciously and went away.

We began to move slowly along the walls and to look
at the paintings. Behind us the crowd ebbed and
swirled. These are my memories, Papa. No, I'm not saying that these paintings represent the truth; they repre-

sent how I feel about things I remembered when I was in Paris. They're not the truth, Papa; but they're not lies, either. Remember you told me about the village burning and the people who died? Remember you told me about the way he always traveled afterward? Remember you told me about your father and how he suddenly began to travel? Remember—? The crowd seemed strangely noisy. I heard whispers. The noise swelled, diminished, swelled again. I glanced around. People were staring at my parents. I looked at my mother. She had become aware of the level of noise and movement around us. She turned slowly. The crucifixions were on the opposite wall, but she could not see them for the dense crowd. Then my father turned. He was taller than most of the people in front of the crucifixions. He looked straight over their heads. The upper portions of the two paintings were visible. I saw my father staring over the heads of the crowd directly at my mother's face on the crucifixions. His dark eyes narrowed. He looked puzzled. He began to move through the crowd, leaving my mother and me behind. I took my mother's hand and followed. Her hand was cold and moist. There were more whispers. People moved aside. I saw my father stop in front of the paintings. My mother and I came up beside him. My mother stood between us, staring at the paintings. People were looking at us and at the paintings. There were still more hushed whispers. Then silence closed around us. I saw people in distant corners of the gallery become aware of the silence and begin to edge toward us. We stood there, staring at our own faces in the second painting. I had my hand on my mother's arm. I felt her shudder. Her eyes were wide and disbelieving and her mouth was open, and she stared and shuddered and seemed not to know what to do or say. I felt the crowd begin to press in against us. "Hey," someone whispered loudly. "That's them." The crowd stirred, then was silent. Through the silence came the soft music of the quartet. There was a long frozen moment of waiting. Then my father moved toward the paintings. I saw him bend to read the titles. His shoulders stiffened. Then he saw the red labels and the name of the museum that had purchased the paintings. He straightened slowly. He turned and looked at me. His face wore an expression of awe and rage and bewilderment and sadness, all at the same time. I remembered that expression. During the months of my mother's illness, I had drawn her once sitting in the sunlight of our living room, and he had watched me from the doorway, watched me using cigarette ash to give life to the contours of her body and face. He had had that same expression on his face.Who are you? the expression said. Are you really my son? He had not spoken to me then. He did not speak to me now. He took my mother's arm and led her through the silent crowd. He walked slowly, and with dignity. He looked straight ahead through the crowd, walking with deliberate slowness. I followed. I saw Anna Schaeffer's face somewhere in the crowd. I saw my father push the elevator button. My mother kept staring at me in astonishment and disbelief. My father looked at the elevator door. The door opened. We stepped aside to let a wave of people move by us into the gallery. We were alone in the elevator as it went back down. My father would not look at me. The elevator operator, an elderly man in a crimson uniform and cap, stared at us curiously. Downstairs, we pushed through the crowd in the hallway and came outside on the street. It was cold. Sunlight bathed the tops of the buildings and slanted across the intersections.

"Papa—"

But he was not listening. He stood on the curb, hailing a cab.

"Mama—"

"There are limits, Asher." Her voice trembled and her eyes were wet. "Everything has a limit. I don't know what to tell you. I don't want to talk to you now."

A cab pulled up to the curb. My father opened the door. My mother climbed inside. He sat beside her and closed the door in my face. He did not once look at me. The cab pulled away. I stood at the curb and watched the cab move into the stream of traffic. I shivered in the wind. I stood there a long time; then I went back upstairs to the gallery.

I remember feeling more and more tired as the day wore on and thinking I could no longer endure the noise and the compliments of the crowd. Finally, it was over. Waiters moved through the silent gallery, picking up dishes and glasses. The bartender was closing up. The quartet was packing away its instruments.

Anna Schaeffer stood beside me. "Congratulations," she said. "It was a fine day for you, Asher Lev."

I did not say anything.

"The apprentice has become a master," she said quietly. Then she said, "Come in tomorrow. We have business to discuss."

We shook hands. She did not ask me about my parents.

I remember coming home that night and finding the apartment empty. I slept fitfully and thought I heard my parents come in but I was not certain. In the morning, I woke late and they were gone. I went to the gallery. Only about a dozen people were there. It seemed barnlike and empty. The paintings drooped from the walls, parodies of masters I could not begin to follow. I did not look at the crucifixions.

I came back home after dark. The apartment was empty. There was a note from my mother. They were eating at my Uncle Yitzchok's house. There was food for me in the refrigerator. I ate and went to bed and heard them come in hours later and go straight to their room. They were not home when I woke the following morning.

That was the day the *New York Times* carried the review of the show, together with photographs of the two crucifixions. It was a kind review. I stood at the newsstand on the parkway looking at my copy of the *Times* and saw my father reading his copy at his desk. I saw him discovering the review. I saw him looking at himself and my mother in the second photograph. I walked along the parkway. I thought I saw people looking at me. I came into the Ladover building and went upstairs to my father's office. I found him behind his desk, speaking into a telephone. He was talking in Yiddish about a trip to San Francisco. There was an open copy of the *Times* on his desk. He looked at me from across the desk. His eyes were sharp, clear, dark. His lips stiffened. He did not stop talking. He swiveled in his chair and turned his back to me, still talking into the telephone. I stood there for a long moment, staring at his small dark velvet skullcap and his thickset shoulders. Then I went back downstairs and came outside.

I do not remember what I did the rest of that day. Nor do I have a clear memory of what that Shabbos was like, though I remember the three of us were together in the apartment for the meals. There were no quarrels. There was very little conversation. Once I tried to talk to my father about the paintings. He threatened to get up and walk out of the room. "Aryeh," my mother murmured. "Please." Her eyes wore a dark tortured look.

The following week, *Time* and *Newsweek* carried stories on the show, along with pictures of the crucifixions and photographs of myself and my parents. To this day, I do not know how they obtained photographs of my parents. Had a photographer been in the gallery with a camera that Sunday? I asked Anna Schaeffer about it later that week, and she shrugged. The stories were about Asher Lev, painter, the Ladover Hasid who had put his family into a crucifixion. Leading Catholics had been asked for their reactions to having an Orthodox Jew use the crucifixion in his paintings, and they had responded, some of them quite unkindly. There were faintly lurid overtones to the stories—Freudian evaluations regarding my relationship with my parents. But the technical analyses of the paintings were well done and very favorable.

I saw my father reading the stories. I wandered around the apartment, then took the subway to Manhattan and went up the tall stone stairs into the mansion-like building off Washington Square where my mother taught Russian affairs. I asked for her class and came to the door and peered through the small glass panel. She sat behind her desk, lecturing. I came quietly into the room and sat in the back of the room. I saw her stare at me, hesitate, then continue. There were about twenty students in the class. My mother was talking about Russian foreign policy during the First World War. She lectured in a soft voice. There was the sound of pens and pencils against paper. Then a student glanced at me, looked away, then looked back, her eyes going wide. She leaned over and whispered to the young man next to her. "Asher Lev," I heard. "Asher Lev." There was a stirring throughout the room. Heads turned. My mother stopped her lecture and looked at me from across the room. I felt my face burning. I got up and went out and took the subway home.

That Shabbos, people turned their backs to me in the synagogue. The Rebbe came in during the service and sat down in the chair near the Ark. I could see his eyes beneath the prayer shawl. I could see him scanning the people in the synagogue. I saw him looking at me. For a long time, he sat near the Ark looking at me across the expanse of the synagogue. People saw him looking at me. After the service, the mashpia would not return my greetings. He walked past me, his eyes filled with pain. Yudel Krinsky murmured a response but gazed at me in silent bewilderment. My Uncle Yitzchok brushed by me angrily. I ate with my parents in a heavy silence. I tried to talk about the paintings. "I will walk out of the room," my father said. "I warn you. Do not destroy my Shabbos."

"Asher, please," my mother said. "Not now."

We did not talk about the paintings.

The next day, the Sunday *Times* carried another review of the show, a lengthy and serious attack against my entire painting style, against the essential integrity of my efforts, and especially against the crucifixions. It was a long carefully composed and well-reasoned article written by the man who had once accused me of having a dangerous affinity to Picassoid forms and then had changed his mind. Now he accused me of a regressive flirtation with the clichés of literary painting. Once again, there were photographs of the two crucifixions.

Anna Schaeffer called me during the morning. It was a vicious slanderous review, she said. At least half a dozen painters had called her to say they were writing to the *Times* in my defense. I was to be brave, she said. The vultures were out. I had to learn to abide the vultures.

My mother came into my room that afternoon and stood near the doorway. I was at the window, looking out at the dirty snow in the yard below.

Had I seen the review in the *Times*? she asked softly. "Yes."

My father wanted to know if I was all right, she said. "Yes."

Was there anything she could do? "Yes."

What could she do?

She could listen, I said.

She hesitated. Then she came slowly into the room and sat down on my bed.

I tried to explain it to her. Somewhere in the middle of it all, it became clear that I was not succeeding. She would accept what I had to say. But she would never understand it. To do what I had done was beyond comprehension. She would not even dare try to explain it to my father. What could she explain? The crucifixion had been in a way responsible for his own father's murder on a night before Easter decades ago. What could she possibly say to my father?

She went out of the room. A few minutes later, I was called to the telephone. It was Rav Dorochoff. The

Rebbe wanted to see me. Now. Yes, now. In his office. I went out of the apartment and into the cold afternoon sunlight of the street.

I remember Rav Dorochoff's dark anger and the brusque way he ushered me into the Rebbe's office. I remember the Rebbe's long burning gaze and the silence that filled the space between us. He had read everything. He had followed the papers and the magazines. He understood everything. He sat behind his desk, gazing at me out of dark sad eyes. The brim of his ordinary hat threw a shadow across his forehead.

"I understand," he kept saying. "Jacob Kahn once explained it to me in connection with sculpture. I understand." Then he said, "I do not hold with those who believe that all painting and sculpture is from the sitra achra. I believe such gifts are from the Master of the Universe. But they have to be used wisely, Asher. What you have done has caused harm. People are angry. They ask questions, and I have no answer to give them that they will understand. Your naked women were a great difficulty for me, Asher. But this is an impossibility." He was silent for a long moment. I could see his dark eyes in the shadow cast by the brim of his hat. Then he said, "I will ask you not to continue living here, Asher Lev. I will ask you to go away."

I felt a cold trembling inside me.

"You are too close here to people you love. You are hurting them and making them angry. They are good people. They do not understand you. It is not good for you to remain here."

I said nothing.

"Asher."

I looked at him.

"Go to the yeshiva in Paris. You did not grow up there. People will not be so angry in Paris. There are no memories in Paris of Asher Lev."

I was quiet.

"Asher Lev," the Rebbe said softly. "You have crossed a boundary. I cannot help you. You are alone now. I give you my blessings."

I came out of the Rebbe's office and walked past Rav Dorochoff's angry gaze and out of the building. I walked for hours then beneath the naked trees of the parkway along streets that had once been my world but were now cold and gone from me. Sometime during the walking, I stopped in front of a mound of snow and with my finger drew in one continuous line the contour of my face. Asher Lev in snow on a cold Brooklyn parkway. Asher Lev, Hasid. Asher Lev, painter. I looked at my right hand, the hand with which I painted. There was power in that hand. Power to create and destroy. Power to bring pleasure and pain. Power to amuse and horrify. There was in that hand the demonic and the divine at one and the same time. The demonic and the divine were two aspects of the same force. Creation was demonic and divine. Creativity was demonic and divine. Art was demonic and divine. The solitary vision that put new eyes into gouged-out sockets was demonic and divine. I was demonic and divine. Asher Lev, son of Aryeh and Rivkeh Lev, was the child of the Master of the Universe *and* the Other Side. Asher Lev paints good pictures and hurts people he loves. Then be a great painter, Asher Lev; that will be the only justification for all the pain you will cause. But as a great painter I will cause pain again if I must. Then become a greater painter. But I will cause pain again. Then become a still greater painter. Master of the Universe, will I live this way all the rest of my life? Yes, came the whisper from the branches of the trees. Now journey with me, my Asher. Paint the anguish of all the world. Let people see the pain. But create your own molds and your own play of forms for the pain. We must give a balance to the universe.

Yes, I said. Yes. My own play of forms for the pain.

Later that afternoon, I called Anna Schaeffer at the gallery. It was another mob scene, she cried exultantly. I would have to see it to believe it.

I told her I was returning to Europe.

There was a long silence. I could hear the noise of the crowd through the telephone.

"Will you stay to the end of the show?" she asked.

"I'm leaving tomorrow, Anna."

"Where will you go?"

"I don't know. Back to Paris. I may go to Russia."

She was very quiet.

"I need new faces. And there's the Hermitage in Leningrad and the Matisses in Moscow."

"Yes," she said. Then she said, "You will let me know where you can be reached."

"Yes."

"Goodbye, Asher Lev. When you get to Paris, you should wear the beret."

I said nothing.

"Goodbye, Asher Lev. Good luck."

I went into the kitchen and told my parents. My father stared at me and said nothing. My mother began to cry.

I called and made a reservation on a flight to Paris for the next night. I remember nothing else about that day. I came awake in the night and heard my parents talking softly in the kitchen. I lay in my bed and wondered what they were saying.

I woke in the morning and prayed. My parents were not home. I made myself breakfast. I wandered about the apartment and walked the streets. I had lunch alone in the apartment and supper with my parents. I packed my bags. We stood at the door. My mother was crying. My father stood next to her, tall, heavy-shouldered, his eyes dark—and moist, I thought. He said nothing, but he shook my hand. "Please write," my mother said. "You'll write?" She looked tiny and fragile. "Have a safe journey, my Asher," she kept saying. "Have a safe journey."

I came out of the apartment house. It was cold and dark. I looked up. My parents stood framed in the living-room window. I hailed a cab and climbed inside. It pulled slowly away from the curb. I turned in the seat and looked out the rear window of the cab. My parents were still watching me through our living-room window.